THE WIND CAVE BOOK III

THE

BATTLE

MICHELA
MONTGOMERY

A POST HILL PRESS BOOK

ISBN (trade book): 978-1-61868-913-9
ISBN (eBook): 978-1-61868-914-6

THE BATTLE
The Wind Cave Book 3
© 2015 by Michela Montgomery
All Rights Reserved

Cover Design by Martin Kintanar

Post Hill
PRESS

Post Hill Press
275 Madison Avenue, 14th Floor
New York, NY 10016
http://posthillpress.com

For all of the dreamers, the poets, the writers and the actors who dream of seeing their name in print or on billboards. And for my family, who loves me regardless of whether my name is in lights or not.

CHAPTER ONE

Edgar was whimpering with fear and Gigi was still draped over Percy's shoulder. He stood frozen in the middle of the destroyed train car while the machine gun fire continued outside. Instinct took over.

"Percy," I said, tugging at his arm. "Lie her down underneath the seats so only her legs show." He did as I asked, and I turned to Edgar. He was staring at the broken bodies of Sasha and Phillip and I knew he was in shock. I turned his face towards me and heard a few more shots being fired, but fewer screams.

"You have to listen to me. No matter what happens in the next ten minutes, I need you to be absolutely still."

I pushed him down onto the floor of the car and hid as much of him as possible behind one of the seats, hoping he understood me. My legs, still covered in blood, were going to provide me with camouflage for all four of us. Running my hand down the length of my leg, I swiped it across the back and sides of Gigi's legs that stuck out from underneath the armrests of the broken seats. Pushing Edgar underneath the seats on the other side of the car, I tugged at his pant leg until his leg stuck out where a window used to be. I wiped my bloody hands across his pant leg quickly.

We could hear voices coming and occasional single shots being fired which, in my mind, could only mean one thing. People were being shot, execution style, while trying to escape. Running was not an option.

"Percy," I whispered fiercely, and pointed to the far corner of the car, "get down and back." Before he could go, I swiped my hand across my other leg and then on his arm. My blood smeared bright red over his forearm and I pointed to the floor. "Have it sticking out from under the seat. Go!"

Knowing that by now my legs looked like an autopsy and my hands were covered in blood, I crawled three seats down from where I'd hidden Edgar and draped myself backwards and upside down over the edge of a seat so that my legs would be really visible to anyone who crawled up on top of the car to see inside.

My heart pounding in my chest, I heard the sounds of footsteps on the rocks coming close to our car. Edgar whimpered and I silently pleaded with him to be quiet. If someone volleyed shots into the car without crawling up, we were all four dead. I was taking a calculated risk that they wouldn't waste ammunition unless they saw a bunch of Americans hiding, cowering. I didn't intend to give them the satisfaction.

The car shifted as someone hoisted themselves up over the edge of the car. I could hear their footsteps as they walked up and down the car, scanning for survivors. With any luck, the only thing he'd see was a very dead Sasha and Phillip, and a few bloody limbs from under some seats. My face was the only thing someone couldn't see, as I'd slid my face behind a cushion. I was contorted so I wouldn't have to fake the face of a corpse. I squeezed my eyes closed and waited to hear machine gun fire.

I thought about Camilla, and the necklace that I wore. I thought about Ano and Jazz thousands of miles away. I thought about Matt, and Carrie and Charlie, having picnics where it was safe; and about Carlie, possibly fighting for her life right this very minute as I was. I thought about anything that would keep me from moving, anything that would take me away from where I was right at this very minute. Oddly enough, as my body lay across the broken seats of our train car, I thought about my parents.

The footsteps walked up one side of the car, the entire length, and down the other. We could hear foreign voices yelling, calling to each other, and I held my breath. I couldn't open my eyes. If I opened them we were dead. If I opened them, everything happening around me was real and I would scream. I shut my eyes tighter until the footsteps stopped. The car shifted and we heard him jump down from the top of our car.

Footsteps from all around us echoed and I wondered what was happening. Surely they had no need for a wrecked train in the middle of nowhere. Where were we? How long had it been since we'd left the station? An hour? Two? Fifteen minutes went by and the voices got softer, as if from a distance, but I didn't move. From next to me, Edgar's soft whimpering continued and I shushed him as quietly as I could.

After another fifteen minutes my legs and back were aching from the odd angle. I felt the dried blood on my legs and resisted the urge to move them. Another fifteen minutes and all we heard was silence. No voices, no gunfire. I wasn't sure that we were alone, wasn't sure it was safe to move. Someone could be posted to remain behind to make sure no survivors escaped. If that were the case, we were dead.

I swallowed; my mouth felt like dried cotton, and yet I kept still. The seconds ticked by and I wondered how long we should wait before moving. From where I lay, I could make out Gigi's legs underneath the seats. She hadn't moved, and it wasn't a good sign. Although I'd never been big on praying, I silently asked God to spare her life, for the sake of the two grandsons who could not lose another member of their family.

From across the car, Percy called in a low voice. "Kate?"

"Yeah?"

"What'd you think?"

I hadn't moved. I didn't know. I wasn't sure. We'd have to find out eventually, however, and it had been nearly an hour since we'd crashed and at least a half hour since we'd heard any movement or voices.

"One of us will have to go check it out," I whispered. "I'll go."

"No, Kate."

Edgar whimpered from next to me, and we both shushed him before he got too loud. "Percy," I hissed, "think." Like I had back in the cave, I reminded him of his responsibilities as opposed to mine. "Stay here," I said quietly. "Take care of Edgar and Gigi."

"No." His voice was above a whisper and I knew I'd have to reason with him quickly or someone would hear us.

"I'm not strong enough to lift Gigi out of here if something happens to you. Please..." I implored, and from the silence, I could tell he was thinking about what I was saying.

I was thinking through my exit of the train car. There was no easy way to do it. I'd have to climb up and lift myself out, making my body visible from any and all angles. Even if I hopped down fast, the noise alone would alert someone that I was here. And they'd come looking for more survivors. Oh, God.

"Percy," I whispered, knowing he would hate what I was about to say, "if you hear a shot..." My throat was closing up, knowing that I was likely spending the last minutes of my life right now with him.

"Stop," he said quietly but firmly.

"Stay put until you're sure they're gone."

He was quiet for a minute more, but finally responded, "I will."

"Call Carrie. Tell her what happened."

His voice was hoarse and it broke when he answered, "I will."

I sat up slowly. My head spun from being vertical, and I swayed for a moment before moving my legs from the armrest. Edgar's eyes peeked out at me from where I'd stowed him.

"Kate?" he whispered. His voice sounded as if he was five, and I put a finger to my lips.

"Ssshhh. Quiet, Edgar."

Before I climbed out of the bus there was something I needed to do. As quickly as I could, I reached back and unfastened the clasp of Camilla's necklace from around my neck. I walked to the rear of the bus and Percy slipped his upper torso out from underneath the seats to reach for me.

"No, stay down. Stay there." It was going to be harder for me to leave if he came out, and I could touch him. I placed the necklace into his hand. "Keep it safe."

His entire face registered pain, but he nodded.

As quietly as I could, I climbed up onto the upper row of seats and prepared to stick my head out of the window to the train car. I listened for any sound around us. From below me, Percy whispered for me to be careful.

I lifted myself up and out in one swift movement onto the top of the car. In the same second my body flattened itself against it, knowing it was a long drop to the bottom. I turned my head to the side facing the underside of the car. From where the tracks had turned, I saw seven or eight of the cars that had derailed; abandoned. The crumpled bodies of people were lying scattered on the ground where they had been shot.

Don't look, I told myself. *Just slide down.*

Seeing no one, I inched to the edge and held onto the lip of the bottom of the car and slid one leg over. The rest of my body followed, and soon I was dangling down off the edge of the train car.

Just let go, I thought. *Now!*

My fingers obeyed and I dropped to the ground, a five foot drop from where I had been hanging. Pain shot through both of my legs and I crumpled to the ground.

There was no hiding now. I was a rabbit out of the hole, waiting to be shot. I leaned my body against the side of the car, only visible now from one side of the landscape. The overturned car kept me hidden from anyone on the other side of the accident scene and I prayed that the insurgents that had done this had moved on. There wasn't any movement from this side of the car. No one in sight, no other signs of life. Only the sound of the wind whistling around me. I got to my knees painfully, swaying slightly. I couldn't pass out. Not now. Holding my breath, I walked carefully around the overturned car. I slid against the exterior, and the scene before me nearly destroyed me.

Bodies. Trails of them; some on top of one another, some singular in their post mortem state. Not more than five feet from me lay the bodies of two women that had been in our car with us; who had been shot as they'd exited the train. My stomach lurched and I turned away to lay my face against the cool metal of the train to keep from vomiting. After breathing deeply for a few seconds, the convulsions in my stomach ceased. I could do this.

Steeling myself to face it, I slid the remainder of the way around the train car. Far to my right was the engine car. Black smoke still billowed from its windows. Behind our car were at least five others, all turned in different directions. Bodies littered the area around the crash site, some hanging out of windows, as if they'd been shot trying to climb out of the train, and others face down on the ground in groups. Reflexively, my stomach lurched again. I dropped to my knees and was sick against the train; heaving again and again until I had nothing left. I spat and wiped my mouth with the back of my hand. Horrible shudders ran through my body. I had to get back to Percy.

Convinced that we were believed dead, the monsters that had done this had moved on, like locusts, to destroy human life elsewhere. On the side of our car was a ladder. The cuts along my legs broke open as I climbed to the top of the car. I was able to climb over and around until I could hoist my body up and slide back down into the belly of the overturned shell. My feet touched a chair and I climbed down until I stood where a window used to be.

Percy didn't wait for me to call all clear. He was out and holding me before I could utter a single word. I couldn't tell if he was crying or just shaking really hard, but his hands were rough against me as he touched my back, my face, my hair. I clung to him for a second, barely aware that my legs had begun to throb.

The sound of Edgar crying had me pushing against Percy to get to him. "Edgar," I called softly, still afraid to use the full volume of my voice, "come here."

He shook his head from underneath the seat and Percy reached his leg and pulled him out until he cowered against the floor. As if he weighed nothing more than a child, Percy lifted him to a standing position and wrapped his arms around him. "It's over," he said again and again until Edgar returned the embrace tentatively.

Unable to kneel with the cuts on my legs, I sat down and reached for Gigi, who was still unconscious. Percy set Edgar on the opposite side of him so his view of Sasha and Phillip's bodies was blocked. He knelt beside me and helped me maneuver her out from under the seat.

I lifted my fingers to her neck and felt a pulse. I flipped Percy's wrist over for his watch and he held it steady while I counted.

"Weak," I announced after a moment.

I looked around for my backpack. "I have a small medical kit." I reached above Phillip's broken body and dislodged my backpack from where it had been flung during impact. Pulling it free, I unzipped the top and pulled a white plastic medical kit from inside. "Here," I said, grabbing a packet of smelling salts and breaking it open, "put this under her nose."

Percy waved it under Gigi's nose with no response.

Oh, God, I thought. *What if she doesn't wake up?*

Another moment went by, and finally her eyes fluttered open.

"Gigi," Percy urged, "stay still."

She turned her head one way and then the other, looking around us. She was confused, and touched her head lightly. "Wha...what happened?"

Not wanting to complicate things, I stuck to the simplest explanation. "The train derailed," I said. "Do you remember?"

She touched her head again, and I pulled my penlight from my med kit and looked directly at her. "I want you to look right here," I said, holding a finger up in front of my nose. "Can you see my finger?"

"Y...yes."

"All right, look right here." I shined the light in and out of both eyes.

Percy looked to me. "Well?"

"Lie back, Gigi. Good."

She turned to Percy. "What happened, Percy?"

"The train derailed, Gigi," he repeated, and she nodded, a confused look still on her face.

"Gigi," I said, "look at my finger and follow it, please." I moved my finger in front of her face and peripherally, and then switched hands. "Good."

"Percy?" Gigi touched his arm.

"Yes, Gigi?"

"Where's Edgar?"

"He's right here, Gigi," I said softly and pointed to Edgar's legs that stuck out from where we'd sat him behind the chairs.

"Where are we?" she looked around. "Why did the train stop?"

Percy looked at me in panic. "Does she have...brain damage?"

"I think she has a really bad concussion. Her pupils are equal and reactive."

"What does that mean?"

"If she had brain damage her pupils would be slower and wouldn't constrict when light touched them."

"Why does she keep asking the same question?"

"It's really common with a bad concussion. She needs medical attention."

"Yeah, we need to get the hell out of here."

I looked behind him. "If you can open that door, we won't have to lift her out of the top."

"Is there anyone out there to hear us?"

"I didn't see anyone," I told him, and then thought of all the corpses lying on the ground outside the train. I stood and walked to the end of the overturned car. "Percy, keep Edgar on the side where we overturned. The underside of the train."

"Why?"

I inclined my head in Edgar's direction. He understood. "How bad?"

I bit my lip and exhaled hard. "Bad."

"All right. Let's go."

I approached Edgar, who had been quiet the entire time, and reached out to him. "Okay, you need to stand up now."

His eyes were enormous, staring straight ahead. I recognized that look from a boy I'd seen on one of my rounds that had witnessed his father being shot in South Philly. Edgar was in shock.

Keeping my tone neutral, I said, "We're going to do the same thing, together. I'm going to do it with you. Are you ready?"

He looked at me and nodded. In front of us, Percy had managed to get the door that went from car to car halfway open. It was wide enough for us to slide out without crawling out the top of the overturned car.

"I'm going to hold your hand the entire time," I said, "and I'm not going to let it go."

As if in a trance, Edgar watched my hand as I slowly moved it towards him and took his in mine. I'd seen the hospital shrink do the same thing with the boy that night, and was amazed it had worked. Now, if only I had the same luck with Edgar.

"Okay? Let's go."

I helped him stand and didn't let go of his hand as we walked side by side towards Percy, whose eyes were wide at the sight of his nearly comatose brother.

"Almost there," I said. We stepped through the door, ducking between the metal door and the rail and ending up outside of the train car.

Keeping my body turned so Edgar could only face one direction, I held his hand and steered him towards the underbelly of the train car. "Good. Now, we're going to sit here," I said, lowering him to the ground. His hand still clutched mine and I nodded to him. "Good job, Edgar, very good job."

The sight of the few bodies lying haphazardly near us elicited cries from Edgar, but I limped around to stand in front of him.

"Don't look. I want you to look at Gigi. Keep your eyes on her and don't look this way. Got it?"

Percy sat Gigi next to Edgar and I tried to pull my hand from Edgar's grip. He began to cry. I sat on the ground next to him. "I'm not going to let you go. Percy, get my pack and my kit from the floor and bring it here," I said, and he disappeared into the train car.

Gigi stared out blankly to the greenery around us. "Where are we?" she asked again.

Percy returned and dropped my pack and my kit at my feet. "Edgar, can you help me?" I asked him, and my free hand reached to open the kit. "I need to bandage my legs. Can you help me do that?"

I didn't wait for his response, but my legs were filthy and without bandaging them, the lacerations would continue to break open and bleed. At this point, infection and scarring were likely. Percy helped open gauze pads and bottles and I tried not to cry out when the alcohol hit the open wounds. Tears formed in my eyes and I bit my lip, breathing through my mouth. Pain seared through my legs and I grabbed Percy's upper arm and held on until the worst of the pain passed.

Pain filled Percy's face as he and Edgar helped me wipe the gashes across the front of both my legs. I pulled at Percy's hand when he began to wipe the wounds a second time. "Percy, please. Enough."

The cuts were deep and both legs were still seeping blood, but it was clotting and drying fairly well. When both legs had been cleaned and dressed, they were throbbing and my head hurt badly. I sighed with relief when Percy closed up my medical kit and zipped it back into my backpack.

"We need to get away from here," I said, trying to keep my voice even. I had no pain medication with me, and the thought of standing and walking more than a few feet was enough to make me want to cry.

"I don't know where we'll go," Percy said, looking out toward the train tracks beside us.

"We could backtrack," I suggested. "We're not more than an hour or two from Philly.

"They were likely on their way to Philly. And, you'll never make it." He looked at my legs. "I can carry you."

"No, Percy. Gigi might need you to carry her, or at least help her walk."

In the distance, the sound of jeeps approaching made my heart start racing. Percy heard it too and we both stood at the same time. Billows of dust came out from the distance, and I grabbed Edgar's hand and screamed at Percy.

"Move! Now!"

Edgar's cry was loud. He put his free hand over his ear and I pushed against the car and stood. I pulled Edgar to a standing position. Percy helped Gigi to stand and half carried, half pulled her behind him, with me leading the way. As fast as I could, I was making my way to the end car, past the twisted cars on the tracks, with people hanging out of them.

"Don't look, Edgar!" I screamed to him, and hoped he could hear me as the sound of jeeps got louder. Pain tore through my legs as I ran, pulling Edgar along with me, the sound of Percy following close behind.

The last two cars were the baggage cars. We were fifty feet from the first one when the roar of the jeeps filled our ears. If we could make it to the baggage cars, there might be enough metal around us to protect us, even if only for a few minutes. After that, I knew, we were dead.

They were coming fast, and overtaking us. Sweat dripped down my back and I broke into a near sprint, pain ripping through my claves, to get to the safety of the baggage car before they could begin firing on us. I could feel pain rip through my calves as my feet hit the ground. With any luck, we might get there before they entered the perimeter and saw us running. No such luck.

From directly behind us, we heard a voice booming over a bullhorn, "Stop where you are! We repeat! Stop where you are!"

I skidded to a stop. That voice was speaking *English*. We stopped and turned, our arms in the air as no fewer than five jeeps approached and surrounded us, and ten more streamed past them to surround the perimeter. The dust from their jeeps billowed around, all four of us pressed tightly against one another.

Soldiers stood in the rear of each of the jeeps, two with mounted automatic weapons, all three armed to the hilt. As the dust began to clear, I caught sight of something I'd never been so grateful to see in all my life. On the side of the third jeep was the American flag and the letters ARNG. Army Reserve National Guard.

"We're American!" Percy called out, and a soldier stepped from the front jeep and gave a signal to the other two jeeps to circle and look for other survivors.

After they pulled away he stepped down and approached us. Edgar screamed and pressed his face against my shoulder.

The soldier stopped where he'd landed out of the jeep. "Command Sergeant Major Hillson, United States National Guard." Sgt. Hillson turned to the men in the other jeeps and made a circular motion with his index finger. "Perimeter search!" he called. The jeeps went swarming by us and dust billowed around us once again.

I tried to quiet Edgar, and Sergeant Hillson looked at the four of us standing against the train. I could feel blood dripping down inside the bandages and I shifted weight from one leg to the other.

"Are there more of you that got out?" he asked, pointing to the remaining train cars. He raised his voice when none of us responded. "Are there more of you?"

I responded slowly, knowing that only I'd seen the massive slaughter on the other side of the train. "I don't think so," I said shakily, and Sergeant Hillson swore under his breath.

"Somebody get me a medic!" he shouted, looking down at my legs, which were covered in blood from my knees to my ankles. The bandages I'd put on them had torn open as we'd run. Blood had soaked through the bandages and was dripping into my shoes. He reached for the walkie talkie on his belt. "Medic at the front of the line. Civilian casualty."

I managed to quiet Edgar, but he still clung to me as if terrified the soldier was going to start shooting at any second. Percy helped Gigi to sit, and her head lolled against his shoulder.

Another man approached Sergeant Hillson, saluted, and confirmed the news I'd already suspected. We were the sole survivors.

A large Army truck came towards us and two medics ran out, carrying a stretcher. They headed for me, but I pointed to Gigi. "Take her first," I told them. "Loss of consciousness and possible head trauma. She needs a head CT and oxygen."

Gently, they loaded Gigi onto the stretcher and carried her to the back of the jeep. The three of us turned to follow them, and Sergeant Hillson touched my shoulder to stop me. "I need to ask you some questions."

I motioned for Percy to go with Edgar and Gigi, but Percy didn't budge.

"I'll stay," he said.

A soldier approached with a blanket and wrapped it around Edgar, who continued to cower at the loud noises all around us.

"Percy, please take him over to the medic," I begged. "Get him checked out. You can talk to Sgt. Hillson after I do and I'll stay with Edgar."

Reluctantly, Percy walked to the medic truck with Edgar and I turned to Sgt. Hillson.

"What's your name?"

"Kate. Kate Moore." I shifted my weight again and Sgt. Hillson motioned to one of the medics.

"All right, Kate, what was the origin of this train?"

"Philadelphia, Pennsylvania."

"What was your destination?"

"Um, Virginia."

A medic directed me to sit on the passenger side of the jeep while he examined my legs. As he peeled the bandages away from my wounds, spots danced in front of my eyes. I clutched the side of the door for support.

"How long ago did this happen?"

"We left the station at about eight this morning. We had only been on the train for an hour or two before… there was an explosion, and we felt the train leave the track."

Two soldiers joined Sergeant Hillson to stand in front of me and listen, and I answered their questions as best I could.

The medic regarded Sgt. Hillson. "Sergeant Major," he said and waited to be acknowledged. "We need to take her to the hospital."

I was nauseous and felt weak. I leaned heavily against the seat next to me, unable to protest as the medic lifted me in his arms and lowered me to the stretcher. Percy appeared beside me.

"Edgar?" I asked.

"Sedated and in the medic truck." Percy looked to the medic who was stringing an IV into my arm. "How is she?"

"She's lost some blood and she'll need a surgeon to repair those cuts on her legs."

Sgt. Hillson nodded to the medic, who lifted me with the help of a Corpsman.

"Sergeant Hillson," Percy asked as he climbed in his jeep. "Are you going to follow them? The men who did this?"

"Yes we are."

Percy looked at the destruction and death that surrounded us. "God help you."

The jeep started up and he commanded the medic to get me to the hospital. "God help us all," he replied, and his jeep swerved quickly around the rear car of the train in pursuit of the murderous band that had over an hour's lead time on them already.

CHAPTER TWO

Two nights of working the graveyard shift and sleeping all day had Carlie's internal clock confused. They arrived back at David's flat at two a.m. hoping to get at least six hours sleep before having to go in again; not knowing when or if the attack would come.

They entered the flat in the easy silence that comes when you know someone so well that speech isn't always necessary. David locked the door; silly now because of the deserted city, but comforting to Carlie nonetheless. She never thought she'd be the kind of girl content with domestic life. The kind of girl who wanted to cook dinner and lie on the couch together with a glass of wine and talk for hours. Never, that was, until she met David.

He was everything she wanted in a man, in a partner, and a friend. She needed someone strong, someone who could challenge her both physically and mentally. The more time they spent together the more time she craved, until she was content simply being next to him throughout the day. Deep in her heart, in the place she would never admit to, she knew it was more than friendship, more than companionship. Carlie had finally found the man who 'got her', and she was completely, hopelessly, and irrevocably in love.

They slid into his bed, side by side, neither one of them having adjusted to the new schedule. Stripping off his scrubs, David flipped the covers over both of them. Carlie had not even bothered to disrobe before crawling onto her side of the bed and laying her head down on the pillow next to his. David slipped an arm over her waist and pulled her to him; the simple act of having her against him was enough to lull him into a comfortable sleep.

Two hours later, Carlie's eyes blinked open. Her stomach was churning and she barely made it to the bathroom before she threw up. Within seconds, David was beside her. "What's going on? Are you okay?"

She pointed towards the door. "Out." She leaned against the porcelain of the lid.

Grabbing a washcloth from the cupboard, he rinsed it with cool water from the sink then placed it on the back of her neck. "Relax."

She sat on the floor until her stomach calmed, and then wiped her mouth, flushed, and got up, , swaying.

"Easy," David said and held her gently by the waist until she'd steadied herself.

Carlie smiled weakly. "God, I'm sorry. It's my nerves. I'm not sleeping well, and I can't help thinking about it. All the time."

"You sure you're okay?"

"Yeah. I'm fine. Let's go back to bed." She brushed her teeth and rinsed her mouth before following him back to bed.

David clicked off the light but couldn't relax. Sighing, he rolled to her. "Carlie."

"Mmmhmm?"

"Have you been eating something I don't know about?"

"No. Dave, I'm fine. Just nerves, like I said."

"That's the third time you've thrown up this week."

She let out an exasperated sigh. "And I barfed before I took the USMLE, too. Nerves. I get nervous. I have a nervous stomach. That's all."

David was silent for a few moments, and then, unable to sleep, he rolled onto his back. "Carlie?" he whispered, and she didn't respond. "Carlie," he tried again, and this time she stirred and rolled towards him, slipping an arm over his hip. "I need to ask you something."

Her voice was tired. "What?"

This was not the kind of question he had ever wanted to ask a woman. "When was your last period?"

Carlie giggled softly, something striking her funny in the way he said it. "Shut up," she said, and continued laughing.

"I'm serious, actually."

David leaned back to smooth her long brown hair back from her face, and she suddenly stopped laughing. "I just had it."

"I don't remember you *just* having it," he commented. "When?"

The smile that had been on her face faded and Carlie got an irritated 'I can't believe you're doing this now' look in its place. "Um, let's see." She held up her hands and counted on her fingers. "Okay, it was about um, three weeks ago. Happy?"

"How are you figuring that?"

"Because I started the same night right after the first Boeing warehouse collapsed." She gently slapped him on the chest. "You're an idiot." She rolled back over but he wasn't letting it go.

"That was *seven* weeks ago. Not three. Three weeks ago was the bus accident. The one that killed the five people in the diner. *Seven* weeks ago Boeing collapsed. I know because I had a meeting with the chief that day to discuss the offer we'd received for more help from Bellingham."

"No, it was—" she stopped dead.

"*Seven*," David repeated. "Weeks."

She moved away from him. "I know I just had it. I know I did."

"Do you keep a planner or something with it marked?"

"No, I used to, but not since I came here. I haven't had time. Besides," she said, turning towards him, "we've been careful every time."

David's face relaxed and he moved against her, kissing her neck softly. "*Every* time?"

"Yes. I'm..."

"The shower? On my birthday?"

Oh. Well, maybe not *every* time. She gritted her teeth. "Dave, it's not possible. I'm not having any signs of pregnancy."

He sat up in bed and folded his arms across his chest. "Really?"

"Really. I *am* a doctor. I would know."

"Mmmhmm. Okay. Vomiting three times in a week."

She shrugged. "Nerves."

"Telling me yesterday that my salad smelled like rancid fish."

"Um, it did."

"You're exhausted."

"No more than you are."

He sighed. "Do your breasts hurt?"

"Nope."

"Carlie, would you do me a favor? Just to appease me?"

She sighed heavily.

"Will you let me do a draw on you and test your HCG levels when we get in tomorrow?"

It wouldn't hurt, and it would make him stop obsessing about it, so she agreed. "Yes, fine."

He smiled. "Thank you."

They both lay back down, but neither one of them were going to go back to sleep. She turned away from him onto her side and slowly, mentally counted in her head. No, she simply had been wrong. Remembered it wrong. She couldn't be pregnant. Her hand slipped to her chest and gently pressed against her breasts. They weren't sore exactly, it was more like tender. Like right before your period kind of tender. She smiled at that thought. She was probably really close to getting it. Any day now. However, her eyes stayed open and she couldn't relax.

Behind her, David lay awake with his arm draped over her hip. They'd been careless; reckless...he was a complete fool. Most days he waited for the evening to come, when she was completely his. There was no caution in the way he'd fallen for Carlie. Something inside of him had come back to life when he met her, and he'd become addicted to it. *But, my God...he thought. She's twelve years younger them me. We're not married. We're in this war zone, waiting for death to find us.* He'd never considered the possibility of becoming a father. Ever.

However, the thought of being a husband to Carlie and a father to their child? He could only be that lucky. The look on her face told him that she wouldn't be happy tomorrow if the draw came back positive. If she was carrying his child. *His child.* Even the sound of it in his mind made him smile. He set his jaw. She'd be even less happy when he drove her to the bus station himself and put her on the next bus back to Denver where she'd be safe. Where they'd *both* be safe.

Without warning, an explosion rattled the windows in his flat so hard that they both flew up out of the bed. They ran to the window and scanned the darkness for light; signs of activity in the distance. From the horizon, a light flashed, and an explosion sounded several seconds later. The glasses in David's cupboard rattled and Carlie was slipping her shoes on as fast as she could, David climbing back into the scrubs he'd worn minutes ago. He called over to her.

"What the hell do you think you're doing?"

"Coming with you."

She pulled a rubber band around her hair, securing it into a bun behind her head. David had warned her that a ponytail was easier to grab, and so she wrapped her hair as tightly as possible at the nape of her neck.

"The hell you are." He grabbed his physician's badge from the nightstand and stalked through the kitchen towards the front door.

She met him at the door and stood against it, mouth in a hard line. "You leave me here," she warned, "and I'll be on the front lines searching for you." Her chest rose and fell with each breath, and her heart was beating a mile a minute. "You leave me," she said again, "and the war out there will be nothing compared to what you find when we both come home alive tonight."

He set his jaw at her stubbornness, but knew he'd never keep her here. And having her close where he could protect her was better than nothing. "Get your gun," he said through gritted teeth. "And the extra clip from inside the drawer. There's a war going on outside."

David slipped one of the heavy jackets he'd bought a month ago on her, and zipped it up. They descended the stairs from his flat and took their first steps out into the war zone. They ran the three blocks to the trauma center in the dark, lit only by the occasional flashes of light from bombs exploding in the Sound. Maria and Ynez were both behind the front desk, and two of the three attending doctors greeted David as he walked in through the door.

The chief wore an Army jacket with the words MEDIC emblazoned on the back, and was busy packing the remainder of the red emergency kits they would use in the field.

"Chief," David greeted him and helped him fill the remaining items in the extra kit.

Four more residents joined Carlie to stand against the counter.

"I'm hearing friendly fire being returned." David said, addressing them all.

"The only way we're going to be of any help is to go out there and attend to our men, our soldiers who are fighting for us and dying, right now. The battlefield is downtown Seattle and we're taking the Bellingham bus in as far as we can go."

He sighed, and the chief handed each of them a bright red medic kit. "It has stretchers and if we're lucky, they won't bomb it before we can load it with American soldiers and bring them back here. The order of triage on the battlefield is this; no pulse, move on. Amputation; tie off and load onto the bus asap. Heavy bleeder; pack it and rack it. Get them on the bus. Get them back here. Save as many as we can and get all of our asses out of there safely." He looked to their faces. "Any questions?"

They were all silent.

"Make sure you have extra ammunition and your safety is off. Get on the bus." The chief's voice was quiet, and they all grabbed their kits and filed out of the trauma ward and onto the bus bound for downtown Seattle.

The ride was bumpy. One of the two former medics who had driven the bus the last few months to and from the unit to Bellingham had stayed. He knew the back roads, the ones that weren't blocked, and they swerved and swayed together, sitting on the floor of the bus, headed towards the sound of those bombs. The sound got louder and Carlie wanted to cover her ears by the time the bus came to a complete stop alongside an old building that used to tower over the Seattle skyline but was now, in fact, an empty shell – half its former size. They could hear the rat-tat-tat of machine gun fire from the distance, but it was getting closer. David looked at her, his face filled with fear – but not for himself.

"Remember our location!" the medic yelled. "I'll be waiting here! I'll be crouching fifty feet from the bus and I'll have extra stretchers outside."

They all exited to the rear, in pre-determined teams, carrying a stretcher each. From their position, they could see all of Seattle Harbor, and all stood in awe and terror at what they saw. No fewer than three large battleships were in the harbor, and at least five smaller ones; mostly headed for shore. Black smoke billowed up from one of the smaller ships and Carlie had no idea if the ones headed for shore were friendly or not. They ducked as low as possible as they approached the crest of the hill. The streets of Seattle were being used to fight this war, and they were about to enter the fray.

On their stomachs, they looked down on the scene below them. Carlie's stomach lurched and her first inclination was to run. Machine gun fire actually hit the building to their right and they flung their hands over their heads and pressed closer to the dirt.

From where she lay, Carlie could see groups of men approach from the harbor, and the sound of gunfire echoed off the empty streets. One at a time, a line of men ran from the cover of one building to another no more than two hundred yards below her. She caught her breath in her throat when she recognized the color of their uniforms and the shape of their helmets. They were American. Another explosion sounded and something hit the corner of the building the soldiers were coming from. Carlie covered her head once again as pieces of the building fell all around them. The sound of machine gun fire joined the sound of something else: voices calling out. The sound of men dying.

Next to her, Rob and Tate grabbed their stretcher and pulled their collars up high. Both men crawled on their bellies to crest the hill.

"Now!" David said to her, and he pulled the stretcher forward, and her along with it, over the crest.

With every shot, she worried that she'd been hit or that David would go down. Low to the ground they ran, then ducked behind the cover of the opposing edge of the building that had been hit moments ago. Three men lay fifty feet from her, and David pushed her back against the building with his hand before she could react.

"Stay!" he commanded, and ran out to the first soldier, grabbed a leg and dragged him back behind the shelter of the corner of the building. "Mannis!"

Carlie ran forward and grabbed the other leg and managed to pull him to safety with David. She felt for a pulse while David and Rob ran out and retrieved the second soldier. His helmet was missing and she looked in his face. He was so young. Younger, even, than her. The entire right side of his face was covered with blood and shards of glass, but his pulse was strong. She reached behind her and slid her bag towards her. He was screaming, his hands trying to pull at the glass that had embedded itself in his chest and face.

"Stop," she said, her voice shaking badly. "I'm going to get you out of here." Another explosion sounded near her and she covered the soldier's body with her own.

"Who are you?" he cried out. "Where's my captain? He was right next to me!" His head rolled back and forth and he cried out in pain.

"Be still," Carlie urged and flipped open the top of her kit. "I'm an American doctor. You're going to be all right." She tore open one of the prefilled syringes with morphine in it. Remembering what David had told her, she tore open the front of his shirt and flipped over his dog tag. No allergies. She injected the syringe into his shoulder and his cries gradually diminished.

David and Rob returned with the second soldier, lifted the first patient onto the stretcher, and went to retrieve the third. From the crest of the hill she saw the second two teams run out low to the ground around another building further away. Gunfire echoed all around her and Carlie crawled to the second man and felt for a pulse. The upper half of his thigh was gone and he was bleeding, badly. His pulse was weak, but there.

She reached for a tourniquet in her kit. She tore open the front of his shirt and flipped over the tag. "Hey! Donald! Come on!" She wrapped it tightly around the leg at the hip and saw the gush of blood slow. She grabbed a battle pack and tore it open, pouring it on the gaping wound until it stopped bleeding altogether. Pulling the second stretcher closer to her, she laid it out next to him as David and Rob came back together, without the third soldier.

"Where is he?" she asked, and the ground rocked with the detonation of a bomb nearby.

"Gone!" Rob shouted, and he and David pulled the second man onto the stretcher. He looked around quickly. "Where the hell is Tate?"

"He was right behind you!!"

They looked behind them, to where the third soldier lay and saw Tate's leg draped over his body where he'd fallen.

"NO!" Carlie shouted.

David made a grab for Rob as he ran back out to Tate's body. He half pulled, half carried him back, the front of his medic jacket covered in blood.

"No, no, no, no..." Rob said over and over, and David tore open the jacket and saw where the bullets had entered, and exited.

"He's got a pulse, he comes with us." David looked to Tate and then Carlie.

"I've got Tate. Carlie, you get the back of the first stretcher, Rob get the front. Follow me and stay down, Goddamnit!"

They rushed to do as he'd commanded. Carlie struggled under the weight of the first body on the stretcher. Her medic kit was strapped to the handle and she moved her hand against it. At a lull in the gunfire, David signaled to them to move.

Carlie ran, trying not to trip. She held the two poles of the stretcher up to the crest of the hill. They ran with everything they had, Rob half pulling Carlie most of the way. Her arms strained and pain shot through right to her shoulder with the weight of the body and the incline of the hill. Ahead of them she saw David, Tate slung over his shoulder, cresting the hill and running even under the weight of another man. The sound of shots behind them got louder, but she couldn't turn to look back.

Somehow they made it. Frank ran to meet them and helped David load Tate onto a stretcher and onto the bus. Rob and Carlie loaded the second stretcher and ran back outside at the sound of approaching footsteps. The second team ran, stretcher between them, Dan yelling the whole way like a paratrooper. Carlie helped the third team onto the bus with another stretcher when they saw the chief and Marco headed for them, an injured soldier in each of their arms.

"Lost the stretcher halfway down the hill!" he called and they rushed to help him.

As they loaded the last of the five bodies onto the bus, Carlie looked around them. "Hey, Frank!" she called out in alarm. "Where's David?"

"Went back down. Said something about a second stretcher."

Frank was busy setting up the soldiers on the lower racks so that if they were fired on, they wouldn't be injured worse than they already were. Carlie ran around the bus holding her breath. Like a shot, they appeared, David and Todd, at the top of the crest, the soldier with the massive leg wound between them.

"Go!" he was calling to them. "Start the bus! Go!"

They clambered on the bus just as something was fired into the building next to them, shattering glass everywhere. Pieces of it fell on the bus as David and Todd were pulled inside and the soldier slid into the last holding space underneath the safety net.

"Frank, move this thing!" David screamed, and the bus roared to life and turned the opposite direction that they had come.

It seemed to Carlie that they would have to backtrack to return to the trauma center but she didn't care. As long as they were away from the machine gun fire and bombs. The bus surged back and forth as Frank navigated at a breakneck speed out of the hot zone, back towards safe territory.

Within five minutes she felt the ride even out and they were turning back in the direction of where they needed to be. They were all crouched down next to the men they had saved, and the sound of pain was all around them as they drove quickly towards the trauma center.

CHAPTER THREE

"Matt," Carrie called, "bring me that basket from the car and the pie cutter."

Returning with both, he set them down on the table of food that the women had set out. Born and raised in California, Matt had never been to a barn raising, or a town meeting, or for that matter – anything having to do with a town. Looking around him, however, he couldn't understand for the life of him why not.

Carrie waved at a few of the new people passing by.

"Can't let a soul go by without an introduction," Charlie muttered. Matt grinned and bit his cheek to keep from laughing.

"I'm so glad you decided to come!" Carrie said and nodded towards Charlie. "This is my husband, Charlie." She motioned to the couple in front of them that looked to be a little younger than she and Charlie. "This is Mandy and Greg..."

"Craig," he corrected.

"Craig Oppengard." She smiled at them again. "And their son...uh... Peter?" Peter nodded in acknowledgement. "And their daughter Sarah."

Peter and Sarah were older; in their early twenties from the look of them; in any case much too old to be traveling – or moving – with their parents.

Carrie turned to Matt. "And this is our..." she didn't really know what to call Matt, and with a laugh, he finished for her.

"I'm a friend of the family," he said, and shook Craig and Mandy's hand. Sarah smiled at him and Peter looked bored with the whole process.

"How are you liking it in Fall River so far?" Carrie asked Mandy.

Charlie whispered in Matt's ear, "Should have been a tour guide."

"It's very nice," Mandy said, though it wasn't quite sincere enough to be convincing.

"Sarah, Mandy tells me you're a teacher."

Sarah was petite, around five feet tall with golden brown hair and really fair skin. The freckles on her nose made her look younger than she likely was. "I am...was...an elementary school teacher. Before we left Texas."

"We need a teacher around here," Carrie said, although she had no idea if the school was open or not.

"What do you do, Matt?" Craig asked, and Matt leaned against the side of the truck with Charlie.

"Right now I help Charlie out on the farm."

Charlie clapped him on the back. "We'll make a wheat farmer outta him yet."

"Yay," Peter said under his breath, and turned to look the other direction.

"What about you, Peter?" Matt asked, and tried not to dislike the guy after only having met him thirty seconds ago.

"Before we made the spectacular decision to move here?" he asked, and his parents' eyes dropped. "Played ball for the Longhorns."

Matt didn't miss a beat. "Yeah? What's your major?"

"Economics," he said. "But I was thinking of changing. Maybe pre-law."

"That's what Matt was studying. Before...well," Carrie said, "you know."

"Yeah?" Peter asked. "Where?"

Knowing it might shut him up, Matt looked him in the eye. "Stanford."

It worked. He shifted his gaze to something else, and Matt got a nudge from Charlie that said it wasn't nice to tease the tourists.

"Y'all were a lawyer?" Sarah asked, wrinkling her nose up as she tilted her face to look at him.

"Nah, not yet. Hadn't taken the bar."

"But you weren't there. When the bomb went off."

"No, I wasn't."

"Lucky for you," Mandy said.

He smiled. "Yes. Lucky for me."

"You live with family?" Sarah asked Matt.

"I live with Carrie and Charlie," he answered. "But I'm thinking of building my own place when I get my own land."

Craig motioned to Mandy. "We liked the idea of that, too. Starting new somewhere safe."

Matt wondered if there was such a place nowadays, somewhere safe nowadays, but he stayed silent and thought about the telegram Katie had sent to Carrie yesterday. By now she was in Virginia. With Percy. His jaw hardened and he looked at the ground.

"Y'all didn't move here with your folks?" Sarah asked, pushing him a little further, and he liked the Texas lilt to her voice.

"No, my uh, dad didn't make it and my mom got sick." It was the best way to describe what had happened, and the only way he could explain it to a stranger. "She's with my brother back in Boston."

Sarah smiled at him. Matt looked away, but Carrie caught it and smiled. "So you're not married, Sarah?"

Charlie, who had been sipping iced tea, nearly choked, and Matt pounded hard on his back.

Sarah laughed and looked directly at Matt. "No, ma'am, I'm not married."

Carrie grinned brightly. "I see."

"Are you married, Matt?" Sarah asked when Charlie stopped coughing.

"Not yet," Matt said evenly and her smile faded a little. "My girlfriend is in Philadelphia right now, so..." he shrugged. "I'm waiting for her to come back."

If looks could kill, Matt would be dead on the spot from the daggers Carrie was shooting him. Charlie smirked and sat back down to sip his tea. So help him, his wife was gonna marry Matt off, even if it killed him. He chuckled at the thought.

Carrie looked off into the distance, her hand shielding her eyes against the sun. "What on Earth?"

Charlie and Matt looked in the same direction. "What is it?"

"It's Tom. What's...he's running. Matt," she held her hand out to him, "hurry. He looks like he needs help."

Matt ran towards Tom, and caught the older man in the street. He was carrying no fewer than ten pieces of paper, all telegrams – but handwritten and scrawled on the paper that he normally typed them on.

Jefferson Trent caught up with Matt and they both helped Tom walk towards the picnic benches set up at the edge of the old park. Twenty people gathered around him. His face was beaded in sweat and he was wheezing.

"Slow down, Tom," Charlie said and looked around. "Mark Lindblade here?" he looked around. "Doc Lindblade?"

"I've...got to tell you....something..." Tom said urgently, shaking the crumpled pieces of paper in his hands. "Everyone! I've..." he tried to catch his breath he coughed again and again until he could actually speak.

Carson handed him a glass of water and he took a hurried drink, dribbling water down the front of his shirt. He looked around him at the people of Fall River. "We're getting messages..." he began quickly. "From all over. Emergency signals."

A collective cry went up through the crowd, but Charlie's booming voice rose above them. "Let him talk! Shut up a minute!" He looked back down to where Tom sat on the edge of the bench. "Go on."

Tom's hands still clutched the telegrams as if his life depended on it and Matt thought Tom was going to cry as he read the first out loud. "At seven-thirty eastern time," he took a gulp of air, "two buses traveling into New York were attacked and all passengers on board were killed."

Matt began to sweat. What did this mean? Was Jazz right? Had the battle begun?

"At nine-thirty eastern, a train from Philadelphia was attacked and all passengers on it..." he began to sob, but finished in broken breaths, "were shot."

Philadelphia. No. Matt took a step backwards and the Earth tipped. *Oh my God. No, it simply couldn't be. She was on a different train. She had to have been. It couldn't have been hers.*

"Militia entered Florida near what used to be the Space Center," Tom continued, "and gunned down hundreds of local residents in the outlying areas."

Several people covered their mouths, others leaned against the shoulder of a neighbor and began to cry. Tom began to give accounts that he'd received through the wires of attacks on every coast, from nearly every point of entry to the United States.

"What about our armies?" someone asked. "Where are they?"

Tom looked helpless and broken. "I'm sorry," he said, and gathered the pieces of paper together. "This is all I have right now." He stood shakily. "Emergency warnings have been sent to all postal stations through the code. Stay inside. Arm yourselves. God be with you all." His voice broke. "I'd better get back now. I'll call any of you I can if I hear anything else." He walked back, muttering to himself and wiping across his face with his arm, tears streaming down his face.

Everyone was silent for a half second, and then pandemonium broke out among the crowd. Matt made it to Carrie in under a second, and picked her up in his arms.

"Charlie!" he called above the crowd. "Get the truck!"

He carried Carrie to Charlie's truck and they drove back to the farm in silence. Carrie cried silently against Matt's shoulder and Charlie sat gripping the steering wheel as if it was the only thing holding him together.

Matt reached for Carrie's arm and helped her into the house. He turned to Charlie as the screen door closed behind her. "I'll be needing a few of those guns we talked about."

Charlie was silent for a second. When he responded, his voice was quiet. "You gonna go fight 'em all, chief?"

"Nope. But I'm gonna find her. Even..." Matt's lower lip actually trembled, "even if it means all I do is find her body and bring it back here to bury."

Charlie whistled softly through his teeth. "How you gonna get there? No busses gonna run now that we're under attack."

Matt thought about this, but didn't immediately respond. "You gonna walk? Drive?"

He didn't have a car, and couldn't very well take the only one that Charlie and Carrie had to go find Katie. Tears filled his eyes.

"She can't...can't be..." he said, and Charlie pulled him into a firm embrace. Matt's entire body sagged and he sobbed into Charlie's shoulder.

Charlie wasn't a crying man. He could remember three times in his whole life that he'd cried. Two were the births of his sons, and the last was the death of his mother. As he stood there holding Matt against him, tears welled up in his eyes and he cursed everything going on around them.

"I need you here, son," Charlie said, his voice rough, and pushed against him gently until Matt stood straight again. "In case things go bad."

Matt's head sagged still, and tears rolled down his cheeks. "I shouldn't have let her go with him. If I'd never let her go..."

"That's horse shit," Charlie said, and leaned a hand on his shoulder. "Now you listen. She had her own way of doing things, and her own mind. You don't know that her train is the one that got...well, the one that got hit." That seemed to comfort Matt some, and he nodded. "Until you know for sure, we're not gonna think of it like she's dead."

From inside, he could hear the sound of Carrie crying, and he pointed towards the door. "C'mon. Go in. She needs you bad right now, to talk about Kate."

They entered the room where Carrie sat, Kate's letters spread out across the table. She held her last telegram in her hands. "She said they were leaving early," she wailed with great, horrible sobs. "They wanted to get an early start."

Matt knelt down next to her and Carrie buried her face in his shoulder. "She's not gone. She's not gone," he chanted. "She's not. She can't be."

Carrie didn't respond, and Matt pushed her away to look at her. "There were so many trains leaving this morning, I bet she's in Virginia by now." He didn't believe it, but he kept saying it anyway. "I'm gonna go into town and I'm gonna send a telegram to the post station there in Virginia near the address she sent you. I'll send it every hour if I have to. I *will* get a response."

This seemed to soothe Carrie, who wiped her eyes with her hand. "Charlie, I want you to go with him and send word to the boys."

"All right, Mother," Charlie said, and handed her his handkerchief.

"Tell them to be safe. To take care of themselves. And tell them..." she began to cry softly again, "tell them to come home if they can."

"Okay," Charlie said. "We'll do it tomorrow."

"No," she said. "Now. Today. Please?"

"I'm not gonna go leaving you, or anyone else, alone. Not with everything—"

"Charlie Blackhawk, I know how to shoot a gun better 'n most men you know, and I pity the poor son of a bitch who comes through my door." She sniffed again and, although it wasn't funny, Charlie couldn't help but smile.

"All right, Mother. We'll go. I'll take the pie and give it to Tom. He'll likely need food tonight, since I doubt he'll leave the station at all."

Carrie turned back towards the letters scattered across the table. When Matt stood, she touched his hand and he leaned down to her again. "What is it, Carrie?"

She reached up and gripped the front of his shirt to pull him closer. She spoke to him softly, pleading, "Find our girl."

Charlie and Matt drove to the post station quietly. The entire way, Matt wondered what he should say in his telegram to get Kate to come home. He couldn't send a telegram to the uncle to simply confirm the death; he wouldn't allow himself to do that. Charlie was right. He had to go on the assumption that it hadn't been her train that got hit. If Kate was indeed alive, and in Virginia, what could he possibly say that would make her come to him?

"Charlie," Matt asked, "you think the busses are still running out of Wheatland?"

Charlie sighed before responding. "Not sure, chief. You thinkin' of goin' somewhere?"

Matt looked out the window and didn't answer.

"Folks most likely won't be leavin' the Midwest. We're a lot safer than the outlyin' areas, that's for sure."

"I suppose." Matt's brows knit together in concentration. "But if I wanted to—"

"Gas is even more scarce now, if the war's started. You can't get to her. You know that, don't ya? Even if it wasn't her train—"

"Then I'll go to the address in Virginia and find her there."

Charlie's mouth set in a hard line. "Ain't no damned train gonna go to into a war zone! Everyone's comin' this way! Not t'other way around!"

"I've *got* to, Charlie," Matt said, his voice desperate. "I can't have lost her. I just can't." They were silent for a moment as they neared town. "I knew he wouldn't take care of her. Not like I could." His hatred for Percy burned hot and he clenched his fists.

Charlie turned down Maple and his voice softened some. "I know but there's nothin' gonna be gained from that right now. Send her a telegram in Virginia. If she's there, she'll respond."

Matt's laugh was bitter. "Yeah! You think Percy will ever let her respond to a 'just want to make sure you're okay' telegram from me? He's better off if I think she's dead. Think about it, Charlie. Even if I send a telegram begging her to send a reply, what are the chances he'll let her respond? Or that she'll even *get* the telegram?"

Charlie said nothing, only gripped the steering wheel in thoughtful silence.

Matt's jaw hardened as he thought of Percy – the entire reason Kate had been going to Virginia in the first place. His heart fell. She couldn't be dead. It couldn't be her train. It had to be another. If they had been on another train, and were in Virginia already, Percy would never let her leave… voluntarily.

Matt considered the possibilities. As they pulled into town, it struck him. At first, he mentally shook off the idea. It was dishonest. More than that, it was dangerous. But it might be enough to get Kate to leave Virginia and come, if she was alive. Alternatively, Matt worried that if Kate did come, she'd be at risk by traveling on another train that could also be attacked.

The thought paralyzed him. However, at least she'd be traveling to a safer part of the country, and once she was here, he could protect her. It was a day and a half by train from Virginia to Wheatland. Surely the Midwest was safer than the coast. Charlie was right. Trains were traveling *away* from the coast, not *to* it. Those telegrams Tom had read were proof. She simply wasn't safe in Virginia. Matt needed her safe. He needed Kate beside him.

"Oh Jesus," Charlie muttered under his breath, and they both looked at the post station. It was flooded with people, pushing to get inside for either news or to send a telegram of their own. It was complete pandemonium. Charlie and Matt alighted from the truck and Charlie pushed inside against the mob of people who were swarming against the front desk where Tom looked about ready to have a stroke. Pulling a chair from the corner of the room, Charlie stood on it and whistled loudly through his teeth several times until the roar quieted to a murmur.

"Hang on, all of ya!" he looked around to people crowding around the front desk, holding their messages in their hands. Their faces were much alike; worried, scared, tearstained. "What'ya doin?" Charlie asked. "War's out there, not in here. Tom's doin' his best. Now. We're gonna line up. Single file!" he said, pointing to a man who was trying to push through the crowd. "Tom will help you one at a time! Till that happens, shut up!"

Matt looked around at the people who had crowded into the post station who respected Charlie and would obey him.

"You get loud and Tom can't hear what you need to send. He can't help you. Any of you!" He stopped and his voice got lower. "Now, Tom and his son have been here all morning without a break. Someone, go get 'em some water, or a soda, and a sandwich from Peterson's." No one moved. "Whoever brings it back gets seen next," Charlie said.

Three people ran out of the station and Charlie winked at Tom. "All right, Tom. Go ahead."

A grateful look spread across Tom's face, and he nodded thanks to Charlie. Matt slid into line to wait his turn. A few minutes passed and the three people returned with food, soda, water and, true to Charlie's word, were slid into the front of the line. Charlie stood to the side, watching the crowd as they filtered up to send their telegrams, one at a time. Behind him, the telegram machine was clicking with messages coming through. Tom's son Martin sat next to it, writing down every word and sending messages when it paused.

When Matt finally got up to the front, it had been more than an hour and a half. Tom looked like he'd fought a war. His normally jovial face was gray and the creases around his eyes were deep.

"Hey, Tom," Matt said, and Tom actually curved his lips into a slight smile in response. "These are going to Charlie's boys." He handed Tom the two short messages that Charlie had written out, asking both boys to send word that they were all right, or come home. Matt slipped a third message across the counter. "This one's going to this address in Virginia."

Tom read the last piece of paper and looked over to Charlie, who was busy talking to a neighbor. "You, ah, sure this is correct?"

"Yes," Matt said, then lowered his voice. "Just send it, all right?"

Tom added it to the top of the stack to be sent. Matt walked out of the post station, with Charlie following a few minutes later. It would take three hours before Martin would get to the message being sent to Kate in Virginia, and another five before it was typed out in Virginia and sent out for delivery.

No longer delivered in cardboard, the paper telegram was folded and sealed in a small envelope, and it read:

```
To:  Kate  Moore  c/o  Thomas  Oliveri,  21
Colonial Fredericksburg VA

From:  Charlie  Blackhawk  55  Shoreline  Hwy
Fall River, SD

Carrie has fallen ill

She is asking for you to come

Urgent, please respond

Charlie
```

CHAPTER FOUR

The first phase of the frontal attack was massive. When their combined fleet entered U.S. territorial waters – both on the East Coast and the West – it was done as a massive coordinated effort. They received their first warnings when they breached the 12 nautical mile belt, but at that point, the threats from the United States to cease their advance and retreat to neutral water were useless.

They knew ahead of time where the U.S. had their largest warships, which were targeted by their cloaked submarines. Under heavy siege, the warships and destroyers could not both defend themselves and attack the ships passing to land on U.S. soil. With many of their Nimitz Class aircraft carriers in the Gulf or Middle East, the chances of a massive nuclear response to their attack would be minimal. In addition, it was widely known the United States stationed much of their fleet – including many destroyers – of the coast of Virginia in Norfolk. For that reason only, Virginia was the first and most heavily hit target.

Fortunately, not all of their ports would be so heavily guarded. Seattle and San Francisco, which had been initial detonation points of interest, were ideal landing patterns for their fleet of Amphibious Assault ships. Carrying a bulk of their army to their shores, the fleet would be able to both arrive as locusts and destroy any opposition raised in such remote locations. This was why the initial nuclear strike had been planned so carefully, and the second wave of the attack delayed with precision timing; the cities that had suffered the most egregious attacks would be sparsely populated, easier to re-enter and unlikely to have any military presence. They were the perfect wound to infect.

With half of their fleet on the East Coast and the remainder on the West, they had thought strategically about how to get the advantage. With submarines coming in three different waves on five different shores, they could accurately give a firm location of the U.S. ships to destroy. Their location would be sent to the command post and they would be eliminated one by one by China's DF21D's. As each of the coastal cities was attacked – and by then their existing fleet was being destroyed – the U.S. would try and call on their outlying fleet to come to their aid. With the final subs hiding in outlying waters, the location of the incoming ships would be easy to transmit. China's ASBMs had the capability to strike a moving capital ship with ballistic missiles, and were deadly accurate.

The combined power of their five countries' armies, along with the amount of "purchased" firepower from countries that swore no allegiance to their cause – but also didn't offer opposition – would be so overwhelming to the U.S. that there would be no way to defend against them. And that was just the attack by sea. Once their men hit land...the battle would be all but won.

When news of the Pennsylvania train attack reached New Orleans, Ano went to bed and stayed there the entire day. Michelle and Grandma Vesper brought trays of food in to her, and she sent them away without touching a bite. Jazz stayed in the garage with the uncles, following what little they could on the short and long wave radios. Another cousin brought a CB and got in touch with some truckers who had driven through some of the eastern coastal cities on their way to another destination. What they were told was not good.

With the minute amount of information gleaned from all sources, it was clear that the United States had known and was prepared for the insurgents' attacks. No one was prepared for the number of civilian casualties occurring up and down both coasts. The U.S. appeared to have a plan, but since no one knew who was organizing the military, the details of the defense remained a secret. Many television stations were back up, but most were in the Midwest and south, where little or no fighting had been reported. All those stations were getting second, third, and fourth hand reports, and repeating what they could verify on the air.

The main facts were clear; the U.S. was under heavy attack. Its borders were being infiltrated by armies of many countries intent on doing as much damage and destruction as possible before they were exterminated. The streets of most cities were empty. People stayed in their homes unless they absolutely needed to leave, and even then it wasn't advisable. Everyone asked the same questions: Where are our military leaders? Why haven't other countries come to our aid when we've helped them time and time again?

The question on everyone's mind, but one that no one would verbalize was the worst: Will our armies be enough to defeat the insurgents that started this war in the first place?

The day before the war began, Ano had received Kate's telegram. She sat down to write her a long letter about hers and Jazz's plans to go to seminary. The letter sat unfinished on top of the small desk in the room she and Jazz shared. She'd closed the drapes, not wanting to see the sunlight or have any intrusion on her thoughts. They'd heard reports of the first three attacks, but after hearing the train from Philly had been bombed and all its passengers gunned down, Ano had had enough. She lay on her side in bed, spinning her wedding ring around and around on her finger. She thought about Stanford and all the dreams she'd had in college – where she'd go; what she'd be. And she thought about Kate.

Kate had been headed to Virginia with Percy. Her eyes narrowed even at the thought of that man. If she was being truthful, Ano had never liked him. Never understood what Kate saw in him; never believed it would matter. In her mind, he'd redeemed himself because, after all, if it hadn't been for him, none of them would have been alive after the first bomb hit San Francisco. Then again, it was Kate's idea for him to do his thesis on the cave in the first place, so she'd chalk that one up to Kate and not *him*.

If Kate had stayed with Matt, she'd be in South Dakota with Carrie and Charlie. She'd be happy, and safe. But she hadn't. Ano rubbed her eyes with the heels of her hands and tried not to cry again. Kate couldn't be gone; she simply couldn't. The train wasn't hers. It had to have been a different train. And Kate had either not made it onto her train, or had already made it to Virginia when that particular train was attacked. In her heart she feared the worst, and simply couldn't admit it out loud. Kate could not be dead.

Ano had thought through every plan of action she could possibly take, from telegrams to Virginia and Pennsylvania to hiring one of those locators to try and get to Kate. If Ano could reach her, she could find a way to bring her back here to New Orleans. Away from the coast. Away from the war. Away from Percy.

Danger followed that man like a damn magnet, she fumed. First the Wind Cave, now this? How could he keep Kate with him in good conscience? She didn't understand it. A soft knock sounded at the door and her grandmother came in.

"C'mon baby," Grandma crooned and sat down on the edge of the bed. "Don't make Grandma worry. Come downstairs. We havin' supper in 'bout twenty minutes."

Ano shook her head, but didn't turn. "I'm not hungry."

Grandma Vesper sighed and got off the bed. For a second Ano thought she'd left, but she closed the door to the bedroom and walked around to sit at Ano's feet. She rubbed them with her soft hands and Ano relaxed. "She's okay, chile."

Ano's lip began to quiver and she nodded silently.

"When your grandpa died..."

Ano's ears perked up. Her grandmother rarely ever spoke of her grandfather's death. In fact, in years past, it was a surefire way to make Grandma Vesper cry merely by mentioning her husband, who had died many, many years before.

"...I just closed up." Grandma Vesper rocked back and forth, and Ano relaxed with the feeling of her grandmother rubbing her feet and rocking on the bed. "Ev'body said for me to grieve. But I couldn't. I wasn't ready." She hummed for a few seconds more. "I didn't cry much that first month. Or the second. And then," Ano wasn't sure if it was a chuckle or her breath catching in her grandma's throat, "I was doin' laundry one day while you were in preschool. An' I reached into the dryer and pulled out one of his socks."

She laughed gently at the memory, a soft throaty laugh. Grandma Vesper sniffed, and Ano knew she was crying.

"I held it and held it, and cried and cried. Didn't think I'd ever stop." She sighed and wiped the tears from her eyes. "Nobody can tell you how to grieve, baby girl." She took a deep breath. "You lost a lot lately. Lost a home. A school. Your dreams."

Her grandmother's voice had a hold on her now, but instead of going on, she began to hum. Ano recognized it. It was Kate's song, the song her grandmother used to hum to Kate when she would come. Tears squeezed out between Ano's shut eyelids and she lay on the bed crying silently.

"I don't know how," she said, speaking between sobs, "how I can keep going without her. I love her. So much, and..." her grandmother's hand never left her feet as she cried and talked, "now it seems like everything I loved is gone."

Grandma Vesper was likely the wisest person on Earth. She listened, and hummed, and rubbed Ano's feet, and when Ano's breaths were coming in shuddering breaths, she finally spoke. "Your generation never really been through a war," she said.

Ano started to disagree, but Grandma held up a hand for her to listen.

"I been through Ko-rea. I been through Vietnam. And lemme tell you, those weren't no paper wars."

"What's a paper war?"

Grandma Vesper chuckled. "It's a war you read about in the paper, like it's some damned TV show. Who's doin' what to who today." Her lower lip quivered. "My brother, he died in Ko-rea. Nearly killed my momma. We saw his friends come home, missin' arms and legs...sometimes eyes." She stopped for a moment, thinking. "People o' your generation are soft! Spoiled! Sitting in front of damned computers playing games while there's people dying!" She mumbled to herself for a minute, and then said, "When my brother was in Ko-rea, we listened every day. *Every day* to the TV. *Every day* to the radio. When they comin' home? When they comin' back? President's on, what's he gonna say? When's Travis comin' home?"

Ano turned over and wiped her eyes.

"Baby, listen. I been through wars. I know what's comin'." She hesitated, wondering if her granddaughter could take what she was about to say. "War brings only one thing...pain. And lots of it. Pain to the people who's in it, pain to the folks waitin' back at home for their children to come walkin' back through the door."

"I'm so tired of being scared. And worried."

"I know," Grandma Vesper said. "So are we all. It's war, baby. This time, all men gotta fight. All men gotta rise up. We come from way worse than this. We'll survive. Times like this, you gotta thank God you're not in New York or L.A.! You imagine what would have happened if you and Jazz wouldn't have found your momma and me? And Lively?"

Ano tried not to smile. "Jazz says the enemy would have given Lively back."

Grandma's throaty laughter filled the room. "I do love that boy. Lively is our secret weapon, though," she teased, and tilted her head to look at her lovely granddaughter. "I love Kate like she's my own, and I can't think she's gone. You thought we was gone, and look!" She raised her hands up to the heavens and smiled back down at Ano. "Grandma's still here."

"I don't like just sitting here. It's like we're waiting for them to come attack us."

Grandma Vesper nodded, understanding. "I know, it's hard. And even harder to feel joy." She scooted closer to Ano, and smoothed the long bangs from around her face where they'd fallen. "You gotta focus on the good in your life right now. We alive – and together. You got a husband who loves you!"

Ano smiled.

"And a Grandma who wants you to come down and eat!"

Ano actually did laugh at that, and allowed Grandma Vesper to sit her up and give her a hug. Another knock sounded on the door and Jazz peeked his head in.

"Sorry," he said, "I thought you—"

"Come on in now, don't let Grandma scare you 'way!" she chuckled and got up off the bed. "I gotta get back downstairs before Lively add more salt to that jambalaya."

"Actually," Jazz said, pointing towards the door with his thumb, "she just asked Michelle to get more cayenne pepper."

Grandma Vesper's mouth set in a hard line. "I'll kill that woman. Lively!" she shouted and hustled out of the room.

Jazz shut the door behind her and sat on the bed. "How you doin'?"

Ano shrugged. "Okay. A little better I think."

"Wanna come down to dinner?"

Ano looked to where her grandmother exited. Even from upstairs they could hear Lively and Grandma Vesper having it out over cayenne pepper. Jazz snickered and Ano laughed a little. "I think dinner's gonna be late."

"Maybe so," Jazz said. "I'm sorry. I been leavin' you alone a lot lately."

She shrugged. "It's ah-right."

"No, I been spending too much time with your uncle in the garage."

He lay down on the bed next to her. Her face, even without an ounce of makeup, was the loveliest thing he'd ever seen.

"Jazz," she said, "I wanna try to get in touch with Kate. I gotta know if she's okay."

"Okay, baby. Anything you want."

"I want you to take me to the post station tonight."

"Not after dark. We'll go tomorrow morning."

Ano sighed, but conceded. "First thing."

"First thing," he assured her. His hand smoothed along her arm, then back up to her neck. She closed her eyes, it felt so good.

"You hear from Matt?"

"No," he said, "only that one letter right after he got back." His fingers slid to the top button of her blouse and her eyes opened at the touch.

"You write him back?"

"What am I gonna say?" He unfastened the second, then the third button on her shirt and their eyes met.

"You could say," she slipped her hands down to where his shirt was tucked into his jeans, "that you think Kate's alive. And that she'll come around."

Five buttons, six. One hand slid inside the shirt and wrapped gently around her warm breast. "Uh huh," he said, and pulled her closer to kiss her neck. "What if I don't think she'll..." he slid a hand behind her knee and pulled one long leg to recline over his hip, "...come around?"

Her fingers nimbly unfastened the buttons on his jeans, but Ano kept her eyes locked on his. "Then you lie." She leaned in to kiss him, her lips warm against his own.

"Lie?" He slid his hands underneath her shorts and tugged.

"Mmmhmmm." Ano pulled the bottom of his shirt up and Jazz removed it the rest of the way, revealing his incredibly broad chest. She traced it with her index finger, and said hot against his ear, "Lie."

"Thought you told me never to lie." His hand came to rest against her.

Her head was tipped back and her mouth was open. She felt the pressure increase. "That's right...oh...um...no lying. To me."

Smiling at the pleasure he was giving his wife, Jazz rubbed his hand against her and leaned down to taste the skin on her neck. "Okay," he breathed, "I'll write him back."

Downstairs, even above the ruckus Lively was making, Grandma Vesper could hear the creaking of that old mattress and smiled to herself, thinking that everything would work itself out in the end.

Chapter Five

There was no end to this trail, and we were in the dark. Where was my flashlight? My lantern? Why couldn't I move faster? My legs were moving through sand as I ran. Suddenly I stopped and looked around me. I was alone. Then from a hundred feet away I saw someone and rushed to get to them. Percy? Edgar? I had to get there. What if they were alone?

My hands were shaking, and I was sweating horribly. My mouth was dry, and I couldn't call out to them. It was getting darker and I tried to hurry faster but my legs wouldn't carry me. I looked down. My legs were covered in blood, streaming down into my shoes, making it impossible for me to run. Please, I thought, just let me make it to them.

I got closer. It was one person, short and fragile looking. As I got within ten feet of her, I realized my horrible mistake. Her back was to me and standing right in front of her was one of the enemy soldiers. I tried to scream but nothing came out. He raised his M-16 pointed directly at her middle. As if separated by glass, I pounded against the air in front of me and tried to scream again. I was too late. Bullets sprayed from his gun, making sick pelting noises as they hit her squarely in the torso. As she fell I ran for her, kneeling next to her body. Her face turned towards me. Something was wrong. The face of the girl...was my own.

"Kate! Kate!" Percy was shaking my shoulders. "Kate! Wake up! It's a dream!"

Not expecting to see someone in front of me as I awoke, my first thought was fear and I pounded at his chest with my fists. "No! Get away from me! Help!"

His hands easily deflected my blows, and held my hands by the wrists until I stopped struggling. Breathing like a wild animal, I looked around me. Was this a dream? Or was I safe? My throat was dry and I looked around us. I wasn't alone. His grip on my wrists relaxed, and I swallowed hard. Percy was sitting next to me in a large four-poster bed. The entire room was dark, save a light he'd left on in the bathroom behind us.

"It was a dream," he said, waiting for me to calm down.

My chest was heaving, my heart beating like a jackrabbit. He released my hands. I remembered now. Remembered the ride to the Army base, and Percy's call to his uncle. The rest of the day was mostly a blur. I remember being taken into the hospital with Gigi and Edgar, but only snippets since then. I looked down at myself. I was wearing a white nightshirt but...I reached down to my legs, which felt...odd.

"No." Percy reached for my hands.

"I want to—"

He pulled my hands from the thick bandages that covered my lower legs. "No. Stop."

My legs hurt, and itched badly. I tried to pull my hands free from his grasp.

"Kate," he said sharply, and the look on his face told me that he wouldn't release me until I stopped trying to touch my legs.

I felt as if I was going to cry. "I need to touch them." My voice sounded like a child's. "Please," I pleaded, "they hurt. They itch."

"Okay. Hang on." Percy reached around me to the nightstand and pushed a button on the unit that reminded me of a garage door opener.

A nurse opened the door to our room literally seconds later. "Mr. Warner?"

My eyes opened wide. I had a nurse? What the hell had happened at the hospital?

"Kate's legs itch," Percy told her. "And she's in pain."

"Yes, sir." She left and returned a moment later with a medical kit, much like the one Carlie had brought down with her in the cave. She pulled a syringe from the kit and I held my hand out to stop her.

"What is that? Wait. What are you giving me?"

She hesitated, a placating smile on her face. "I'm giving you an injection of hydroxyzine for the itching and a second of methadone for the pain."

"NO!" I tried to climb out of bed and overtop of Percy, but he held me firmly in place.

"Kate," he said calmly.

"NO!" I pushed against him and tried to move my legs but they were both heavy and wrapped tightly. "I don't want any narcotics." I turned towards Percy, frantic. "It'll give me more nightmares. Please."

"How about the hydroxyzine? For the itching?" The nurse's tone was bland.

I shook my head. I'd be able to tolerate the itching, and didn't trust rent-a-nurse as far as I could throw her. Percy waved her off, which irritated me because technically her duty was to me - the patient. She left as quietly as she'd entered.

His grip on me relaxed and I pulled from his grasp, massaging my shoulders. "She could have helped you," he said, and when I didn't respond, Percy sighed and ran a hand through his hair. "Lie back, Kate. Just relax."

I couldn't relax. Everything in the room was unfamiliar. Nothing in here was mine. "Where are we?"

He lifted a pillow behind me and pointed me back to it. "Lie back, please."

"Where are we?" I was getting irritated, but I did as he asked. "Why are my legs bandaged?" I asked. "And where is Gigi? And Edgar?"

He took a breath. "This is my uncle's house. Gigi is still at the hospital. They wanted to keep her for observation. She had a small hematoma. My uncle has the very best doctors caring for her."

"Is she going to be okay?"

"The doctors say that it's shrinking. She should be home in a few days. Maybe a week."

"What about Edgar?"

"He's down the hall from us. Two doors down. They gave him something to sleep. He was frantic when they took you into surgery."

Instinctively, I reached for my legs. "Surgery?"

"Three hours of surgery to repair your legs."

I hated to sound vain at a time like this. "Am I...is it going to leave scars?"

"They don't know. My uncle had a plastic surgeon stitch them back up. He says you might hardly notice. If," he added, touching my nose lightly, "you can keep your hands off them."

"Please don't call that nurse again," I said quietly. "I don't want to take anything that gives me nightmares."

"All right."

I couldn't relax. The dream was too real. The pain was too fresh. My breathing slowed, and I looked at Percy next to me in bed.

He slid back down under the covers. "Better now?"

It wasn't better. Not even a little. However, my heart wasn't racing as badly, and Percy was next to me in this massive, overpowering room.

Because I hadn't answered, Percy sighed and massaged the bridge of his nose next to me in the dark. "C'mon, Kate. Lie back please."

"Did the U.S. win? I mean, is it over?"

"No," he said, and his eyes began to close. "No, it's not over. But we're safe here."

His face relaxed back into sleep, and finally I was able to relax a little myself and look around. The large four-poster bed I shared with him took up a huge amount of space. Old world tapestries hung from each corner of it, like royalty. I didn't like the feeling of it, and missed the comfort of the bedroom I'd shared with him at Gigi's.

"You actually have to *close* your eyes to attempt sleeping," he said, his own eyes closed. "Works better that way."

Sliding down under the covers with him, I worried that once sleep had claimed me, the nightmares would return.

When I opened my eyes again, the thick, heavy curtains were open and Percy was gone from bed next to me. I sat up and looked around. No rent-a-nurse. So far, so good. I wiggled my toes, and felt twinges of pain along the front of my calves. But I *could* move them, and I was going to see if I could walk on them.

I pulled the heavy covers back and looked at my legs. My calves, covered in thick, long gauze pads and surgical tape, were twice their original size. I reached out hesitantly and touched them. The itching had ceased, but they hurt. Badly. Above the knee where the surgical tape ended were purple and black marks and I winced at how bad they looked.

The door to the bathroom was behind and to the left of the bed. I was going to have to get up. Carefully, I slipped my legs over the edge. Only my calves were bandaged, and I didn't think it was going to alter anything if I slid my feet down to the floor. I felt around with my feet and couldn't feel the floor, so I pulled myself back up to sit on the edge of the bed. I was at least three feet from the ground. This was not going to be easy. From across the room, I spied a step stool, about two feet high, which clearly should have gone to the edge of the bed.

"Good morning," Percy said as he entered the room carrying a breakfast tray for me.

"It would have been good, had I been able to get out of bed."

He slid the tray onto my nightstand and reached in to lift my legs back under the covers.

"Percy!" I protested. "I have to be able to pee!"

"All right." Like I weighed nothing, he picked me back up in his arms and walked to the enormous, oversized bathroom. Setting me down directly in front of the toilet, he stood next to me and I looked back at him, hand on my hip.

"You can go now," I said, motioning towards the door.

"If I leave, you'll try walking to the door."

"And that would be bad because?"

"Kate, the longer you're on your legs, the more at risk they are for breaking open and scarring," he said impatiently. "You don't want to go back in for another surgery, do you?"

He knew he had the advantage, and I gritted my teeth. "Fine. I won't walk."

"Thank you." He exited, closing the door behind him.

I barely had enough time to pull back up my underwear, the door opened again.

"Wow, that was a great three seconds you gave me."

"You're trying to irritate me," Percy said, picking me up in his arms once again. "By refusing to take care of yourself."

"Where are my pajamas?" I asked, ignoring his comment.

"What pajamas?" He slid me into bed and replaced the heavy comforter over me.

"My blue ones. The ones you hate."

He busied himself with stacking pillows up behind me so I could sit up to eat the breakfast he'd brought.

"Percy."

He pulled the tray across my lap, removed the napkin from underneath the silverware, and patted my arm as he put it next to me.

"You threw them away didn't you?"

"Our trunks were kindly recovered by the Army and brought here to the house last night." His tone was clipped, and I sensed I was achieving my goal of getting under his skin enough to let me in and out of bed myself. "Although the insurgents had rifled through them, I highly doubt they would have thought your pajamas anything more than rags." He smiled. "They are likely still stuffed inside the inner pocket of the trunk that you and I share."

He reached over and removed the silver plate covers that were over my food.

"Scrambled eggs," he said and winked, possibly in an effort to be charming. "Um, toast. And fruit." He placed the food covers on the nightstand, and handed me the small garage door opener from last night. "The top button summons the maid, and she can remove your tray when you're done. The middle button summons the nurse." He looked at me with a raised eyebrow. "If you can behave yourself, summon her if you are in any pain. And the third—"

"Wait, wait, wait," I said, holding up my hands. "Where are you going to be?"

"My uncle is taking me over to see Gigi at the hospital. And then he's taking me to the science lab where he works."

For a minute, I said nothing. I just stared at him. He was dressed in a dark blue suit and dress shirt. His tie was fastened securely in a knot and he looked amazing. But so formal. So unlike my Percy. I looked down at the tray. "All right."

"I'll be back tonight," he said, and I'll tell you everything about it. I promise."

I looked back up to his face. Staggering. He was actually going to a lab. Had it not dawned on him that yesterday we were nearly killed? Clearly, this fact had escaped him.

"All right. Can you have my backpack brought up?"

"Yes," he said. "Why?"

"Because my medical books are in it, and I'd like to start studying again."

His face darkened, but he nodded. "Of course."

"Thank you."

We were quiet for a moment, and then he picked up a fork and handed it to me. "Eat," he said gently. "Your breakfast is getting cold."

Not only had Percy completely removed the three-foot step ladder from the room entirely, but apparently the staff was on strict orders to keep tabs on me so that I did not try to get out of bed. Once I had my backpack brought up to my room, the day was looking up considerably. My overnight kit allowed me to brush my hair and pull it back into a ponytail so it was out of my face when I read the next chapter in my anatomy book.

Three sections and two hours through my first chapter, I was bored. I flipped the covers back and rolled onto my stomach, rummaging through my backpack. Clearly, before Percy had them bring it to me, he'd ransacked it for potential problem items and removed them. Like my medical kit. I sighed. I was going to be stuck here all day. Alone, in this room. With nothing to do and no one to—

Scrambling to a sitting position, I pressed the first button on my garage door opener. The door swung open ten seconds later and Olivia entered. "Yes, ma'am?"

I sat back in bed, trying to look like I was behaving. "Is Edgar in his room?"

"The youngest Mr. Warner is having lunch and then has an appointment with the nurse."

That wasn't going to work. I wasn't going to see Percy's little brother get stuck with that jab-happy freak. "Bring the youngest Mr. Warner to my room, please. *Before* he sees the nurse."

She hesitated, then nodded and left the room.

Within five minutes the door opened again, and the top of Edgar's head peeked out from the door. "Edgar!" I called from the bed, and he visibly shrank and cowered. *Oh, no.* Okay, I was going to have to soft shoe this one. "Edgar," I called softly, and waited until he saw me in the bed. "Come here."

For a moment, he looked around, as if confused, until he saw me sitting on my bed. "K...Kate?" He said it as if he didn't trust that I was real.

"C'mere," I said.

He came to the edge of the bed and studied me for a moment. "Are you all right?"

"Of course I am." I patted the bed next to me. He hesitated. "It's okay."

He looked at my legs, covered in heavy bandages. "Do they hurt much?"

I forced a smile, even though they did throb considerably. Enough to make my head ache. "Not bad at all."

He stood next to the bed, as if assessing whether it was safe to come sit next to me.

"C'mon, Edgar, it's okay." I patted the bed again.

He smiled finally, climbed up onto the bed, and looked at my books strewn across it. "What's all this?"

"Stuff for college."

He flipped open the cover of my lab book and saw my scrawling of notes. "And this?"

"A lab I did back at Penn."

He looked around the room for a moment and then, seeing that it was only us, began to relax. "Where's Percy?"

My brows knit together. "Didn't he come see you this morning?"

"No."

I didn't like that, but perhaps Edgar had been asleep when Percy left.

"I didn't sleep well. Bad dreams." He lowered his eyes and I was surprised he would admit something so private to me.

"Me, too," I said, and bumped his shoulder with my own.

He flinched away from my touch, and something inside me twisted into a knot.

"Hey, you want to watch a movie?" I asked. "There's a DVD player over there and a whole shelf of movies."

His face relaxed nodded bit. "Yeah. Okay." He rummaged around the shelf for a few minutes, then held up a comedy. "This one?"

I had no idea what movie it was, but really, it didn't matter. "Looks good." He set up the movie as if it was the most normal thing in the world, then climbed back onto the bed next to me.

We watched the movie for a half hour in relative silence until Edgar moved his pillow a fraction of an inch closer to me. Slowly sliding my hand, I rested it on my thigh, which brushed up against Edgar's shoulder. He didn't move, the touch was so slight. A few minutes later, I moved my hand until it was gently against his shoulder, and then flattened my palm until it rested against him.

I reached up and touched his shoulder gently, then began rubbing small circles. I thought he'd get sick of it and ask me to stop, but he didn't. We sat there for a few minutes, just the two of us, me rubbing his shoulder. His body sagging from exhaustion and lack of sleep, he drifted off briefly then woke with a start.

He turned to me apologetically. "Sorry."

"Why don't you lie down this way?" I scooted back up against the pillows Percy had stacked for me earlier, and stretched my legs out in front of me. "Lie down and put your head right here." I pulled a pillow over next to my hip. "I'll rub your back."

"I'll hurt your legs," he said cautiously.

"The bandages are all the way down there," I said, pointing to my calves.

Tentatively, he lay down, his gangly legs sticking off the side of the bed, and I traced small circles on his shoulders and back. "Have you ever met your uncle before?"

"A long time ago, but I don't remember him."

I thought that was odd, but I wasn't going to make a big deal about it.

"Have you seen Gigi?" he asked.

"No, but Percy was going to see her at the hospital this morning, I think."

"Mmm."

Edgar's head got heavier and I his body relaxed. The movie continued to play on the large flat screen on the wall, but as Edgar's breathing normalized, I reached for the remote and turned the volume down low enough to be considered white noise.

I played with the curls all over his head, running my fingers lightly through them. His hair was longer than Percy's, and had more red in it.

After a half hour, I saw the rhythmic rise and fall of his chest, and heard the soft sound of his snore and knew he was asleep. I touched his soft curls, and the perfect skin on his cheek, marveling at how different from Percy Edgar was in personality. I wondered if Edgar was more like his father than his mother. Unfortunately, I would never have the chance to find out.

The door opened and the nurse entered. "I'm supposed to give Mr. Warner his medication now."

I looked down at Edgar, sleeping at my hip. "He doesn't appear to need any medication," I said, and tried to smile.

"I have my orders, Miss."

"I'm afraid those orders will have to change, *nurse*." I said it with the very tone I'd heard doctors at Penn use, and it worked.

Looking down at Edgar sleeping in my lap, she responded, "I can wait until he's awake to give him his medicine."

"Good." I bit my tongue against telling her to run along and find someone else to stick with a needle.

She watched us for a moment. "I'll need to know the minute he's awake."

"What medicine is this that he needs so badly?" I asked.

"Versed."

The hair on the back of my neck stood up. "That's a sedative."

She nodded, a slight smile on her face. "That's correct."

"May I ask why the youngest Mr. Warner needs a sedative?"

"You'll have to take that up with the elder Mr. Warner."

"Believe me, I will."

I kept Edgar with me all day, reading books, talking and playing card games from a deck I had in my backpack. Edgar insisted on having his dinner with me in my room, and began to chatter on about sports he'd played at Avon, friends and things he used to have in his old room in Manhattan. We talked about subjects he liked and I tried to draw him out as much as I could, carefully avoiding what had happened on the train.

By eight o'clock, he was asleep again and I was reading my anatomy book. A movie was playing with the sound low.

The door opened again. I half expected it to be the nurse, whom I'd sent away three times already throughout the afternoon, but it was Percy. And he looked pissed. I closed my book quietly as he came to stand by my bedside. Sliding the tie from around his neck, he unbuttoned the top of his dress shirt and looked over at the sleeping figure of his brother by my side.

"I come home," he said, the anger clear in his voice, "to find that my instructions for *you* to rest have been disregarded, the instructions for *my brother* have been ignored, and the nurse my uncle hired tells me you actually *refused* to allow her to treat either one of you!" His nostrils flared, and his tone was tight. "May I ask," he said, folding his tie in half, "why this is?"

I wasn't accustomed to being spoken to like I was five. Nor was I going to sit here like Percy was my father and be scolded like I was an errant toddler. I set my book aside and began stroking Edgar's hair again.

"May *I* ask," I said calmly, "why you would leave without saying good morning to your brother? Or why your instructions included a sedative for a perfectly healthy teen? Or why your instructions for either one of us included isolation and removal of my medical kit from my personal bag?"

He didn't speak for a full minute. He'd been gone all day, and now he was back, and the first words from his mouth were in anger.

"The instructions are for your recovery. And that of *my* brother." The inflection in his tone was unmistakable. Percy turned on his heel. He stopped at the door and looked back at me. "I'll have our trunk and your medical kit brought up immediately." The smile was gone from his face. "You can cut off your bandages, or whatever you're going to do, and I'll just help you deal with the scarring." He stood, his hand on the doorknob. "I'm going down to have supper with my uncle. Good night, Kate."

The door was closed before I had the chance to respond. True to his word, the trunk and medical kit were brought up within the hour, but Percy did not return. An hour went by, then two. Still no Percy. Sliding Edgar over to Percy's side of the bed, I looked down to the floor far below me. I had to go to the bathroom, and I'd put it off as long as I could.

Edgar had helped me down from the bed earlier that day, but the swelling in my feet and legs had been less and it had seemed easier to get up and down with Edgar's help. With Percy not coming back in and Edgar asleep, I was going to have to do it on my own. Grabbing the edge of the comforter, I lifted, pulled and looked down. Underneath was the rail of the bed, halfway between the bed and the floor.

"Okay," I said, "I can do this."

My calves and feet were badly swollen, and they hurt as I stepped onto the rail of the bed. Holding onto the tall corner poster, I lowered myself to the floor, trying to keep my legs as straight as possible. Finally on the floor, I was immediately sorry. My feet felt like they had needles in them, and I inhaled sharply with the pain. Each step towards the bathroom felt like daggers through my legs and I was panting by the time I made it to the doorframe. I stayed in the bathroom for longer than I should have, but my legs had hurt so badly that I needed to rest them before I tried making it back into bed. Unable to put it off any longer, I stood.

"Oh, God." I leaned against the counter for support. One step at a time, I shuffled towards the bathroom door, each step causing me immeasurable pain. I reached the doorframe of the bathroom just as the bedroom door opened and Percy's tired face emerged.

I prepared myself for him to admonish me as I stood there clinging to the doorframe. Instead, he rushed over to me, scooped me up in his arms and carried me back to bed.

"I should have taken you while I was here," he said. "I'm sorry." He looked down at my feet. "Oh, Kate."

"I know," I said, embarrassed, "they look awful." My feet, more than double their normal size, were bluish and purple.

I could tell he was irritated, but his tone was softer now. "Why, didn't you let the nurse look at this today?"

"Because there's nothing that can be done for simple edema."

He sighed. "Edema."

"Edema, or swelling in the feet or ankles, can often be complicated by prolonged periods of standing, surgery to the feet or calves, and is often found in the elderly. If the condition—"

"Okay, okay." He sighed, and rubbed his eyes.

"Sorry. I can't help it."

He motioned towards Edgar. "He stay in here all day?"

"Yeah. Slept a lot, though. He said he had nightmares last night."

"Guess you two have that in common," Percy said.

"Everything scared him today. The sounds outside, the tray rattling." I played with one of the curls over Edgar's ear, and wrapped it around my finger. "It was like he was worried he'd wake up and find he was back on the train."

Percy didn't say anything for a long moment, just sighed and massaged the bridge of his nose.

I turned to look at him, my voice low so as not to wake Edgar. "I'm sorry if I caused problems today. Your instructions didn't make any sense, though, and I really felt isolated."

"The instructions were for your own good. And Edgar's."

"I don't see how sedating him would have helped. He says the medicine gives him nightmares."

"I'll speak to his doctor about that. But you're not his doctor. And you can't go changing orders like you are."

That stung, and I turned my face from him to look at Edgar. "I'm not going to sit idly by while his *doctor*," I said with frost in my voice, "prescribes medication for him that is both useless and counterproductive. He needs more than drug induced sleep."

I don't know what upset him more; that I questioned his adherence to the doctor's order or that I refused to accept that his instructions were for the good of either Edgar or myself.

"Gigi comes home tomorrow," he said, his tone still distant. "You'll have someone to make you feel less isolated."

My eyes found his again. "You won't be here again tomorrow?"

"No. My uncle thinks there is a good chance I could help them at the lab. Discussing countermeasures for chemical warfare, if that's used. They think it might be."

I hesitated, not wanting to get confirmation of what I feared he was going to say. "So this isn't a temporary thing? You're going to be working with him? Your uncle I mean?"

Percy sighed, clearly not wanting to delve into this subject now. "This is my chosen field."

It dawned on me that he wasn't talking about one more day, or even two more. He was talking about a permanent change. "But you have to go through...don't they have to hire you or something for you to work there with him? Security. Background check. That kind of stuff."

He nodded, wouldn't look in my eyes. "Mmmhmmm."

"Percy."

"Yes, they do."

He didn't have to say it; I knew what had happened. "You're already going through background checks, aren't you?" I looked up at his face but he wouldn't meet my eyes. "And this is what you want?"

I knew that look on his face, the one that indicated he wasn't going to discuss it with me. He knew it wasn't what I wanted, knew I'd be irritated.

"You should get some sleep," he said, and leaning towards me, he kissed my forehead lightly.

I felt as if our coming here was orchestrated; part of his master plan from the beginning, even before we left the Wind Cave. I turned my face from him. He wasn't going to discuss it; it wasn't his way. No matter how much I wanted him to, he'd made his decision. Now it was up to me to either deal with it...or not.

CHAPTER SIX

"Surgery one needs more O neg!"

Carlie threw a used sponge into the waste container next to her. "Where's my suction?" she asked Maria, who was trying hard to do three tasks at once.

Carlie wiped the sweat from her face with her arm. She'd been at this for over twenty hours, and awake for nearly thirty. Carlie was on the verge of collapse. After this one, she was done. No matter who walked through that door, they'd have to wait. Or die. She couldn't do any more.

They'd done three runs total to the front, and brought back twenty-four men. Of those twenty-four, eighteen had made it. Five hours after they'd begun, the Army medics in the field saw them, accompanied them back to the trauma ward, and set up shop. It looked like an Army base with all the helicopters flying in and out and soldiers lying everywhere. She was grateful when they'd stopped going to front lines; in fact the soldiers put a stop to that pretty much after their third run.

"Civilian personnel drop back!" was the most common phrase screamed at them when they dragged another soldier from the battlefield. She knew that they'd been right. What she'd seen today was nothing short of barbaric. But what she'd done today was heroic, if not more.

"Maria," she said, steadying herself against the table, "you need to..." she pulled off her mask and spun around, in time to vomit into the waste container behind her. She cursed and vomited again.

Maria shouted instructions at the Army nurse in the hall, "Get me an orderly in here stat!"

Carlie felt as if she was going to sink into the ground. Her legs shook and her stomach lurched. She thought back to the last time she'd eaten. Two Army officers had given her some of their rations in the hall. Truth be told, it had smelled awful, but she'd thanked them and eaten it out of necessity. Obviously, it hadn't agreed with her.

"Mannis, out of here, now!" David stalked into trauma one, stripped off his bloodstained apron and gloves, and motioned for Maria to dress him in another. He moved to her patient, who only needed his wound closed before he was ready for recovery.

"I'm almost done with—"

"You're done NOW. Scrub out, doctor!" he said, and slipped into the gloves Maria was placing on his hands. "Wait for me in the on-call."

Carlie pulled off her apron and gloves and shoved them into the contaminated waste bin, which badly needed emptying. Stalking through the washroom, she kicked the door closed behind her, glaring at David through the window between the two. She scrubbed out, dried her hands, and rinsed her mouth out before walking down the hall towards the on-call.

There were men everywhere in the halls. Lining the trauma ward, in every triage room, and behind every curtain. Army doctors swarmed around them as she passed. The on-call room greeted her like an old friend and she pulled open the locker, frantically needing something on her stomach. As she remembered, a package of saltines lay in the corner and she stuffed three of them in her mouth. They were stale and they were dry, but they likely wouldn't come up. She couldn't find the beef jerky, but she did find three granola bars and she unwrapped them one at a time, consuming them as if possessed.

As she polished off the third one, the door behind her swung open. *Shit.* She swallowed the last morsel and crumpled the empty wrappers in her hand.

"Dr. Mannis."

She turned to face David, hand behind her back. She worked to swallow the last of the granola bar before speaking.

A small smile tugged at his lips. "You're in the on call room...bingeing."

She rested a hand on her hip. "I do not binge. I'm having a snack."

He held his hand out in front of him. "Wrappers, please?" She gave him an innocent look and he pointed to the corner of her mouth. "Chocolate."

"Shit." She wiped her mouth and handed him the three wrappers. "I was so hungry." Her voice truly filled with remorse, she added, "I'm sorry about getting sick. The soldiers gave me some of their rations and—"

"You threw up again."

"David, you don't understand!" she pleaded. "It's not that! I ate some Army rations and they tasted like...like dog food! They made me sick."

David listened patiently for a moment, and then said, "You've been up for well over twenty-four hours. There's an Army jeep outside and I'll wager they'd take us the three blocks to the flat. It's away from the hot zone. We'll get some sleep. You need to rest."

"I just needed a little snack and—"

"You need sleep and real food. What you're doing is not good for you, or the—"

"Don't you say it." Carlie pointed a finger at his chest, and pushed past him into the hall.

Side by side they walked towards the entrance of the trauma ward until David grabbed her by the arm, anchoring him to her. A white haired man turned to face them, actually smiling when he saw David.

"Dr. Windsor."

"Commander Unger." David's grip on Carlie's upper arm didn't loosen, but he motioned to one of the jeeps outside next to them. "I wonder if one of your soldiers would be so kind as to lend us one of your jeeps for a few hours."

His look was one of concern. "Where do you need to go? You know we're not allowing any civilian personnel—"

"Our flat is about three blocks from here," David interrupted. "We need some food, and rest."

Commander Unger called to a young man nearby. "Private, take the good doctors to their home, post yourself outside their door, and then accompany them back safely to the hospital."

The young soldier saluted. "Yes, sir!"

"That's not necessary," David protested.

Commander Unger's face became serious, and he leaned close to David. "With what you did here today, it's the least I can do to thank you. The Army owes you a debt of gratitude."

The private held a hand out toward the jeep and David casually saluted the Commander. He and Carlie slipped jackets and helmets before climbing in the jeep to go home.

"You should have asked him in," Carlie said, kicking off her shoes after they arrived. "He's tired, same as us."

"He wouldn't be able to," David said. "He's on duty."

Carlie walked through to the kitchen, her only thought right now of food and decent water. After that, she could fall into an exhausted sleep for five or six hours.

Obviously with the same idea, David helped her rummage through the cupboards and dump edible contents on the counter. When he turned back from the cupboard, he saw Carlie scoop an entire spoonful of peanut butter onto a slice of wheat bread and take a bite.

"Oh, God," she said, chewing with her eyes closed. "This tastes so good."

He stood watching her for a moment. He reached for the bread and made himself a cheese sandwich. She reached past him for a banana and peeled it back, offering him a bite.

"You hate bananas," he said.

"It's just that I'm so hungry," she said and finished chewing. "I'm just happy it's not Army rations."

David shrugged. "I ate them. Tasted fine to me."

"You're used to them. I'm a civilian, remember?"

He laughed. "Honey, I haven't had rations in twenty years."

"Well, whatever. They still tasted like dog food."

Carlie polished off the peanut butter sandwich, downed the last of the water in her glass, and then reached for the package of cookies in front of David.

"You might wanna slow down before you get sick again."

"No, I feel better now. I'm still hungry though." She dug the spoon into the peanut butter once again and actually began to eat it off the spoon. David tried not to wince.

"What?"

"Nothing."

She opened the container of milk and poured a glass. When she put it to her lips, she turned and spat it into the sink.

"What's wrong?"

"Milk's rancid."

He reached for the container to sniff it. "No, it's fresh. I defrosted it last night."

She lifted it to pour it down the sink, and David stopped her. He took her glass and took a drink.

"Tastes fine."

Carlie screwed the cap back on. "Don't blame me when you're the one with your head in the bucket next time." She reached for a cookie and smeared peanut butter on it from her spoon. David watched her from the edge of the counter, a slight look of amusement on his face.

"Do you want some water to wash that down?"

"Mmmhmm. Yes, please."

He filled her glass and handed it to her while she licked the remainder of the peanut butter off the spoon. "Okay," he said, "Since you feel better, you mind doing something for me?"

She popped another cookie in her mouth and put the milk back in the fridge. "Sure. What?"

He pulled a box from his doctor's bag and placed it on the counter between them. "I need you to pee."

Her eyes went to his and she chewed the last of her cookie. "I told you—"

"That's great. So when the test comes back negative? You can say I told you so."

She looked down at the box. "Fine," she said, snatching it from the counter. "I'm going to take a shower. And then I'm going to get some sleep."

"Okay."

Ten minutes later when Carlie still hadn't emerged, David decided to go on a recon mission to retrieve her. Walking to the bathroom, he knocked on the door. "Hey. You in there?"

He heard her sniff. "No. Go away."

He couldn't help but be a little excited. "Carlie..."

"I said, go away!"

"You need to sleep."

He could hear her blow her nose and run the sink. The door opened and she appeared, box gone, nowhere in sight. He leaned his head in and looked around. "Where's the test?"

She walked past him towards his bed. "I threw it away."

"May I ask why?"

"It was a fucking dud, that's why."

"I see."

Removing her scrubs and bra, she flopped down on the bed. His mouth hung open at the sight of her bare body. She reached under the pillow for the little nightshirt she normally wore, pulled it on, then turned around to face him. "What?"

David slid his scrubs off, pulled his shirt over his head, and closed the blinds before slipping into bed beside her. "Nothing." She was pregnant. He didn't need to be a doctor to know that. Seeing her naked and completely ripe was enough to make him...

"David! God!" She moved a half foot away from him.

"What?" he said innocently. "I'm sorry, all right? Carlie, I'm sorry."

Gently, he pulled her against him, trying to fight the surge of feelings flowing through him.

"How can you..." she pounded her pillow with her fist. "You won't feel like that when I'm huge and..." she began to cry, and he suppressed a smile, turning her onto her back.

"Yes, I will."

She hiccoughed. "All men say that! It's total crap!"

"Listen to me," he said gently, and smoothed the hair from her face. "I know this isn't how you may have planned things to work out."

She made a scoffing sound and rolled her eyes.

"But things happen for a reason. And this isn't a bad thing." He turned her to face him, both of them lying on their sides.

"For you!" she said, hitting him in the chest. "I'm not done with my residency! How am I going to finish and do my specialty when I'm pregnant?" She sniffed. "And raising a baby...alone."

The last word came out so softly that David barely heard it. "You're not alone," he said, his voice thick with emotion. "You won't *ever* be alone."

Carlie's sniffles turned to stifled sobs. "Now I'm this...this single mom with—"

"Carlie," he said, "you won't be a *single* mom."

She pushed against him, hitting him in the chest. "You think this is how I wanted it to be? You offering to stay with me simply because—"

"I'm not offering to *stay with* you, Carlie," he said. "I'm not talking about *sticking around*. I'm talking about being together. A family, marriage, everything."

Carlie snorted in derision and sniffed through her tears. "Yeah, and I really want you to throw marriage out like this because you feel guilty that you—"

"Stop it," he said firmly. "This has nothing to do with guilt, pity or anything like that."

"Yes it does!" she said, and continued crying.

He stopped her mouth with a kiss. It deepened and her crying slowed.

"Carlie, I want to marry you because I love you." He looked into her eyes. "And because I can't live without you."

"You don't mean that," she said, still unconvinced, tears still squeezing out from behind her eyelids.

"I *do* mean that," he said, pulling her tighter to him. "More than you know."

"And what kind of mother takes her fetus into a battlefield!" She buried her head in his shoulder and sobbed.

David knew it was more than pregnancy talking, knew it was more than exhaustion. Carlie was twenty-five, dealing with situations and things that she should never have to see, never have to deal with. She was scared, she was pregnant, and she felt alone. Doing the only thing he could, David wrapped his arms around her and let her cry until they both fell asleep as the rain began to fall outside.

CHAPTER SEVEN

It had been twelve days and they hadn't received a telegram back from Kate. In the beginning, Matt had ridden with Charlie every day to the post station to see if there had been a reply. After five days, they resigned themselves to calling as opposed to driving all the way into town. Even though they had the gas tank on the farm, it wouldn't last forever, and Matt knew they had to conserve where they could. Plus, the ride home empty handed was simply too painful. After ten days, they barely talked about it at all.

Reality had begun to sink in. The 'what ifs' were rampant, and Matt spent a lot of time working in the fields like a dog. It worried Charlie and Carrie alike.

"Take him his lunch," Carrie said. "And tell him to eat it this time."

"Will do," Charlie said. He finished his iced tea and stood, donning his hat and accepting the basket that held Matt's lunch.

"I'll need you both in early tonight," Carrie said.

He paused at the door and looked back. "Yeah?"

She nodded and turned back to the sink.

"Mother?" Charlie's eyes narrowed. She was up to something.

"Yes, Charlie?"

"We havin' company I don't know about?"

"I invited the Oppengards for supper tonight."

Charlie swore under his breath and looked out at the field towards Matt. "You trying to make him go insane?"

"It's not good for him to spend so much time alone. We both miss Kate, but..."

Charlie came back in and set the basket on the table. He lowered his voice. In their thirty plus years together, he'd rarely raised his voice to his wife.

"Mother," he said, a cross tone to his voice, "no matter what you think, he's doin' more than missin' her."

"Charlie..."

He held his hand up to her. "Lemme finish, now." He sighed heavily. "If I ever lost you," he worked the muscles in his jaw, "I'd be about the sorriest son-of-a-bitch that ever lived. I'd stop eatin' and throw myself into my work, and I'd..." he paused and pulled his hat from his head, "I'd be dead inside."

"He's too young to be—"

Charlie took a step towards his wife. "You used to tell me that love had no age, and love had no time limit."

Carrie sighed. "Well I meant *us*." She came to him, and wrapped her arms around his middle. "I'm sorry. I shouldn't have invited them."

"Maybe if the boys had come home you'd be more at ease."

"Yes," she agreed. "I wish they would have come home."

Truth be told, Charlie wished the same. However, both boys were in Iowa with their wives, and both were safe. For now. He sighed. "I know, Mother." He thought about Matt working out in the field, and how insane it would drive him that Carrie was ambushing him.

"I suppose it's too late now to un-invite them?"

"Oh, *that'd* be neighborly."

He chuckled and looked down at her face. "All right, then. I'll warn him. But none of your matchmaking with Sandra."

"Sarah."

He winked at her as he walked toward the back door. "Whatever."

Matt saw Charlie coming from inside the house and leaned on his shovel for a rest. "You ready to get that next row done?"

"Nah. You gotta start eatin' or she's gonna skin me." He handed Matt the basket. "Here."

"Thanks."

"I'm not a delivery boy, chief. You gotta start eating."

Matt took a bite of the cold chicken leg Carrie had sent out for him. "All right."

Charlie sighed. "Gotta tell you something." The poor kid was gonna want to kill Carrie, and he couldn't rightly blame him. "And you're not gonna like it."

Matt stopped chewing and his face blanched.

"No, no, nothin' like that," Charlie quickly assured him. "It's just, uh, we gotta get cleaned up early tonight."

Matt paused, chicken leg halfway to his mouth. "Why?"

Charlie swore under his breath and looked uncomfortable. "We got... Carrie, well, she..." he looked away then back to Matt. "Carrie invited the Opperheinmers over for supper."

"The who?"

"Those folks we met at the picnic the other day."

Matt tossed the chicken leg back into the bucket and looked out towards the field. He'd been set up enough in his lifetime, he knew what it felt like. And he didn't like it any better now than he did then.

"She doesn't get it. Does she?"

Charlie didn't say anything. He hated to admit it, but he thought Matt was right. Carrie *didn't* understand what he was going through. At all.

"Finish up your lunch," Charlie said, and pulled his work gloves from his back pocket, "and let's get some work done."

Matt stood in front of the closet in the cottage. Normally after he and Charlie were done for the day, he'd take a shower and slip on some shorts and a t-shirt. But they had company coming. However, he reasoned, it wasn't *his* company, was it? Better to be comfortable. His mother's words echoed in his mind, for one of the last parties they'd made him attend before he'd gone to Wind Cave.

"No, the blue shirt, with the tie. Dress shabbily and people remember what you wore. Dress well and they remember who you are."

Kate had never cared what he wore. Never asked him to dress up. Never cared if he wore his torn Metallica shirt in bed while she read. She was so easy to be around, to talk with...to love. And he had. He reached for a pair of shorts. That was it, wasn't it? He loved her. So much that it hurt inside just to think of the rest of his life without her. He didn't have it in him to dress any nicer tonight. He'd been a show pony his whole life. That life was what had lost him the best thing that ever happened to him. He wasn't about to go back to being a show pony now. Not for anyone.

Carrie had pulled out all the stops for supper. They were eating at the kitchen table, but she'd added a leaf in it so they'd all fit around it. He could see the apple pie cooling on the counter, and smell Carrie's cranberry chutney from the door. He leaned down and kissed her on the cheek when he entered.

"Smells good."

She stopped for a moment and looked at what he was wearing, but Charlie shook his head at her, and she didn't say a word.

"Gonna need some more flour by the end of next week," she said. "I traded the Holbrooks some of our eggs for more milk, but I'll need a few more pounds of whatever flour they have at Petersons."

Matt popped a morsel of chicken in his mouth from the tray on the counter. "I'll drive in and get it for you. Need to mail a letter to Jazz anyway."

"Thank you, Matt."

A knock sounded at the door, and Matt rolled his eyes at Charlie in amusement. Charlie was actually washed, shaved, and dressed in a nice shirt. Show pony, indeed. He smirked and Charlie leaned in towards his ear before going to the door.

"Keep it up, Chuckles. I'll have Carrie sit you next to Samantha."

"Sarah."

"Whatever."

The Oppengards all came in, dressed nicely. A little *too* nicely, Matt thought, but he didn't say anything. They were from a big city, and he knew how different Fall River was from city life. It would be hard to adjust. He shook Craig and Mandy's hands and then Peter's. Sarah stood a little back, a white and yellow flowered sundress swinging with each move she made.

"Hi, Matt," she said and extended her hand to shake. "It's nice to see you again."

Matt smiled and shook her hand, then looked back to Peter. "You up for a little pigskin before supper?"

Carrie's eyebrows went up, Charlie's mouth dropped, but Peter smiled. "Why, sure. You got a football?"

"Found one in the barn today," Matt said, clapped him on the back, and followed him outside.

Carrie's face fell and it took every ounce of effort Charlie had to keep from laughing out loud. He'd found a way to outsmart Carrie, something Charlie had never been able to do in more than thirty years. He turned to Craig. "Can I get you a beer?"

After offering to help in the kitchen and then listening to polite conversation between her mother and Carrie, Sarah went out the back door to watch the boys play football. She noticed there was nowhere clean to sit, but smoothed the back of her dress down anyway and sat on the top step. Matt and Pete were laughing and tossing the ball back and forth, making fake plays and screaming at each other when they missed. She hadn't seen a smile on Pete's face since they'd moved from Texas, so it was good to see him actually enjoying himself.

October had come to South Dakota, and with it, cooler temperatures. The last of the Indian summer had faded with September, and she remembered the heat from Texas, and the faces of her students that she would likely never see again. The leaves had turned lovely gold and red colors, and the wheat that they'd planted swayed as the breeze came up. Pulling her sweater around her shoulders, she looked out over the landscape and sighed. This was sure different from Texas.

Carrie's face peeked out from behind the screen door. "Sarah, will you tell the boys to get cleaned up for supper, please?"

"Yes, ma'am." Sarah descended the steps and walked out to where the game was being played. There was more talking going on than anything.

"Hey y'all!" she called, and waved for them to come in. "Carrie says get washed up. Supper's ready."

Pete tossed the football back to Matt, who stood a few feet from him. "Play after?"

"Count on it."

Pete walked towards the house, and Matt turned in the direction of the cottage. He sighed when Sarah followed and fell into step right beside him.

"Have you heard from your brothers?" she asked Matt. "Is everything okay?"

He tossed the ball in the air as they walked. "Yeah. They're both fine." He didn't need to tell her that his relationship with both of his brothers had been horribly strained since Kate left him in Los Altos, that he blamed Paul for making Kate leave, and ultimately, for her death. He couldn't go into that, didn't want to say it out loud to anyone. Those were the thoughts he had when he was working in the fields, the things he went over in his mind while he and Charlie looked for land; things that she could never, and would never get. Things that only Kate would understand.

"Have you heard from your girlfriend in Philadelphia?" Her tone was innocent, but Matt knew why she asked. He'd seen girls like Sarah a hundred times; at school, at parties, and pushed at him by his parents. Vanilla cake girls with no substance or fire. Nothing like Kate.

"No, not yet."

"I'm sorry."

"Me too." He stopped at the cottage and set the ball down on the bottom step.

"How long have you been together?"

Forever. It seemed like he'd been with Kate for years, but in reality, it was a very short time. "Um, since June."

"Oh, wow. So... not long."

He kicked at the rocks next to the steps leading into the cottage. "I guess not."

"You meet her at Stanford?"

He thinking of the day he'd met Kate. "Yep." His heart broke a little remembering how he had told Kate the story in Wind Cave. She hadn't remembered him.

Sarah sighed. Matt was giving her one-word answers, which was never a good sign. "Are you planning on going out to visit her?"

"That's hard to say." He couldn't very well tell her that he had plans to go see her when he still feared the worst.

"Well, I hope you hear from her soon."

He was quiet for a second. "I guess I better go in and wash up," he said, which he hoped would be her cue to leave.

She looked at him, a hand on her hip. Her golden brown hair flipped around her face as the breeze picked up, and she tucked a strand of it behind her ear. "Matt?"

"Yeah?"

"I'm not so bad, you know." She said the first part quietly, as if afraid of his response. Then her blue eyes flashed back at him. "I'm not just some young schoolteacher from Houston with no spark and no life." She lifted her chin a little. The way she did it reminded him of Kate. "Just so you know."

A smile tugged at the corner of his mouth. "Thanks for letting me know."

"And if your girlfriend doesn't...well, if she stays in Philadelphia, I wouldn't mind having the chance to get to know you."

She was forward. And attractive. And sweet. All the things his parents would have loved. So would his brothers. A regular Miss Texas. But she wasn't Kate. "Thanks," he said lamely.

He watched her walk back to the house. He'd been alone way too long. The woman he needed wasn't walking back in the house. The one he needed was...where was she? He didn't know. He'd need to know really soon. He needed to find out, one way or the other. When Matt turned to go into the cottage, Carrie's frantic voice from the kitchen swiveled him towards the house and he broke out in a run.

He hit the screen door and flung it open, seeing Charlie grabbing his keys from the hook on the wall.

"What happened?" Matt asked, looking from Carrie to Charlie.

"C'mon, boy, let's go," Charlie said to him. He inclined his head towards the Oppengards. "We'll be back directly. Sorry for the interruption."

Matt pushed through the kitchen and caught a hold of Charlie's arm, looking at him questioningly."Tom just called," Charlie said with an edge in his voice. "Virginia sent a telegram back."

Chapter Eight

"You should wait for Percy," Gigi said, seated at the small table in the corner of the room.

I slipped my old faded pajamas into my backpack. "I know."

"You're going to be in trouble when Percy gets home!" Edgar said, but still didn't leave my side. Since the first day we'd come to Percy's uncle's house, Edgar and I had been inseparable. "Wish I could go with you," he mumbled.

"I do, too, Edgar."

"It's too dangerous," Gigi said quietly. "Think about what happened the last time. Think about what *could* happen. Percy would go crazy if something happened to you."

I stopped folding the shirt in my hands. "You actually think he'd notice?"

"Edgar," Gigi said softly, "bring me my hand cream from my nightstand. The lemon one."

"All right, Gigi." All arms and legs, he lumbered from the room.

Turning towards me, Gigi asked, "Will you close the door, please?"

Percy had inherited that same tone, the one he got when he was about to impart something important. I did as Gigi asked.

"Come here, and sit down for a moment."

I walked slowly to the table, and sat next to Percy's grandmother. The long, straight nose that both Percy and Edgar had came from Gigi, as well as the shape of their faces. I smiled at the resemblance. Gigi sat forward and set her hand on the table.

"My son Robert, was always an entrepreneur. Always busy. Always working a deal. Making things happen. When he married Camilla, he changed for a little while. They became very close, and started a family."

My brows drew together. I was pretty sure I knew where this was going. "But they had an arranged marriage. Percy told me—"

"The Warner men have always come from arranged marriages," Gigi said. "Ever since, oh, as far back as I can remember."

"But yours wasn't."

She smiled at me. "I was the exception. Three generations before me, and everyone after me. Just because something is arranged doesn't mean it's passionless." She turned her face towards the window, as if considering the next thing she was about to say. "And just because a man shows passion and then...forgets to show passion, doesn't mean he doesn't still love you."

Like a ton of bricks it hit me. "Is that why Camilla came to stay with you so often?"

She nodded sadly. Of course. She was lonely. All of her boys gone, her husband was in the city all the time, working, and she was left in this enormous Manhattan palace...alone.

"Camilla and Robert had so much passion in their marriage when they were together," she said. "And such good times."

"I'm not leaving for good," I promised her. "I'm going to see a friend who has fallen ill."

"You know what he'll do when he comes home and finds you're gone."

"Gigi," I said, imploring her, "I can't stay. I don't belong here. I'm going crazy."

"Your legs aren't healed," she said, pointing down to the bandages that still covered both calves.

"The stitches are out, and I know how to properly clean the wounds."

Gigi looked at me pointedly. "And you could just leave him? Without saying goodbye?"

"You don't understand."

"I'm old, my dear, but I understand far more than you think."

I stood, then sank back down into the chair. "I'm useless here. I do nothing but sit and wait for Percy to come home. I read chapters that I've read three times, see movies that I've watched ten times, and then, when he finally decides to come home, he's..." I looked at her and shook my head. "Sorry, I...never mind."

"No," she smiled, urging me on, "go on. He's what? Preoccupied? Distant?"

I felt selfish saying it. "Yes." I couldn't tell her the rest. That he hadn't touched me in the entire two weeks we'd been at his uncle's house. That the one time I'd tried to be close to him, he'd apologized and said he was tired and had gone to sleep. I was alone, even when we were in the same room. I couldn't take it anymore. I felt invisible. And I'd never felt that way next to Percy. Not ever.

"Have you asked him if you could go to the lab with him?" she asked.

"No."

"Or if he'd consider telling you about his work? What they're doing? Thomas said that Percy is doing very well. That he's—"

"He doesn't want to talk about it with me."

Gigi tapped her fingernails on the table lightly. "Or have you not asked?"

My face turned to hers sharply. "I've asked. He's just not—"

She held her hand up. "I want to tell you something." Her eyes cast down at her lap, then back up to my face. "I taught Camilla how to be a good wife. A good *Warner*." She said the name with a great deal of pride. "I can teach you, too."

Wait a minute. A good *Warner*. A good *wife*? "Percy doesn't want to get—"

"I think you are a wonderful match," Gigi said. "A good, strong match. You're a fine woman, and a wonderful mother figure to Edgar."

The thought of Edgar softened my features and seeing that, she smiled.

"He loves you, you know."

"I care for Edgar, a great deal. But he'll be in school soon. He said that—"

"Yes, Thomas will find a teacher and Edgar will begin lessons here at the house until things resume normalcy. By then, you may be starting a family of your own."

My boyfriend's grandmother had just mentioned marriage and pregnancy in the same thirty-second period, and I was getting nervous. It wasn't that I'd never considered marrying Percy, I just hadn't considered it happening anytime soon. And certainly not by arrangement.

"Gigi," I said, trying to put it delicately, "I've never really wanted to have children." Also, and this wasn't something I was going to add, but marriage hadn't been really high on my list of priorities, either.

She nodded, though, not fazed at all. "Times have changed, Kate."

"Yes, I know. I just don't think I'd make a very good wife."

"Neither did I! Neither did Camilla!" Gigi laughed, as if I'd made the greatest joke in the world. "But I've seen you with Edgar." Her eyes sparkled and she laid a hand on my knee. "And I've seen you with Percy."

I considered, for a brief second, marrying Percy, and bearing his child. Or, if I listened to Gigi, *children*. I didn't know what to think. I had so many dreams that didn't include either marriage or children. But I had very few dreams that didn't include Percy.

The door behind us flew open and Edgar's flushed face appeared in it. "Kate!" he said, and Gigi held a hand up to him.

"Edgar, that door was closed. That indicates a—"

"I'm trying to tell you something!" Edgar's voice broke in the middle and when he opened his mouth to speak again, Percy was standing in the doorway and moved him gently aside.

His face was tense, his brows knit together. "Edgar, go downstairs and complete the assignment I gave you this morning."

"But the tutor isn't coming until—"

One look from Percy and Edgar fairly withered. "All right." His tone said he'd far rather stay to witness Percy scold me, but he lumbered off down the hall.

"Gigi, I'd like a word with Kate, please."

Gigi stood up shakily, and I helped her to her feet. She patted me on the arm like the soldier who had led the lamb to slaughter. "Remember what I said," she whispered and walked through to exit the room, closing the door behind her.

Percy didn't say anything for a long moment. The sound of his dress shoes echoed on the hardwood floor. I stayed where I was and watched him pace and loosen his tie.

"It is my understanding that you were driven to the post station today, and sent a telegram to South Dakota." He looked directly at me. "Is this correct?"

"It is."

Percy looked down at my backpack that sat half packed against the large chest of drawers. "Going somewhere?"

"As a matter of fact, I am."

"Are the two mutually exclusive events?"

"They are not."

He sighed and unbuttoned the top button on his dress shirt. I wondered who'd called him, who I'd have to thank for that. I didn't have to ask—everyone was getting direction from either Thomas or Percy.

"You've made plans to leave. When were you planning on advising me of this?"

I glanced down. He leaned against the bed and massaged his eyes. When he spoke, his voice was soft. "Kate, do you understand what it is I'm doing here in Virginia?"

"Of course."

"Could you enlighten me, then? On what you believe I'm doing."

"You're working with your uncle in—"

"Incorrect."

"You're learning how to combat chemical—"

"Incorrect." He paused. "One more try?"

His professor face was on now, and it was beginning to piss me off. I narrowed my eyes at him. "Why don't you tell me, since I am so profoundly misguided?"

He walked towards me. "What I am doing is starting a new life here. Doing something in the field that I planned to continue in. The field," he raised an eyebrow at me, "we both pursued."

I wasn't going to argue with him at this point, so I let him continue.

"Our lives at Stanford are gone. People's lives everywhere are changing. Ending. I'm trying to make a new beginning." He reached me and touched my shoulder. "For us. We talked about this in Wind Cave. We discussed—"

"We discussed doing it together!" I said, my voice raised. "How included do you think I feel when you won't even discuss the work you're doing, the life you're supposed to be building *with me*?"

"You're right," he conceded. "I've been pre-occupied."

"And how attached do you think I feel to this life if I never get out? Never do anything with my days?" I hesitated, knowing the next part might be too much sentimentality for him, but it had to be said. "Never spend time with you."

His face softened. "I should be paying more attention to you." It was phrased as a statement, but he said it as a question. I nodded and he smiled, as if something had been settled. "I'm going to make a concerted effort to do so. We can discuss you getting out more over dinner tonight, together."

"No, my train leaves in four hours."

His brows knit back together. "But you're not leaving."

"I have to."

"No," he said. "I agreed to spend more time with you, and—"

"That doesn't mean I'm staying. I still have to go see Carrie. She's sick, and asking for me."

"Then send her a telegram with your best wishes for a speedy recovery."

"You know how attached I am to her."

"I do. I also know that it is dangerous to travel, and she is not *alone* in South Dakota."

"Oh, please," I said, and moved around him toward my backpack.

"You were going to leave without so much as leaving me a note?" he said, and I didn't miss the inflection of what he was saying.

I spun to him, my eyes angry. "Don't you dare compare my leaving you to my leaving Matt."

"I wasn't," he said and walked to me, pulled the shirt from my hands and set it back in the drawer. "However, it hasn't escaped my attention that Charlie sends for you and you jump at the opportunity to go there, despite the fact that you were almost killed on a train less than three weeks ago."

That stopped me. I turned towards him slowly. "May I ask how you knew that it was *Charlie* who sent for me?"

Percy didn't say anything for a moment.

"I found the telegram yesterday. On your uncle's desk. Folded in half."

"And why were you looking on his desk?" Percy asked.

"Because Gigi asked me to get her a pen and a piece of paper and that was the only place I could think to look." I crossed my arms over my chest. "Silly me."

Neither of us spoke, but Percy's eyes remained locked on my face.

"Tell me you didn't know it came over two weeks ago."

"Kate, I didn't want you to worry."

Now I was mad. "So you deliberately keep something like that from me?"

"Perhaps I made an error in judgment. I wanted to you heal. To get stronger before I told you."

"Well, I'm definitely stronger now."

"You are not strong enough to go," he said, closing the top drawer of the dresser for emphasis.

"I walk all around the house, I walk the estate with Gigi. I clean my own wounds. I'm plenty strong."

Something flickered behind his eyes. "I wasn't talking about your legs."

That stopped me, and the fire went out of my tone. "Oh."

The muscles in his jaw were working furiously. "I don't want you to go."

Despite my ire, my reply was soft. "I know."

"It's too dangerous."

I laughed softly. "The train ride or being near Matt?"

There was pain in his eyes. "Both."

"I know. I've thought of that."

Percy slipped his hands around my waist and pulled me closer to him. It was the first time he'd touched me without necessity in over a week and I was sinking. "Don't go," he said into my hair.

Knowing it was the only thing he hadn't tried, he lowered his mouth to my neck, flicking his tongue against my skin.

"Stop it," I said and pushed against him. "That isn't going to work."

Percy's arms held me fast; his hands encircled my waist and lifted me on top of the dresser. His face was right next to mine, but I turned away. He reached for my chin and tipped my face up to his. Closing the gap between us, his mouth was hot against mine and I convinced myself I was going to stop. I pushed against his chest, but he tasted so good, and I'd missed him so much. My hands slid up and wound through his hair and I found myself kissing him back.

Like being caught in a current, a wave overtook me as he crushed me to him. I was drowning. My hands tore at his shirt, pulling it from where it was tucked neatly into his dress pants and I slid my hands underneath the fabric, digging my fingers into his skin. He pushed my skirt up around my waist, lifting me with one arm and pulling my bikinis from me with the other. My fingers found and released his belt and his dress slacks dropped to the floor. He pressed me against the wall next to the dresser.

Percy and I had never had sex like this, and I wondered if we should stop. How could it feel so good, and be so wrong at the same time? I could feel him against me, and I wanted him so badly.

"Percy, we should—"

His mouth was over mine before I could finish and I wrapped my legs around him as he entered me hard, holding my back against the wall. Breaking apart from the kiss, I cried out. His mouth moved down my neck and my legs tightened around him, and he whispered hoarsely against my cheek, "Tell me to stop, Kate."

My fingers dug into his shoulders. "No, don't, Percy. Don't stop."

His hands dug into my waist, our hips colliding with each stroke. Every second I got closer to the edge until his thrusts quickened, and I gritted my teeth against the explosion that I knew was coming.

Percy called out when he came, and I joined him seconds later. His hips slowed, and the softness of his kiss increased. Without pulling from me, he carried me to the bed, ascending the three steps to lie on top of me. I waited until my breathing returned to normal before saying anything.

"Percy," I said, and he kissed me again, so softly it rendered me mute. So many thoughts ran through my mind that I was dizzy. Worry over Carrie and Charlie for sending the telegram. Fear over being so close to Matt where I would have nowhere to hide from what happened between us. Fear over leaving Percy, the train ride to South Dakota, and fear over his expectations for us in the future.

"Don't go," he repeated again, even though his voice had softened considerably.

I knew I was making a decision that might have detrimental effects. But I had to go. And somewhere inside him, he knew what I was going to say.

"I have to go to her. I might be too late already."

He sighed and kissed my neck, and I marveled that he didn't pull from me. "If you're going to go," he said, "I'm sending some insurance with you."

"What insurance?"

He chuckled and touched my cheek. "You didn't really think I'd let you go alone, did you?"

I smiled brightly. "You're coming with me?"

His whisper was low in my ear. "I think I just did that, honey."

I grinned and squirmed underneath him and felt him react to my body. "Then what?"

"Let me worry about keeping you safe. But..."

"What?"

"Stay away from him." The finality with which he spoke left no room for interpretation.

"I'm not going there for him," I assured him. "I'm going there—"

"For Carrie, I know. I don't trust him, Kate. And neither should you."

I kissed the edge of his chin. "You could always accompany me yourself."

"I have Gigi to look after, and duties here that require my presence. Virginia is not safe. We're lucky they moved through here without more death. More damage. I need to stay and do what I can." He paused. "I owe it to my Uncle."

My heart fell. Despite being against him physically, I still felt a barrier between us that I could not breach.

"Finish packing. I'll expect you back here in one week. Unless things worsen, and in that event, I'll send a telegram."

I was pleased that we wouldn't have to fight over it. Happier still that I would be with Carrie by the end of the week.

"Kate," he said, moving against me.

I slid a leg around his hip. "Yes, Percy?"

He slid his tie from around his neck and leaned down to kiss me. "I don't think I'm making it back to the lab today."

Wrapping my other leg around him and gasping as he began to move inside me, I nodded in agreement.

CHAPTER NINE

"He did *what*?" Ano's voice was loud and nearly deafened Jazz sitting next to her.

"Baby," he said, closing his eyes. "Please."

She stood, glass of juice in hand, and began to pace. "That man is a fool!" She set her glass of juice down on the counter and turned to him, her long legs peeking out from her shorts.

Her mother came into the kitchen, touching Jazz on the shoulder as she walked by in her bathrobe. "Morning, baby."

Both replies came at the same time. "Morning, Mom."

Michelle filled the teapot, looking from Ano to Jazz and then back to her daughter. "Somethin' goin' on that somebody wants to tell me about?"

"His dumb ass best friend got a brilliant idea in his head and now—"

"Hey. Do not call him—"

"I do not need to—"

"Stop!" Michelle held her hands up to them both. "Ano, don't disparage the man's best friend." She turned to Jazz. "What'd that boy do now?"

"I went to the post station this morning to send Kate another telegram to her uncle's house," Jazz said. "And I got a telegram from Matt saying," he sighed, "that Kate's on her way to South Dakota."

"She's okay? Kate's okay? Oh, that is such good news!" Michelle's face lit up and she looked from one face to the other. "Why aren't you happy about this? Kate's okay! That's amazing!"

Ano looked at Jazz. "Yes, it's amazing."

"So, why is she on her way to...wait, where did you say she was going?" Jazz's shoulders sagged. "South Dakota."

Michelle shrugged. "Still don't see the problem."

Ano crossed her arms over her chest. "Not yet, you don't."

"She's going because Matt sent a telegram to her *as Charlie*, saying..." he hung his head.

"Go on," Ano said, pointing to her mother. "Uh huh."

Michelle felt sorry for him. "Jazz?"

"He pretended to be Charlie and told her that Carrie was sick so she'd come."

Michelle covered her mouth with her hand and closed her eyes. When she opened them, she looked from one to the other and blew a breath out in a long whoosh. "Well," she said, putting a piece of bread in the toaster, "it's gonna be an interesting week at Charlie and Carrie's house, I'll say that!"

"*Interesting*, Momma? For real?"

Grandma Vesper came in and sat down at the table next to Ano. "Mornin', baby girl."

"Mornin', Grandma."

"What would you have the man do, Ano?" Michelle said. "He was desperate for Kate. And now maybe they can work things out. And I thought you liked Matt?"

Grandma Vesper turned around. "Miss Kate's alive?" She slapped Ano's shoulder playfully and did a hip shake. "Praise Jesus! I knew it!" She saw Ano's expression and asked Jazz, "Why's she so mad?"

"Because lying to Kate 'bout Carrie's only gonna make Kate mad and send her right back to Percy," Ano cut in.

"Wow," Jazz said, impressed. "You actually said the name without, you know..."

"Shut up."

Grandma Vesper looked at the three of them. "Miss Kate's alive and gonna get back with Matt?"

They all three shook their heads and responded simultaneously. "No."

Grandma nodded her head. "Good."

Ano looked at her with her mouth open. "Grandma!"

"I like that Percy! He's a fine lookin' man!"

Ano covered her face in her hands and Michelle turned back around to her toast, which had popped out of the toaster. "Mama, that's just wrong."

Jazz was laughing, and Ano slapped him lightly on the shoulder. "OW!"

"So, what'd you say?"

Jazz shrugged. "What?"

She pursed her lips at him, a sure sign she didn't believe the smoke screen he was about to put up. "You sent him one back," she said, making a circular motion with her hand, "and told him...?"

Jazz shrugged. "Mom, could you put in another piece of toast for me?"

"Jazz Taylor!"

He turned to her with a smile. "Mrs. Taylor?"

"It wasn't enough we found out Kate's okay. Now you gotta go messin' in her business."

"Leave that boy alone." Grandma Vesper stood and ruffled Jazz's hair as she moved to get a glass of juice.

"Thank you, Grandma." He smiled at her.

"You're not getting out of that question so easy," Ano hissed in Jazz's ear.

Michelle buttered two pieces of toast and handed one to Jazz. "You hear back from the seminary?"

"Yes, ma'am," Jazz said. "They have a space in the spring."

Ano looked at him. "Why didn't you tell me?"

"Because it doesn't matter right now!"

Michelle reached for a bowl and began to search for cereal in the cupboards as Uncle Robert came in and said good morning to all of them.

"I hear you say you got into Seminary?"

"Yes," Jazz said.

Uncle Robert nodded. "Well, ah-right."

"Thank you, sir."

"Jazz," Ano said, "the train up there's likely to be safe. We could—"

Uncle Robert accepted the bowl of cereal Michelle handed him. "No. Nobody leaves this house till the fighting's done."

Lively came shuffling into the kitchen and Jazz covered his face with his hand. "There's no peace for an ol' woman to get some rest around here!"

"I'm surprised Percy let Kate go on a train," Michelle said. "After what happened."

"Who got on a train?" Lively asked.

"Miss Kate."

Uncle Robert thought for a minute. "Her husband let her get on a train?" He shook his head. "Damned fool."

"She's not married," Ano said, and turned to her mother, who was busy making hot cereal for Grandma Vesper and Lively. "I don't think he had a choice, Momma."

"Who didn't?"

"Percy!"

Lively mumbled something about all of them being 'damned fools' and shuffled to the coffee maker.

"What, you think Kate just got on without telling him?" Michelle stirred the cereal into the bowl and poured in more milk.

"Miss Kate better watch out 'for she gets herself killed this time!" Grandma Vesper said, and Uncle Robert agreed heartily.

"No," Ano said, "Kate probably told him that Carrie was sick. And that she was going. Period."

Jazz shrugged. "Why aren't you happy about this? Now Kate's gonna be with Matt!"

Uncle Robert pointed to him with his spoon. "Unless she don't make it."

Several 'uh-huhs' and 'okays' were heard about the room and Ano gritted her teeth. "She won't *be* with Matt if she finds out he lied to get her there."

"She's a jackass if she stay with a man who lie to her!" Lively said loudly, and Jazz covered his face with his hand again.

"So write her a letter and tell her how you feel," Michelle suggested to Ano. "Tell her you think Matt only did it to keep her safe. To keep her from harm's way. Maybe she'll believe you."

"By the time the letter gets there," Grandma Vesper said, "you might as well be sendin' smoke signals."

Uncle Robert interjected again. "If she makes it at all!"

Ano's temper flared. "Kate's gonna be up there all alone. With Matt."

Jazz covered her hand with his own. "She'll be okay."

"What did you say to Matt?" Ano asked, locking her gaze onto his.

"I wished him good luck, and told him to be careful."

Ano looked down at the table and didn't speak for a moment. When she spoke, her voice was quiet. "Matt made it down here on a train without any problem."

"That was before the fighting broke out."

"Yes, but if *he* did—"

Uncle Robert pointed at her with his spoon. "Nobody leavin' this house until the fightin's done."

No one commented on that, but Ano got up from the table to go back to her bedroom. Jazz was three steps behind her.

"Hey." He followed her into the bedroom and closed the door behind him.

"Hey," she said back.

He crawled onto the bed and lay down next to her. "Baby, your uncle's right. It's not safe. And the trains are—"

"She's hurt. And she's walking into a trap. If Matt will lie to her to get her to South Dakota, he'll lie to get her back."

"She's a grown woman, Ano."

"She's my best friend."

"I know that. But think clearly. She's alive and probably safer at Carrie and Charlie's in South Dakota than at Percy's uncle's house in Virginia."

"Safer from the war," she said, "but not from herself."

He got an incredulous look on his face. "What in the world does that mean? Anobelle, you need to let Kate make her own mistakes and—"

"I am," she said quietly. "But she's new at this, Jazz. She's never been in love before. Her heart is easily confused. You don't know her like I do."

"You're right, I don't," he admitted. "But she's going to have to learn to stand on her own two feet sooner or later."

"It isn't standing on her own two—arrgh!" She sat up and hit the mattress with her fist. "Kate doesn't know how to deal with guys like Matt. And guys like..."

"Percy," Jazz finished for her.

"Thank you. She just doesn't. I'm scared for her. And I miss her, Jazz. So much. She's alive. And I ..."

"I know, baby," he said, and rubbed her back with one hand.

She sat up, reached for his hand, and held it to her heart. "When I married you," she said somberly, "I promised to honor and obey you."

"Mmmhmm."

Her eyes found his and she pleaded with them. "If you *tell* me as my husband not to go, I won't go."

"Wait," Jazz said, backing up from her. "What d'you mean, you *won't* go? You heard what your—"

"He's my uncle. You're my *husband*."

"Yeah, but—"

"I need to go to Kate. *Need* to go to her. She's gonna go crazy when she finds out Matt tricked her. She'll be scared, confused..."

"There's a war on!"

"I know!"

Jazz reclined on his elbow and looked at his wife. "Baby, with everything going on, food is going to start getting harder to buy and—"

"All the more reason to go! Uncle Robert will have two less mouths to feed!"

His tone softened. "And you could leave your mom? And Grandma Vesper?" He paused for a moment and let the weight of his words sink in. "You thought you lost them once."

"You've been telling me that New Orleans isn't being seen as a 'point of entry' for the enemy."

"That's true, but that's just on the radio reports. We have no idea if the radio is a hundred percent accurate."

Ano reached for Jazz's hand. "My cousins are here, Uncle Robert is here, and nothing is going to happen in this little suburban area. Jazz, the worst thing that's going to happen is that food is going to get harder to come by. I highly doubt that the enemy is going to parachute into a suburb that's an hour from the coast."

Jazz looked at his wife's face, pleading with him to relent. "You sure this isn't just something to get you outta this house for a week?"

She smiled sweetly at him and came in close. "Now, why would you say that?"

He pulled back a little more and eyed her cautiously. "You're a wily creature, Ano Taylor."

She batted her lashes at him. "Thank you, Mr. Taylor."

"I still can't let you go."

Her face dropped. "Why not?"

"Because if somethin' happened to you, I'd..." he turned towards her and slid her hair off her shoulder. "I couldn't take it."

"So come with me."

"Hell no."

"Why not?"

"Because! It's too dangerous!"

"There have been almost no attacks on any of the Midwest states! None of them!"

"Yeah, 'almost' no attacks. Now's a bad time to test that theory."

She sank down onto the bed and grabbed his hand again. "Please, Jazz?"

"No."

"Carrie and Charlie have that spare room."

"No."

"Last time we pushed the beds together..." she leaned forward and kissed him softly on the lips.

"I remember," he said, but didn't move.

"You could spend time with Matt."

"Uh huh."

She sat back, none of her arguments working. "What do I have to say?"

He smiled at her. "There's nothin' you can say to—"

From downstairs, Lively's voice was heard above anything else. "Those two damned fools in their room again! Pretty soon, they gonna have a baby, and then there'll be *no* peace for an old woman!"

Jazz clenched the muscles in his jaw. "Ah-right," he agreed. "I'll talk to Uncle Robert."

CHAPTER TEN

"Doctor Mannis?"

Carlie moved to the bedside of one of the soldiers in recovery.

She stepped to the end of his bed, pulled his chart from the hook, and looked up. "Yes, uh...Private Jacobs?"

"My head's itching. Bad."

She looked to the chart and noted that his bandages needed changing soon anyway. "Maria?" she called towards the triage desk.

"Does it look better?" he asked.

"Hang on a second," she said, and unwrapped the bandages from his head. As she got closer, there was more blood that had seeped through the gauze pads. Her face darkened.

"You needed me, Dr. Mannis?"

"Yeah, I need you to get Doctor Phillips for me."

Maria turned to go, then asked, "Do you know what he looks like?"

The soldier smirked. "Major Phillips is tall. Thin. And he's got a purple wristband on."

"There you have it," Carlie said. "Go get him. Stat."

"My head bust open again?" Private Jacobs asked Carlie.

"You're fine, lie still please." She got to the wound and removed the gauze pad and saw seeping of blood along the length of the incision.

"Doctor Mannis?"

"Hi," Carlie said. "You're Doctor Phillips?"

"Yes." He came in and leaned over to view the soldier's wound. "Ah, Private, I warned you about letting beautiful women look under your bandages."

The private smiled. "Yes, sir."

He looked at the seeping incision and sat down next to the soldier. "Look here," he said, clicking his penlight into each eye, and then had the soldier follow a finger to test his peripheral optical ability. He nodded at Carlie. "Get him prepped and into Surgery One," he said, and started walking away.

Carlie bristled. "I'll have a *nurse* get him prepped. I'll meet you in Surgery One, and I can assist you."

He stopped and pivoted on his heel. "I'm sorry, *doctor*. I didn't mean to offend you."

Carlie slid her pen back into her pocket. "Apology accepted."

He stood where he was as Carlie called around him, "Maria?" She pointed to the private. "Surgery One."

"Yes, Doctor."

Carlie walked towards the far end of the hall, where she'd been going before the private had called her.

The major caught up with her. "So," he said, smiling, "what made you stay?"

She walked towards the cage for more methadone. "I wanted to help. Instead of hiding and waiting for someone to save me."

He leaned against the door of the cage and she inclined her head for him to move so she could open the door. "Some people would say that's very brave," he said.

"Or very stupid." She moved to the other side of the cage. "Careful. It's got a sharp edge."

He opened the door to let himself into the cage with her. "Which would you say?"

She removed three vials from the shelf and turned to look at him. He was a little too close. "Um, doctor," she pointed behind him. "I have to get through."

"Major," he reminded her. "John Phillips."

"Major."

"You're a clinical resident here?"

She pursed her lips in irritation. "No. I'm a *surgical* resident."

"I see."

He was a good-looking guy, taller than average with nice blue eyes. "I, uh," she pointed to the door, "still need to get through."

He moved quickly to allow her room to pass. "After you."

She walked down the hall, the major right beside her. A young soldier with a helmet and full gear ran down the hall toward the major and saluted quickly. "Major Phillips, Commander says he needs you now, sir."

The major barely looked at Carlie before double timing it out the front doors of the triage and into what used to be their loading zone for the Bellingham bus. The pop shade tents they'd used were gone, and everywhere she looked there was activity.

Medics ran past her and retrieved wounded from inside the trauma ward. Catching sight of the white haired commander she and David had seen before, she ran to him.

"Commander," she said over the roar of the jeeps pulling in and out, "what's going on?"

He gave instructions to a soldier near him and turned to face her. "We have a breach in the line," he said, and when she shook her head in confusion, he said, "They got through! The enemy got through! We have to move out. Get to one of the transports outside and get in it!"

She ran back inside. *David.* The trauma ward was transformed from a few moments ago; it was now emptying out of both personnel and wounded. Soldiers loaded the wounded onto trucks, which drove away to be replaced by other trucks. She ran through the halls searching for other faces she knew.

"Maria!" she screamed, seeing Maria prepping the private for surgery. "Get him out of here. They're going on a transport. Get yourself to safety!"

Carlie ran down the hall, pulling her fellow residents from where they were, pushing them towards the exit. Each time she asked about David but no one had seen him. Fewer and fewer people remained and she still hadn't found him. She ran through each of the surgery rooms and found them empty. She wasn't leaving without him.

"David!" she screamed, turning circles in the middle of the hall, which moments ago had been packed with bodies. "David!"

"Civilian personnel, evacuate!" A soldier grabbed her arm and pulled her towards the exit and she fought him, pushing against him with everything she had.

A second soldier grabbed her, dragged her by the waist out of the med unit, and forced her into the back of the second to the last of the waiting transports. The rear hatch closed, a tarp fell down over the top, and everything inside went black.

Hands from behind her pulled her up to a sitting position and onto the hard wooden seat within the transport. The combination of movement, swaying, lack of air and close proximity of people were doing nothing for her stomach, and she was grateful when the rear flap opened even slightly, for the fresh air it brought in with it.

After a half hour, she asked the soldier sitting next to her, "Where are we going?" He didn't answer her, and she turned the other direction. "Do you know where we're going?"

A voice across from her answered, "Secure location."

"Where is that?"

There was some snickering from all around. "I'm sure if they told everyone that, ma'am, it wouldn't be secure no more."

She nodded in the dark. "Oh. Of course."

Her mind was whirling. She had no idea where the other residents had gone. No idea where David was. Were all the transports going to the same location? She doubted it. In any case, if they didn't, how would she find David? The movement and the darkness in the transport was soothing after another half hour, and she felt herself leaning against the soldier next to her. "Sorry," she said, and righted herself.

From beside her, the soldier's soft voice replied, "S'okay. You smell real nice. Go ahead and lay your head against me, ma'am. I don't mind."

She tried to lean forward instead of to the side, but the angle hurt her stomach and before long, she was leaning to the side again, against the shoulder of the soldier with the soft voice. A jolt awoke her when the transport finally stopped.

"Where are we? Are we there?"

The rear tarp opened and the gate was lowered. The soldier next to her looked back to her. "Keep your head down and follow me." He reached above him. "Here, put this on."

"Thank you, uh…" she looked for the name on his uniform.

"Staff Sergeant Derrick."

"Thank you, Staff Sergeant Derrick."

He plunked a helmet on her head, which was so large it covered her eyes. Stumbling to get out of the transport as fast as everyone else, she nearly fell, but was caught by two soldiers on the ground. Tipping the helmet back, she was able to look around. Temporary tents were set up all around her, along with three tents that looked like command posts, and a really large one she guessed was to house the soldiers.

Transports were driving in and emptying soldiers out like worker bees, and they rushed to help secure the new location. Everyone, it seemed, had a job. Everyone except her. She approached a tall man in a heavy artillery jacket and tapped him on the shoulder.

With a surprised look he turned around and she was face to face with Major John Phillips. His previous smile was gone, and in its place was worry. "What the hell are you doing here?"

"I don't know. They threw me into the back of a transport, and..." she shrugged.

He cursed. "Follow me. Doctor."

The ground was muddy, and her tennis shoes that she'd been wearing were no match for the deep holes she was trudging through. He approached a tent and stood at attention until called at ease and allowed to enter by the officer inside.

"Major Phillips."

"Sir."

The middle-aged man in front of him looked at Carlie with an irritated expression. "Are we in the practice of picking of strays, Major?"

"No, sir."

"Then kindly tell me what this young lady is doing here."

"Oh, I'm—"

"I was speaking to the major," the commander said tersely.

Carlie listened silently as the major explained who she was and where they had come from. He accepted the information from him, then turned back around to the table he'd been leaning over when they'd come in. She didn't want to ask him if they should just stand there, for fear he would yell at her again, so she stayed silent, waiting while he seemingly did nothing but read some stupid map on a table. Was anybody going to talk?

"Doctor," the commander said, rising and walking towards her, "you are in a hot zone. Do you understand what that is?"

She nodded mutely, and then, not knowing if she should address him or not, she added, "Yes. Uh, sir."

"The rest of your unit, the ones who were smart enough to get on the *correct* transport., are in another location."

"Yes, sir. Okay."

He stood in front of her, weighing his options. "It'll be dark soon, and not safe for the transport of civilian personnel."

Surely he wasn't suggesting she was going to have to stay here? She didn't quite know what to say, and she looked to Major Phillips, who stared straight ahead with his hands clasped behind his back.

"You'll need to stay here until a reasonably safe time can be found to transport you to rejoin your medical unit. I will let you know when that can take place. Until that time, you may assist Army personnel in the care and wellbeing of our soldiers. Major Phillips, find the good doctor somewhere to sleep tonight." He nodded curtly. "Dismissed."

Major Phillips took her by the upper arm and led her from the Commander's tent. He didn't release her until they were a hundred yards from him, and Carlie looked around her, her helmet falling from her head. Pulling the helmet from her, Major Phillips adjusted the straps and slapped it back onto her head, securing it under her chin by a strap. She followed behind him like a lost dog.

"Wear that at all times, even when you sleep."

"Okay." She was struggling to keep up with him and her shoes were caked with mud, thick and black.

"Latrine over there," he pointed, "medic tent, there." She looked in the vague area he had pointed her and nodded, even though she had no idea what he'd pointed out. "I'll find you somewhere to sleep."

He turned on his heel and she called after him, "Major?" He didn't respond. "Major Phillips?"

Stopping, he swiveled around, the look on his face serious. "Yes?"

"I need to...where's the...um..."

"Spit it out, doctor."

"I need to pee!" she said loudly, and there were several soldiers that laughed as they passed by.

Major Phillips grinned and pointed animatedly towards the far corner of the compound. "Latrine."

"Is that the women's latrine, or the...?"

He walked away, chuckling and shaking his head.

Her evening was difficult. She had no idea where anything was, and as a result, was little help to the medical personnel who seemingly had everything down to a system in a very short amount of time. She hadn't brought her medical kit, her bag, or even her purse. She didn't even have her identity card, which was back in her locker in the trauma ward. The thought chilled her that if she died, she'd have nothing to identify her at all.

Her stomach was growling by the evening, and most of the men had crowded into one barracks tent or another. She was too scared and cold to continue wandering around looking for somewhere to go, and so she settled for a small cot in the medic tent, next to a wounded soldier. It was hard, and her thin white jacket gave her no warmth whatsoever, but at least she was lying down.

Within a half hour, her teeth were chattering and rain began to patter on the roof of the tent. She tucked her knees up to her chest and tried to drown out the distant sounds of artillery coming from where they'd been mere hours ago. A hand tapped her shoulder and she opened her eyes.

"I think we can do better than this." Major Phillips said. "Come with me, *Doctor.*" She picked her helmet up from the ground and slipped it on her head as they walked outside and across the compound. It was still raining lightly. Pulling the flap aside and allowing her to pass, they entered into a tent with three cots in it. He pointed to one. "There you go. Courtesy of the United States Army."

She stood shivering and nodded her thanks to him as she walked to the corner and sat on the edge of a bare cot.

"This is soaked," he said, unbuttoning her doctor's jacket. "Take it off."

He hung it on the makeshift hanger dangling from the center pole, reached for a blanket from one of the other bunks, and tossed it to her.She caught it and said, "Thank you." Still shivering, she turned to lie down.

"Have you had any food?"

Her hair was soaking wet and she wrung it out at the ends. "No."

He looked at her quizzically. "I'm amazed that you stayed." He sat and patted the place next to him on his cot, then leaned over to retrieve two plastic packets from his pack. He offered one to her. "And even more amazed you survived."

"What is that?" she asked, her teeth still chattering.

He reached around her and grabbed another blanket and wrapped it around her shoulders. "MRE. Do you want one?"

"Yes please," she said, hoping it didn't taste as bad as her previous experience with Army food. "What's an MRE?"

He tore both packets open and handed her one. "Meal, Ready to Eat."

She thanked God there were crackers in it. There was something that smelled really bad and looked kind of like beef jerky. Her stomach stopped growling as she drank thirstily from the canteen he handed her. Thunder sounded from overhead and she cringed.

"It's only thunder," he said, half laughing, and regarded her with curiosity. "I'm confused how you can brave through five hours on the front lines rescuing Army men," he said, crossing his arms over his chest, "and be afraid of a thunderstorm."

She couldn't very well tell him that things had changed for her between then and now that the knowledge that she was pregnant made everything different. She couldn't tell him that she'd been having a relationship with her attending and that had really been one of the main reasons she'd agreed to stay in the first place. She concentrated on her meal and when she'd finished, Major Phillips offered her some of his. Carlie gratefully accepted, and after eating his crackers – but leaving the beef jerky looking meat behind – she thanked him and crawled onto her cot, dragging the blanket over her.

Somewhere in the night, the artillery got closer, the explosions sounding like horribly close thunderclaps. The rain was still pelting the tent when she awoke, her stomach churning. Running outside, she fell to her knees and was sick, the rain soaking her back and hair once again. Major Phillips was up the second he heard her leave and ran after her, retrieving her from the mud, carrying her back to the tent.

He set her on the edge of her cot and reached for a towel from his pack, rinsing it with water and then gently wiping the dirt from her hands and face. Carlie was clearly not okay. She sat on the edge of the cot, tears rolling down her cheeks while Major Phillips wiped the mud away.

He sat back on his heels, and regarded her carefully. "Sometimes the MREs take a little getting used to."

Tears ran freely down her cheeks, and the rain had soaked her hair. "It's not that." She sniffled for a minute, wondering if she should say it out loud. If she said it out loud, it became real. He waited, as she took a shuddering breath and looked into his eyes.

"I'm…I'm…pregnant."

CHAPTER ELEVEN

President Riley paced the floor of the second story room he occupied with three Navy Seals, his wife, and daughter. With the breach of his location in Gatineau Park, and then again in Ottawa, they had sequestered themselves in the northern Adirondack Mountains, in a cabin known only to a few, but guarded by many. Still, with so little preparatory time to arm the cabin, he felt exposed and continually on edge.

The arrival of intelligence was announced, and the door opened. As always, Albert Riley still had a loaded handgun mounted to the drawer in the desk he sat behind.

Deborah Simpson always entered a room with an air of self-importance that Albert loathed. He'd kept it in check because they'd served in Congress together many years ago, and truthfully, she wasn't someone you wanted to make an enemy.

"Mister President."

"Deb." He stood and greeted her with a handshake, motioning for her to sit in the chair across from his desk. "Please."

He poured them both a drink and then unceremoniously toasted to the success of the United States.

"Mister President," she started, "I have the notices from Strategic Alliance, and the final reports in on the remaining members of the House and Senate."

"How many left?"

She opened her notebook. "Of the four hundred thirty-five members, we've been able to locate one hundred ten."

Riley removed his glasses and massaged the bridge of his nose. "The Senate?"

"Luckily, we have heard from fifty-five."

"Just over half."

"Yes, sir."

"And the Strategic Alliance?"

Deborah handed him the notices and leaned back in her chair, sipping her drink. "I think you'll find the intelligence on page four critical."

He made a non-committal response and continued reading the brief. After reading page four, he set the document on the edge of the desk. "This isn't possible. We've been developing those weapons for a year now. General Pattison said they were operational a month before the first attack." He tapped his finger on the table. "This report is wrong."

"If that report is wrong," she stated, "then what stage are we at with their deployment?"

Riley took a sip of his drink and did not answer.

"Where is General Pattison?" Deborah pressed. "If I can communicate the report's errors to him, then I can clear them up with the Alliance."

"Those weapons are operational," Riley said quietly. "I know they are."

Deborah leaned forward, setting her glass down close to his. "Sir," she said, taking the report from the table, "read paragraph nine carefully. I think you'll find—"

"Mister President." The Navy Seal that had been standing five feet behind Deborah's chair advanced, weapon out.

"What the hell?" Albert raised his hands above his head.

"Not you, sir," the Seal replied, his weapon trained on the back of Deborah's head. "Her."

"Deborah?"

"Yes, sir. Her hand hovered over your drink just now, sir."

Albert leaned back in his chair as the other Seals in the room advanced on them both, pulling Albert behind them and training their weapons directly on Deborah.

Her expression calm, her perfectly manicured hands indicating no sign of nervousness, Deborah smiled back at Albert. "I did nothing of the sort. Mister President, we've been friends for twenty years."

Even with three guns aimed at her head and heart, he thought, she could still lie. The SEALS pulled her to her feet, removed her suit jacket, and searched her.

"We've never been friends, Deborah," he said. "You've always been a cast iron bitch who would sell out your country for the almighty dollar."

One of the SEALS pulled a walkie-talkie from his belt. "The nest is compromised. The eagle must fly. Repeat, Eagle is on the move." He turned to Albert and held up a small device retrieved from Deborah's shoe. "It's a PLB, sir."

Five more SEALS opened the door, fully armed. "We have a transport for you and your family, sir. We have a narrow window, Mister President."

Albert removed his handgun from underneath the desk and grabbed the briefcase that never left his side. SEALS swarmed around him, packing up everything in the room.

"Good luck, Albert." Even down on her knees, the compound emptying around her, Deborah had a smug tone.

"I don't need luck, you worthless shell of a human being." He paused next to her before leaving the room. "But you will, when they find you here and discover you didn't deliver me...and that I didn't tell you where General Pattison has those weapons."

Finally, he saw his words hit their mark. Fear crept into her face as she knelt on the floor, a gun trained at her head.

"You might consider drinking whatever you put in that glass when we're all gone. It'll be better than what they have in store for you."

President Riley retreated from the room, the remaining SEALS flanking him, leaving Deborah kneeling on the ground, waiting for a death that was too good for her...and approaching fast.

When Percy said he was sending me with 'insurance', I never anticipated this. Knowing him as I did, I shouldn't have been surprised. Sitting beside me on the train, Edgar glanced over occasionally and grinned, happy that he'd escaped a week of the tutor his uncle had hired, happy he was going to be with me for a whole week, happy with the secret knowledge of whatever Percy had said to him out of my earshot when we'd said goodbye at the train station.

I had no doubt that Percy was unhappy sending his only surviving brother as my chaperone, however, I couldn't help but think Edgar was serving a double purpose. Without me there at home to entertain and educate Edgar, he'd be underfoot with Percy and Gigi. Edgar had packed his bag and Percy had accompanied us to the train station. Percy had kissed me and told me to be careful, that he'd expect me back in a week, and told Edgar he'd expect to hear from him daily. I looked at Edgar's grinning face. I wasn't exactly sure what Percy was up to, though I had a pretty fair idea.

The train ride was long, and Edgar and I shared a sleeper car with bunk beds. Edgar is fifteen. And he's really good at being fifteen. About five hours into the train ride, I was wondering if he would make it to sixteen. Ever. We traded bunk beds three times. After he was certain that the top bunk was, in fact, the best, he began to draw. Then talk. Then hum. And I learned something interesting about having a sibling. They're *never quiet.* Finally, when I began to focus on the circulatory system and the train crossed through Ohio, Edgar blessedly fell asleep.

I read through the night, dropping off into a light sleep a few times. I opened my eyes when we left Indiana and entered Illinois. The chilly sun rose on the horizon and Edgar was snoring softly in the bunk above me. It seemed odd to me that siblings could have certain things that were alike, and others that were so different. In that regard, Percy and Edgar have the same manner of sleeping. Both sleep on their sides, normally only on their back when they awaken. And, as I'd discovered while taking care of Edgar, they both snore. It's not the horrid, resonating snore that makes others wonder if a wild animal is about to attack, but a soft, comforting sound of really deep sleep.

I got up and dressed in the bathroom, washed my face, and brushed my hair. Thankfully, I didn't have to be quiet or worry about waking Edgar. Unlike his older sibling, Edgar couldn't be woken unless forced. And occasionally, not even then. In short, Edgar slept like the dead. In that way he reminded me of Ano. Stuffing my faded blue pajamas into my backpack, I sat cross-legged on the bed and pulled my anatomy book from my bag. Though it lay open in my lap, I couldn't concentrate.

The threat of attack on the train had ended as we left Ohio, and now Indiana stretched ahead of us like a welcome friend. The landscape comforted me after the long months of Philadelphia pavement and manicured trees. I cracked my window and got down on my stomach next to it, shivering as a slight bit of the Indiana air reached my face.

Beyond us, the treetops were just barely lit by the sunlight. By the end of today, we'd be entering Iowa, the wheat and corn on the plains swaying in the breeze, as if they were welcoming me back to somewhere I had once belonged. As if I was coming home.

I'd sent the telegram to Charlie asking him to pick me up right after I'd bought my train ticket and knew my approximate arrival time. I had no idea then that Charlie would be picking up two of us. Carrie wouldn't be able to accompany him to the station due to her condition, and I prepared myself for the worst, just in case.

Edgar woke up grouchy, and it was a chore to get him ready to disembark. The last two days of traveling with him by train had worn on me. I was tired of the constant motion of the car and the horrid boxed food on the train. I tried to reiterate to Edgar that we were traveling there for Carrie, and he needed to be helpful while we stayed with them, but I think my words fell on deaf ears. I now know why people complained about having siblings. How had Percy done this with four brothers?

Ready to throw him onto the tracks, I hustled Edgar out of the train as soon as we stopped moving and I scanned the depot for signs of Charlie. We stood, our bags at our feet, waiting.

"Where is he?" Edgar asked, and his voice broke at the end.

I sighed. At this rate, I would not make it more than a half hour on the ride to Charlie and Carrie's house. "Edgar," I began.

"Well, there she is!" Charlie's voice echoed to me across the depot. I turned. Charlie stood, exactly as I remembered him. I ran to him, flinging myself into his arms. It wasn't usual for Charlie to give hugs, but he crushed me to him and swung me back and forth in greeting.

Tears squeezed out between my eyes as he hugged me and it felt like years since I'd seen him. He set me down, his smile wide. "Hey there, Missy."

"Hi, Charlie."

"You got a bag? Lessgo!"

"Um," I held up my index finger to Charlie, "hang on." I walked back to where Edgar stood with both our bags. "Charlie Blackhawk, this is Edgar Warner." I looked up into Charlie's surprised face. "Percy's brother."

Wonderful man that he is, Charlie extended a hand to Edgar, and the two shook in greeting. "Look just like your brother! Anyone ever tell you that?"

"Yes," Edgar replied, "they have."

Charlie picked up my backpack. "Truck's over here. C'mon."

We loaded our bags in the back and walked around to the cab. Before he opened the door, Charlie held me back for a second with an arm around my shoulders and whispered in my ear, "I didn't know you were bringin' company."

I whispered back, "Neither did I."

Charlie opened the door to the cab. Barely waiting for the door to open all the way, Matt slid out of the truck and stood, facing me. The sight of him after all this time literally took my breath. It had been weeks since Ano's wedding and yet he looked years different. Leaner, browner, but still Matt.

"Katie." As if he couldn't help himself, he pulled me into a hug that was unmistakably Matt. I stiffened and pulled away, and he let me go easily. He looked at me, his entire face glowing. That is, until he looked directly behind me and saw Edgar. His face immediately darkened.

"Matt Skylar, this is Edgar Warner. Percy's—"

"Brother." Matt shook Edgar's hand. "Ya look just like him."

"I know."

Charlie stood by the door, knowing that the presence of Edgar had complicated a whole lot more than any of us would care to admit. "We're not all not gonna fit in the cab," he said, and Matt nodded to Edgar.

"Edgar can sit in the back, right, Edgar? Let Charlie and me catch up with Kate?"

"No," Edgar said. "I don't think so." The expression on his face made him look like Percy and at that moment, it dawned on me exactly what instructions he had given to his younger brother. I also knew I was going to kill Percy when I got back to Philadelphia.

"Sorry," Matt said, "what?"

Edgar crossed his arms over his chest. "Can't let you do that, *Matt*." He said his name with a distaste that only comes when one brother has given another brother entirely too much information. "You can sit in back, and *Charlie* can catch up with Kate."

Charlie covered his face with his hand and looked at both boys. "All right," he said, his expression hardening, "I'm gonna solve this. Matt, you ride in back first, Edgar, you take second half. We'll stop halfway and get some lunch for everyone and some coffee for whoever rides in back."

"I'm only fifteen."

"Then it's high time you started drinking somethin' stronger than milk," Charlie said. "Get in."

The first half of the ride was fairly quiet, Charlie giving me hardly any details about Carrie and I was wondering if he didn't want to say too much in front of Edgar, or if it was because she was worse off and he didn't want to frighten me. I lightly dozed off for an hour onto Charlie's shoulder and awoke as we pulled into an A&P for lunch. After we all grabbed a sandwich, Matt and Edgar walked to the truck to trade places. Matt removed his heavy jacket and tossed it to Edgar as he climbed in back.

"That'll keep you warm."

"Matt!" Edgar called, and Matt turned as I climbed back into the cab of the truck.

"What?"

Edgar leaned down over the side, their faces close together. "I'll be facing towards the window. Just in case."

Unfazed, Matt said, "Keep your mouth closed. Sitting like that you'll swallow a lot of bugs." He was still laughing as he climbed into the cab next to me.

I turned to him as Charlie climbed in and started the truck. "Was that necessary?"

"Kid's as cocky as his older brother, so help me God."

"Matt..." Charlie warned.

He turned towards the window as we headed back out onto the highway.

Finally sure that Edgar couldn't hear us, Charlie cleared his throat. "There's somethin' we've gotta talk about, now that it's just us."

Matt sighed, and I sensed that the worst had happened. I was too late. Carrie had sent for me, and it had taken too long for me to get there. I nearly began to cry.

"I knew it." I took a shuddering breath. "I'm so sorry, I should have been here earlier for Carrie."

Charlie glanced at me, then to Matt. There was actual anger in his face. "See what happens when ya act before ya think?"

Matt looked out the window, not speaking to either of us. I looked at Charlie, then Matt. "What's going on?"

"*Genius* here got so worried when we didn't know if it was your train that was hit that he—"

"I was half out of my mind, Kate," Matt pleaded. "You have to believe me."

"What do you mean?"

"The telegram," he said. "The one you got from...Charlie."

I nodded slowly. "Yeah?"

He closed his eyes. "I...I sent that."

I inhaled sharply through my nose and concentrated on the road in front of us for a long moment. "Are you telling me," I said, my voice soft but dangerous, "that Carrie isn't sick?"

Charlie's mouth was set in a line and his expression said that he knew what Matt had coming to him, and he wasn't going to intervene.

"Yeah," Matt responded.

My fists were curled into balls. I'd never wanted to hit someone the way I wanted to hit him now. I turned to Charlie. "You knew about this?"

"Noooo! Don't go getting me mixed up in this. We only found out what he'd done after we got your telegram and Matt had to explain it to me and Carrie. By then it was too late and your train had already left, or we would have sent you back a telegram saying not to come. Too dangerous."

"You better thank Edgar when we get out of this truck," I said to Matt between my teeth. "He is the only thing keeping me from kicking your ass right now."

Charlie chuckled.

"I acted before I thought," Matt said contritely.

My voice went up an octave. "You put *me* at risk! You put *Edgar* at risk! You scared the shit out of me thinking Carrie was sick! How dare you use my love for her to lure me here for...for what?"

Matt nodded, knowing he deserved my venom. "You're right," he said. "You're right, Kate. When I got your telegram...sorry, *Carrie* got your telegram, about Percy moving you to Virginia, we all knew it was a bad idea. Then we found out that a train had been hit, and Carrie and I, we freaked out. We thought it was your train. I kept thinking that if I would have kept you here then you wouldn't have been in danger. If you would have come home where it's safe..." his voice trailed off for a moment. "And when I heard that your train had been hit, Kate, we didn't know if you were alive or dead. I worried that Percy wouldn't respond if it wasn't an emergency. I just wanted you here where it was safe." He turned to stare out the window and didn't say anything more.

Charlie's hand slid down and squeezed my knee. Charlie wasn't supporting Matt, that was for sure. However, I could tell from Charlie's response that my accident had taken a greater toll on Matt than I could see right now, and he wanted me to go a little easy on him.

"As you can see, I'm fine," I said in an even, temperate tone.

"Are you?" Matt asked, looking at me now. "You weren't hurt?"

I wasn't sure I was ready to talk about this. I hadn't told anyone about it yet, though my nightmares had continued. Hadn't even discussed it with Percy, not that he'd been around much before I'd left anyway.

"I got some...cuts. On my legs." I looked out the front window. "Glass and stuff. They're healing really well, though."

"We heard that everyone on board..." Charlie trailed off.

All three of us were silent for a moment and my heart began to race a little as I thought back to that horrible day. There was no way I could tell them. No way I could tell anyone what had happened. "I...they..." I had lost my voice and tried to keep my mind form drifting back to that horrible day.

Charlie patted me on the leg again. "S'okay, Missy. We'll talk 'bout it later."

I couldn't speak for a few minutes. I worked on staying in the present, and not remembering the train. All the bodies. The sound of...

"I'm sorry, Kate."

The cab of the truck was silent once again. Gently, Matt reached over and took my hand in his and laced our fingers together. From right behind us, a loud knock sounded on the glass and we turned our faces to see Edgar, shaking his head and pointing to our hands.

I laughed, taking my hand back into my own lap. Matt glared at Edgar, and Edgar shivered, but smiled as he reclined against the truck once again.

Charlie motioned with his thumb towards the truck bed. "What d'we tell the whelp?"

Poor Edgar. He'd only been here a few hours and already he had a lot to overcome. "I think if we tell him the truth, I'll be in a lot of trouble. And so will you."

Matt sighed and leaned back in the cab, simultaneously slouching down, which caused his leg to rest against mine. Without looking behind us, he asked, "You don't think he'll mind, do you?"

Yeah, I thought he'd mind. Very much.

"By the way," he said, tipping his head to the side so his face was inches from my cheek, "You look amazing."

I smiled. "The things you do, Matt Skylar. So help me."

CHAPTER TWELVE

Charlie wasn't sure how he was going to explain the very un-sick Carrie to Edgar, so when we pulled into the driveway, Matt and I decided to keep Edgar busy out front for a few minutes while Charlie went in and explained the 'Edgar complication' to Carrie. We agreed that within a day or so of my arrival, Carrie would have a miraculous recovery, possibly including a trip to a "doctor" in town, and all would resume as normal. We had a plan.

Matt and I took Edgar down to the end of the drive to get mail, even though we both knew they went to the post station instead, every day. Coming back empty handed from the ten-minute detour, we were unable to detain Edgar any longer and grabbed the bags to head inside the house.

Everything, from the sound of the screen door to the smell inside, was the same. I looked around for Carrie. I even called her name. Charlie came out into the kitchen from their bedroom and looked at me directly. "Carrie's in bed. She'll see you now."

I signaled for Edgar to wait for me. Thankfully, his expression was solemn. This is what he'd been brought for - to deliver me to my sick surrogate mother. By allowing me out of his sight to see Carrie, he was completing part of his mission. I ran through to Carrie and Charlie's bedroom right off the kitchen and closed the door quietly before being spun around to face a very well, very healthy Carrie.

"My girl!" she said excitedly, although she was whispering. She pulled me into a hug. The kind that only Carrie could give and not come off as awkward.

I clung to her. I rested my head on her shoulder and twisted into her arms. I wanted to cry, to sink into her lap and never let go. And after over two months of not seeing her, of writing her every other day and telling her every wonderful, horrible, terrifying thing I'd been through, that's what I did. She led me to the edge of the bed and gently took me in her lap, letting the tears flow, not knowing or caring if they were from sorrow or joy.

She pulled a quilt over the top of us, kissed my head and held me, humming something quiet until I was either too worn out to cry any more or finally aware that she was real and right in front of me. When I leaned my head back to look at her face, her cheeks were wet and her eyes were rimmed in red.

"Thought I lost you," she mumbled, and tears slid silently down her cheeks.

"Me too."

She brushed her lips against my forehead. "You're here."

I nodded, unable to speak. The tears came again.

"You're home."

I'd never heard those words and had them register as they did at this very minute. Lying against her, wrapped in her arms, the handmade quilt over me, the truth of the statement struck me in its clarity. I was, indeed, home. As if regressing back to toddlerhood, I snuggled down against Carrie, the tears still wet on my cheeks.

For a long while we sat together, not talking, not crying. This is what I'd needed. All those days I'd been in Los Altos with Matt's mother. All those lonely walks I'd taken to the post station. The fifteen-mile ride to the bus station that horrible morning I'd left Matt. The long train ride to Penn State. The day I'd found out Ano was getting married. The day I'd said goodbye to Matt at Ano's uncle's house. My last few long, lonely days in Virginia. And pretty much every day after the train accident.

I'd never understood what girls at Stanford meant when they'd cried and said they missed their mothers. I shrugged when Ano told me that only her mother would understand when something had gone horribly wrong during the day. I doubted the sincerity of people who claimed their mother could make them feel better 'just by talking to them'. Lying in Carrie's arms, or perhaps by divine intervention, enlightenment on this issue was finally mine. Regardless of the fact that it had taken twenty-two years, finally, I had a mother.

"I hear you brought a friend," Carrie said into my hair and I snuggled against her.

"Percy's brother."

"Ah." She didn't say anything more for a few minutes, and I could tell it was my turn to do a little explaining.

I sat up a little, although Carrie kept a hold of me and occasionally stroked the hair from my face or tucked some hair behind my ear.

"He didn't want me to come alone," I said, and traced along the pattern of the quilt with my finger.

"Because of Matt." She didn't say it with malice, but I could tell she didn't approve. "Doesn't he trust you?"

I laughed, a little. "Oh, he trusts *me*," I said.

Carrie nodded. "I see."

"I guess he has every reason to distrust Matt. I mean, look what he did to get me here."

Carrie stroked my arm softly. "About that..." She looked into my face. "I was pretty mad when he showed up here, after I got your letter. I put him through hell the first two weeks he was here."

"Oh yeah?"

She was trying not to smile. "Made him sleep in the barn the first week."

I giggled, and then covered my mouth. "You did not."

"Yes, ma'am, I did." She tucked a strand of blonde hair behind my ear. "But then I saw that he..." She stopped for a minute, deciding what to say.

"He what?"

"He loves you. So much more than I thought." Her eyes caught mine and held them. "The day we found out about your train ...he died a little that day, I think."

I thought about Matt in the other room. "Yeah. He seems different."

"He is."

"I'm not here to work it out with him. I came for you."

She smiled. "And here I am!" She hugged me tightly and kissed my head. "So are you in love? With Percy, I mean?"

"I am, yes."

"Does he make you happy?"

I replied with no hesitation, "He does."

She sighed. "So you're considering staying with him in Virginia?"

"Oh, Carrie. I'm not sure. Everything is so mixed up." Staying in Virginia came with a whole bunch of complications. I thought about Gigi, and the talk we'd had about marriage, and children, and Percy being so distant. And the type of marriage I could look forward to as a 'Warner wife'. I realized I'd been silent too long.

"I think we have a lot to talk about."

A soft knock sounded at the door and Charlie came in. "Feelin' better?" We both chuckled and Carrie helped me stand. "I think it would help things if you let the whelp meet her."

"He has a name, Charlie," I chastised him.

Charlie shrugged. "So?"

I smothered a giggle and planted a mock punch in his shoulder.

"I'll climb under the quilt to meet the whel...to meet Edgar."

I followed Charlie out to the living room where Matt and Edgar were literally standing facing each other, arms crossed over their chests. Even at fifteen, Edgar was nearly six feet tall.

"Edgar," I said, and motioned for him to follow me. I'm sure it helped the story a little bit that I looked like I'd been crying the better part of an hour, which I had been. When I brought him in to Carrie's bedroom, her eyes were still really red as well.

"Carrie, this is Edgar Warner. Edgar, this is Carrie Blackhawk."

Edgar tried to smile at Carrie, who was snuggled down under the quilt. If I knew Edgar, he was taking mental notes on how sick she was for a report back to Percy.

"I'm so glad you could come with Kate," Carrie said, and her voice was a little hoarse. *Nice touch*, I thought.

He nodded politely. "Thank you for having me. I hope you'll feel better soon."

Carrie nodded a little too enthusiastically. "Doctor says with more rest and some medicine I'll be up and around later this week."

I scrunched my eyebrows together and she sank a little lower in the bed and coughed.

"But I've been sick for a while now."

A serious look on his face, Edgar replied, "Yes, I know."

"All right," I said gently. "Carrie is going to rest for a little while, and we're going to make dinner for her." I shoved Edgar out her bedroom door and she pointed to the kitchen.

"Pot pie," she said. "In the fridge."

I gave her the thumbs up before closing the door. "Carrie, we'll see you after you've taken some of your medicine."

"All right."

I closed the door and smiled at Edgar, who looked at my tearstained face, a little concerned. "Are you all right?" He put his arm around my shoulders as we walked through the kitchen.

"I'm fine," I said. "So glad we're here."

"Oh no!" Edgar looked to the clock. "I was supposed to send a telegram to Percy when we got here! "He's going to kill me!"

"Edgar, it's fine. The postal station is only fifteen minutes from here."

He tugged on my arm. "Can we go?"

Charlie could always be counted on to take advantage of an emergent situation. "All right, whelp. Get your coat and let's go."

Edgar moved for the door and then stopped. He looked to Matt, then me again. "Kate," he said, "come with me."

"I need to stay here and fix dinner for Carrie."

Edgar looked at Matt. I could tell he wasn't going to leave with Matt still in the room. From behind Edgar, Charlie barked at Matt.

"What're you standing around for? While Kate visits with Carrie, I need you to go out and get the rest of that work done in the barn."

Matt headed out the back door. "Yes, sir."

Charlie nodded towards me. For Edgar's benefit, he added, "Don't let her get out of bed till she's had her medicine, Kate. Stay right by her side."

"I will," I said somberly.

Charlie pushed Edgar through the front door and into the truck, and we heard it roar to life and pull out of the driveway. Within minutes, Carrie's bedroom door opened and the back porch door creaked a crack.

"We all clear?" Matt called.

Carrie walked over to me, embracing me in a full hug. "He seems nice."

Matt snorted. "You should spend some time with his brother."

Carrie and I both shook our heads.

"What?"

"I hope you're better behaved when Jazz and Ano get here tomorrow."

I spun back to Carrie. "What'd you say?"

"That's right," Matt said. "I didn't tell you."

"*Ano is coming*?" I jumped up and down and clapped my hands like I was five, earning a laugh from Matt.

"Glad that makes you happy, sweetheart."

The endearment was too much and I stopped. His face fell a little."Ugh. Sorry. I forgot for a minute."

Carrie brightened. "Which means, with all these healthy boys to feed, I've gotta get cooking before the whel...before Edgar comes back."

"Nice, Carrie."

"It's kind of catchy."

"Kate," Matt said, "we've got a little more than a half hour if Charlie times it right." His eyes pleaded with me. "Take a walk with me?"

This is what I'd feared from the first moment I'd gotten the telegram.

"Go on," Carrie said. "I'll cover for you."

We walked out the back door towards the field and I took in my breath. Everywhere, as far as the eye could see, was wheat. "Oh my gosh."

Matt followed my gaze. "I know. Incredible, right?"

I nodded mutely and he reached out and took my hand. "C'mon."

As if we were old friends, we walked side by side on the well-worn road through the two main fields of wheat. It was as high as my hip, and I marveled at it as it moved with the breeze. "You did this?"

He smiled and I could see in his face, the pride at what he had done out here with Charlie. Rightfully so. When I'd left they were plowing and planting. Now, three months later, the wheat was growing in thick and strong. We fell into an easy pace together along the path, and he didn't let go of my hand. Like before, he was always touching me.

"If I told you how many times I walked out here thinking of you..." he shrugged, "I think I'd embarrass you."

I didn't say anything. I couldn't. He knew it, but it didn't dampen his mood. "Why are Ano and Jazz coming?"

He laughed, and I'd forgotten the rumbling sound his laughter made in his chest. "I think Lively was driving Jazz crazy. And I know Ano was crazy worried about you when she heard about the train. There's not a lot of activity where they're at, so they decided to come for the time you're here."

I was enjoying this. The way we talked together, the easy conversation we always seemed to have. We walked a little farther. "You said your legs are getting better. What happened?"

"I had surgery. Right after the train accident. They're healing."

"I see."

"Your mother?" I asked. "How is she?"

His face darkened a little and I could tell this wasn't friendly territory. "John says she's doing fine."

"Good." I wasn't going to ask about his brothers. I thought that might be opening up a can of worms and really, I was enjoying our conversation too much to go there.

"What about Carlie?" he asked, obviously happy to avoid the topic of his brothers as well. "Have you heard from her in Bellevue?"

"The last letter I got from her she said she was..." I stopped. The last letter I'd gotten from her I hadn't finished reading. I hadn't finished because...

"Kate."

I'd been holding her letter. I'd showed it to Percy. "Yeah?"

"You were saying, 'She said she was'... what? The letter?"

My chest hurt. I had been reading the letter when the explosion had sounded. And then the screaming started.

"Kate?" He turned me to him and shook me gently. "What's going on? Is Carlie okay?"

"Matt, can we talk about Carlie's letter later?"

"Sure, Kate. 'Course we can."

I swallowed the bile back in my throat. "Thanks."

I didn't want to think about the train. Didn't want to think about it now. Matt squeezed my hand. "It's okay," he whispered.

I looked around us. I needed to change the subject. The breeze came up and I shivered.

"I love it here."

Matt stripped off his long sleeved shirt. "You never dress warm enough. I swear."

"No, you'll freeze," I said, looking at his tan arms and muscular chest against the thin white undershirt he wore. He handed me the shirt and I stood there with it in my hands for a moment. It was still warm from his body.

"I never do." He laughed. "Kind of like when we went into the city that day and..."

"Oh, it was so cold!"

He was laughing now, with his whole body. "Everything on your body was standing like BAM! At attention."

"Yes, thank you, I needed to be reminded of that."

He reached out and helped me slip his shirt over my head and pull both of my arms through. I was drowning in it, but it was warm and...I inhaled. It smelled like him. I hated how good it smelled and how much I'd missed the smell of his skin. A knowing look crossed his face as he watched me and I turned away from him.

He was still chuckling. "That was a good day," he said, keeping his tone neutral. "Walking by the water with you, the breeze off the bay."

"Freezing our asses off."

He laughed and tugged at his shirt as if to straighten it. His hand came up and touched my arm. This wasn't safe. Percy was right. It was way too familiar and obviously way too soon to be...

"Gave you my shirt that day, too. Remember?"

The sight of his face in the sunlight made my heart ache. Badly.

His voice was low and he wore an easy smile. "And I *still* didn't freeze."

"No, you didn't." I bumped against him. "But you got a sunburn."

"Yeah," he said. "I did." I could see the smile on his face but he didn't say anything for a long while.

Realizing my stupidity, I knew why. He'd had a sunburn, a bad one, on his arms and neck. We'd gone back to Jim's house and slathered aloe all over him until he complained that it felt slimy and had gotten in the shower. With me. For the better part of two hours.

I blushed. "Oh, God, that was... I'm sorry." Even if I'd pushed the memory from my mind, my body could still remember. Butterflies crowded in my stomach.

He stopped and looked toward the house. "Me, too. About a lot of things. But not about that." He took a step towards me. "Not about one minute I spent with you." He reached up to my face, and I didn't flinch when he touched my cheek with his thumb. Encouraged by this, his other hand smoothed down the hair that swirled around my face from the breeze. "I've..." his voice broke a little. "I missed you, Kate. So much."

We walked on a bit farther in silence, a world of unspoken things between us.

"What happened to med school?" he asked.

"I had to quit," I admitted, and I could hear the longing in my voice.

"To go to Virginia?"

"Yes."

Matt sighed. "You think you'll go back? Do you want to go back?"

I thought about everything that had happened since I'd left Penn. "I don't know," I admitted with a laugh. "For right now, I'm not sure which direction to take."

He looked at me, a little hope in his eyes. "That's okay. You don't have to know right now. Maybe the right thing is waiting for you to find it."

I wasn't so sure. Our walk slowed and the backs of our hands rested against each other. His hands were warm but he didn't move any closer. I examined his face, smiling at what I saw. His face was different. Not the soft carefree face of the pretty boy law student who'd been down in Wind Cave for the better part of a month with me four months ago.

"You've changed."

"In a lot of ways." His face held expectation and it twisted my heart in two.

I looked up into his face. "Matt, I'm with Percy. You know that, right?"

He sighed and we started walking again, toward the house. "Yeah, I saw. At Ano's wedding."

It was out there. I'd said it. Now he knew.

"That doesn't change anything. I know what you see in Percy. I get it. And I don't blame you for leaving me in Los Altos. But he's not right for you, Kate."

"Matt, I don't want to—"

He stopped me with his hand and took a step towards me. "I don't want to make things hard on you." He looked down for a moment and then back up into my face, his expression intense. "But he'll never know you like I do. He might *appreciate* you." The way he said it held every ounce of the distaste I knew he felt for Percy. "But he won't *love* you." He was right next to me, and he stroked my cheek gently. "Not like I do."

There it was again. He loved me. Said the words in such a causal way that it twisted my heart until it hurt. His touch felt so good.

"Matt, I can't." I took a deep breath. "When I left Los Altos—"

"I was a complete idiot," he interrupted. "I never should have let you go." Knowing there was a deeper meaning behind it, he added, "If you were ever mine again, I'd never let you go."

The words hurt, because I knew he was referencing Percy, who had released me to come back here. "Oh, Matt, you don't understand."

"Wait. Listen to me. The part that you didn't get to hear. The part you missed on the stairs..." he took a step towards me.

"Kate?" Edgar's voice called out from the back porch and Matt cursed under his breath in frustration.

"Is it me, or does his voice need to change already. How old is he, seventeen?"

I started laughing. "Not even sixteen. Now, hush." I raised my voice and held up a hand to him as the house came into sight. "I'm here, Edgar."

Edgar came towards me and looked irritated. His face looked exactly like Percy's with the brows scrunched together and I felt like laughing. "I thought you were supposed to stay with Carrie?"

"Carrie was doing fine and Matt and I came out a couple of seconds ago to get some air."

Edgar fell into step right between us. "I sent Percy the telegram."

"Congratulations. Would you like a medal?"

Edgar glared at Matt. "My brother said you'd be like this."

"Oh yeah?" he said absently. "What else did big bro have to say?"

"Matt, stop."

Edgar opened his mouth to respond and I slipped my hand into the crook of his arm. "Edgar, Carrie needs some help in the kitchen. Take me in?"

He hesitated, unsure if he should spar with Matt or do as I'd asked him. Thankfully, he wasn't as firm in his hatred for Matt as his older sibling. He looked down at me with a slight frown. "What are you wearing?"

I looked down at Matt's shirt. "It was cold, so—"

"I think you should take it off."

Matt turned and swore under his breath.

"Edgar," I said with a slight warning, "be nice."

"I don't think my brother would like to hear that you're wearing another man's clothes." "It's hardly something you need to report back on," I said, slipping off Matt's shirt and handing it to him.

Edgar nodded in approval. "Thank you, Kate."

"Ugh!" I tugged on his arm. "Tattletale. Let's go." He opened the back screen door for me and I walked in ahead of him.

Before he could follow me, Matt grabbed a hold of the back of his shirt, holding him in place for a second. "Don't think that being fifteen will save you from the ass whooping you deserve if you keep this up."

Edgar turned to Matt with the exact same expression that Percy wore on his face when challenged. His eyes narrowed and his voice was as low as Matt's. "I'm trained in fencing and boxing, as is my brother. But I think my brother told me that you might already know that." He smiled and entered Carrie's kitchen, right on my heels.

CHAPTER THIRTEEN

There had been a heated discussion over the sleeping arrangements that night. Edgar insisted that I sleep in the boys' room, which had two twin beds, and Carrie insisted I sleep out in the cottage, for more privacy. In a final concession for peace, Matt agreed to sleep in the boys' room in the twin bed next to Edgar while I took the cottage. I had resisted both options, and really simply wanted to sleep out on the couch in Carrie's living room. It was warm and close to everyone, and since I hadn't been sleeping much anyway, I would be able to read as late as I wanted. Also, I didn't want to have to send a telegram to Percy saying Matt had killed his brother in his sleep.

The cottage was filled with Matt's things. His clothes, his books, everything out there reminded me of him. The scent on the pillows was unmistakably Matt. It was, I'll admit, a little overwhelming. For the first hour, I paced and looked around at how the cottage had changed. For the next few hours, I flipped through pages in my anatomy book. About two in the morning, still with all the lights on, I turned the faucet on in the bathroom and tried to relax and clear my mind. I was here. Safe, in the cottage. I wouldn't sleep, I would just doze. *Think light sleep.* I lay down on the bed. *Relax.* My eyes began to flutter closed. I was here. I was...

Alone. And running. And it was dark. I could feel the ground underneath my feet in the brush next to the train. They were gaining on me. Single shots were fired all around me and I could see people being shot dead in my peripheral vision. They fell to the ground as I ran past them. Others were screaming. I ran faster but my chest hurt. The sound of screaming and gunshots filled my ears. Louder. And louder. My chest hurt. They were going to catch me this time. This time, I wasn't going to make it. I wasn't going to get away. The sound of shots and that scream...loud. Screaming....so loud...

"Missy! Kate!" Charlie turned to Matt. "Go get Carrie! NOW!"

Carrie had heard me and was on her way out to the cottage. Charlie shook me. "Kate!"

I hit him, pushed against him, and a scream tore from my chest as I fought against him, to get free from his arms. And then I saw his face. Carrie ran in and pulled me into her arms. I pushed back against even her, wondering if she was real. *Which one was a dream?* I looked around, my eyes wild, and slowly, gradually began to relax against Carrie.

"Shhhh," she said, and I took a deep breath. "Shush now."

"No," I said, my heart beating wildly. "They're going to...I have to run. I'm..." I looked around. *Was this a dream, too? Or was the other one a dream?*

"You're here. You're safe. No one's going to get you."

"No, I have to run. They'll catch me," I said, my voice muffled against Carrie's shoulder.

Edgar bounded into the cottage, hair askew and clad only in his shorts and a t-shirt. Seeing me in the middle of the bed, he ran a hand through his hair and looked at me. "Dreams again?"

I nodded, my heart pounding out of my chest.

"*Again?*" Matt asked, having watched the whole scene. He was now aware of why I looked like I hadn't slept in weeks. "This happens a lot?"

Edgar came to sit on the edge of the bed. He didn't touch me, but sat next to me, as he always did when I'd had one of my nightmares. "Yes. They're getting better though." He looked up to me. "Right? Getting better?"

My shirt was soaked in sweat. "Of course. They're getting better."

Carrie's face was worried and she turned to Edgar. I'm not sure she trusted me to give an honest answer. "This is *better*? What was it like before?"

Edgar's face creased with worry. He didn't know Carrie; wasn't sure if he should relate family business to her. "She couldn't sleep at all for a while. So they gave her medicine. For a while."

"*Sedatives?*" Matt's voice exploded from the corner of the room, and Charlie reached out a hand to quiet him.

"Only for a few days."

"What do you do now?" Carrie asked calmly. "When she has one of these episodes?"

"Percy lets her work them out. He says that they'll go away in time."

Matt's voice was hard. "He lets her *work them out*. What does that mean, exactly?"

Edgar narrowed his eyes at Matt. "What were you doing in Kate's room?"

Charlie held a hand up, his chest still heaving. "Now, look. Matt and me been up since the crack of dawn and were walkin' in to get breakfast when we heard Missy start screamin'. Kate, you talk to a doctor 'bout this?"

I nodded, but it was Edgar who answered. "Percy has medicine for her, but..." he looked at me, wondering if it was safe to give the people around us personal information.

"I don't like to take it."

Carrie smoothed the hair from my eyes. Even my hair was wet, soaked with sweat. "What's the medicine do?"

I took a shuddering breath. "It's supposed to suppress deep sleep, so you don't get the severity of nightmares. Makes me feel like I'm sluggish all day, and sick to my stomach. I don't like it."

Carrie looked over to Edgar. "You get these too?"

He looked around him, as if not wanting to admit to any weakness at all. "Not any more. I got them bad for about a week. And not any for a while."

Matt came to kneel beside me, and put a hand on my leg. Edgar opened his mouth to protest. Before he could, Matt snapped, "Relax for a minute. Don't hurt yourself." He turned his face up to mine. "Are the dreams all the same?"

Percy and I didn't talk about my nightmares. I think it was fairly obvious what they were about and really didn't see the need in rehashing them.

"I'm gonna splash some water on my face," I said to the people around me. "Sorry I scared everyone. I'm going to try and take naps from now on."

"There's nothing to be sorry for, honey. You need sleep," Carrie said, her face creased with worry.

"I'll be fine," I assured her, though I don't think I was fooling anyone.

Edgar got off the bed. "All better now, Kate?" he asked.

"All better, Edgar."

"She is sure as hell not '*all better*'," Matt snapped, and Charlie rested a hand on his shoulder.

Edgar waited at the door for a minute, the other three faces around me not convinced in the slightest that it was even a little bit better. He cleared his throat, hoping they would follow. I smiled at Charlie, in an effort to confirm that it was all right to leave. Charlie leaned down, tugged at Matt's sleeve, and the three men stood at the door.

"We'll be out here if you need us, Missy."

Matt's expression was worried, and he hesitated leaving.

"See?" Edgar said to him. "She works it out."

Looking like he was going to go for blood, Matt opened his mouth to respond and Charlie directed him by the head, pushing him out the door ahead of him. "C'mon, let's go hit somethin' with a hammer."

After they'd left, I pulled away from Carrie. "I'm fine. I just need a shower. It fades. Always does."

She nodded, her face saying she didn't remotely believe me. Her voice was soft, motherly. "What does Percy do when you have these dreams?"

"Like Edgar says, he's been very patient. He lets me get it out of my system and we go back to sleep."

Her face said she wasn't pleased with my response. "Maybe we should talk to Doc Lindblade while you're here. Just in case."

I managed a smile. "If it'll make you feel better."

"It will."

"All right." The sun was coming up, but my room was chilly. "I'm going to take a hot shower and then come in to help with breakfast."

Warily, she got off the bed. "All right. I'll wait for you in the kitchen."

Just before she got to the door, I stopped her. "Carrie?"

"Yes, honey?"

I blushed, embarrassed I'd caused so much trouble. "I'm sorry."

Her face softened and she came back over to kiss me on the head once more. "Don't you worry. You're home now and it'll all work out. You'll see."

She left the room and the screen door closed softly behind her. I pulled back the covers and slipped my legs from the bed, needing to get as far away from the dream as possible. Clad in my faded blue pajamas, the bandages on my legs reminded me I needed to change them. Peeling them off one by one, I stood and walked to the shower and turned on the hot water. The initial sting I ordinarily felt when water touched the wounds wasn't as bad today, and I comforted myself with the fact that they were finally healing.

Finished in the shower, I wrapped a towel around my body and walked to my backpack to retrieve my medical kit. I'd brought only jeans, so my scars wouldn't be visible to anyone. Maybe in time even I could forget about them. The screen door opened and my hands went around myself modestly, regardless of the fact I was wearing a towel.

"Hi," Matt said, and closed the door to the cottage. His eyes flashed down to my legs and I saw his expression. I turned quickly so my back was to him.

"You need to go." He didn't move from behind me. "Matt!" I yelled, embarrassed he had seen the long, scabbed over wounds healing on the fronts of my legs. "Go!"

He didn't say anything and I didn't know if it was because I was standing naked underneath my towel, or because he'd been so disgusted by the long scars across my legs. Either way, I repeated myself.

"Kate," he said, and I could hear the change in his voice.

"I don't want your pity," I spat, my back still to him. "Get out. They're healing and I need to bandage them. So just..." my venom died when his hand touched my shoulder, damp from the shower. "Please get out." My tone was harsh and I stopped myself from saying anything more. "Matt," I begged, "please go."

"Turn around."

I shook my head. Even Percy didn't get to see my legs without bandages. I changed them when I was alone, when no one could see. I could feel him behind me and I squared my shoulders. "This is something I do alone."His arms went around my waist, chin on my shoulder. "I will." His arms tightened. He didn't make a move to go under the towel, didn't try to turn me around. I could feel his warmth, and I could feel his breath on my neck.

"You do a lot of things alone," he teased. "Why don't you let me take a little bit of this one?"

"I have no idea what you're talking about."

His feathered his lips against my neck. "Let someone comfort you. Tell you it's okay."

My voice sounded dead. "It's not okay." Part of me wanted to add that it might never be 'okay' again. Anyone who looked at the multiple scars that ran down the length of my legs knew that I was anything but okay. They were still red and angry looking, and there were days when the hard scabs tugged and hurt. Days when they split open if I didn't put enough antibiotic ointment on them. Days when I wondered if they would ever go away, kind of like the nightmares. Always there to remind me that things would never, ever, be the same.

"Then we'll make it okay. But you have to let someone in and tell them about it. To make them go away."

I fought back the edges of the dream. "No." My voice came out in a whisper.

"I'm so sorry," he said, and I realized what he meant at once.

"They're healing."

"Your *legs* are. Are you?"

I allowed myself to relax a little against him. "Some days are better than others," I said truthfully. The feeling of his arms around me made me know it was a safe time to ask. "Are you? Healing, I mean."

He chuckled, and tucked his chin tighter against my shoulder. "If you'd have asked me that a week ago, I'd have said no."

"And now?"

His hands gripped my waist through the wet towel. "*Right* now?" I could feel his smile against my bare shoulder. "With you in my arms I could rule the world. No problem."

I laughed gently at his response. "The things you say, I swear."

He joined in my laughter, and didn't say anything for a long minute, just stood holding me. His hands were wrapped around me, warm and strong. It felt safe, and he didn't make a move that would disrupt the easy comfort of the embrace. Finally, he sighed and his arms wrapped clear around my body.

"Promise me that you'll tell me about the nightmares."

"I can't."

His voice was tender, soft in my ear. And all Matt. "You used to tell me everything. You still can." Matt kissed my neck gently, squeezed me once more and left the cottage, the screen door closing behind him.

Chapter Fourteen

"Well, that was a fun trip." Jazz muttered under his breath as they disembarked the train and set their luggage down in front of them.

"Oh please let Charlie be here," Ano said and Jazz couldn't help nodding in silent agreement. However, when they looked around the station, Charlie was nowhere in sight. Ano covered her abdomen with her hand.

"You want some more Motrin?" Jazz asked.

She smiled weakly. "No, it'll be fine. Sorry, Jazz."

"Baby, you can't help it. It's fine."

Charlie's face appeared from the mouth of the terminal and Ano waved him over. He pulled his hat off and smiled widely as he greeted them. "Well, if it isn't the mister and missus. Congratulations, you two."

"Thank you," they said, almost together, and Ano stood carefully and picked up her duffle bag.

Charlie led them back to the truck, helped them load their luggage into the bed, and pulled Jazz aside as Ano climbed in the cab.

"Everything okay?"

Jazz's face looked haggard, like a man who'd spent the last twenty-six hours at the gates of hell. "Monthly bill came early."

Charlie half smiled. "Welcome to marriage. Get in."

Once settled, they began the long ride back to the farm and Jazz was anxious to hear how the first day between Matt and Katie had gone.

"You and Carrie doin' okay with World War Three at your place?"

Charlie chuckled. "Lot more than you know, Ace."

He paused and looked at Charlie. "Why? Something happen?"

Charlie chuckled. "We got a, uh, interesting situation back home."

"She's pretty pissed, huh?" Ano remarked. "Poor Kate. I'm gonna kill that man."

Charlie chuckled even louder. "You gotta get in line. Kate brought a friend."

"Wha...Percy's here?"

"No, not Percy. His younger brother Edwin. Edward."

"Edgar."

"Yeah, that's the one."

Ano made a face at Jazz. "Why'd she do that?"

"I don't think she had a choice in the matter."

Jazz started laughing. "Man, Percy kills me. He kills me!"

"I don't get it," Ano said. "What am I missing?"

"Percy sent Edgar along with Kate so he could stay back at home, care for their grandmother, and continue his work," Charlie explained. "I think he sent Edgar to make sure Matt...behaves."

Ano smiled to herself. "I'm sure Matt loves that."

"Like I said," Charlie told them, "it's an interesting situation."

"Kate knows, though, right? That Matt tricked her?"

"She knows. The whelp doesn't. So a few more days and Carrie's 'doctor's' gonna 'switch her medicine', and she'll take a turn for the better."

"You all are playing into this?" Ano said, her voice rising. "That's unhealthy!"

Charlie shrugged.

"Just tell Edgar that there was a mistake, and—"

"Percy's got him sending daily telegrams."

"Daily?"

"Yep," Charlie said. "Daily."

Jazz and Ano both pursed their lips and were silent for a moment, thinking the situation through. "Percy's gonna kill Matt."

Under his breath Charlie said, "My money's on Matt."

"You told Kate, didn't she—"

"I think Kate's got a lot going on in her head right now," Charlie said and Ano froze.

"What does that mean?"

He shrugged.

"Charlie," she asked quietly, "what does that *mean*?"

The crow's feet around Charlie's eyes deepened and stood out on his leathery brown skin. "I think that train ride...I think somethin's wrong."

"You mean, like she's still freaked out or something?" Jazz asked.

"No, I mean like she's still not over it. I don't know. Some folks go through bad times and they can't move past it."

"Why, what did she say to you?"

Charlie sighed. There was no way he could describe what had happened to Kate this morning. He'd been thinking about it the entire ride to the station and still couldn't figure it out. "Wasn't what she said," he told her. "It's that she's...not right. Somethin' is just wrong."

Ano patted his arm. "Well, I'm here now, so everything with Kate's gonna be all right. Jazz, trade places with me. I need some air."

Scooting underneath him, she traded places while Charlie smiled at the antics of women. Newly wed. He remembered. Some days it seemed like last week; some days it seemed every day of the thirty years it had been. He chuckled and looked at the couple next to him.

Jazz, worn out from trying to comfort his wife, and his wife worn out from simple female biology. Yep, he remembered those days. They'd have more to come. Some better, some worse. Days when they'd want to kill each other, days when they hold each other up. He wouldn't trade one day of it, not for anything.

Chapter Fifteen

It was dusk by the time I heard the tires on the gravel drive. Ano was here and I got to spend the rest of the week with my best friend. Life was good. She got out of the truck with a big grin and I ran to her.

"I'm so glad to see you," she said, embracing me tightly. "I was so worried that you—"

"I know," I said into her shoulder. "I'm fine."

"I'm so glad!" she said and hugged me harder.

"I'm happy you're here," I said, releasing her and looking into her face. She looked worn out. "What's wrong?"

She hugged me again and whispered in my ear, "'Member when we went to the art museum and I was so stressed, and what happened in the..."

"Card shop?" I said, grimacing, and she nodded.

"Yeah."

"Oh, man..."

Jazz slid from the cab of the truck and I waved at him. He pulled me into a hug and whispered in my ear, "Tell me you got some Midol or, you know, ultra-strength female knockout shit in your bag."

"Gotcha covered."

"You're my new hero."

"C'mon," I said to Ano. "Let's get you guys set up in the cottage."

"The cottage?"

"You're married now. You need to have a little privacy."

"No need for that this week, if you know what I mean."

I giggled. "Yeah, yeah. C'mon."

Carrie was up today, having told Edgar her medicine was really kicking in. She'd thankfully had become 'overtired' halfway into the afternoon and we'd retreated into her bedroom and she taught me to knit.

She was up again, and pulled Ano into a hard hug. "Well, look at you, Missus Taylor!"

Ano smiled brightly at her and hugged her back. "Hi, Carrie! Thanks for letting us stay!"

"Well, honey, are you okay?"

I snickered. "I need to get her some stuff from my bag."

"I see," Carrie commented. "All right, well, feel better."

Edgar, my constant shadow, had come to stand next to me and I rubbed his shoulder as I introduced him.

"Ano, this is Edgar."

Ano turned to find him literally flanking me. "My gosh," she said, pointing at him but looking at me. "He looks just like—"

Now irritated at having heard it so many times, Edgar cut in, "Percy. My brother. Yes, I know."

"Personality runs in the family," Matt said from behind her and pulled her up into a huge bear hug.

"Matt!" she said. "Oh, yuck!" she said, pulling back from him. "You're all sweaty! Ugh, gross!"

"Been working outside all day." He laughed and grabbed me into a bear hug as well. "Am I sweaty?" he growled and picked me up with one arm.

"Yuck!" I said, pushing away from him as well and Matt nuzzled my neck quickly before Edgar stepped towards him, reaching a hand out, indicating that Matt should put me down.

Ano muffled a laugh and grinned at Edgar. "You *are* Percy's brother."

"Yes," Edgar said. "I am."

I pushed Edgar backwards by his stomach and took Ano by the arm. "Let's get you set up in the cottage."

Matt had moved most of his things into the spare room this afternoon while Charlie went to pick up Ano and Jazz. I tried to help, but since Edgar wouldn't leave my side, it became more of a hassle than it was worth. After his things were moved out, I had Edgar help me change the sheets. Ano and Jazz would have fresh ones tonight to sleep on and I would be able to stay up and read on the couch.

"Here," I said, pulling an assortment of drugs from my bag. "Pick."

"Oh, you're a lifesaver." She pulled two blue tablets from my hand and washed them down with a glass of water. "Don't tell me, you too this week?"

"Any day now, so I brought everything."

Ano pointed to herself. "A week and a half early."

I shrugged. "Stress."

"Yeah. Or my body knows I was comin' to see you."

Well-known female phenomenon. When women room together, live together or are close together for long periods of time, their cycles link. It's like satellite hookup with different receivers. No one understands this, but all women know about it. Ano and I had been on the same cycle for four years. Until now.

"Well," I laughed, "you can blame me, then."

She sat down on the queen-sized bed and looked at me. "You look tired. You doin' okay?"

"Yeah, you know. I have a bodyguard, but..."

She laughed. "What happened there?"

"Percy's getting protective in his old age."

"Sending his little brother to whup up on Mr. Skylar. Has the man no shame?"

We both laughed and I flopped down on the bed next to her. "How's married life?"

She grinned. "Good."

"Oh, yeah? How are Mom and Grandma holdin' up? They asking for grandchildren yet?"

"Oh my God, so help me, if my mom warns me one more time to 'be careful'..."

"So, no plans for a little Taylor?"

"Are you kidding? I'm finishing my Masters and Jazz is goin' to Seminary. After...well, after the war is over."

"Seminary? So, he decided?"

"Yup. He got accepted for spring."

"The fighting will be over by then," I reassured her. "It can't go on for another three months." Silently, I prayed for that to be true.

She offered me a small smile and scooted back on the bed next to me. "We're lucky we got to come at all."

"I feel guilty that you risked coming, but I'm so glad you're here."

"Me too. Thought for a while there Uncle Robert wasn't going to let us come."

"What changed his mind?"

Ano played with a string on the quilt. "I think it was mostly Jazz telling him I would find a way to leave anyway and having him come was just assurance we would come back."

"Is there anything happening? In New Orleans, I mean?"

Ano clasped her hands in front of her. "No. Thank God, nothing yet. But they keep saying 'any day now' and it was driving me crazy. Like sitting waiting for the sky to fall."

"I know. Life in Virginia was so restrictive. I couldn't go anywhere. We didn't leave the house barely at all, except for a walk in the back garden once or twice a day."

"Is that because they have curfews or something?"

"No."

"Then why couldn't you leave the house?"

"Well, because there was this...this..."

Ano's eyes narrowed. "Girl, you are *not* trying to lie to me right now."

"No, it's just that the first week or so I was in bed because..."

"Because why?"

I ignored the question. "And then after that, Percy was gone all the time and I was with Gigi and Edgar."

For a moment, Ano didn't say a word, though her smile had diminished. "Percy was gone? Where did he go?"

"To the lab to work with his uncle."

"Without you."

"Well, yeah. I wouldn't have been a lot of help, anyway."

"Really, why not?"

I had no answer and Ano knew it. I fiddled with a strand of thread from the quilt on the bed.

Ano scooted closer towards me, her knees touching mine. "How is it, living with him?"

I was not ready to talk about that yet, not having finished processing my feelings all the way through. "Fine."

Ano rolled her eyes at me. "Fine? Not a day gone by in three years when you haven't seen or talked to or about that man at least once and now you're living with him and it's *fine*? Baby girl, please."

I thought back to the first night in Gigi's house with Percy. "At first, it was wonderful." I closed my eyes and remembered waking up with him. "It's just the war and everything that's happened. He's under a lot of stress."

The headache that never seemed to leave me was now beginning to pound.

"*He's* under a lot of stress," she repeated.

"He said that he is busy making a life for us. The life we talked about in the cave."

"Do you want that? Kate, we're not in the cave anymore. If what you want has changed, then tell him."

"We can talk about that later," I said. "Let's change the subject."

"Okay," she lay down and we rolled on our sides, face to face. "You gonna tell me what happened with the train?"

"Oh my God. What about it?" I knew Charlie had likely told her I was going crazy and that I needed professional help. I also knew I couldn't talk about it yet. Not even with Ano.

"Kate."

"Ano, I can't. I'm sorry."

"Why not?"

I thought of any reason she'd accept. Finally I said, "I'm not ready."

"But you're okay? You didn't get hurt?"

"Got some cuts on my legs but they're healing. And I'm having a few nightmares, but nothing that won't go away in time."

She sighed and I could tell she wanted to push a little further. "Nightmares. About the train crash?"

"Ano, I'm not ready to—"

"All right," she said, holding her hands up in surrender. "I'll leave it alone for now."

"Thank you."

"Not forever though. You and me gonna have a sit down really soon. And then nothing's off limits, y'understand? Not the dreams, not the train, and not Percy."

"Okay. I promise."

Darkness was settling over the cottage and I heard the crickets from outside. I was relieved when Ano started talking about Lively, and how much she irritated Jazz. We talked about Grandma Vesper and Uncle Robert, and how angry he'd been at Jazz for letting Ano convince him to come. She told me about her honeymoon, and how they had been able to pretend life was normal for the two days they'd been in Florida. I loved hearing it all. Darkness in the room settled over us and the sound of Ano's throaty laugh made me relax. It was like we were at Stanford, side by side in our dorm room, safe, talking about everything and nothing. Right here, next to my best friend, my eyes began to close. I was safe. I was right next to Ano.

Chapter Sixteen

"Mmm, Carrie that smells so good!" Ano said. "Can I help with anything?"

Carrie gestured towards the stack of carrots on the vegetable sink. "You can peel those if you want."

Jazz was talking to Edgar on the couch, telling him and Charlie about reports they'd heard on the radio in New Orleans. Matt wandered in and looked around. Walking to Ano, he asked her, "Where's Kate?"

"Fell asleep 'bout twenty minutes ago." Ano didn't see the worried exchange between Matt and Carrie. "I swear that girl's worn out. Looks like she hasn't slept in weeks."

Matt pointed to Carrie as he headed out the back door. "Keep the whelp inside." Even before he got to the cottage he could hear Kate talking, mumbling in her sleep. Her words were frantic, very few of them making sense. He opened the screen door and looked at her lying on the bed, covered with a quilt that Ano had draped over her.

Kate's legs moved back and forth, and her head thrashed side to side. Then her body was still for a moment. Matt sat on the edge next to her, wondering if he woke her suddenly if it would be better or worse.

A soft, strangled cry came out of her mouth. "Percy, they're all dead." She mumbled something else, and her legs moved like she was running. "They're—oh my God! They're coming!"

Matt had never heard Kate frightened. Not like this. It destroyed him to know there was little he could do except pull her from whatever cavern she'd fallen into and retrieve her as best he could.

"Kate," he said, and shook her arm firmly. "Kate," he said louder, knowing a gentle nudge wasn't going to be enough. Shaking her was doing no good. It was going to take something else. Something drastic. Careful to avoid her flailing arms, Matt lay down next to her and tugged her against him, quilt and all. He wrapped his arms around her and said loudly in her ear, "Wake up. Do you hear me? Come back! You're safe!"

She struggled against him, and he knew she was going to scream. When the scream started, it scared him as badly as it had the first time he'd heard it. This time, however, he knew it was worse. Kate was watching people die. She pummeled his chest and struggled against him, but he held her firmly and pressed her head into his shoulder.

"It's okay! It's okay! Stop now, Kate. You're—"

"Help me!" she screamed, struggling against his grasp. She screamed again into his shoulder and hit his chest with her fists. She was waking up, he could tell, and her struggling was becoming weaker. Matt never released the iron grip he had around her. Footsteps coming from the house sounded and the screen door to the cottage opened behind them.

"Matt!"

Kate was waking up now, in his arms, crying hard, and he threw a leg over the top of her body and hugged her against him. "Shhhhh," he said in her ear, and waved the person at the door away. "It's okay, Katie. It's okay."

Edgar's voice came from behind him. "Let her go."

Ano was there, pushing past them to get close to Kate. "*What the hell was that*? Is she all right?"

"Nightmares," Carrie said, pulling her wrap around her shoulders.

Ano moved to come towards them but Matt held out a hand for her to stop. Jazz rested a hand on Ano's shoulder. "Let him take care of her."

Edgar clenched his jaw tight and tried to move past Jazz, who stood in his path to the bed. "He has to let her go."

Matt smoothed the hair back from Kate's face and kissed her forehead softly in the dark as she shook in his arms. Through clenched teeth he said, "Get him out of here, or so help me God."

Charlie took control. "Edgar, in the house. Let him calm her down."

"Let her *go*," Edgar said again.

Saving Matt from getting up and killing Percy's only remaining brother, Jazz grabbed Edgar's arm. "Let it go tonight, little brother. He's not gonna hurt her. C'mon."

Carrie and Charlie ushered everyone from the room, Edgar complaining the entire way. When Kate's body started to relax against him, Matt released his grip enough to lean her head back and sweep the hair away from her face. She took in a few shuddering breaths.

He kissed her forehead and cheeks, wet with tears. "It's okay. It's gonna be okay." Her body, so achingly familiar, was warm against his hands as he slid them inside the quilt and traced circles on her back; he felt the rigidity start to leave her.

"I'm so sorry," she said. "I was lying with Ano, and we were talking. ...I was so tired. I didn't think I would fall asleep. I just needed to close my eyes for a minute."

"Relax," he said, his voice rumbling in his chest. He snuggled her tighter against him. "Shh. You're safe now." Matt was surprised when she buried her face against his chest. "Is this why you look like you haven't slept in weeks?" he asked.

"I try not to. Mostly, I catnap, not for long. I didn't mean to fall asleep."Matt rubbed her back gently. "I've got you now. Shhh."

Matt's resolve to do the right thing was crumbling. Kate, her body safe and warm, was against him where she'd belonged all along. He'd promised Charlie that he wouldn't do anything dishonorable while she was here. Promised Carrie he wouldn't make it harder for Kate. Promised himself he would step aside if Kate told him that Percy was her choice.

And yet lying here with her, there wasn't an honorable thought going through his mind. He worked to keep his hands at her waist, to place brotherly kisses on her forehead instead of opening his mouth against hers. He was suddenly glad for the quilt between them so she couldn't feel what the closeness was costing him.

Kate took another shuddering breath and relaxed against his chest, surrendering to the strength of his arms. With her head against his chest, her body against his, the muscles in his jaw tightened as he fought his body's reaction to having her in his arms after all this time.

"I think I'm okay now." She sniffed a few more times before pushing against him and pulling her arms from the quilt.

"Okay," he said, though didn't move his leg from over the top of hers, or pull his arms from around her. "Can we stay like this for a minute?"

He could barely see the outline of her face in the darkness, but traced her cheek with his finger. She worked her arms free of the blanket and Matt rubbed his thumb against her cheeks, still damp from her tears. Her face was perfect in its every detail. How many times had he lain in bed at night thinking about having her next to him in bed again? In his arms, against him...underneath him. His entire body was rigid.

"We should go in. Thank you. For..."

His sarcasm was unmistakable. "For not letting you 'work through it' alone?"

She exhaled. "I hate this."

"I know."

She had to know what came next. He couldn't imagine she didn't know. She was too close to him; the smell of her skin and the feeling of her body underneath him were too much. His hand slid behind her head and his mouth covered hers before his heart could skip another beat. Even as he did, she was pushing away. Knowing she would break the embrace soon, he flicked his tongue against hers quickly, the taste of her enough to make him groan. She pulled back, and he released her quickly. For one horrible second, he didn't know what she was going to do. He heard her voice, low and quiet to him in the darkness.

"No. I can't."

"You're right, I'm sorry." Matt said. "I shouldn't have."

Kate sighed, and he slipped his leg from over the top of her. They both sat up and she removed the quilt from around her. He was damned near in physical pain wanting to kiss her again, but he held it in check.

Charlie's voice from the other side of the screen door startled both of them. "You're gonna have company in about three seconds, so whatever you're doing, I'd stop." He looked at Kate. "You okay, Missy?"

"I'm okay, Charlie."

"All right then."

His footsteps retreated and another set was heard approaching. The screen door opened and Edgar flicked the lights on and looked at them both, sitting on the edge of the bed.

"Are you all right, Kate?" He was talking to her, but his eyes were locked on Matt.

She blinked with the sudden flare of light in the room. "I'm fine, Edgar. Go in. I'll be in in a minute."

His red brown curls were in disarray, a sure sign he'd been running a hand through his hair. "I made a promise to Percy not to let anything happen to you."

Kate stood, smoothing her shirt down and wiping her eyes with the sleeve of her shirt. "I'm fine. Nothing 'happened' to me. It was just another nightmare. I'm okay."

Not retreating one inch while she was close to Matt, Edgar asked, "You sure?"

"Really, it was only a nightmare, Edgar." She walked towards him. "Matt was trying to help. He wasn't hurting me." She patted him on the shoulder as she passed him.

Matt stood and walked towards the screen door, but Edgar blocked his path. He spoke to Matt through half gritted teeth. "From now on, you keep your hands off her."

"We're not going to be friends," Matt said, leaning back against the bathroom door frame, "are we, Ed?"

Edgar shook his head slowly. "No, we're not."

"Good." Matt's face brightened. "Then it doesn't hurt me to tell you something." He took a step toward him, and was surprised when he saw Edgar retreat, just an inch. "Your brother sent a boy to do the job of a *man*." Matt's face was hard as he looked down at Edgar standing on the top step of the cottage. "Protecting Kate is a *man's* job. Put *that* in your telegram."

Edgar's jaw was hard, and Matt could see he was angry. "Kate is going to be my sister someday," he said, and knew he'd hit his mark.

"Is that a fact," Matt said, eyeing him carefully.

Edgar nodded. "Yes. That's a fact."

Matt's smile returned and he pushed Edgar gently aside to leave the cottage. "Not if I can help it, Ed," he said softly. "Not if I can help it."

CHAPTER SEVENTEEN

General Zhen was troubled. Even with the U.S. Naval forces engaged and taking on heavy casualties, they refused to retreat, even in locations where they were completely outnumbered. Their entry into Virginia had been seamless; perfectly executed. Their journey north had cost them more casualties than planned; for such small territories, the population was remarkably concentrated. The sheer power of their Air Force had been underestimated. The number of soldiers in their armies had been grossly miscalculated. However, what had been the most detrimental wasn't the losses they were sustaining in the air, or even at sea. It was that the citizens of the cities they encountered. They were fighting back, in some cases, overwhelmingly so.

In Maryland and Pennsylvania, they had not counted on their own extreme casualties and in many cases had to re-group before pressing on. Their supporting countries were not bolstered by this, and replacement troops had not been as plentiful as had been promised. Countries were wavering in their support as they saw the United States defend – and even retaliate – against the aggressions by their coalition of armies. It was a difficult political reality. No one wanted to be seen by the U.S. as a conspirator if their efforts failed, but everyone would want to be seen as a friend to the coalition if they were victorious in the end.

If they could succeed in locating the U.S. president, then their victory would be assured. But each time their intelligence was close to executing him, he escaped, sometimes with minutes to spare. Once the U.S. president was killed, there was no one next in line to take his place. With no one to direct the resistance, the U.S. Army would crumble within weeks. Great trouble had been taken to locate their generals and admirals. In the event that the president *was found and executed, their generals and admirals would be next, to prohibit any possibility of coordination between military factions.*

Zhen moved a marker across the map into Ohio. Perhaps it was time to drive a knife through the heartland of the country; prove their strength. He leaned back in his chair and contemplated this show of force without involving the other three coalition leaders. They had not been as successful in battle as Zhen, and they lacked the firepower – and, he thought frankly, the stomach. The Midwest would surely be an easier defeat than the outlying states had been.

Within hours, more troops would be arriving, and within days the next wave of bombs would be dropped at his command. He had only to send the coordinates and give the order. Zhen pushed a marker from Ohio south to Kentucky, weighing his options. The first wave of bombs was slated for Pennsylvania. But what if their attack drove through the center as opposed to finishing off the remaining states where the battle had begun? Would that be spreading themselves too thin, or cutting off the enemy's means of obtaining reinforcements? The U.S. National Guard was coming from somewhere. Surely, it was their nation's heartland that was the source.

With a slide of his hand, Zhen made his decision and smiled. Their armies would create a wall around the defeated U.S. territories and strangle them. The new targets would frighten the resistance out of the bordering states – hopefully assuring that no further civilian hostilities would be tolerated without dire consequences. The U.S. would sink to its knees and they would emerge – the new empire amidst its ruin. And once again, Zhen would bring honor to his country.

Carlie awoke to the smell of smoke and the sound of artillery in the distance. The cots around her were all empty, and she could hear that the rain had stopped outside. She sat up and stretched. Her back ached and her head hurt. She checked her watch. Oh, no. That couldn't be right. 9:05AM. She stood and the heavy artillery jacket that had been draped over her fell to the floor. She turned it over and read the patch on the pocket: Maj. J. Phillips

She looked around. Tacked to the center pole of the tent was a note. Carlie pulled it down. In heavy black scrawl it read:

Doctor,

Stay inside, possible enemy fire expected today. Breakfast MRE on my cot. Eat. Rest. Take care of junior.

John

She folded the note. She had to pee, and her stomach was, once again, growling. The latrine was clear on the other side of the compound, and John had told her to stay in. Looking around, Carlie made up her mind. Donning the heavy jacket that John had draped over her last night, she zipped it up to her neck and buckled the helmet underneath her chin. Even with no rain the trail to the latrine was a mess, and her tennis shoes were black with mud by the time she got there. Thankful she'd remembered the jacket, she hung it up on the opening to the stall for a modicum of privacy while she did her morning business.

The trek back to her tent seemed much shorter, now that the pressure was off her bladder. The sound of bombs was still in the distance; thankfully not as close as last night. She ducked into the tent and unsnapped her helmet.

"Where the hell have you been?" a cross voice asked, and she pulled her helmet off to see Major Phillips in front of her.

"I had to use the latrine."

"My orders were to stay inside." He unbuttoned the jacket she wore and slipped it from around her shoulders. "You do not leave the interior of this tent again unless you are accompanied by myself or other secure personnel."

Carlie stood, hand on hip. "Major, can you tell me if all of the civilian guests of the U.S. Army are treated this way?"

He tossed the jacket on the end of his cot and turned back to her, a smile tugging at the corner of his lips. "Only the pregnant ones."

"I see."

He pointed to her cot. "Sit."

Her hand went up and she saluted him. "Yes, sir."

He chuckled. "You're, uh, saluting with the wrong hand."

"Some soldier I'm turning out to be."

"I'll have to court-martial you later." He tore open the Army green packets and handed them both to her. "Here, I got you one of each. Let's hope they work out better than dinner last night."

She waved off his concern. "It doesn't matter what I eat. By evening it comes up anyway."

"Good to know." Clearing his throat, he removed a packet from his shirt pocket and handed them to her. "Here, take these."

"What are they?"

"Multi vitamins, I got them from the med unit today. I think you're supposed to be taking something when you're pregnant."

She accepted them from his hand. "How do you know all this?"

He sat on the end of his cot, facing her. "Six nephews. My sister's kids." He raised his hand. "Uncle John."

"Holy crap! Six? All boys?"

He laughed, and she liked the sound of it. "Yeah, my brother in law, he was really hoping for a girl."

"Yeah, obviously." She tried not to stuff the food in her mouth, but she was so hungry.

"I hate to ask, but are you married? Do you know who the father—"

"Oh!" Her face colored. "Yeah. I do. My...boyfriend. And, well, kind of my attending."

"Ah. Donald."

"*David*. Doctor David Windsor. No, we're not married. Kind of just... happened."

"He was in your unit then."

There was something odd in the way he said it. "Yes. "I'll be rejoining my unit shortly, correct?"

He didn't immediately respond and she stopped eating. "Major?" she prompted, studying his face. He didn't look away, like most men would have. He was a doctor. A military doctor and used to giving bad news.

His eyes held steady on her. "The transport carrying your medical crew went to another location yesterday."

"Yes, I know that." She hesitated before asking, "What happened to them?"

"Their compound came under enemy fire this morning."

Carlie concentrated on breathing in through her nose and out through her mouth. "And?" She felt dizzy, and a little sick.

"I think we should take it easy today, stay inside and—"

Carlie rested a hand on his forearm. "John?"

He breathed deeply. His face remained calm. "I'm so sorry."

She looked at her lap and said nothing. *David. Maria. Ynez. Tom.* Everyone she had been with for the past few months. She gripped the edge of the cot. "Do you have a list of wounded yet?"

"There were no wounded."

Carlie's heart stopped cold. "I see." Her head felt odd, and she could hear a buzzing in her ears. "Maybe David wasn't with them."

"We haven't received reports from any from the other transports of civilian personnel that—"

"Maybe he wasn't with them!" she repeated. "He wasn't!" She screamed it at him, the strength of her own voice surprising her. "He couldn't have been!"

Carlie tried to stand, but her legs wouldn't support her. She began to rock back and forth, arms across her middle. From the distance, the sound of artillery fire got closer and she heard the sound of soldiers running.

John didn't know what to do. He cursed under his breath and walked to the flap of his tent to look out. "Stay here," he said, grabbing his helmet from the cot next to her. "Carlie, show me you heard me."

She looked up to him and nodded briefly. And just like that, he was gone.

Behind the waistband of her scrubs was the belt that held David's Glock. Pulling it out, she slid the safety to 'off' and set it on the cot within reaching distance. She could hear shooting, like the first day they'd done the transport. It didn't sound like the gunshots you hear on TV. It sounded more like...weird popping noises. And the machine guns. David had been right; it was nothing like she'd ever imagined. Not in her worst nightmares.

The extra clip was in her bag, back at the trauma center. She turned the gun over and popped the clip out as David had taught her to many times. It was full. The sound of artillery fire got louder and she heard jeeps loading up with men inside the compound. It was coming closer. She lay on her side, gun above her, mulling over the options in her head. Waiting for someone to come into the compound and kill her, possibly take a few of them out before she, too, was shot to death. That was clearly option one.

She listened to the orders being shouted to the men outside. Option two, get up. Go out into the compound and fight. She was going to die anyway. At least she could succeed in the one thing she'd said she wanted all along; she was going to die for the freedom she had enjoyed every day. It had sounded a lot better in theory than in practice.

Option three was the worst, and of course least enjoyable option. She had option three tucked safely in its little plastic capsule between her skin and her bra, should that horrible moment arise.

The jeeps ground through their gears and orders were called out really close to her tent. The sound of a heavy transport rumbled and then another, and she sat up on the cot. Reaching for the Glock, she tucked it back into the holster under her scrubs and walked to the door. Peeling back the flap, she saw the camp being struck from one end to the other. Tents were being dismantled fast; men scrambled like worker bees to strike what had been assembled a few short hours ago. Without hearing it from any source, Carlie knew there had been another breach. Men were coming here to kill them. Something inside of Carlie snapped into place.

Crossing quickly to her cot, she picked up her helmet and snapped it under her chin. Kicking the one cot to the side, she saw another jacket like the one John had worn, but smaller, and she slipped it on. The sleeves were long, but it fit better and it had a small holder inside for a weapon. She slipped the Glock out from behind her waistband and into the inner pocket of the jacket. She grabbed the last three packets of MRE crackers and stuffed them into the pockets at the front of her jacket. There was an option four; something she hadn't considered. Something she'd learned from David. Option four was to be a soldier. To die defending the country she loved.

John appeared at the flap of the tent. His face had smears of mud on it, and something between surprise and relief showed in his face when he saw her standing, ready to go.

"Let's go. Now. Follow me as fast as you can."

Carlie kept her eyes locked on the back of his helmet as they moved through the maze of soldiers who were all frantically trying to break everything down and pack it into large transports. John pointed to some green heavy boxes a hundred feet away. "Private, lock those comm boxes down on transport one!"

"Yes, sir!"

Moving fast to a smaller, covered transport, John lifted her up into the back. "Stay in here and don't move. This one's next and I'm on it." Within minutes, men filed up into the back, all heavily armed. She was pushed to the very end, the last one inside a truck lined with a dozen soldiers. The tarp was released over the sides, the rear gate was slammed shut, and Major Phillips threw himself into the back with them, still yelling orders. The tarp slid down and again, the inside of the transport was encased in near total darkness.

Carlie could see him moving towards her, and a soldier made room as John sat to face her. The roar of the transport was loud, and it rolled from side to side as they hit potholes and rocks leaving what had been the command post. Even if he could have talked to her, told her where they were going, she wouldn't have heard him. The roar of the engine was too loud, and the sound of artillery made it impossible to think of anything but where she was right at that moment. There wasn't room to think about David now, or mourn him as he deserved. There wasn't time to think about their baby or one second ahead of where she was right now. Her immediate concern was to stay alive. Barring that, everything else would come after.

Within twenty minutes, an explosion rocked something close to their transport and everything came to an immediate halt. John slid open the window between their compartment to the driver's compartment. "Status, Sergeant!"

Before he could answer, machine gun fire was heard from outside and John shouted to the soldiers around her.

"Engage! Engage! Go, go, go!"

Men emptied out faster than they'd gotten in, the covering to the transport quickly pulled back. The soldiers didn't wait to file out the back. They were sliding out any opening there was, and answering the original gunfire with their own. Carlie pulled her only weapon from her holster and jumped out the back, rolling on the ground as David had taught her. John caught Carlie by the back of her jacket and ran for the safety of a building with ten others.

The front transport exploded and all of them hit the deck, safely behind the side of a cement building. Pieces of the transport landed around her, and she looked up from where she lay to see soldiers firing their weapons from in front of their cover. John pointed to two of them, and then to the transport next to them. They ran, slid behind it, and pulled avocado shaped balls from the front of their jackets, halting to turn and throw them in the direction of the original fire.

They exploded and the two soldiers ran back, rolled, and landed square in front of Carlie. All three of them got up off the ground and she moved to the back of the group. She had no idea if this was an ambush or something they had expected. More shots, machine gun fire, then a few more shots and... silence. An American voice called something out, and another American voice answered, not far away. The soldiers in front who had crouched down began to stand, and the soldiers in front began to move towards the Major.

As they moved forward to the edge of the building, Carlie glanced behind them.

David had taught Carlie a lot of things. He'd taught her to shoot with deadly accuracy; he'd taught her some minor hand-to-hand combat; and he'd taught her not to panic in emergent situations. However, he had never prepared her for the moment that she'd actually be called upon to use the skills he'd taught her. The actual moment she would discharge her weapon so suddenly and violently that it would scare even her.

In that one moment, it was just her, facing three enemy soldiers. And the sound of her weapon firing over and over.

CHAPTER EIGHTEEN

I handed Ano my little zipper packet that only yesterday had been full. "We'll go into town today and get more."

"You sure you don't need any?" she asked.

"We switched this month. Yours came early; mine's late."

"Okay," Ano said, "then I need to go into town."

My eyebrow went up wickedly. "We could send the boys into town to get it."

"Yeah, I'd love to see what Jazz would bring me back! No, thank you."

"Ah, one of the many joys of married life. Getting him used to your cycle."

"Uh...no," she said.

"All right," I said, headed for the house, "let's get Carrie. She said this morning she needed more sugar."

Inside the house, the men all sat around the radio, which Charlie had placed in the middle of the coffee table. Jazz and Matt sat listening from the couch, Charlie from his recliner, and Edgar cross-legged on the floor.

"Carrie," I asked, "what are they listening to?"

She was wiping off the counters from making another pie and held a finger to her lips. "Supposed to be an announcement about the war this morning."

I walked to the living room and leaned against the doorframe. Matt patted the couch next to him. When I passed Edgar, I saw the look on his face and patted his shoulder as I passed by him.

"Hey," he said, his voice low. "You sleep okay last night?"

"Yeah. I did. Thanks."

Last night, once Edgar fell asleep and was snoring, Matt had come out to the living room and sat on the end of the couch to keep me company. We talked, joked, and laughed for hours until I could hardly keep my eyes open. And finally, when I couldn't postpone sleep any longer, he'd sat on the floor next to the couch, right beside to me planning to wake me if I started moving or talking. He didn't have to. For the first time in weeks, I slept through the night without a nightmare.

I'd woken to see Matt's head leaned back against the couch, nearly in my lap. His mouth was open and he was sound asleep. For a minute, I watched him. I remembered waking up next to him, and all the mornings we'd wake up tangled against each other at Jim's house. Softly, gently, I'd touched his face. He woke up in shock, his face clouded over and then he turned to look at me. He'd smiled widely, and rested his head against my hip. Before Edgar could wake up and find him gone, he kissed my forehead and returned to the room they shared.

Everyone's eyes were on the radio, listening to the announcer, who was repeating the same information over and over. Everyone's eyes except Edgar's. His eyes remained focused on Matt's hand which, as soon as I'd sat down, had slid over the top of the couch behind me and now loomed dangerously close to wrapping around my shoulder.

In the kitchen, Carrie reached into the cookie jar and retrieved some cash. Watching her fold the cash into the apron pocket, Matt slid a small roll of money into my hand. "Don't let her pay for groceries."

I smiled and quietly assured him I wouldn't.

Ano asked me, "You ready?"

"Yep."

Matt's arm slipped around my shoulder and he pulled me close enough to whisper in my ear, "You guys just going to the store?"

"Yeah," I whispered back. "You need anything?"

The corner of his mouth quirked up. Knowing every word he said was being mentally recorded for posterity by Edgar, he responded, "Just you." His face was inches from mine and I smacked his leg, knowing he was doing it solely to irritate Edgar. Rolling my eyes I stood, only remotely aware that the hand that had been around my shoulder slid down my body as I did so. I thought Edgar was going to come unglued. Ano and Carrie grabbed the keys and I walked out the front door with them, Edgar fast on my heels.

"Kate!"

"What's up, Edgar? You need anything at the store?"

He silently fumed in front of me and took a step away from the front screen door. "Come here, please," he said, his hand in the small of my back guiding me away from the earshot of the other men inside, his voice low and his eyes cast downward. "I don't like it when you let Matt touch you... like that."

"Edgar, I know what Percy sent you here to do. And you're doing a great job. You're keeping me safe. You need to know that Matt doesn't mean any harm."

"Kate," he said, his voice pleading, "he's..." his brows came together and his voice went low. When he did that, he looked exactly like Percy, making me care for him all the more. "He's trying to...I think he wants to..." he shifted his weight from one foot to the other, uncomfortable with the subject matter. "I don't think his intentions are to be *friends*. If you get what I mean."

His face turned red and I nearly fell over. Edgar, for all his fifteen years, clearly didn't understand that I knew far more about what he meant than he did. Ano honked the horn and I held up my index finger once again and turned towards Edgar.

"Matt's trying to irritate you," I said with a slight smile. "He's only messing with you. Matt and I are trying to be friends. That's it, okay?"

He nodded, obviously unconvinced.

"Now," I said, putting on my very best Percy voice, "I'm going to the store. Do you need anything?"

He shook his head, still looking down.

"Sorry you came?"

His head snapped up and he looked down into my face. "No," he said firmly. "I'm not."

I reached up to an errant curl that had found its way across his forehead. "Good." Smoothing back his hair, I looked up into his eyes. They were the same as Percy's. Those wonderful, washed out blue eyes that one day some woman was going to melt into, just as I had with his older brother.

He noticed that I was wearing the locket that Gigi had given me for my birthday, and his expression softened. "You miss him. My brother." He turned to walk me to the car.

"Yes, I do."

"I know he misses you, too."

If only that were true, I thought. If only Percy missed me half as much as I missed him. He retreated as we pulled out of the driveway.

"He's gonna be a handsome man if he ever grows into that body," Carrie remarked as we watched Edgar walk back into the house.

"Or that voice," Ano giggled.

"Yes," I said after the mop of curly red-brown hair disappeared behind the screen door. "Yes, he will."

The announcement came a half hour after the women's departure, and was repeated over and over on the AM station Charlie had found. They all listened to it in its entirety three times before shutting the radio off and sitting for a few moments in silence. In reality, very little new information had been relayed. What they'd been listening for, and really what everyone was tuning in to hear, was word about a president. A leader. The person who, at the moment, was at the helm of the United States, leading us through this war. And after news about the battles, the victories and the losses, the only news was that our militia was strong and 'an end was in sight'.

"Well," Charlie said, his voice somber. "I wish they'd have said more."

"I don't think they can right now," Jazz told him.

"Yeah," Charlie said.

"There's someone directing this war," Matt said. "But they're not gonna say so until its safe."

A knock sounded at the front door and Charlie glanced at the clock. "Girls back already?"

Edgar hopped up and opened the door, then stood dumbfounded at the sight on the porch in front of him. He couldn't move, he couldn't breathe. He was lucky he was still standing. Behind him, he didn't hear Charlie ask him three times who it was, and so Matt jumped up and pushed him aside, darn near knocking him over.

"Oh, hey, Sarah."

Sarah stood at the front door, a basket in her hands. "Hi, Matt. My mom wanted me to drop some knitting books off for Carrie. And..." she held up the basket in her hands, "I brought you some...well, I baked."

Edgar stared at the small woman in front of him, mute. Matt looked at Edgar to his left, popping him lightly on the back of the head. "Out of the way, Ed."

Matt pushed the screen door open allowing her inside and Jazz stood, along with Charlie, to greet her. Edgar stood next to her in awe. Sarah wasn't more than five feet tall, her thick, golden brown hair curled up at the bottom, and she had a delicate, sweet face. To keep the curls from her face, she had tied a thick white ribbon in it. With a bow. Edgar was fairly sure that Sarah was an angel.

"Come on in," Charlie said, and moved towards the kitchen.

"Thanks!" Sarah looked around at the four men that surrounded her. "Um, is Carrie home?"

"No, she and the girls went into town."

"The girls?" Sarah looked around at Edgar and Jazz, and Matt remembered his manners.

Charlie pointed to Jazz. "His wife, and..." Charlie paused, not knowing how to introduce her, "and...uh, Kate."

She turned to Matt. "Oh!" her face colored a little. "Kate is...here."

Matt nodded, but didn't say anything more.

"All the way from Philadelphia?"

"Actually, we traveled from Virginia," Edgar said, and Matt could see the train wreck that was about to happen.

Sarah looked confused. "*We?*"

As Edgar opened his mouth to answer, Matt said loudly, "Sorry, Sarah, this is my best friend. This is Jazz Taylor. Jazz, this is Sarah..." he paused for a moment, hoping he wouldn't butcher her name, "Oppengard." Matt pointed his thumb to the tall redhead next to him. "And this is Ed."

Edgar, finally having found both his voice and his feet, took a single step towards Sarah and extended his hand. "Edgar Warner." Thankfully, his voice didn't crack, and she shook his hand politely. "Pleased to meet you."

"Hi, Edgar. I'm Sarah. Edgar...that's an old fashioned name."

Edgar blushed. "My parents named us—me and my brothers— after famous writers or poets."

"Edgar Allen Poe?"

"Correct."

She laughed and Edgar joined in.

Matt ushered Sarah to the door. "Okay, well, um, Carrie should be back in, I don't know, about a half hour so..."

"Oh!" she said, and awkwardly handed the basket to Matt. "Well, then here."

Just as awkwardly, he accepted it, and they stood in silence until Jazz took a step towards her. "You live around here, Sarah?"

Matt shook his head at Jazz, who gave him an innocent look like he had no idea what was going on. From where he stood, Edgar saw the exchange.

"I live a few miles from here," she said, responding to Jazz. "We recently moved here from Houston."

Since none of the men standing around him seemed to have any manners at all, and having Sarah there was making Matt uncomfortable, Edgar pointed her towards the kitchen where he pulled out a chair. "Would you like to sit and have something to drink? You can wait for Carrie."

Matt shot Edgar a murderous look.

"Oh, um, thank you, Edgar."

Incredibly comfortable and smooth for someone who moments ago was mute, Edgar pushed her chair in and poured Sarah a glass of iced tea and then one for himself. Charlie watched the entire scene from in front of his chair with an amused expression on his face. These boys were going to kill themselves...or each other.

Edgar set out the sugar bowl in front of Sarah. "Where were you when the bomb hit Houston?" His expression made him look much older than his fifteen years, and he stood at the island cutting slices of lemon for her tea.

"Well," she said, her southern drawl a little more pronounced as she relaxed, "my family was all on a cruise when it happened."

"A cruise?" Edgar pulled out the chair next to hers and sat. "To where?" Matt watched Edgar with disgust.

Oblivious, Sarah was happy to have someone to talk to. "The Caribbean. Have you ever been?"

Edgar spooned a small amount of sugar in his tea. "No, I haven't. We used to spend our summers at my grandmother's house in London."

"London!" Her face lit up and Matt wondered if the drainage ditch next to the wheat was wide enough to conceal Percy's youngest brother's body. Sarah smiled and a small dimple appeared in the corner of her mouth. "I've never been to London." She turned to Matt. "Have you been to London, Matt?"

Edgar smiled up at him and Matt thought he had never looked more like his older brother. At that very moment, he also didn't know which brother he hated more.

"Yeah," Matt said, forcing a smile. "Yeah, I have."

"What do you do, Sarah?" It was dawning on Jazz that Sarah was here to do more than give baked goods to Carrie, and he began to take interest. He moved towards them and poured himself a glass of iced tea as well.

"I was a teacher back in Houston."

"What grade level?" Edgar asked.

"Yours," Matt shot back, and Charlie laughed.

Edgar's face colored bright red but Sarah didn't get the joke.

"No I teach, well, I *taught* second grade."

Jazz sat next to her and observed. Seeing Matt's face, he knew what was going on. Every few words she would glance up at him with a look akin to hero worship on her face. Jazz had seen the look on lots of women; Matt naturally brought it out in them. Jazz grinned. He was stuck here with a wife who seemed to have a terminal case of PMS and he was gonna have some fun with Matt.

"How did you meet my man Matt?"

The dimple in her cheek reappeared. "We met at the picnic a few weeks ago."

"Awww," both Jazz and Edgar crooned simultaneously, and Charlie sat back down in his recliner. There would be nothing more fun that watching Matt get hit by this bus.

Reaching behind him, Jazz pulled the basket out of Matt's hands and flipped open the cloth top. "Chocolate chip." Jazz grinned widely. "That's Matt's favorite."

"Really?"

Jazz lifted the basket by its handle and offered one to Matt. "C'mon man. Have a cookie."

Sarah looked up to Matt, her voice soft. "I made them from scratch."

Edgar looked at Jazz. "She made them from scratch."

Matt plucked a cookie from the basket. "Thank you."

Edgar hadn't taken his eyes from Sarah in the twenty minutes she'd been there. "Did you move here permanently? Or are you waiting for the fighting to be over before going back home?"

"Oh, I think my parents initially made the move here for safety," she actually looked up to Matt before finishing, "but it's growing on us."

Edgar bit into a cookie that Jazz had offered him. "You're a wonderful cook, Sarah."

She blushed. "Thank you, Edgar!" She turned to Jazz. "How long have you and Matt been friends?"

Jazz leaned back in his chair. "About three years. Feels like longer though." Matt kicked the leg of Jazz's chair but Jazz's smile remained fixed.

"And, Edgar," Sarah asked, "how do you know Matt?"

Edgar's gaze drifted up to Matt and he narrowed his eyes. Matt was faster on his feet than Percy's younger brother.

"Edgar is Percy's younger brother," he said. "Percy and I went to school together at Stanford, and we were in the Wind Cave together when the blast hit." Matt turned to Edgar. "Isn't that right, Ed?"

His eyes steadily on Matt's face, Edgar replied, "That's right. Percy is my older brother. And Percy is Kate's—"

"Hello!" Carrie called, opening the front door. Her arms were laden with groceries. Matt jumped up and pulled the bag from her arm. "I saw the car in the drive, do we have company?"

Seeing Sarah at the table flanked by both Jazz and Edgar, Carrie's face blanched a little. "Well, Sarah! What a...nice surprise!"

Behind her, Ano and Kate walked in, both carrying a small bags themselves. Seeing the disaster that was upon him, Matt acted fast. "Edgar, go out and get the rest of the groceries from the truck for Carrie."

Edgar stood. "Sure, *Matt*," he said, bumping shoulders – hard – with him on the way out. "No problem."

As soon as the screen door slammed from Edgar's departure, Matt moved backwards, scooped Kate into his arms, and propelled her towards Sarah. "Sarah, this is Kate."

Kate laughed and pushed against Matt's chest, bag still in her hand. "Matt, stop!" she turned towards Sarah, shaking her head. "Hi, I'm Kate Moore."

Sarah's smile had faded a little as she surveyed the woman she believed to be her competition. "Sarah Oppengard. Nice to meet you." She paused a moment before adding, "It must be hard being so far away from your boyfriend."

Not understanding she meant Matt and not Percy, Kate nodded. "It is. Yeah."

He slipped his arms easily around Kate's waist and she looked up at him. "What?"

He stared at her; the look on his face obvious. "Nothing." Surprising them both, he leaned down and kissed her quickly, taking full advantage of Edgar being out of the room.

"Hey!" she protested, and pushed against his hard chest. "What's gotten into you?"

Matt grinned and warmth spread across his face. "Nothing." His grip around her waist didn't relax at all.

"Well, I should be going," Sarah said, embarrassed. "Mrs. Blackhawk, my mother wanted me to drop these books off to you."

"Thank you, Sarah," Carrie said, taking note of the look of hurt and disappointment on Sarah's face.

Edgar entered as Sarah was leaving. She stopped in front of him and extended her hand. "Edgar, it was nice to meet you."

"You're leaving?"

"Yes, I think so," Sara said quickly.

Edgar, flustered from returning empty-handed from the truck, sighed heavily. "You're not going to stay and visit with Carrie?"

She shook her head, her face flushed. "No, I don't think so."

"I know she'll appreciate the knitting books, even though she's feeling much better now."

Sarah's brows drew together. "Feeling better? Was she sick?"

Edgar nodded and behind him, Charlie covered his face with a hand. "Yes. Very sick. For quite a while now, I believe."

"Oh. I didn't know that." She looked at Carrie, who appeared the very picture of perfect health. "Feel better, Mrs. Blackhawk."

Edgar looked like he wanted to scoop her up in his arms, if nothing more than to keep her from Matt.

"Goodbye, Edgar," she said.

Although she was already out the door, Edgar said, "Goodbye, Sarah."

Chapter Nineteen

Edgar turned slowly and walked through the kitchen. He stopped next to Matt. "There weren't any groceries in the truck, but I believe you knew that."

He hit the screen door hard, descending the steps two at a time. I spun around to Matt, my finger in his chest. "What did you do to him?"

"Me? I didn't do anything!"

"He's hurt and he's mad, Matt, and he wasn't like that when I left!"

Matt held his hands up in mock surrender to me. "Sarah showed up unannounced at the front door and he went all Helen Keller on us!"

Charlie snickered and I shot him a withering look.

"Matt didn't do anything, Kate," Jazz said. "I think Sarah's got a crush on our boy Matt here, and I think Ed's got a little crush goin' as well."

I tossed my bag onto the kitchen table. "Well, what a shock. It's good to see that nothing changes." I was mad at him for hurting Edgar and mad at him for the look of pain I'd seen on the face of that girl who'd left so quickly. "Maybe Paul was right," I said so only he could hear. "The Midwest is full of girls who are just dying to get their hands on a Skylar boy."

His eyes flashed instant pain at what I'd said. "Kate, it's not like that."

"The hell it isn't." I set my jaw. "Carrie, I'm gonna go after him. I'll meet you and Ano in the garden in a little while." When I got to the screen door I shot back at Matt, "Despite what you think of Edgar, he's fifteen, and he can still be hurt."

I ran down the steps of the back porch towards the lanky figure disappearing around the corner of the first wheat field. "Edgar?" I called as I ran, knowing he had a head start, and his legs were a lot longer than mine. I got a stitch in my side halfway out, but kept running.

"Edgar!"

I turned the corner, not seeing him along the path. "Edgar. C'mon, I want to talk. Please?"

"She wasn't really sick, was she?"

I looked up to the top of a small stack of hay bales and shook my head. "Damn you're fast. How'd you get up there so quick?"

He extended his hand down to me and I climbed up next to him. We sat in silence, and I hoped he wouldn't ask again. I'd be forced to answer him truthfully; I couldn't lie to Edgar.

"Kate," he prompted, and I rested my head on my knees.

"Oh, Edgar," I said. I raised my head to look out over the fields of wheat. "I'm sorry."

He laughed, but it came out harshly. "That you tricked me? Or that you lied to my brother?"

"No, that when I got here, Charlie told me what had happened and I didn't trust you. I should have told you what happened, but I was afraid that you'd—"

"Tell Percy?"

"Yes."

"So now that I know Carrie wasn't really sick, what happened?"

I told him the whole story, about Matt and Carrie hearing the news of our train, and about Matt feeling like it was his fault if I was dead. We talked about Carrie and how she'd cried for us, and that I was sure when Matt sent the telegram to Virginia, he expected an urgent response, not for me to get on a train. Edgar, like Percy would have, listened to my story quietly, without judgment. When I'd finished, he looked out across the wheat waving in the wind.

"He still lied."

"Well, Edgar, sometimes people say things to get other people to do what they want." I was thinking of Percy, and of how he'd moved us to Virginia to be safe, and we had ended up almost getting killed in the process. "No matter what it ends up costing."

We were quiet for a few minutes, just the two of us. It was a crisp October day; the sky was a perfect blue and the sun was high, and it wasn't a degree over sixty.

"So, ah… Sarah seemed really nice." I had no idea what to say to Edgar about girls, or if he even wanted to talk about girls. Or if Percy had already had this talk with him…about girls. I was in uncharted territory.

"She's lovely."

Oh, boy. I had no clue where I could go with this. Percy would be much better at this than me. "She was very pretty."

Edgar cleared his throat. "There's this boy at Avon, Dylan. He's a lot like Matt."

"Oh, yeah?"

Edgar laughed a little. "Calls me Red." His face colored.

Although I'd gotten better at it, I still kind of sucked at comforting. "Well," I said, "he's..." I searched for something that Ano would say and, coming up with nothing, I laughed. "I don't know what to say about that, Edgar. What does Percy say?"

"He says they called him the same thing."

"Really? I didn't know that."

"Mmmhmm. Will had the brightest hair of any of us though. *Really* red!"

We both laughed. I was actually happy to listen to his memories of his family. It made me feel like I could know them, just a little bit.

"And John? What about him?"

"John's hair was brown and red, like Dad's. Percy's is getting browner like Dad's. It's not as red anymore."

I bumped shoulders with him. "I never minded that he had red hair."

"Really?"

"Nope."

He asked the next question tentatively. "Do you mind the curls?"

"Are you kidding?" I turned towards him and ran a hand through the back of his thick hair. "I love Percy's hair. And yours is just like his."

"So do girls..."

I could feel his embarrassment and it made my heart ache for him to go through this without his mother.

"I mean, when girls see..."

"If a girl won't date you simply because you have curly red hair, she's not worthy to be on your arm."

He glanced away. "Girls like Sarah, they go for boys like Matt. Not, you know..."

His voice trailed off and I marveled at his fifteen year old logic. "Do they have girls at Avon?"

"No!" He laughed as if I'd made a really funny joke. "No way!"

"Okay. Um, then how do you meet girls at school?"

"We have dances, social activities, with the other prep school, Miss Porter's."

I *didn't* know, but I was willing to take his word for it. "And Miss Porter's is all girls?"

"Yes." He took a deep breath and then told me, "Homecoming is this month. Well, *was* this month. I don't even know if I would have attended."

"Were you going to ask someone?"

"I'm...most of the girls at..." he sighed. "No."

"Do you like anyone? A girl at school?"

He said no, and I silently thanked God for small favors.

"One of my roommates, Peter, he asked a girl to homecoming last year."

"Uh huh. And?"

Edgar frowned. "It, ah, didn't go so well."

"So you decided not to ask someone because Peter got shot down?"

"No, Charlotte Ascott would have gone with me."

"Well, why didn't you go with her?"

He leaned back onto his elbows and stretched his long legs out in front of him. "She *has* to. Because of our families, not because she really wanted to."

This was a whole new arena for me. "So your folks were close to the Ascotts?"

"Ugh, it's complicated."

"You didn't like Charlotte enough to ask her?"

"It isn't that." We were silent for a minute, then, "I saw Sarah and... Have you ever gotten the feeling like, you see someone and think that they are the most..." He pressed his lips together. "Never mind."

"When I was a sophomore, I met this guy in one of my classes. I couldn't breathe for the first half hour. I dropped three beakers because he got me as a lab partner, and all I wanted to do was stare at him."

Edgar smiled knowingly. "You're talking about my brother."

I grinned back. "I am."

"And did you feel...?" his hand went to his stomach and I knew exactly what he was going to say.

"Like I was going to explode? Like there were butterflies as big as birds in there?"

Edgar nodded. "Yeah."

He went from pink to bright red in ten seconds, and I was pretty sure Percy hadn't had this talk with him yet. Nor had anyone, from the look of it.

And since no one had ever had this talk with *me*, we were both in for a real learning experience.

"If Sarah...went to Miss Porter's, assuming she was fifteen and not...I don't know however old she is. Would you have asked her to go to Homecoming?"

He thought for a moment. "I don't know."

"Don't know how to dance, huh?" I chuckled a little.

He turned to face me, his face completely serious. "I know how to dance. Quite well, in fact."

"Really? Oh. Wow, okay."

"Do *you* know how to dance?"

"No, I never learned how."

"Didn't they teach you at your school?"

"No. Ballroom dancing wasn't high on the list of priorities in North Dakota."

"Oh. You never danced with your father?"

Now it was my turn to be embarrassed. I had barely shared these details with Percy. How could I tell his little brother? I winced, remembering how Paul and John had reacted to my background and how most people judged me for where I'd come from. "Edgar, my dad was a plumber."

"So? Is there a rule that says a plumber can't dance?"

I laughed hard and Edgar joined in. "Well, he was a non-dancing type of plumber."

"Oh. Well haven't you ever danced with my brother?"

"Once, at Ano's wedding, but we didn't, you know, ballroom dance." I asked, "Percy can ballroom dance?"

"Of course! Percy's a wonderful dancer. My mother was always asking him to dance with her at our Christmas parties."

I fingered the small pendant around my neck. "Really?"

"Yes. He could teach you, I bet, if—"

"He's busy, now, Edgar." My heart was heavy as I realized the truth of that statement.

He hopped down from the hay bales. "Then *I'll* teach you." He motioned for me to come down and I shook my head. "Kate," he said in a voice much older than his fifteen years, "come down here."

"Uh, no. Edgar, I'm the most uncoordinated person, trust me."

He held out his hand. "I once had to dance with my second cousin Georgette who is both tone deaf and a foot shorter than you." He grinned widely when he sensed that I was wavering. "I'm certain you can't be worse than her."

I was searching for any excuse not to do it. "There's no music."

"The first few times we don't use music. Mr. Chapparelle claps."

"He what?"

"Claps! Like a beat. One, two three." He extended his hand out to me again. "Come on."

"I'm *so* going to regret this." I hopped down off the hay bales and stood in front of him. Ridiculously, I realized my hands were shaking.

"You look nervous."

"I am."

"Why?"

This was one of those social things. The kind of things normally only known if you've been bred and conditioned to learn it. The kind of things you learn when your parents send you to prep schools and you socialize with other prep schools and—

"Kate."

"Yeah?"

Edgar smiled at me and, unknowingly, said the one thing that would relax me. "You're overthinking it."

A smile spread across my face as I thought of Percy. "You're right."

Edgar's face became more serious and he stepped in front of me. "Put your feet...no, like..." he pulled me by the hand until we stood in front of each other, our feet staggered. "Now," he said, and pointed down to his feet. "Watch what I do, and do the opposite."

"The opposite? All right." I looked down.

"Waltz, with a one, two three," he said.

"Wait. Shouldn't we start with a simpler step? Like the box step or something?"

"Um, the *box step?* No."

I conceded. "Okay, the waltz."

His smile returned. "The waltz." We looked down. "Right foot first, step back. Good. That's one. Now, move the left foot...no, the *left* foot. Your *other* left, Kate. Good. Now back and over. See how I did it?"

I moved my left foot backwards and Edgar kicked it to my left with his own. "Ow!"

"And back to the beginning. Got it now?"

"Not even remotely."

He moved until we were side by side. "All right, I'll do the girl part. *Copy me this time.*" His feet moved so gracefully. "Back, back, over. And, forward, forward, over. Again! Back, back over." He repeated the step with me for about five minutes until I was doing it on my own.

"I've got it!" I said, and I started to laugh.

"Now, we'll put the boy steps and girl steps together. Ready?"

I was exhilarated that I was actually learning something from Edgar. "No!"

He moved in front of me. "And, back, back over. Forward, forward...come on, other foot. There. Over. Again."

Within fifteen minutes, Edgar had me dancing the step with him while he clapped the beat. I tripped over my own two feet half the time, but only actually fell once. And without reproach, he helped me up and corrected what I'd done wrong. By the time we walked back to the house from the hay bales, I could actually do the steps to a waltz.

"Thanks, Edgar."

"It was fun." He slowed his steps. "I like being with you, Kate."

"I like being with you, too." I didn't realize how much I meant it until now.

"My brother is lucky to have you."

"I'm lucky to have him."

"It would be nice..." he started, and then sighed when we came into earshot of the garden where Ano and Carrie had clearly gotten sick of waiting and started without me, "to have a *sister* around, and not just a brother."

The reality of what he was saying hit me and nearly broke my heart with its sincerity. Edgar pulled me into a hug and kissed my cheek. "I'm going to have Charlie drive me into town," he said, walking backwards. "And tell Percy that Carrie is feeling much recovered."

I smiled at him. He was such a good kid. "Thank you, Edgar."

He waved and ran through to the house, calling Charlie's name.

***

That evening, on his way home from the lab, Percy stopped at the postal station to retrieve Edgar's telegram. As always, he leaned against the wall inside the station and read it right away. Each day, Edgar had some detail about Matt's behavior that irritated him more than the next. What he read tonight wasn't irritating. What he read was so honest that it took him several minutes to compose himself before returning to his uncle's car.

On the telegram, Edgar had written:

```
To: Percy Warner, 21 Colonial Fredericksburg
VA

From: Edgar Warner, 55 Shoreline Hwy Fall
River, SD

Carrie is much recovered
Taught Kate to ballroom dance in a field
today
She told me about meeting you at Stanford
Mom would have loved her so much

Edgar
```

CHAPTER TWENTY

Voices. Voices all around her. And hands. Lifting her. Everything hurt. Everything. Her entire body was buzzing, as if it had fallen asleep and suddenly been awakened again. Stabbing pain in her shoulder, no, her leg. Her side was hot. Stop. David, make the pain go away.

"Move her now!" Seven men lifted Carlie into the back of the third transport and piled in with him. "Sergeant, get MEDEVAC on the comm now!"

"Yes, sir!"

"Get the private! Go, go, go!"

"Move out! Move out!" John knelt over Carlie's body and the engine of the transport roared to life. "I need lights!"

Six flashlights came on within seconds and pointed at Carlie, lying on the floor between them. Ripping open her heavy jacket, he saw the long sleeved shirt she'd been wearing last night, blood spreading from the wound in her shoulder and one on her side. "Jesus Christ."

"Major?"

"Yeah?" Ill-equipped to deal with a wound without so much as his medical kit, he pulled his knife from his belt and slit her shirt open all the way.

"Her leg, sir."

John looked down at her right leg, which was stretched out between his own. Bright red blood had soaked the thigh of her scrubs. "Son of a bitch! Sergeant I need an ETA on the MEDEVAC location!"

"Five minutes, Major!"

"Fuck five minutes! I've got two injured soldiers and I need that bird on the ground yesterday! Get me there, now!"

"Yes, sir!"

The bullet had actually blown through her side – clean entry and exit wounds, both seeping blood. John reached up and grabbed the hand of the private sitting on the bench next to him. "Hold this, here! Constant pressure!"

Cutting away the shirt from the gunshot wound to her shoulder, he could see the bullet had missed the clavicle by a half inch. From the zipper pocket on his jacket, he pulled a battlefield pack and poured it over the wound in her shoulder to stop the bleeding until she could reach the CSH.

He cut off a long piece of her shirt and lifted her thigh to slide it under and fashion a tourniquet. The transport slowed and he reached forward for a pulse.

"C'mon, Carlie."

Smears of blood colored her pale skin and he winced. What the hell had he been thinking? Reaching up, he tried again for a pulse. It was weak, and getting weaker.

"Where the hell's my chopper?"

He heard the sound of the MEDEVAC outside and tied the piece of shirt around her leg above the wound. The rear flap to the transport opened and they slammed to a stop. John pointed to the other wounded man behind him, who'd been struck in the calf upon returning fire. "Tyler! Get the private to the MEDEVAC! The rest of you, lift her on my mark!"

He slid from the back of the transport, Carlie's blood soaking his pant leg as he did so. "Three, two, one, now!" All hands lifted Carlie's body and carried her to the MEDEVAC, which was landing as they ran towards it. John secured her body onto one of the interior stretchers and pulled the other wounded man aboard.

"Sir! We've got her, sir!" a MEDEVAC doctor said, strapping Carlie down.

"She's a civilian!" John yelled above the sound of the whirling blades.

"Sir?"

"Civilian!" he yelled above the sound of the blades. "And she's pregnant!"

John mimed with his hands and the MEDEVAC doctor gave a thumbs up to show he understood. Watching the chopper take off, John had never wanted to be on a MEDEVAC so badly in his life.

***

"BP dropping, eighty over fifty-five."

"Radio ahead to the CSH, multiple GSW to shoulder, right oblique and upper right femur."

"CSH reports ground crew at the ready, ETA six minutes."

"BP still dropping, seventy over forty-five."

"Putting in a central line."

The MEDEVAC doctor called over to the other wounded soldier. "What's her name?"

"I don't know, sir!"

"She was with your unit, soldier, you don't know her name?"

"No, sir," the private responded.

"Report MEDEVAC has a Jane Doe, civilian female of unknown age. Possible civilian is pregnant, unknown gestational age, over."

"Copy that MEDEVAC 2. Ground crew advised on status Jane Doe."

"Central line in. ETA to CSH two minutes."

"Have HUS standing by, over."

"BP coming up. Eighty over sixty, holding."

"Get some 02 on her."

Moving. She was moving. No more, everything's heavy. David, why is everything so dark? Sharp pain. Lights. A million bright lights and new faces. Moving. Everyone was talking. Still talking and moving. Stop. Make the pain go away.

The MEDEVAC landed at the Combat Support Hospital that had been set up as a safe location, less than twenty miles from where Carlie's trauma ward had been originally. Army surgeons from the Hospital Unit Surgical rushed forward and pulled her body from the MEDEVAC, as well as the private who had been shot in the leg during the exchange.

"Civilian Jane Doe, unknown age. Field personnel reports possible pregnancy. Caught in unfriendly firefight. Multiple GSW to left shoulder, right oblique, and right femur."

"Surgery One is prepped and ready and we have a GYN standing by for possible OB consult."

Carlie was wheeled into Surgery One with a team of two surgeons and four nurses, working to prep her for surgery, drawing blood and triaging her wounds.

"HCG level 82,000 mIU."

"Tell Ron we have a civilian Jane Doe who is— someone get me the gestational calculation on that HCG!"

"It's early. Four to six weeks."

"Christ. All right, call over to the HUB and get a consult on what anesthesia for—"

"BP dropping. Seventy over forty-five."

"Battle pack's not gonna hold much longer."

"We can't go GA for the risk to the fetus."

"Epidural?"

"Do it. Get Ron in here with an epidural stat!" He looked down into Carlie's face. "Jesus Christ. She doesn't look any older than my kid. Twenty-four at best."

"What the hell was she doing in a hot zone in the middle of a firefight?"

"I don't know. All right, Ron's here. Carol, get me the x-rays on that shoulder, thank you."

"Shattered the scapula as it exited."

"Femur fracture, rear exit wound."

"She'll have some good scars to show her kid if we do this right. All right, people, let's go."

***

"I'm looking for a civilian and a soldier who were brought in by MEDEVAC at around eleven hundred hours from Unit Beta Four," John said.

"What's the name of the soldier?"

"The soldier's name is Private Lanskin. The other is a female civilian. "

"Yes sir, I'll check MEDEVAC log."

"Around eleven hundred or eleven thirty."

"Yes sir, I have a Jane Doe and a Private Derek Lanskin that came in on MEDEVAC 2 at eleven seventeen."

"That's it! Where can I find them, please?"

"Private Lanskin is in recovery sixteen and Jane Doe is still in Surgery One."

"She's not a Jane Doe."

"You'll need to go to administration to change her information, Major."

"All right. Thank you."

Can't feel anything. Everything is numb. Didn't think it would take this long to die. Why am I not dead yet? David, the lights still hurt my eyes. They look like the lights in trauma one. Am I back in trauma one? Was it all a dream? Nothing hurts anymore, so maybe it was a dream. Faces. I see faces, but I don't know them. Maria? Ynez? I knew you guys weren't dead. Bad dream, it was all a bad dream.

"She's coming around."

"Relax, Jane. Nice deep breaths. That's it. It's fine. You're doing fine."

"I'm getting ready to close. Have Stella send over the ultrasound machine from the HUB, would you?"

"Yes, Doctor."

"Let's make sure everything is in the pink after she's all stitched up neat and clean here."

"That's it. Open your eyes. Welcome back. I'm going to turn up your oxygen a little here, get you breathing a little better."

"BP Jane Doe one thirty over eighty. Fetal heart rate one thirty."

"Very good."

"Okay, just relax. You're all right."

"Jane Doe heart rate one ten."

"Calm down, Jane. Stop shaking your head. Relax." His voice was strong. Full of authority. "Jane, I need you to relax. Your baby can't relax if you don't relax. So just take it easy."

"Fetal heart rate one-forty."

"Calm down, Jane." That voice again, full of authority. "You're in the hospital and safe. You have to relax."

"BP Jane Doe one hundred twenty over eighty."

"There we go. Easy breaths. We're done now. We'll be moving you to recovery in a few minutes. That's it, Jane. Nice, easy breaths. Jane, if you can hear me, I want you to blink, okay? Good job." He paused. "Jane, you're at Bellingham CSU, Combat Support Hospital. Blink if you understood me. Good."

Another face. "Jane? You had surgery to repair the gunshot wounds to your side, shoulder, and leg. You're going to be fine, okay? Relax. You're in good hands. Your baby is doing fine. Blink if you understand me. Nicely done." The doctor addressed the others in the room. "Nice work people. Penny, dress the wounds and wheel Jane to recovery."

"Yes, Doctor."

He leaned over to look down into Carlie's face. "You were very lucky." His eyes were kind, and he reminded her of her father. "You'll have a very exciting story to tell your girl, or boy, one day. I'll come check on you once you're settled." He turned to the nurse. "Okay, Penny."

The eyes above her, the anesthesiologist's, were gentle. "I turned down the epidural, so that heavy feeling will go away in a couple of hours. All right?"

Carlie nodded and tried to look around her but the heaviness that was in her limbs drifted to her eyelids and she let sleep claim her.

Darkness again. Heavy. Maybe this is death. Maybe it's coming. Maybe then I can see David again.

"Carlie?"

She blinked several times, but it felt like her eyes wouldn't open.

"Carlie."

She recognized that voice. She kept her eyes closed. "Major. Phillips." Her own voice came out in a whisper and she heard a soft laugh.

"Thought you were rid of me, did you?"

She licked her lips. They were dry and cracked.

"Here." He spooned a few ice chips into her mouth. "Only a couple. You can have more if you keep this down."

She accepted the ice chips from the spoon. They were cold, and they melted on her tongue. "Mmm."

"Taste good, huh?"

She tried to nod but her neck hurt.

"Oh yeah, um, don't try to move a lot. Not quite yet."

Her eyes slowly blinked open. "Neck hurts."

"They've got you bandaged up pretty good because of your shoulder there." He spooned a few more ice chips into her mouth.

"What happened?"

John put the cup down on the nightstand next to her bed. "What do you remember?"

"I got up off the ground and turned around." She tried to look above her, but the lights were too bright and she closed her eyes again. "I saw...I don't even know, it was so fast. I can see their faces. But nothing else."

"Do you remember firing on them?"

Panic filled her and her eyes opened. "Were they...enemy...I didn't shoot our guys, did I?"

He laughed. A genuine laugh. "They were unfriendlies. The enemy."

She coughed and he reached for the cup of ice chips again. "Did I kill them?"

"You killed one, hit the second in the stomach. Knocked him to the dirt. And the third one got you before we got him."

Carlie tried to remember. She could still feel the hard discharge and kickback of the weapon in her hand and was finally able to lift her hand and turn it over. "Everything....hurts."

"You emptied your clip," he said solemnly. "Carlie, you saved my men's lives."

Tears squeezed out between her eyelids.

"Listen, I didn't come here to..." he rested his head in his hands. "I'm... God, I'm sorry."

Tears squeezed out between her eyelids. "I can't believe...I never wanted to..."

"I know," he said. "I know."

Her voice came out in a whisper. "I... I killed them."

There was nothing he could say. Nothing he could do to remove that from her memory. The fact that she'd taken two men's lives, despite the fact that they would have killed all of them, was tearing her apart.

"Carlie, listen," he began, "I know that soldiers who—"

"I'm not a soldier," she reminded him. "And I've no intention of being one. *Ever.*"

"Okay," he conceded, "but you have to listen. Carlie, when I met you, you said you'd rather be here than hide. You wanted to be here, fighting for what you believed in. And right or wrong, war is about death." He let that sink in. She stopped crying and nodded. "I know you'll never forget what you did. But there are ten other people who are awfully glad you did it, and who get to see their wives and children because you did. The line between right and wrong is sometimes...blurry, I'll admit. It's not as clean as everyone would have you believe. But right or wrong, you *did* save my men's lives. And mine."

Her eyes met his. "Thank you."

He spooned another scoop of ice chips into her mouth. "What you did was courageous. You acted in the face of lethal danger. Today, you protected people."

He could tell she was thinking about what he'd said.

A nurse came to her bedside. "Jane Doe?"

"No. Mannis, Carlie."

She looked at the chart. "Oh. Ultrasound?"

John looked at Carlie, then the nurse. "May I see the chart, please?"

"I'm sorry, Major, only—"

He flipped over his tag with the physician's symbol on it.

"Oh, I'm sorry, Doctor."

Carlie smirked. "Showoff."

After scanning it, he said to Carlie, "It's a post-surgery ultrasound for fetal activity and heartbeat."

He didn't know whether to stay or go.

"It's all right with me, if you want to stay," the nurse said. "A lot of dads don't get to see the first one, so this will be good."

"I'm not the father."

The nurse pursed her lips. "Oh."

He pulled his chair close to Carlie and said, "If you want, I can come back in a few."

She turned her head toward him, very slightly. "No, would you stay?"

He smiled. "Of course."

The nurse pulled the ultrasound machine next to Carlie's bed. John pulled up her hospital gown and discreetly averted his eyes as the nurse placed the blanket at the line below her abdomen. She pulled out a tube of clear jelly, which she squirted onto Carlie's stomach and pulled the wand from its holder.

"All right. Let's see."

Knowing she couldn't move her head much, John turned the monitor, pulling it closer. After thirty seconds of searching with the wand, there, on the screen, was a little pulsing blip. Shapeless, like a big kidney bean. And in the middle, was a flashing dark spot. Strong. Healthy.

Carlie's breath caught in her throat. Tears ran down her cheeks when she saw her baby's heart on the ultrasound monitor. There he was, David's baby. She was a mother.

"Estimated gestational age five weeks. Not too far along at all. Would you like to know the baby's due date?" the nurse asked.

"Yes."

The nurse flipped a chart out and twisted a dial. "June eleventh."

Her breath caught in her throat and she made a sound somewhere between a sob and a laugh.

"What's wrong?" the nurse asked with concern.

Carlie squeezed her eyes shut. "Nothing. Nothing is wrong." She looked back to the screen. "June eleventh. That's my mother's birthday."

CHAPTER TWENTY-ONE

Baking bread with Carrie is more than just bread, and it's more than merely cooking. It's more like a Superbowl event that involves being together in the kitchen, with a lot of conversation, and no men. The last time we'd all baked bread together, it had been me, Carlie, and Ano in the kitchen with Carrie.

The conversation when you bake becomes kind of a decoupage between personal conversation and food related talk. As I've come to understand under Carrie's close supervision, cooking involves a whole lot more than simply ingredients. It's the way it's mixed, the order you add it in. Timing with bread, like with comedy, is everything.

"Ask Kate about that," Ano said. "She'll be able to tell you lots of stories about my grandma."

I stirred the milk and butter slowly in Carrie's large ceramic bowl. "Grandma Vesper is amazing."

"Well, I think the more people you have helping you in a marriage, the more likely it is to survive," Carrie said.

"Who did you have?" I asked, sliding onto a stool at the island.

"I had Charlie's mom here for...gosh, the last five years of her life."

"She lived in the cottage?" Ano asked.

"Charlie built it for Chepi to live in."

"Chepi?"

"Yes," she said. "Means 'fairy'."

"Wow."

"We'd go for long walks. She was always helping when I got lonely, like when Charlie was out in the fields, when the boys left home." She smiled at

Ano and me. "Lots of people helping you through marriage, life, it's a good thing."

I thought about the people that I could look to one day to help me if I ever decided to get married. Carrie and Charlie. Ano. Her mother and Grandma Vesper. I smiled. Gigi.

"Kate?"

"Hmm?"

"You ready?"

I looked at her bringing the flour tin over and sat up straight. "Oh! Yeah."

"So," Carrie said, pouring in the first cup, "tell me about this job Percy has. The whel...Edgar says he works all the time?"

"Yeah. He works at the science lab in Quantico with his uncle. The one we're living with in Virginia."

Ano poured us all glasses of iced tea. *"All the time?* So you don't see him?"

"He says that'll change."

"He spend time with you at night?" Carrie asked as I mixed. "When he gets home?"

"Um, not a lot."

"That's a 'no,'" Ano told her, and I shot her a dirty look.

"Gigi, that's Percy's grandmother, she talked to me before I left about Percy's mom and it kind of freaked me out."

"What do you mean?"

Carrie poured in a second cup of flour and I pushed the bowl to Ano for a turn.

"She told me that his mom was always lonely. I guess his dad was always working and never around and she made it sound like that's kind of what I can expect. That I'd have kids to keep me busy."

Ano raised her eyebrows at me. "Oh, no she *didn't.*"

"Oh yes she did." We both laughed. "Same ten seconds. Marriage. Bam! Kids."

"Is that what *you* want? Or what *Percy* wants?" Carrie waited until Ano had mixed the second cup in before digging into the flour tin a third time with her cup.

"I don't know. He's mentioned it, like, in passing mentioned it. And Edgar said something to me yesterday about wanting me as his sister."

"This isn't about whether you love Percy," Carrie said with conviction. "It's about whether you'll be happy with him long term. About whether he's good for you."

Ano stopped stirring and pointed to Carrie. "See? There you go."

"He was really affectionate with me at Ano's wedding."

"That was a month ago!" Ano screeched.

"So?"

"Boy should be affectionate with you every *day*."

"Some folks are, some folks aren't," Carrie said, coming to my defense. "Doesn't mean anything, unless you crave physical contact. And if you do and he doesn't, there are bound to be problems."

I blushed, thinking about the sex we'd had the day I'd left to come back to see Carrie. It didn't go unnoticed by Ano.

"Oooooh! What? What!"

I smiled, my face hot.

"What! You can't make a smile like that and then nothing!" She poked me in the ribs. "What!"

I tried not to grin like a fool. "He's not always like that."

"So there's some hot and nasty—"

"Girls!" Carried admonished.

Carrie scooped a fourth cup of flour into the bowl. Mixing was getting harder.

"I'm wondering if med school is what I really want. The crazy hours...I'll *really* never see him then."

"What would you do if you decided not to be a doctor?"

"That's the problem. I'm kind of wondering that myself." I slid the bowl towards her. "Switch."

"How many is that, girls?"

Both of us together said, "Five."

"Would you go back to science?"

"I'm not sure."

"And you don't have to be," Carrie said confidently. "No rule that says you have to have it all figured out at twenty-two. I sure didn't!"

"All right," Ano said, "I'm gonna ask. What about Matt?"

"What about him?"

"He still loves you. And I'm not saying anything about Percy, but—"

"But you've never liked him," I said under my breath.

Ano shrugged. "True."

"I liked Percy just fine," Carrie said. "But what Edgar said about him letting you work out your dreams yourself..." She set her shoulders back and looked directly at me. "Man's job is to be there. To be strong for his wife."

Ano nodded. "I agree."

"That's a shock," I snorted.

Carrie dusted her hands off on her apron. "Go through something like this, you need someone strong, right next to you to lean on."

Ano leaned in to say into my ear, "Kind of like Matt did when you got the nightmare."

"This one makes six. Trade." I sighed. "Matt and Percy are completely different people."

"One's compassionate, one's not."

"That's not it. Percy's compassionate. And caring. He's so different when he's with me."

"Different how?" Carrie asked.

"Um," I floundered, not used to revealing such intimate things out loud. "He's everything I always knew he could be with me."

"Except for the fact that he leaves you alone for twelve hours a day and isn't there when you have nightmares."

I looked at both of them. "Are we forgetting here who it was that was going to ditch me in the Bay Area?" I hadn't meant for it to come out like that, and I lowered my eyes. "Sorry."

Carrie measured out another cup. "I think that you should actually sit down and listen to Matt sometime, let him let him tell you about that."

"Yeah, well, I was there. I heard what happened. Don't need an instant replay."

Carrie looked at me directly. "Maybe there's something you didn't hear."

"Would it matter?"

"Well, seems to me like even if you stay friends it should matter. Clear the air about what happened."

"We can be friends without clearing the air. About that, at least." I twirled the dishtowel around my wrist. "I didn't even think about it after I left Los Altos."

Carrie's voice softened and she scooped another cup of flour into the bowl. "Now, that's not true, Kate."

I knew she was referring to the letter I'd written her when I'd first gotten to Penn. "Okay. He hurt me. And so it was *easier* for me not to think about him."

"That's better."

"Is it hard to be with him now?" Ano asked.

"Actually, no. It's way too easy. Like nothing ever happened. But Matt and I are just different people."

"And you and Percy are the same?" Carrie's face clouded.

"Yeah." I looked from one to the other. "We are."

Ano pursed her lips. "Trade."

The last cup of flour went into the bowl and both Ano and I grimaced. Mainly because seven cups of flour is kind of hard to stir in. Secondarily because I was tired of defending Percy to Ano. To everyone.

"When the train crashed," Carrie began, and I stood up and walked to the sink to wash my hands.

"Actually, it didn't crash," I corrected her. "Terrorists blew up the front car. Or put a bomb underneath it, I'm not sure. But I believe the original cause of derailment was an explosion."

Ano cleared her throat and I could tell that her counselor hat was about to go on. "And then what happened?" she asked gently.

I blew out a deep breath. "Do we have to do this now?"

Carrie flipped the bowl over onto the butcher block island. Bread dough and flour remnants went everywhere. "I think you should," she said, handing Ano the bowl and sprinkling flour on the surface in front of her.

I didn't want to. Every time I thought about it, something hurt. And after I thought about it, I invariably had a nightmare. I'd been doing so well with Matt sitting by my side each night.

"I'm sorry," I said, "I just can't."

Ano came to lean against me, watching Carrie knead the dough. Behind us, the sun was going down and we could hear the tractor still out in the field. "You can."

I pushed against the counter. "I'm gonna go see what the guys are up to."

"You cool your jets there, Missy," Carrie said, kneading the dough against the counter. "You said you were staying to help with bread making, and the bread making isn't over yet. So..." she gestured back towards where I had been leaning and I resumed my position.

"Look, when I talk about it, I have really bad nightmares. I'm not ready to have nightmares again. I'm kind of liking not having them for a change."

"Yes," Carrie said, catching my eye. "I came out early this morning and saw you asleep on the couch. Not having them." She didn't say another word and I knew she'd likely seen Matt, his head reclined against me, sound asleep as well.

"Oh," I said and my cheeks went warm once again.

Ano looked from one of us to the other. "What am I missing?"

Carrie shrugged. "Nothing. Ano, did you wash out the bowl?"

Ano grabbed the bowl and I got ready to dry it. Carrie didn't say anything else about this morning and I was glad. Explaining the fact that Matt had basically been with me every night wasn't going to be easy.

"So you doing better on not having nightmares?" Ano asked me, and I met Carrie's eyes.

"Yeah, I..." I swallowed. "I am."

"Good."

"Sometimes it's all right to give folks a second chance," Carrie said wisely. "Shows you know how to forgive."

I knew what she was saying, as did Ano, who stood at my side while I dried the bowl. "It isn't that I don't know how to forgive," I said. "It's that things have happened and changed me. Who I am, where I want to go."

"Matt's changed, too," Ano offered, and Carrie nodded.

I handed Ano the bowl. "Despite what you think," I said, my voice low, "I know what Percy's capable of. And he would never have let what happened in Los Altos..." I couldn't finish. It still stung.

"Well," Carrie said, handing me the bottle of oil, "that's over and done with. You need to move forward. And if you can only be friends with Matt ..." she smiled, and I knew she meant what she said, "then that's what's going to make you happy."

We smeared oil inside the bowl and Carrie balled up the dough and deposited it inside. I handed Carrie the cheesecloth and she covered it lightly and stuck it in the oven to rise. "Now I'm gonna go get some beans in the garden for supper. You girls mind washing up?"

***

After dinner, Charlie turned on the radio to listen to the war announcements while we did the dishes. The fresh cobbler Carrie and I had made was still cooling on the stove and the kitchen window was open, letting the chilly air drift into the warm kitchen. As we wiped off the counters, Matt came up from behind me, his voice quiet. "Take a walk with me?"

Before I could tell him exactly how ballistic Edgar would go if he saw me try to leave, Matt pointed to the living room where both Charlie and Edgar were sound asleep listening to the radio.

"It's chilly," Carrie said over her shoulder. "And Kate gets cold easy. Take a sweater."

"All right, quit pushing. I'm goin'."

Ano and Jazz shared a knowing smile as Matt and I disappeared out the back screen door into the chilly night air.

"Oh, God." It was crisp and it looked like every star was out in the night sky above us.

"I know," he said. "Some nights, I lie out in the field and stare at it."

We fell into step together, but instead of our regular pattern around the wheat field, Matt steered me towards the trees in the distance. "Wait, where are we going?"

"The creek."

The trees loomed in front of us in the darkness and I hesitated. I'd become increasingly afraid of the darkness, and really wasn't anxious to go in the woods.

"I'm not a big fan of the dark right now."

"Oh. Right. Sorry. We'll go the other direction. C'mon."

We walked out and to our left, flanking the larger of the two fields. "Sorry," I said.

Matt grabbed a strand of wheat as we walked past. "No worries," he said.

Walking together in silence for a moment, I waited for him to tell me whatever he'd brought me out here to say.

"I'm sorry. For the other day with Edgar. I didn't mean to upset him."

"He's a kid, Matt. It's easy to forget because he acts and talks so much older than he is sometimes. But really, he's still just a kid. He's turning sixteen in a month and a half."

"He's Percy's brother."

"Does that make him your mortal enemy?"

"No, it makes him dangerous."

"Dangerous? Edgar?" I shook my head. "Uh uh. No way."

The large stack of hay bales was at the end of the field where they'd been stacked at the end of summer and we approached it side by side.

"You'd never know it to look at him, but he is. He's negotiating from a position of power and he knows it."

"Spoken like a true attorney."

"Former almost attorney."

"True."

The mountain of hay bales lay in front of us and Matt climbed up onto the first bale and extended his hand down to me. "C'mon. All the way to the top."

Grabbing the wire wrap around the second bale I hauled myself up onto the first level. I followed him up and was breathing hard by the time we reached the top bale. I flopped down onto the flat surface of the hay and he laughed; he wasn't so much as winded.

"You haven't worked out in a while."

I stayed where I'd fallen, my arms out in a 'T'. "No kidding."

Matt came to sit next to me and I pushed against the hay to sit up and look around. "I want to tell you something," he said, his face serious. "And I want you to just listen. Can you do that for me?"

I nodded, but had a pretty good idea what was coming.

"What you heard Paul say that day about you, I—"

I turned my face away from him. "Let's not."

"Please, Kate," he said so pleadingly that I stopped. "My brothers don't know me. They were asking me questions about a future that I hadn't even talked to you about. And I know now what I should have done. What I should have said."

I crossed my legs and looked at my hands in my lap.

"I've got a plan now," he said. "It's such a good plan, Kate. Charlie's been helping me find land. I've got my eye on this lot, it's about forty acres."

"Wow."

"I've been learning everything that I can. And I know I've got a lot more to learn, but the economy will come back. And without big businesses running the farms, it'll be back the way it used to be. When independent men could ask a price and get it."

"And this is what you're going to do?"

"Build a house and raise a family. I didn't know it then, what I wanted to do, but I know it now." He scooted closer. "You were right about what you said at the wedding, about telling them to go to hell. I should have, and I've regretted it every single day since the day you left. If I told you how many times I've gone over and over that day. I knew you weren't okay. When I went back downstairs to my brothers I knew it and I was...I was a fucking coward."

I'd never heard him talk like this and it caused me to actually stop and think about what he was saying. "I can't let you take all the blame."

"Wha...?"

I held up a hand to him, but still didn't look in his eyes. "While we're, you know, clearing the air? I should have talked to you that day after I'd heard what Paul said. And I didn't."

"Can I ask why not?" His tone told me he was afraid of the answer.

My laugh came out bitter. "Because I was ashamed. And I hated that. I blamed you for making me feel ashamed of who I was, of what I was."

"Man, I thought I couldn't feel worse than I did a few minutes ago."

"Not trying to make you feel worse."

"I know."

"The thing with Paul, with what happened, I think it got me to take a hard look at myself. At where I was going. And, as much as I hate to say this, I think I was just kind of following along after you because it was easier than going out on my own. I don't know, safer, maybe."

"That might be what you're telling yourself, but that's not why you stayed with me."

My head came up and I looked directly at him in the dark. "All right, since you seem to have all the answers. Do tell."

He rested his arm on his knee and looked out over the wheat fields below us for a minute, and then finally he turned back to me. "Because," he said, and looked me in the eyes for the first time that night, "no matter if you can admit this to anyone or not, even yourself, you fell in love with me, and it scared the hell out of you."

I felt like someone had kicked me in the stomach. I couldn't breathe, I couldn't speak. He was still staring at me, but I couldn't look at him. If I looked at him, I was going to react. All of my thoughts were mixed up inside me, what Matt was saying, what Carrie and Ano had said, what Gigi had said. I had to process. I needed time to think.

"The thing is, Kate," he said and his voice was suddenly hoarse, as if he was close to tears, "I never stopped loving you."

I could hear him trying to take measured breaths. It couldn't be. He wasn't. I wasn't going to believe it. As long as I didn't look at him, I could stay neutral. Detached.

His hands reached for my ankles and he spun me to face him. Off balance, I put my hands out to my sides and steadied myself. And then, I looked up. Right at him.

"Matt Skylar, are you crying?"

He smiled at me, wiping one of his cheeks with the sleeve of his sweatshirt. "I sure as hell am."

Despite the awkward circumstances, I laughed. As did he. "I was your first, for a lot of things," he reminded me, and I was grateful for the dark because of my blush. "You were *my* first too."

"Yeah," I said mockingly and pulled the sleeve of my sweatshirt down over my wrist and wiped his other cheek. "Your first what? The first girl you ever got stuck underground with, maybe."

"No." He sat forward, an arm on either side of me. "Don't you know? Kate, you were my first *real love*."

The brashness of hearing it spoken out loud and the raw emotion he delivered it with was simply too much. Whether it was that I needed to reassure myself that there really was nothing still there, or that I was on emotional overload, I didn't withdraw as he leaned forward and placed his hands on either side of my face. Knowing what was coming, I closed my eyes as he leaned forward and his mouth met mine. Something between a groan and a sigh came from his mouth the minute our lips touched.

As if we'd never kissed before, the touch was tentative, almost cautious. His tongue flicked against mine quickly, testing whether I would respond or withdraw. The minute I tasted him again, I knew I had miscalculated my strength and ability to assess the situation dispassionately. I was, in fact, in deep trouble. No longer cautious, his hands slipped behind my neck and back simultaneously, and the weight of his body pushed me back against the bale below us.

"Kate," he whispered against my mouth, and this time his kiss was more insistent; unyielding. Everything about him was so familiar; his taste, the weight of his body, the feel of him against me. I hated how much I didn't dislike it. Hated myself for not telling him to stop. Hated myself for needing to be touched, kissed, and held.

His lips were on my neck; biting, teasing against my skin. A whimper escaped from my mouth when his mouth came back to mine, covering it, devouring me thoroughly and passionately. And as much as I shouldn't have – I was kissing him back. I needed to taste him, to feel him. His hands slid underneath my behind and pressed me against him, molding my body to his so carefully it made me ache.

"Say my name," he murmured against my hair. "Please, Kate?"

My hands slid against his chest, feeling every angle, every muscle, and I bent my head to taste his neck. He tasted so familiar and yet, so different. I flicked my tongue against his and he groaned. We kissed with a familiarity that was so pure that it almost hurt.

"Please, Kate," he implored against my neck. "Just once."

He deepened his kiss, pulling me against him. As if being pulled into a vortex, I opened my mouth, slightly, against his. It was enough. I could feel him against me and arched my back. He put his hand underneath my sweatshirt and held me to him. Everything he was doing felt so good; his hands on my body, the near incoherent words he was whispering in my ear, his lips and tongue on my own. What was worse – he knew it.

This time, Matt wasn't going to give me the chance to think. "Remember Carlie's uncle's house?" he said seductively against my hair. Not waiting for me to answer, his hips pressed harder, rhythmically against my own. "Taking a bubble bath with all the lights off."

He took one of my hands and held it against him; he was fully aroused.

"Up against the wall of the shower," he said, and I could feel the burn from his mouth against my neck, "until you said my name over and over."

Oh God did I remember that. Involuntarily, I nodded and did the very thing I'd been resisting for a half hour. The very thing Matt wanted. I said his name.

Every part of him reacted to the sound of my voice. His mouth, gentle before, now opened hard against mine, capturing me in a heat we hadn't had before. The pressure of his hips, gentle before in their rhythm, now held me firmly against the hay bale. His hand slid between us, unfastening the top buttons of my jeans. Moving beneath my sweatshirt in an instant, Matt's hand pulled down the strap of my lace bra while his mouth opened against my breast. My fingers dug into his back as he continued his assault of kisses on my body. I opened my mouth to protest when his teeth grazed over me, my fingers wound themselves into his hair and I gasped – both from pleasure and shock.

This, I remembered. The feel of him. The taste of him. Feeling as if he was everywhere, needing him inside me. The rhythm of his hips urged me forward and carried its own beat, drowning out everything else around us. His hands moved over me with an urgency he hadn't had before. Matt covered my mouth with his, his tongue no longer content with flicking gently against mine. The heat from our kiss was burning my lips and quickly moving south.

"I've wanted you for so long," he said, pulling my sweatshirt off completely and lowering his mouth to my breasts.

"Oh, God, Matt."

"That's it, Kate, yes. Say my name again."

I suddenly realized with blinding clarity what was about to happen as he unfastened the remaining buttons on the front of my jeans and then reached to the front of his own. I knew what came next. He shrugged his shirt off and his chest pressed against mine, his hand tugged at the top of my jeans to slide them over my hips. I knew the feeling we would have the minute he entered me and a wave of guilt washed over me.

"No, st-stop," I said, still not sure I wanted him to.

His breathing erratic, his body hard against mine, he groaned, "What? What's wrong?"

"I know this is going to sound awful, but we have to stop, Matt. We can't do this."

He exhaled hard, not moving from his position against me. Kissing me again, he allowed his tongue to graze over mine and I groaned. The taste of him was so familiar and warm that I closed my eyes, my objections fading.

"You sure?" he breathed, resting his forehead against mine.

"No," I said, "I'm *not* sure. I know I have to though."

His chest was still rising and falling, and it took a few minutes before he pulled away and rolled to the side. He placed a hand behind my neck and pulled my face closer to his. "It's not just me," he said, "I know it's not only me. You feel it too. Tell me that you feel it, too."

"I do. I hate it, but I feel it."

He laughed. "Well, that's a testimony if I ever heard one."

My soft laughter mixed with his, and I rested my head against his shoulder.

"I understand," he said. "It's okay."

Not quite ready to release me, Matt pulled me closer to him.

"If you keep doing that," I warned him, "I'm not going to be able to stop. When you touch me, I can't think."

"Maybe you shouldn't think anymore." He pulled my lower lip into his mouth.

"Oh God, Matt."

"I know." He kissed me hard. "Tell me you want me. Just say it once so I know this is real."

Internal objections to the contrary, I obeyed and he laid his head back against the hay bale. He pulled me close once again, kissing me deeply. "And why *aren't* we having sex right now?"

I ran a hand through his hair, a soft smile touching my lips. "Because the minute it was over, we'd both regret it."

Matt made a face.

"Okay," I conceded, "*I'd* regret it."

"I don't think you'd regret it." Matt said wickedly. "Trust me, you'd enjoy it. We were always really good in that department."

"All right, counsel," I said, "I'll stipulate to that."

From a distance, we both heard our names being called and sat straight up on the hay bales like two teenagers caught in the act. "Edgar." We said it at the same time and furiously got ourselves together, fastening our jeans and pulling on our sweatshirts. We hustled down from the top of the bales to the path next to the field. Matt pulled hay out of my hair as we walked. Rounding a corner, we heard Edgar call our names again. My heart was still beating awfully fast and I was sure I was still flushed.

"We're here, Edgar!" I called. The reality of what had just happened was setting in and I felt as though I was Judas walking back to the house.

"Where've you been?" Edgar asked when he came around the corner and waited for us to approach.

My heart was beating furiously and I could still feel the burn of Matt's kisses on my body. "Went for a quick walk. Matt showed me the other field and—"

Edgar's voice was irritated; as if I was the teenager and he was the elder. "It's cold out here, Kate. And you shouldn't be walking at this time of night."

"Okay, Edgar."

"Carrie's serving cobbler," he said, relieved that he'd found us walking with Matt's hands nowhere near me. "She wants you to help her."

Edgar fell into step with us and the lights from the house came into sight. "What were you doing out here this late?"

"Just talking." I said, biting my lip against the lie.

"Jazz found some cards. Want to play a game?"

"Sure, that sounds fun."

Matt reached for my hand as we passed the barn. "Hang on a second," he said.

"I think she's had enough of the night air for now," Edgar said, pulling me by my other arm.

"Guys," I admonished, "I can make decisions for myself. Let's just go in and eat some cobbler. Okay?"

Matt nodded silently.

I walked ahead of them into the house. "Thank you."

I could hear their footsteps behind me as I pulled open the screen door on the back porch, but not the exchange that took place after the door slammed shut.

"Send a telegram to your brother today?"

"Yes. I send him one every day. He likes to know how Kate's doing."

"I wonder if you'd send him a little message. From me to him."

Edgar eyed Matt carefully. "Depends. What's the message?"

Matt's smile went all the way to his eyes and his gait was relaxed as they ascended the steps to the house. "Tell him he was right."

"Wait, what?" Edgar said in confusion.

"Yeah. Tell him that 'Matt says you were right.'"

"Right about what?"

Matt blew out a breath and stretched his hands above his head. "Tell him, 'definitely sugar.'"

Edgar shook his head. "I don't understand."

"Yes, I know," Matt said. "But your brother *will.*"

CHAPTER TWENTY-TWO

"And here are your pre-natal vitamins."

"Thank you." Carlie accepted the small paper cup with her good hand and took the vitamins.

"You finished with your breakfast?"

"Yes," she said and an orderly took the tray away. Carlie looked out the window and felt the sadness come over her again.

The nurse pulled the curtain around her bed, snapped on a set of gloves, and began to lower her to a horizontal position. "Going to dress the wound at your side."

Her side wasn't as bad as her shoulder, or her leg for that matter. But the drainage tube in her side never seemed to lie flat, and the iodine soaked gauze stung all the time. She didn't complain about the pain. At least it was real, and it gave her something to focus on other than her thoughts.

"Take a deep breath," the nurse said and pulled the old gauze from inside the wound. The stinging sensation brought tears to Carlie's eyes.

"Good job," the nurse said when she'd pulled a long piece free. "It's healing nicely."

"Have you heard anything?" Carlie asked, trying to keep her mind off the task at hand. "About the fighting?"

The nurse dropped one long strand of used gauze tubing into the waste container with her forceps. "Well, we managed to hold the line for the last three days," she said. "And I found out last night that there's a destroyer in the Sound that blew one of their subs to Kingdom Come."

Carlie tried to focus on the news and not the fresh gauze the nurse was dipping in iodine. "Thank God. That's good news. Maybe now the fighting will all be over." Even as she said it, she knew that, at least for her, it would never be over. She would think about it for the rest of her life.

The nurse wrapped the gauze around the forceps and looked into Carlie's face. "The father?" she began tentatively, and paused, possibly wondering if Carlie could handle questions about her condition.

Carlie smiled sadly and turned her face to the ceiling. "David."

"That's the baby's father's name?"

"Yes. We were working the Seattle Med Center before…when the fighting began." She sharply took in a breath as the iodine hit her open wound.

"So he wasn't a soldier?"

Carlie gritted her teeth against the pain. "Not active duty. He was a soldier, but it was a long time ago."

The nurse didn't say anything for a few moments and Carlie was grateful when she put fresh pads over the wound and taped it to her side once again.

"Shall we do the shoulder now?"

Carlie turned her face to the side and allowed the gown to be pulled past the heavy bandages that covered her shoulder. The pain shot through her as the nurse manipulated her forward and pulled the bandage free.

"Looks good. Clean."

Carlie was silent once again. She had tried over these last few days to push the depression aside, but it was always there, constantly threatening to overwhelm her. And lately, she wished she could give in to it. Alone. She was alone, and bringing someone else into the world who would already have lost a parent. A tear rolled down her cheek and she briskly wiped it away.

The nurse replaced her gown and touched Carlie's shoulder gently. She left through the curtains that surrounded Carlie's bedside and returned moments later to continue dressing the shoulder.

For the first time since she found out she was pregnant, Carlie felt herself unable to control the emotions surging through her. Her days were nothing more than endless hours of going over the last three months with David in her mind. She saw his face in sleep so many times that when she woke, she swore that it was all a bad dream. Until she felt the pain. Then, like oil being poured over her heart, it all came back.

The nurse snapped the gloves from her hands and discarded them in the waste container. "Is there anything I can get you?" She pushed the curtains away from Carlie's bed and stood for a moment, waiting.

Carlie continued staring out the window. "No thank you."

After a few moments, the nurse touched her good leg. "Well, I see that you have a visitor, so I'll leave you to it."

Surprised, Carlie turned her face to the foot of her bed.

"Hey, thought I'd come see who the new girl in town was." He extended his hand for her to shake. "Curtis Washington."

She shook his hand and he came to sit on the stool next to her bed. "Are you the orthopedist?"

He smiled at her, a lovely white smile set off by his perfect ebony skin. He reminded her of Jazz, though he was older, taller, and heavier. But there was a charisma about him. A pleasantness.

"No, I'm not. I did come by to chat with you about your wounds, see how you're doing."

"So you're a shrink." Carlie frowned and caught a sob in her throat. Great. Now the nurse thought she was crazy. Would they would lock her up and take away the baby too?

"Well, I'm not fond of the word 'shrink', but I'm on staff here to give guidance and listen. Betty thought maybe you could use someone to talk to."

"Who?"

"Your nurse."

"Oh. Well, thanks, but I'm not good company right now."

"Perfect! I'm never good company, so we'll get along."

She sighed. He wasn't going to go away. She'd sent for enough psych consults to know when she was being set up. "Look," she said, her voice low, "I'm not having thoughts of hurting myself, I'm not a danger to anyone, and I'm not hoarding my medication to take my own life, or that of my child. So I don't. Need. Company. Right. Now."

Curtis' face remained bland. "Well, Carlie...may I call you Carlie? I'm very glad to hear all that, but I'm not here to evaluate your mental status. You see," he unzipped his jacket to reveal a clerical collar, "I'm more of what you'd call an advisor."

"Shit." She covered her mouth with her good hand. "Um, sorry."

"S'okay," he said, scooting closer to her bedside. "I've heard worse." When she didn't speak, he touched her arm gently. "So, you're pregnant?"

Carlie teared up, but she nodded.

He smiled. A Jazz smile. Perfect, even, comforting. "I love babies. I have seven nieces and twelve nephews." He tipped his head to the side. "Do you want to talk about how you got in here, Carlie?"

She shook her head.

"Okay, how about the baby's father. Did you know him well?"

"Yes," Carlie said tenderly.

"Were you married?"

Tears again welled up in her eyes. "No. I had ...we just found out when the fighting started."

Curtis laid his hand on the rail of her bed. "Did the baby's father pass recently?"

The way he said it was less harsh than asking if he'd died. Carlie nodded. Curtis' eyes closed for a moment. "I'm so sorry for your loss."

As if those words unlocked the floodgates, tears began flowing freely down Carlie's cheeks. Curtis said nothing at first, but the hand resting on her rail moved closer to her own.

He allowed her to cry for a moment and then asked, "What was his name?"

"David," she sobbed.

He repeated his name. "David."

For a few moments, neither of them spoke. Carlie continued to cry, and Curtis pulled tissues from the bedside table, handing them to her. Gratefully, she accepted them and wiped her eyes.

"I can't seem to get a hold of this," she admitted. "I keep waiting for this to stop. Or to be a bad dream. But all it is is pain, every single day, and the sounds of the bombs. I just want it all to stop."

Curtis took the used tissue from her hand and replaced it. "That's understandable, Carlie. You've lost a lot."

"Of all the emotions I should have right now, all I can feel is..." she stopped short and bit back the word.

"Go on," he urged, "all you can feel is...?"

Carlie didn't speak.

"I'm not writing any of this down, Carlie, and it's just you and I talking. So, please...go on."

"Anger," she spat out. "So much anger it's scary."

"Anger at the war? The baby's father?"

"All of it! I'm helpless lying here in this bed! And I'm alone. He left me in the OR and I tried to find him."

"I'm sure you did."

"I did!" She sat up, then winced when pain in her shoulder forced her back against the bed. "I called his name over and over. Where the hell did he go? And more importantly, why didn't he try harder to find me?"

"You have every right to be angry."

"He knew I was pregnant." She looked out to the window again. "And still...he left me."

"Is it possible that he was looking for you, too?" Curtis asked, and gently wiped the last few tears from her cheeks. "Perhaps he was looking for you and you were missing each other."

"If only I would have found him. Maybe waited for the last transport. I don't know."

"And if you had found him, what would have happened?"

"We would still be together. Still be alive. Unless..."

"Unless?"

"Our medical team, the entire transport was," she hitched a breath, "killed."

"I see."

"They said that David was on the transport."

"If you had been with him, then you, too, would have been killed. And your baby."

"I guess so." She didn't want to say it out loud, but part of her wished they *had* died together. It would have been worth it, if only to have him for a few hours more.

"It's an awful price to pay," Curtis said.

"What is?"

"Wishing you could have been with him when he died. Sacrificing three lives for the sake of not being alone now."

She stared at him as if he was clairvoyant. How could he possibly have known what she was thinking?

"I...I didn't say—"

He chuckled. "No, you didn't. However, your eyes say a lot more than you do, Carlie. I can see how much you loved him."

"I did."

"So many people have lost so much since the war began. Loss, unfortunately, is a part of our lives now."

"I lost my mother in the first blast."

It was the first time she had said the words out loud; words she hadn't uttered, even to David.

"I am so sorry," Curtis said kindly. "Were you close?"

"Yes. Yes, very. She was my best friend."

"Where did she live?"

"In the city. Just over the Bay Bridge."

He allowed a moment of silence to pass between them before asking, "Where were you when the bombs hit San Francisco?"

"I was down in a place called the Wind Cave. It's in South Dakota. My friends and I went there for this four day excursion and it turned out to be much longer."

"You were spared because you were down in this cave when the blast hit?"

"Yes."

"Where are your friends now?"

Carlie's expression softened. "All over, really. Matt's still in San Francisco with his family. Kate is in Pennsylvania. She's going to med school there."

"Oh? Was she in med school with you?"

Carlie laughed lightly as she thought of Kate and her endless list of medical questions. "No, we got to know each other in the cave and I kind of convinced her to pursue medicine. She shows an amazing aptitude for it."

"She sounds very bright."

"Ano and Jazz are in New Orleans with her family. You remind me of Jazz, actually."

"Really?" He smiled. "How so?"

"He wants to become a pastor, or...well, something religious. He's got the same way about him as you do. Comforting. He's a good guy."

"What about Ano?"

"Ano's going to be a psychiatrist. She's so driven, and she can really make you talk – even when you don't want to." Carlie played with the edge of her blanket. "And then there's Percy."

"You and Percy are close?"

"No, we used to date. But he and Kate are really meant to be together. They're in Pennsylvania right now."

"Are you in contact with them?"

"I haven't written since before the reports started to come in about the start of the war. Maybe a month. I don't know."

"Do you trust them?"

Carlie responded without hesitation. "With my life."

"Then you should write them."

Her eyes filled with tears once again. "And say, what, exactly? I'm alone, wounded, pregnant, and have no place to go?"

Curtis smoothed the edge of her blanket. "That sounds like a good start. If they are as kind and good as you say they are, they will offer you help and solace."

She considered this advice for a moment, and the tears stopped coming. "Which hand do you write with?"

"My right hand." She held it up. "Lucky it wasn't this arm that got shot."

He reached into his bag for a few pieces of paper and a pen. "I will mail this for you when you're done. Write to one of them, or all of them, if you need to. I can always get you more paper."

Carlie stared at the blank sheets in front of her. "I don't know where to begin."

He placed his hand gently on her arm. "How about starting with, 'I'm alive'. Because right now, you must focus on the many things you do have. Your life, and that of your baby, are the most important right now." He stood, his hand resting gently on her shoulder for a moment longer.

She picked up the pen. "Curtis?"

"Yes?"

"Thank you."

"People are here for you, Carlie. You just have to accept their help, love, and support."

Carlie turned the first sheet of blank paper toward her and began to write. 'Dear Kate...'

Chapter Twenty-Three

"I can't believe you took all these! It's so beautiful in Florida." Lying on my stomach, I was flipping through the photos of Ano and Jazz's honeymoon with him.

"Fishing, swimming, snorkeling. You have to come with us next time."

"Maybe I will."

Ano's voice echoed from the tiny cottage bathroom behind me. "So did you get in trouble with Edgar last night?"

"No, it was fine. We were walking by the time he found us. Wait, that came out wrong."

Ano giggled and peeked out from the bathroom door, flat iron in her hair. "No, that sounds 'bout accurate."

"Shut up!" I flipped the page. "Hey, what's this one? The one with the little cabana."

Her throaty laughter echoed in the bathroom. "Oh, that was a little stop we made on a walk on the beach."

"That's just sad."

"I know." She giggled. "So? You gonna tell me what happened or not?"

"Ugh." I rolled onto my back. "We finally talked about what happened in Los Altos. There. Happy?"

"Yeah. And?"

"And now I know where he is and he knows—"

She moved to stand in the doorway, hand on hip. "You gonna make me go all commando on your ass?"

I laughed. "No."

"Good."

"I think he's still in love with me."

"No kidding. The only one who didn't know that was you." Ano put the flat iron down and walked in to sit on the end of the bed. "Lemme be clear," she said, her doe eyes large. "Did you get busy?"

"Uh, yuck for you asking like that."

"And still, she doesn't answer!"

"It felt so... I couldn't. I mean, I didn't want to!"

"Which one was it?" Ano asked. "You *couldn't* is a whole lot different than you didn't *want* to."

"I'm with Percy now," I said out loud, as if to reaffirm it.

"But something happened?" she prodded. I didn't respond. "So you feel guilty about cheating on Percy?"

"Wait, wait. I didn't say we did anything! We talked!"

"Nothing else?"

Unfortunately, I sucked at lying. Even more unfortunate was the fact that Ano knew it. "We kissed. That was it."

"*Just* kissed?" Ano's eyes locked on my own.

"We...kind of...it was a little more than just kissing."

"For real? What happened?"

"We were talking, and then he tells me he never stopped loving me."

"Okay. What'd you say?"

"Then he kissed me."

She moved her hand erratically, waving for me to get to the point. "And then? What'd you say?"

"There, uh, wasn't a lot of talking after that."

"Ah."

"Yeah."

"Were there..." her eyebrows went up, "clothes removed?"

Slowly, I nodded my head. "Well, yes, but..."

Ano sighed. "Kate."

"I feel so guilty this morning, Ano. We were so close to doing it. And part of me..."

"What?"

"I feel really bad telling you this. But when he was kissing me, part of me wanted it to be Percy."

"No! No, really?"

"Sorry, it's the truth."

"That's just sad. You didn't tell him that, did you?"

"Ano, I might not be any good at relationships, but I'm not *that* stupid."

"You said *part of you*. What about the other part?"

"Oh, that part wanted him. Really badly."

"Hmm." She thought for a moment, and turned towards me. "But you didn't?"

"No. We were close, I'll be honest. If Edgar hadn't come out and called us..."

"You never said whether you loved him back?"

"No," I said, looking away.

"Do you?"

I shrugged.

"One of these days," she said, "you gotta get past that block. Let someone in. *Say* the word."

"It's only a word. Saying it doesn't mean anything." She sighed and I managed a smile. "Okay. I get it."

She harrumphed under her breath. "Then decide if he's what you want." She pushed her counselor hat pushed aside, and her best friend one was now firmly affixed. "It's not whether he's sorry 'bout what happened, it's whether you can get past it and move on."

"That's not it," I said. "It's whether I want to try again with him. To take the chance he'll... I don't think I could take him hurting me again."

"Do you think he would?"

I laughed, but it sounded a little bitter. "I didn't think he would the first time."

Ano came to sit on the edge of the bed next to me. "Ano, when I'm with Percy— *before* we moved to Virginia—he was...everything. Everything I'd always known we could be together."

"Really? Percy?"

"Sensitive, tender, caring...he is all those things. In private."

Ano pursed her lips. "And now?"

"It's like he's a completely different person."

Because she'd had a lot of relationships, Ano knew her subject matter much better than I ever would. She was overqualified to give me advice, but as always, was happy to guide me in the right direction.

"You have a stronger connection to Percy?" she asked as a question, but I knew she was really asking me to think carefully about both men.

"Percy and I used to have so much in common. And then..." I swallowed hard, "the train...the war happened. And everything changed."

"Any chance he's having trouble processing what happened, too?"

"No, it's like he is proceeding as if it didn't happen!"

Her counselor hat was officially back on now. "Some people cope with things by pretending they didn't occur. Victims of violent crimes often do that because the reality of what happened to them is too awful to process. They shut down that memory, move on as if it didn't happen at all. But," she said, stroking my hand gently, "they are processing it and it will resurface. Trust me. It always does."

"So you're saying one day Percy will have a breakdown?" I asked in disbelief.

"No," she said sarcastically and with a slight shove to my shoulder, "I'm saying that some people process in their own time. Percy will deal with the train ride in his own way. What happened to you was such a shock to your system that its coming out in other ways as well."

"My dreams?"

"That's right, baby girl. And to get past those dreams, you're gonna need to tell someone about them. Like me." She smiled her brilliant smile at me and I laughed.

"The dreams will go away too. In time." As much as my bravado sounded so sure, I wasn't exactly certain that was the case.

"They might," she said, "they might not. I want to know why if you're so close to Percy, you haven't shared the dreams with him."

I actually laughed out loud at her question. "Oh, I think I've *shared* them with him. I'm sure he felt like I was sharing quite enough when I'd wake up hitting him or fighting him. Ano, he put a pillow between us because his chest had bruises all over it."

"You serious?"

With a sad expression, I nodded. "When I left I wasn't sure whether he was distancing himself from me, or I was pushing him away."

"Were you?" Ano asked.

"What? No!"

She held up her hands in mock surrender. "I'm jus' sayin' is all. You do not have that great of a track record for letting people in."

"True."

"If you weren't connecting because of the dreams—"

"No, no, that wasn't it," I cut in. "The dreams were difficult but there was something else between us. Something I couldn't get past. It was killing me not to be close to him. It's like I have trouble breathing without him. And I know you think that's unhealthy."

"I didn't say that," she said. "The thought of living without Jazz," she covered her heart with her hand, "makes me stop breathing."

"I don't feel like that about Matt. It would hurt, but it's different with Percy. Without him," I shook my head, "I don't think I could function."

Ano's mouth curved to a slight smile. "You ever say any of this to Captain Wonderful?"

"Uh, no."

"Maybe you should."

"I'll think about it."

"In the meantime," she giggled, "no more hay bales till you decide what you're gonna do!"

"Thanks."

She laughed out loud, stood, and shimmied her hips. "Mr. Skylar don't need to be gettin' his groove on with you until you're ready."

"Ugh!" I play kicked at her with my bare foot. "You're entirely too frisky this morning." And then, with the sudden realization of what that meant, I smiled at her. "Ah! Will Jazz be a happy man tonight?"

She walked back into the bathroom, retrieved a small bag, and tossed it to me on the bed with a smile. "There. I won't be needing the rest of these for another month. If you need extra, now you have them."

I tossed the bag onto the corner of the bed. "Thanks."

Ano stood at the corner of the bathroom door watching me for a minute. I turned back onto my stomach and flipped to the next page in the phot album she'd brought. I turned to look at her. She was standing in the doorway, staring at me. "What?"

She walked towards me curiously. "We been here seven full days."

"Yeah, so?"

"You...started yet?"

"No."

She walked over to kneel in front of me. "No? You're not worried 'bout that?"

"It's a few days late. Not the first time that's ever happened."

"Mmmhmm. How many?"

"How many what?"

She sighed. "You know Goddamned well how many what."

I sat up. "I don't know, a little over a week."

Ano sat down on the end of the bed. "So you were supposed to start—"

"Trust me, the only time we weren't careful was the day before I came here."

"Which was seven days ago."

"No, it would be…I came here the day before you. So, I guess it'd be eight days. No, nine. Or was it…? Wait."

She was mentally doing the math, right along with me. "Eight days from when you came or eight days from when you were supposed to start? Now I'm confused."

"Ano, stop!" I looked around us. "I need my purse. I've got my thing in my purse."

"It's in the kitchen. I'll get it." Ano ran out of the cottage and I heard her in the kitchen causing a commotion and then she hit the screen door with my bag over her arm. She was beside me and dumping my purse out across the bed within thirty seconds.

"Nice," I said, watching her.

"What?"

"Could you have made a bigger deal out of it, do you think?"

"Just get your thing."

I rifled through the contents of my bag and pulled out the planner. Flipping through it, I found my last red notation and pointed to it. "Right there."

"What the hell is 'Marge'?"

"Oh. The nurse that took care of my dad always used to tell people her Aunt Marge was visiting when her cycle started. So, I started using instead of Aunt Flo. Sounds better."

I wrinkled my nose and Ano giggled.

"Okay, so…" We lowered our heads together and counted, and then recounted. And then recounted again.

"Oh." I said, realizing how long it had really been.

"Yeah. You sure? 'Bout that being the only time?"

"Trust me," I said solemnly. "Until that day he hadn't touched me since the attack."

"Well, then it's the stress, of the attack and the surgery, and everything else you got goin' on."

"I know. That's why I'm not worried."

Her tone was cautious, but I could tell she still wasn't ready to let it go. "You feeling all right?"

My laugh rang out through the cottage and I pushed her shoulder. "I'm not throwing up, I'm not sick. I'm fine! In fact, I've slept better in the past three nights than I have in, well, in a while."

"You wanna go into town?" Ano asked after a moment of silence. "Just in case?"

Part of me wanted to, to make sure, and to give me that piece of mind. She had me a little freaked out. Another part of me knew the medical probability of getting pregnant the day or even few days before my period was very slim. And finally, I didn't want to know. The complication of what knowing entailed was too much. I shook my head. "Nah. I'll wait."

"I wish you'd go get a test so we could be, you know, positive."

"Or not positive, as the case may be."

Ano didn't laugh. "You're sure?"

"Ano, I'm fine."

"Okay. You know your body better than anyone."

"I look at it this way," I rationalized, "when I was going through finals, I actually skipped over my period entirely."

"I won't say anything. But if you don't start in the next couple of days I'm driving you down there myself."

"Okay," I conceded. "I'm gonna send a telegram to Percy today, telling him we're staying longer. With that train in Ohio getting bombed, Charlie's not letting me go anywhere anytime soon."

We resumed looking through the photos in the album, unaware that under the window Edgar had heard every word of the last five minutes of our conversation.

Going to town with seven people in one pickup truck is not an easy event, especially when four of those people are women. Because we were trying to conserve as much gas as possible and not make unnecessary trips, all of us piled into the truck. Ano and I were both going to send a telegram. She and Jazz had decided to stay with Carrie and Charlie with all the fighting and activity going on, it was safer. Charlie had made sure he drilled it into all of us that we weren't going to even think of leaving until the United States was whole again, or we all had been there so long we had to build houses on his property. I think Carrie was kind of hoping for the latter.

Carrie and Charlie were in the cab and Jazz, Ano, and the rest of us were all stuck in the bed of the truck for the fifteen-minute ride to town. I was sitting between Edgar and Matt; ironic at best, uncomfortable at worst. When we parked, Matt hopped over the side and reached up for me, and Edgar literally pushed his hands out of the way.

"Are you crazy?" he said, pointing me to the end of the bed. "She could fall. And hurt herself. Kate, go out the back."

I raised my eyebrows at him. "You wanna re-phrase that?" Edgar was kind of taking this protective little brother thing a little too far.

Edgar sighed. "Please Kate? Come to the back of the truck."

I didn't want any drama so I hopped over the tailgate myself.

"Anything you want me to tell my mom or grandma?" Ano asked Jazz, kissing his lips before she and I walked three blocks to the post station.

"Nope. Got a few things I wouldn't mind sayin' to Lively, but I don't think you wanna send those in a telegram."

Ano shook her head and Jazz laughed. Matt punched him in the shoulder.

"Hey!" Matt called to me. "You goin' with her?"

"Yes," I replied.

"Tell Percy I say hello," he said with a wide grin on his face.

Charlie grabbed Matt by the back of the shirt to drag him towards the hardware store at the corner, and Jazz trailed after them.

"What?"

"That mouth's gonna get you in trouble," Charlie said.

I could hear Matt's laugh echo from down the street.

"Edgar," Carrie called, and I turned around to see Edgar following us, instead of Carrie.

"What's wrong, Edgar?" I said. "You're supposed to go to the store with Carrie."

"Do you need anything? Is there anything you need at the store?" he asked shyly, his hands in his pockets.

"Nothing I can think of." I placed my hand on his forehead. "You feeling okay? You look flushed."

He pulled his head away from my hand. "I'm fine."

"Okay," I said, walking backwards towards where Ano stood waiting. "I'll tell Percy you say hello. Okay?"

He walked back towards Carrie, torn between what he should do – his duty to his brother, and not wanting to betray his new friend and sister.

All arms and legs, he walked next to Carrie down each aisle. From their cart, it looked like she was feeding an army. Edgar had money from Matt,

Jazz, and Kate to give to Carrie for contribution toward the food bill, which lately had been staggering.

"There's no more of that cereal, they must be out of it. Well, we'll have to find something else." Carrie continued to look at the shelves, some of them empty and others half-stocked.

Petersons was the only market in town, and with supply lines being affected all over, they were lucky to get food at all, even for the price they were charging. Many things they traded their neighbors for; eggs for milk, vegetables for fruit, and the like. But so many things had to be bought.

"I think we need a...Edgar, is something wrong?"

He raised his head. "No, I'm sorry. Did you need me to reach something for you, Carrie?"

She stood, can of soup in her hand, and regarded him. "You all right?" her hand went to her hip. "You and Matt been at each other again?"

"No, ma'am."

"Edgar, I raised two boys and I know that look."

He sighed and took a step towards her, having to lean down quite a way so their conversation was private. Unlike his normal demeanor, Edgar was fidgeting. "Suppose...you knew something. About someone in your family. And perhaps if, well, someone else might need to know that information. Or—"

"I don't do well with 'maybe's'. Just tell me what's going on and I...are you all right? "

"It's not me."

"Kate?" He nodded, but didn't look up. "Is this because she took a walk with Matt the other—"

"No. No, they were just walking. I think."

Carrie had seen the blush on Matt's face when they walked through the door and doubted very much that walking was the only activity, but didn't say anything to Edgar to the contrary. "Then what is it? Nightmares again?"

The knowledge was killing him, and he had no family here at all to consult on what to do. Kate trusted Carrie. This once, he was going to have to do the same. "I think..." he lowered his voice and said something in Carrie's ear.

Carrie pulled away from him like he'd slapped her and looked at Edgar. "That can't be true."

"I didn't mean to hear them," he said, his voice filled with regret. "But now I think maybe I should tell my brother. That he should know, should be here and...and be with Kate."Carrie thought for a moment. It couldn't be true. Kate would have told her if something like this had happened, wouldn't she? She couldn't very well go to Kate and ask her if it was true. That would clearly betray Edgar, who had confided in her. Edgar had trusted her with this knowledge; came to her not knowing what he should do. Poor thing. He was in a bad situation, which had just gotten much, much more complicated.

"All right," Carrie said, pushing the cart ahead of them. "We're going to think this through. Hold off on telling Percy. Let me talk to Kate and—"

"No!" Edgar screeched. "She'll kill me! If she thinks I was listening to—"

"I'm the one who sent you out there to get them," she explained, "and I won't let on that I think anything's going on. It'll be easier if we get to the bottom of this without involving your brother. Besides, you don't know what you heard – exactly."

Edgar wasn't sure he agreed, but continued down the aisles quietly for a few moments.

Carrie didn't know Percy well. Even in the few weeks he'd been at the farm he'd kept mainly to himself, talking only occasionally to Charlie. He always seemed serious, reserved. So unlike Kate. Since Edgar was opening up to her, she was going to do what she did best. She was going to dig. "Does Percy spend a lot of time with Kate?"

Edgar shrugged. "He did when we were in Philadelphia."

Carrie placed three bags of flour into the cart. "And now?"

"I think he's really busy right now."

He was clearly repeating what he'd heard Kate say. "I see," Carrie commented.

"She spends a lot of time with my grandmother though."

"Yes, Kate's told me about Gigi."

Edgar's face became serious. "I take care of Kate. When Percy's at work, she's my responsibility."

Her heart squeezed for him as she realized how attached he really was to Kate. To him, this wasn't just some place his brother had sent him, some errand. Edgar had come because his brother had trusted him with something precious. Something valuable. Percy had trusted Edgar with Kate.

Her voice softened. "Percy must love both of you a great deal to send you together to look after each other." He nodded and Carrie smiled, noting the boyhood in Edgar's face was fading and waiting to take its place were the angles of a man. She remembered her own two boys going through this stage. So eager for manhood, for responsibility. Edgar, like his brother, seemed different. Pensive. Serious.

"You're turning sixteen soon," Carrie commented and pulled a large bag of crackers from the shelf.

"Yes. In December."

"When do you go back to school?"

"Percy has arranged a tutor for me when we return to Virginia." His face fell and it wasn't lost on Carrie.

"You decided not to go back to your school?"

"My brother decided that I should stay close. He wants to keep us both safe."

"Yes," she said, watching Edgar's face. "I can't blame him. I have two boys and I worry about them constantly. Percy must worry a lot about you being so far from him."

"No. Percy knows I'll bring Kate back safely. I'm not frightened to take a train back to Virginia."

"Still, it must have been hard to let his only brother go hundreds of miles away."

Edgar looked at Carrie, as if assessing whether she was trying to get him to say something against Percy. "Percy has my best interests at heart."

"Of course he does."

"My brother would do anything to keep Kate safe. He loves her very much." They turned down the next aisle and before Carrie could ask her next question, Edgar added, "She's going to be my sister one day."

Carrie's next question died on her lips. "Really?"

"Of course." He said it as if it had already been decided, as if it was a foregone conclusion.

"I thought that..." Carrie knew she was treading on dangerous ground between what she knew about Percy through Kate and what she could say to Edgar, "...that all the men in your family came from arranged marriages?"

"They do."

Carrie pointed Edgar to the boxes of cornmeal she wanted and waited for him to pull them down and into the cart. "If that's so, then—"

"My grandmother helped arrange most of the marriages in our family," Edgar told her. "She knows that there's no one better for Percy than Kate." Then he said something so out of character for his fifteen years that it stopped Carrie literally in her tracks. "Percy...comes to life when he's around her. Nothing will change that. Not Matt's charm or his looks or his barbs at me or my brother. Nothing."

Edgar was loading the groceries in the back of the truck when we walked back from the postal station. He opened the tailgate and held his hand out to help me in. Instead of taking it, I handed him a piece of paper and stood in front of him, hand on my hip.

"From now on, I get editorial rights on your telegrams *before* you send them."

Edgar opened the piece of paper, read it and, smiling, folded it back and tucked it into his pocket. "C'mon," he said, outstretching his hand again.

Reluctantly, I took his hand and climbed into the back of the truck next to Ano. Crossing from the opposite side of the street, Jazz and Matt came, trailed by Charlie from the hardware store. Before Matt could get into the truck bed, Edgar hopped up and sat next to me. Jazz and Matt climbed in and closed the tailgate behind them. After he'd made sure everyone was in, Charlie started the truck to head back home.

"What'd you say to Mom?" Jazz asked Ano. It was still weird hearing him call Michelle "Mom".

"Told her we'd be home after another week or so. Depends on the fighting."

"Uncle Robert'll love that."

"Oh, I'm sure we'll get a telegram from Uncle Robert really soon," she chuckled.

"What'd you tell Percy?" Matt asked me.

"The same. That we'd be back when it's safer to travel. That we're fine." I kept my tone as benign as possible. The wind shifted and I huddled down in the back of the truck. Looking at the sky, I could tell that rain was headed our way.

Next to me, Edgar moved his arm up and around my shoulders and pulled me to him. "Why didn't you dress warmer?" he asked me and I shrugged, glad for the warmth of his body.

"Didn't think it would cloud up so fast."

"You should prepare better next time," Edgar said, and his admonishment reminded me of Percy. We were quiet for a few minutes, then Edgar whispered into my ear, "What did you really say to my brother?"

"That we'll be back soon. When it's safe."

"And?"

I sighed. Edgar was beginning to know me. A little too well. "And that we miss him."

He smiled at that and tightened his grip around me for the rest of the ride home.

By the time we turned onto Shoreline Highway, the first few drops had begun to fall. By the time we pulled into the driveway, it was sprinkling. When the last bag of groceries had been brought in from the truck, the sky opened up and it began to pour.

I've always been a big fan of rain. The house I grew up in had a metal roof over the porch. When the rain came, it made soft 'ping, ping, ping' sounds until the rain got harder and then it was like a roar. On nights that it rained, I didn't need to turn on the TV. I didn't need to run the water in the bathroom. I only needed to keep the back door open and listen to the sounds of the rain to put me into a deep sleep.

Most of the afternoon I spent inside the house with Ano and Carrie; knitting, talking about everything from Ano's honeymoon to med school. Matt, Jazz, Edgar, and Charlie stayed in the garage, tinkering away on the tractor. About halfway through the day they all came in, surprising us with their loud, happy chatter.

"Who lit a fire under you boys?" Carrie asked as she set aside her knitting and came to fix lunch in the kitchen.

Charlie's face was all lit up and he pointed to Edgar, who had a smear of grease under one eye. "This one's got the damndest mechanical sense I've ever seen. The whelp fixed the tractor!"

Carrie's look of shock was nothing compared to mine. I hopped up from where I'd been sitting on the floor and crossed to Edgar, who was grinning quietly.

"He moved over the top of the engine, popped her out and sat there tinkering while Jazz and Matt," he motioned over to them and then dismissed them with a wave, "well, I don't know what they two of them were doin'."

"Watchin' Boy Wonder," Jazz said, and I knew it was more like they'd been *mocking* Boy Wonder.

"And then he puts it back in, and damned if the thing didn't fire right up!"

"I didn't know you knew about engines," I said, and Edgar smiled at me from across the kitchen.

"I don't picture 'shop' as a big class for boarding school *girls*," Matt said playfully.

"Unlike California, preparatory schools in Connecticut call it Mechanical Engineering. And I'm an excellent student."

"Bless Connecticut ingenuity, then!" Charlie said and clapped him on the back.

"Edgar," I said, "Come here. You've got some—"

"Oh, stop motherin' him," Charlie said, pulling him away from me. "C'mon, the hens will get lunch ready, and—"

"Charlie. Blackhawk." Carrie said with a warning tone.

"Well, when the *girls* have lunch, they'll call us."

The guys went back out to the barn where the rain was hitting the roof and rolling off in sheets. Charlie and Jazz leaned over the tractor and Charlie pointed to where Edgar had removed the hose and filter as well.

"You're kind of a handy guy to have around, Ed," Matt said amiably.

"Thanks, *Matt*."

"Did you, uh, send my message to your brother the other day?"

Wiping the grease from his face with a rag Charlie had handed him, Edgar grinned at Matt. "Yeah. I did."

Charlie fired the tractor up briefly, then turned it off again and let Jazz lower the hinged hood.

"He replied today, as a matter of fact."

"Did he?" Matt remarked.

"He did."

"What did big bro have to say?"

Edgar actually considered showing him the telegram, but thought better of it. Instead, he turned towards Matt, towering over him by at least three inches. "I don't think it bothered him all that much."

"Really!" Matt responded with a look of genuine surprise.

Edgar chuckled. "No. You see, Matt, the sugar cane? It belongs to my brother."

CHAPTER TWENTY-FOUR

"Mr. President, there are hardly words." The admiral slid the proposal back to the president, his expression hard.

President Riley reclined in his chair, hundreds of feet below the surface, in a bunker known only to the fifteen people surrounding him.

"Well, Admiral, I think there are words, but seeing as how we're all short on time, I suggest dispensing with pleasantries."

"Mr. President—" General Jessup began.

Riley held a hand up to silence him. "Jake, I've known you for going on twenty years, and for now, I'm just Albert."

A smile played at the edge of the General's mouth. "Yes, sir. Albert, this is plain lunacy."

"I have to agree, Mr. President," the admiral chimed in.

Assents were echoed from around the table, and Riley reclined and steepled his hands over his chest. "Gentlemen, in the last six months, nine men who have tried to take this office have been murdered. Five more died before they could take the oath. In that time, I have been sequestered, shot at, poisoned, moved into and out of this country four times and finally, stabbed. I understand the tenor of this proposal may appear to you all as drastic beyond measure. Believe me when I tell you it is our last resort."

"Mr. President, the CX-6 will be operational and ready for deployment within two weeks."

Riley turned to General Unger, his eyes suddenly tired. "We don't have two weeks, Jim."

"With all due respect, Mr. President...we must."

Riley stood and walked to the far end of the room. His tall frame, once over two hundred pounds, now hovered at one-eighty. The room remained silent while the president paced back and forth, and finally came to stand at the edge of the large oval table.

"I spoke via satellite phone with Commander Peterson this afternoon. His men are stationed in Los Angeles and have assured me that, without our intervention, the new troops that approach will succeed in breaking our line. In that event, the enemy will be able to link troops with Northern California, and they will move north until they reach Seattle. If this happens, we will lose the West Coast."

"There is a convoy moving west from Denver as we speak," General Greer assured him. "It should reach Los Angeles within three days."

"Those troops may land as soon as tomorrow night, General."

"I know, sir."

"Then it's too goddamned late."

"Mr. President," the General pleaded, "nuclear force being used within the United States could cause massive civilian casualties. It means thousands of American lives, sir."

"You say that like I haven't been given the same studies you have," Riley replied. He sighed and sat again, staring at the haggard faces surrounding him. "All right, let's play this out from a military standpoint. Without nuclear intervention, or at least the threat of nuclear intervention, that new wave of troops will hit the West Coast by tomorrow night. Even with the National Guard moving forces from the Midwest and the south, they won't make it in time to catch the first wave. Can we agree this is a potential risk?"

Nods and grunts came from around the table.

"You all have assured me we can 'hold the line' and are progressing well in individual battles but gentlemen, we are not winning this war by merely holding the line."

"Albert, as much as I hate to be the one to pull protocol, the use of nuclear force can't be authorized unless the Secretary of Defense, a majority of the House and Senate—"

"That's true, Tom," Riley said, sarcasm and anger coloring his voice. "Colin's throat was cut from ear to ear. He's lying dead on the floor of his Georgetown home. Over half the Senate and the majority of the House are dead or missing. We are looking at what's left of our government." He ran a hand over his face. "For God's sake, the Speaker of the House was executed last week when he wouldn't give them our location."

"I know, sir."

"Then it's time to move past pomp and circumstance and take action, for Christ's sake!"

"We are still members of an organized government, Mr. President! Those positions demand that we take the necessary measures to assure that no branch of government—"

"Don't quote the fucking Constitution to me, Robert," Albert spat.

Admiral Johnson stood and removed a pen from his inner pocket. "Gentlemen, Mr. President, this country was founded by men who took action in the face of almost certain death. They did it to protect the citizens of a country that trusted them with the responsibility of their position." He leaned forward and flipped to the back page of the proposal. Uncapping his pen, he signed his name. "I swore to protect this country from all who sought to harm or invade it, by any and all means necessary."

General Anderson stood as well. "The Marines stand behind you, Mr. President. We support defense of this country by any and all means necessary." Taking the pen handed to him by Admiral Johnson, he signed his name and handed the pen to the general to his left.

With a sigh, General Greer held the pen and looked down at the proposal in front of him. "What we are doing today is not an act of bravery. We are authorizing the use of nuclear weapons within our own borders. We may drive the coalition from our country, but the harm we do to our own people may be far greater."

Riley's voice was soft from the end of the table, but filled the room nonetheless. "You hired me to be Commander in Chief, a job I have held now for the past forty-one days. I have grown up in this country with the same ideals as any man sitting at this table. Like most, I guess, I got lost in the politics along the way. This isn't empty politics, and it's not a bluff. Our citizens are dying in the streets defending their country! They know the risks of doing nothing and their actions compel me to do something greater than we have been doing." He stabbed at the table with his finger. "The time for doing something is now. Right now, before another innocent life is taken by these bastards. I know in the past this job gets mired down in red tape, politically correct action, and hopes for reelection. Right now, I'm hoping to make it to next week."

General Greer said nothing, but stared at the paper in front of him.

"Jim," Riley pleaded, "for God's sake. If there was any other way to win this war, I would be doing it. However, the time for diplomacy is past. It's time that America takes back its borders. If that means blasting the bastards to hell, then so be it."

General Greer flipped to the back page of the document, his pen hovering over the signature line. "Those are our citizens we'll be killing, too."

"With this proposal, our casualties should be minimal."

"With all due respect, sir, one American life is too many."

"Oh, for Christ's sake, Jim." The three-star general to General Greer's left took the pen from his hand. "This is war. We all knew how this could end. We've just got to have balls big enough to end it." Leaning forward, he signed his name and handed the pen to the commander to his left.

In succession, each man signed his name until the signature lines were all filled. The silence in the room was deafening. The gravity of the document that had just been signed resonated with each of them.

After signing his name at the bottom, Riley capped the pen and handed it back to Admiral Johnson.

"We have nuclear capability from here, do we not?" No one answered. "Robert?"

The General snapped to attention. "Yes sir, we do."

"Then it's time to do what we must. It's time to end this fucking war."

"Get those comm units under a secure location."

"Yes, Major."

Major Phillips stalked through the new command post that had been set up fifteen miles outside the hot zone, a perimeter they were having luck keeping hold of, for now. He entered the colonel's tent and saluted.

"Come in, Major."

"Yes, sir."

"Are you aware of a civilian casualty we sustained a week ago when a transport came under enemy fire?"

"Yes, sir."

"Are you aware that the same civilian was also a doctor from a trauma unit in Bellevue?"

John nodded curtly, staring straight ahead. "Yes, Colonel."

"And are you also aware that I'm getting reports of a certain major who was responsible for bringing this civilian into the firefight?"

"Yes, sir."

"What the hell happened up there, John?"

"Sir, Dr. Mannis was put into a transport at Bellevue trauma erroneously and approached me at Command 4. I took her to the C.O., who advised her she would be rejoining the rest of her unit the next day."

"Before you could get her there, the breach occurred."

"Yes, sir."

"Why didn't you put her in a comm Jeep traveling to the new location, for Christ's sake!"

"Sir, there wasn't time. The breach happened very quickly and we learned that her unit came under heavy fire that morning as well."

"Casualties?"

John's face remained stoic. "No wounded to treat. Sir."

The colonel cursed under his breath. "I see."

"There was a transport leaving with my men. I was reasonably certain I could assure Dr. Mannis' safety, and I brought her along with us, sir."

"Uh huh." Colonel Arnold Walker stood up and walked around to face Major Phillips. "You're Goddamned lucky she lived."

"Yes, sir."

"How's Private Lanskin?"

"Well, sir, I've seen him twice and confirmed he will regain full use of his leg."

"Good. And the good doctor? How is she?"

"Fine, sir."

He walked around to the desk he'd been using and leaned against it. "Been to see her as well?"

Major Phillips nodded. "Yes, sir, I have. To confirm her condition was stable. They had admitted her as a Jane Doe, sir."

"You've cleared that up?"

"Yes, sir."

"I see." Colonel Walker drummed his fingers on the table and looked straight at Major Phillips. "I see you've got yourself logged out for a ride back to CSH tonight with one of the MEDEVACs. Any particular reason why?"

"I'm...there is..." he desperately tried to think of a good enough reason.

"Don't hurt yourself, Major."

"No, sir."

"You know what I learned about fighting a war, Major?"

"No, sir."

"That it means more to a man who's got something to come back to." He sighed. "You're due to take off in fifteen minutes. I'd double-time it to the pad if I were you."

A small smile briefly tugged at the corner of Major Phillips' mouth. "Yes, sir."

"And, Major?"

"Yes, sir?"

"You ever bring a civilian into a firefight again, you'll be changing bedpans in your own O.R. Are we clear, Major?"

"Crystal, sir."

"Dismissed!"

The ride to the CSH on the MEDEVAC took less than fifteen minutes. Major Phillips had time to stop in the HUB and fill a large tray of food before carrying it to Carlie's recovery room. He backed in to the door, the tray heavy in his hands.

"Room service."

"Oh my God," Carlie said, and laughed. "Who is going to eat all that food?" She sat up a little higher in bed. The bandage that had covered her entire shoulder and neck now covered only her upper shoulder and arm. Large purple bruises peeked out from underneath the surgical tape.

"You are." He moved the tray from her hospital bed over and set the tray of food on top of it. "Your doctor says he's happy with your progress. You're doing well and he can release you in another week."

"That's good news." Her face fell a little and John saw it as he pulled a chair toward her bedside.

"What's wrong?"

"Nothing."

John had been around women his entire life and knew there was 'something' going on, though he busied himself with looking at her chart for a few minutes before trying again. "You're afraid of traveling?"

"I have nowhere to go. I can't travel with the baby. It's too dangerous. My identity card is back in the trauma unit and I have no money, no address, no clothes. I don't know any of David's family's names so I can't contact them to tell them...." She sighed. "I'm sorry, John. I'm not good company tonight."

He handed her a box of tissue from the shelf next to the bed. "No, it's hormones. Perfectly normal given everything you're going through right now."

Carlie wiped her eyes, which had begun to turn red.

"You have options, Carlie."

She made a scoffing noise and rolled her eyes. "Yeah. Options. Sure, I have." She blew her nose and sighed. "I don't know what I'm going to do."

"I don't want you to read too much into this, but my parents live in Kellogg, Idaho. Not more than five hours by car."

Carlie continued to sniffle. "And?"

"I know this sounds crazy. But I can call my parents. They're good people. They'll keep you safe. Until I can come home."

"John, no, I don't need you to—"

"Carlie, listen to me. I've got a place in Idaho. Real near my folks." John's face lit up and he leaned forward. "It's on a lake. You could go for walks every morning for exercise. It'd be good for the baby."

"I can't do that."

"Why not? Because you only met me two weeks ago and I almost got you killed?"

"That. And I don't know you. And I'm carrying another man's baby!"

"Not ideal, I'll grant you," he said and they both laughed. He pulled the tray of food to rest between them. "I'm not looking for you to substitute me for the father of the baby."

"I feel like I'm missing something," she admitted to him. "And I hate it. Like any minute he'll come walking in as if nothing happened. There's no closure, no..." she dabbed at the tears streaming down her cheeks. "That's why I couldn't accept your offer."

"Now hang on," he said. "I'm not asking for you to be over this anytime soon. I'm offering you somewhere safe to do it."

She sniffed, looking down at her hands, which were both bare. Before the war had broken out, David had talked about getting married, about her not being a single mother.

"Carlie," John said softly and handed her a fork. "You need to do some healing. You need some time."

She tentatively accepted the fork. "I talked to one of the chaplains the other day. Wrote a few letters to my friends to let them know I was okay. It's so hard to know what to do."

"I'm asking you to let me help you. Let me be the guy you lean on."

"Why?" she asked.

"The whole 'almost getting you killed' thing wasn't enough?" he quipped and she laughed again.

"Because if it doesn't turn into...something," she began hesitantly.

"Then I'll consider us even. You saved my life, I help you in yours. You'll have an address that you can use until you get Identified again. And there is good medical care close by my house." After a second he added, "For both you and the baby."

She didn't say anything for a minute and John gestured towards the tray of food between them. "Eat, Carlie. You need to keep your strength up."

She stuck her fork into the plate of food in front of her and took a bite. "Thank you."

"Uh, for the food or the offer?"

"Both. But mostly for being here. To help me. Us." Carlie placed her hand over her abdomen. "I have no idea what I'm doing."

"You'll be a natural. Trust me."

"Yeah. Because the decisions governing my life so far have been so stellar."

John chuckled and took a bite of chicken. "Well, some you had control over and some you didn't."

"There are a million decisions coming at me so fast that it feels like...I don't know."

He watched her take a small bite of the food he'd brought. Even lying in the hospital bed, she was beautiful. Her heart shaped face was so lovely and, despite having been in a near-fatal firefight, she was glowing. Although he felt horribly that she'd lost the baby's father, he couldn't help but believe there was a reason they'd been brought together.

"The immediate decisions are easy," he reassured her. "Prenatal care taken care of. There's a hospital very close to my ranch and I'll come up once a month for each of your appointments."

"Oh," she said, a worried look crossing her face, "I wouldn't want you to—"

"Carlie," he said and smiled gently, "it's no problem. Really."

She gave a conciliatory nod and took another bite.

"And then there's a room for the baby and really, several of the bedrooms in my ranch would do nicely with a remodel."

She realized he was teasing her and a bit of the tension eased from her shoulders. "Thank you," she said and John saw how much it took for her to accept help from him.

"You're welcome."

"John?"

"Hmm?"

"How is it going? Out there. Are we winning?"

The common misconception with civilians was the concept of win/lose. In a game, there is a winner and a loser. In a war, it was degrees of losing. There may be a *victor*, but there was no *winner*.

"I don't know. Right now, I'd say we're working to turn the tables in our favor."

"That's a polite way of saying we've gotten our asses handed to us, right?"

"No, that's a way of saying that right now the U.S. has come from a position where we never should have been. Too many of our men were overseas fighting a war that, well, we won't go there. The point is, they weren't at home. We weren't minding the store. And in Idaho, if you don't keep an eye on the horizon, the fox is gonna get through the gate."

"That's what happened here?"

"I believe so."

"A lot of people have been saying we should have pulled out and come home when the first attacks happened."

"I think that's easy to say. Keep in mind, though, there's a lot more going on than you see or hear about. There are a hundred balls in the air and the people really only see three or four. It's easy to make that call when you're seeing a quarter of the big picture."

"So you think we did the right thing then? By waiting?"

"We didn't wait."

"Yeah. I was there. We didn't see soldiers until—"

"You just said it. You didn't *see* soldiers. Carlie, we've been sitting in the Sound for over three weeks."

Her eyes went wide. "What? You've been just sitting there?"

"No, we've been strategizing. This wasn't a reactive decision. The United States was responding to the threats being made by another country. There was, and still is, a struggle for power going on. That's what this is all about."

"So, the real war, the one we don't see, is being fought between leaders?"

"That's a crude way to put it, but yes. Like a game of chess. You don't win the game by playing every move with your king, do you?"

"No."

"Neither does the United States. And right now, strategically, I think we're moving into a position to drive this force back where it came from and ultimately, crush it."

"So we have a president who's calling the shots, though. Right?"

He laughed. "You would never make it in the military."

"John, I'm asking you a—"

"I know." His face softened and became a little more serious. "These are all good questions. Enough, though, for one night."

She saw his face and knew he wasn't able to answer any more of her questions. "All right."

"Baby's hungry, right?"

"Yes." Carlie took a forkful of rice and chewed happily for a moment. "John, do you have to go back to the command post tonight?"

He didn't delude himself that it was because she cared for him. "I do. I'll wait as long as I can before catching the last MEDEVAC back though. I still have rounds to do at the command post."

"All right."

"C'mon. I got you some chocolate cake there but you're not getting it until you finish all your chicken."

Carlie smiled slightly. "Yes, sir."

It was twenty-three hundred hours before he hauled his sorry ass back to the command post, stopped in his tent for two hours' sleep and a shave before heading to do his rounds. The new command post had been set up with a mess hall as well as a better medical facility than the last.

Pulling the first chart on the pile, John sat down at the desk and began to review the patient's history by the light of the lamp.

"Late night?"

He didn't bother to look up. "Yeah. Something like that."

"It's been quiet. Bed five tore stitches out and bed seven's going to be transported to the CSH tomorrow."

John looked up at the man standing in front of him. "Thank you, soldier."

"Doctor."

"Oh." He looked closer. "Sorry, I didn't see your..." The man's face looked haggard. "You're a civilian doctor." John sat back in his chair. "I've been made crystal clear on the fact that civilian doctors are not permitted to remain at command posts. Have you seen the—"

"I spoke with the colonel. He explained it, most prolifically."

John grinned. "I'll bet he did." He sat back and eyed the doctor in front of him. "How long you been here?"

"Came in with a transport this afternoon. Took on heavy fire last week. Been holed up in a building for the better part of three days."

The man looked like hell. "Take any casualties?"

"Yeah, beds six through ten are ours. The rest of us didn't make it."

"I'm sorry."

"Thanks."

"When're they transporting you out?"

"Tomorrow, so I've been told."

"Well, good luck, Doctor..."

The man held out his hand. "Windsor. Doctor David Windsor."

CHAPTER TWENTY-FIVE

"You're going in early this morning," Gigi remarked.

Percy barely glanced up from his cereal bowl as he read the paper. "Yes."

"Thomas going with you?"

"No, I'm going in early to start working on a formula we started last night."

"I see." Gigi allowed one of the maids to fill her cup with more tea. She watched her grandson carefully, stirring in a lump of sugar. In the three weeks since Kate and Edgar's departure, Percy had said less and less to her each morning. He came home late each night after she'd already retired, and their morning conversation was the only one she had all day.

"I didn't think the post station opened this early," she said.

"They close at dusk now, so they started opening—" he stopped mid-sentence, spoonful of cereal and fruit halfway to his mouth. Setting the spoon back in the bowl, he sighed. "Gigi, I'm sorry. I wasn't trying to deceive you."

He watched her concentrating on the plate of breakfast in front of her.

"I'm concerned. And with the fighting getting worse, the bombing this week in California…" his voice was tense and filled with worry.

"I listen to the radio during the day. I know what's going on. I know that we're sustaining heavy casualties in many states."

"Yes."

Gigi took a sip from her cup. "But that's not why you're worried."

Like Percy's mother, Gigi possessed the powerful gift of insight that was dangerously close to clairvoyance.

"You're right," he conceded. "It's not the only reason."

"What did Edgar's last telegram say?"

Obviously, Gigi either knew the instructions he had given Edgar, or she'd suspected it when he sent Kate with Edgar as a chaperone. "Nothing of importance," he said.

However, underneath the table, he clenched his hand into a fist several times. Edgar's last telegram to him had been cryptic, at best. There was something wrong with Kate, or Kate wasn't well. It bothered him that Edgar hadn't been more specific in his telegram, giving vague hints that Kate either was under the weather or something had gone wrong. Either way, Edgar hadn't been clear. It bothered him. And this morning, with a carefully worded telegram, he intended to clear it up, or advise Edgar it was time to come home. Immediately.

"How is her friend? The one who was sick?"

"Much better, according to Edgar."

Gigi ate a bite of fruit, dabbing her mouth with the cloth napkin from her lap before continuing. "She is supposed to return in four days?"

"That's correct," Percy said.

"Well," she said. "Four days isn't that long in the grand scheme of things." She studied Percy out of the corner of her eye while he struggled for a response. "Unless she decides it's too dangerous and she stays longer."

He shifted uncomfortably in his seat. "Yes, you're correct, four days isn't that long. But I won't allow her to stay longer. She and Edgar need to be home. They will come home."

"Mmhmm." Gigi said noncommittally. "Kate seems like she has a way of deciding what she will and won't do all on her own."

"Yes, she does," Percy said under his breath and took a drink of his coffee.

"Sorry, dear, what?"

Percy shook his head. "Nothing, Gigi. Sorry." He glanced at his watch. "I'll be in late this evening again."

He stood, taking a last drink of his coffee, preparing to leave.

Gigi's voice stopped him. "Going in early every morning, staying late every night. You remind me of Robert. A young woman like Kate, she understands hard work."

"Yes, she does."

"And dedication to your chosen field."

"Of course."

"But commitment." Gigi said. "Does she understand commitment?"

His voice wasn't cross, though it was raised slightly. "Kate understands commitment better than anyone I've met."

"Sacrifice?"

"Kate won't have to sacrifice anything to have the life she deserves. Ever."

Gigi smiled softly. "The life she deserves?"

"That's right."

She stirred her coffee absently. "And this life is the one she wants? The one you're working so hard to produce?"

Percy's brows knit together in confusion. "Of course."

"Because she's told you that?"

"Well, no. Not exactly. But, Gigi—"

His grandmother went on, undaunted. "She understands that she'll have to sacrifice to get this life, the one you're working so hard for?"

"Kate won't have to sacrifice anything."

Instead of responding, Gigi shook her head and sighed. "Then perhaps you haven't seen the real cost of the life you want for you and Kate."

Percy had the vague feeling Gigi was irritated with him, though didn't know why. "The cost?"

"One of the last times Camilla and I were together, I met her in New York for lunch. Did she tell you?"

"No." He hadn't spoken to his mother in well over a week before she'd been killed.

"Well, I came up to New York and we had lunch. We saw this businessman come into the restaurant to have a meal with his wife." She spread her hands. "Perfectly normal. Camilla pointed to them and said to me, 'You know I would have given everything I owned if Robert would have spent more time with us. With me.'" Gigi smiled at Percy and stirred her tea. "You see, there is a cost. To everything you do, every choice you make. Robert never learned that."

He sighed. "I am not my father."

"I know you're not. There is still a cost. A cost to you, a cost to Kate."

"Kate has never had a foundation. That's what I'm trying to build for her, for us." He looked up at Gigi, and she smiled thinking he had never looked more handsome than at that moment. Or more like his mother. "I am the last of the Warner men, and I have an obligation to—"

"The only obligation you and Edgar have as Warner men is to carry on the family line," Gigi cut in. "Not kill yourself to rebuild your father's empire. He had everything, and what did it get him in the end?"

Percy thought carefully. "That's true. But—"

"Percy," Gigi said, "if you're working in this field because it's what you love to do, then that's your decision. However, if you're doing it because it leads to," she motioned around her, "all this? You're on a fool's errand."

He didn't say anything for a long minute, then pulled a chair out from the table and sat in it, across from Gigi.

"I remember," she said, finally getting to the crux of what she'd wanted to discuss with him, "when you came home for Christmas your second year at Stanford. You had a terrible argument with your father. Do you remember?"

"Vaguely."

"You'd had...oh, what was that professor's name? Something like Muffin."

"Crumb?"

"Yes, that's it!" Gigi leaned towards him. "He'd told you...oh, let me see." She looked at him out of the corner of her eye. "Do you remember?"

"Not specifically. You're right, I believe that I argued with Father. It's been a long time, Gigi, I hardly even remember now it had so little impact."

"Something about changing your major, as I remember?"

"No, that wasn't it. I didn't want to change my major."

"Yes, yes. I believe you were going to change."

"No, that wasn't it."

"Of course it was. Something about your professor saying you weren't suited for research or something like that."

Percy shook his head, his expression solemn. "No. That wasn't it. I told him I wanted to be a professor. To *teach* science, instead of practicing it with Uncle Thomas. Professor Crumb had said I had a gift for teaching."

"Do you remember what your father said to you?"

"Father told me that I would, well, to continue on the path that he'd chosen. The plan that he...that *we'd* discussed."

Her eyes sparkled. "Odd that you should remember it so clearly, I mean, for something that had no impact on you."

Percy's face lifted to meet hers and she reached out and covered his young, strong hand with her own. "Don't repeat his mistakes, Percy. Your father lost everything he really wanted, and was too big of a fool to do anything about it."

So many times when wisdom is passed down from the aged to the young, something is lost in translation. The message isn't grasped, or it's conveyed in the wrong way. However, in that rare, precise moment that wisdom is offered, accepted and understood, magic occurs.

Percy stood to his full height, reached his tie and pulled it loose. Unbuttoning his top button, he looked directly at Gigi.

"I have no idea if there will even be a need for professors in this country after what's happened. I wanted Edgar to grow up as I did, seeing a father – a man - who had a strong work ethic."

"Professors can have a strong work ethic, too, can they not?"

"I wanted Kate to have a strong, secure..."

He wasn't going to say it. Gigi knew she was going to have to help him through this one. "Husband."

His pale blue eyes came up and met hers. "Yes, a husband, that she could depend on. Not some *teacher*."

"That's your father talking, Percy."

"I suppose."

"The Warner men all come from arranged marriages."

"Yes, I know."

"Had you come home from Stanford, I'd have tried to find a match for you. Someone from New York, someone who suited you."

Percy's face hardened. "Yes."

"I arranged your brother John's match. Then his fiancée decided it wasn't for her at the last minute."

"John told me *he* couldn't go through with it. I spoke with him right after Christmas."

Gigi gave him a knowing look. "The young lady in question spent more time with your mother and I planning the wedding than with John."

Percy looked at her sharply, the point not lost on him. "She felt neglected?"

Gigi nodded. "She did."

Percy thought back to his last conversation with Kate. "And lonely."

Gigi, her point now sinking in, nodded again. "Yes."

"And she called it off?"

"With two weeks to spare, I believe."

The muscle in Percy's jaw was working now. "I see."

"Kate is a strong young woman."

His face softened. "She is."

"She understands you."

A smile touched the corners of Percy's mouth and he looked down at his hands for a moment. "Yes, she does. Quite well."

"She would make a lovely wife, a good companion," Gigi paused and allowed her next comment to simmer for a moment, "and a good mother figure for Edgar."

Percy's shoulders sagged, as if finally being able to expose the part of him that he'd hidden since they'd arrived in Virginia. "She is all those things, yes."

"There's only one question you should be asking yourself right now, Percy. Do you love her?"

He turned to Gigi, his face soft and so much like the Percy she knew and loved as a child. "I do."

"Then, my dear, what are you waiting for?"

He thought of Kate and Edgar and Matt back at Carrie's house, thought of the last telegram Edgar had sent, hinting that all was not well with Kate. He thought of Kate's bravery and her strength, not just in the Wind Cave, but after the train crash. He thought of everything she'd been through that made her who she was. Everything that made her the woman he wanted beside him for the rest of his life, made her the woman he wanted to bear his children and grow old with.

He realized he'd been silent a long time, and he looked down at Gigi quietly. "I don't know what I'm waiting for."

A smile touched Gigi's lips. "Neither do I." She lifted her left hand from her lap and with her right, removed the large, two-carat round diamond ring and examined it.

Percy shook his head. "No, Gigi."

There was a glimmer in her eye and she said, "I was twenty-two when I got this ring from your grandfather. Same age as Kate, I believe. Your mother always dreamed of having one of you boys give this ring to a woman. Dreamed of the day this ring would go on their finger at St. Paul's cathedral." She smiled at him. "I couldn't arrange a better match for you than Kate. Not if I live to be a hundred."

Percy looked at the ring she held out to him, and gingerly took it between his index finger and thumb. As much as it pained him to admit it, as much as he hated thinking in these terms, Matt had been right. He'd sent a boy – his brother – to do a man's job. His job. He'd sent his brother in his place to care for and look after Kate. He'd been so busy trying to build a future that he'd gone against reason, against his better judgment, and let the woman he'd fallen in love with walk away.

After walking someone else's path for so long, he was afraid to forge forward with his own dreams. Afraid, but excited. His future, for once in his life, was a blank page in front of him. It terrified him. All except for one thing. Slipping the ring into his pocket, he raised his eyes to Gigi.

"Will you do something for me, Gigi?"

"Anything, my boy."

"Will you kindly tell Uncle Thomas that I won't be coming into the lab today?"

"I will."

He pulled his tie from around his neck. "I have a train to catch."

CHAPTER TWENTY-SIX

The sound of rain and thunder woke me on the couch with a start. My arm was draped over Matt, who was sitting on the floor next to me asleep, his head back against the couch. A clap of thunder rattled the window and I bolted upright, the blanket falling away from me. Thunder. It was only thunder. My heart was beating wildly and I tried to lie back against the pillows on the couch.

Thunder sounded again and this time I put my fingers in my ears. It sounded so much like—

Matt pulled one of my fingers out of my ear. "What's wrong?"

"Nothing, I ..."

A clap of thunder sounded and I cringed.

"You're not afraid of a little rainstorm, are you?"

"Matt," I said, and I actually felt a little sick to my stomach, "the thunder sounds...I can't, um, describe it, but it sounds like..."

Lightning flashed outside and I shut my eyes tight as the sound of thunder boomed from overhead. A little cry escaped my lips and he was up on his knees next to me in a heartbeat.

"Move over."

"What?"

He pulled the cushions out from behind us on the couch. "Move. Over."

I moved to the side and he crawled underneath the blanket next to me. One arm went underneath my neck and the other over my waist. As if our bodies had a memory, he separated his legs so I could slide mine between them. I could feel his pulse against my cheek.

"Relax."

Thunder sounded again and I thought I was going to die. "Oh, God." I gritted my teeth and shook my head. "It's not real. It's not real."

Matt pulled back from me and looked hard into my face. "It's you and me. No one else. Listen to the sound. Tell me what happened. Get it out."

"Are you crazy? No!"

"Shhh," he said. "Listen. Trust me, okay?"

Another clap of thunder boomed overhead. "I can't, Matt."

"Yeah, you can."

We lay against each other, silent for a moment, the rain beating down outside. He reached up and turned off the light above us next to the couch and smoothed the hair back from my forehead. "You're sitting on the train," he began for me.

"Matt," I said, "please. I can't."

He placed his lips on my forehead. "You have to. I'm right here."

I took one horrible, deep breath.

"You're on the train," he said, and waited.

"And I'm reading a letter. From Carlie. Then we hear this..." my heart began to beat faster, "explosion. Like...thunder."

He rubbed his arm gently against my hip. "Okay. An explosion. Then what?"

"And...I...our car kind of shifted, like...tipped. And I see Edgar. And Sasha and Phillip..."

"Who?"

"Gigi's cook and butler. They had been with her forever."

"Okay. You see them what? What are they doing?"

"They're...Sasha's crying. She's screaming. Phillip's got his head between his knees."

Matt's voice was soft and his hands stroke against my arm. "What are *you* doing?"

"I was...pushing. Pushing against the seat in front of me with my legs. And then...then our car hits the ground. Everything is so loud." I blinked in the darkness, remembering. "It's...so loud, Matt. You can't imagine. Everyone was screaming. Glass shattered...from everywhere."

"Your legs."

"Yes."

"So it's on the side. The train car."

"We slid for maybe a few hundred feet or so. I don't know. Then everything happened so fast. I look over and...Gigi isn't moving. Sasha is... she's dead. Phillip too. Edgar is screaming for us to help him."

Matt hadn't counted on this. On hearing this and actually feeling something for Percy, or Edgar.

"People were crawling out of the windows. Then I hear..." A sob died in my throat.

"Go on, Katie."

"I...I can't."

We were quiet for a minute. I could still hear the screams in my head.

"You're here," He said, his voice, gentle against my hair. "You're safe, and nothing's coming through that door to hurt you."

I nodded, but didn't believe him.

"And then you hear...?" he prompted.

My words came out in a near sob. "Machine guns. Outside. They're... they're killing people, Matt. Executing them. The people that survived the crash and climbing out the windows are being shot."

His arms tightened around me, as if he could shield me from what I had seen.

"It doesn't stop. And it's everywhere. They're firing rounds. And this... it sounds so sickening. So different than you think it's gonna sound like. So scary. Then we get Gigi and Edgar. I knew that we had to hide them. I'm bleeding pretty badly, and I smeared my blood all over Edgar and Percy."

Tears slid down my cheeks and I shook my head against Matt's caress. "We draped ourselves over seats so it looked like...we're lying there like we're dead. And we hear them." I covered my mouth with my hand and shook my head. I couldn't say it out loud.

"Hear who?"

"Single shots. They're...executing people. Outside our car."

"Jesus Christ."

My body shook. I wept horrible, silent sobs against Matt's chest and he kissed my head and held me. He didn't say anything, waiting for me to continue.

"Then we hear this soldier...he jumps onto our car. You can feel the weight of him walking from one end to the other." I waited for another clap of thunder, but the only sound was the pounding rain. "I'm waiting for him to start shooting us. To hear machine gun fire. Anything. He just jumps off the train car and...we wait." I sniffed and the lightning flashed outside once again.

"How long did you wait?"

"I don't know. An hour maybe? More?"

I could hear the loud beating of his heart.

"When I got out to look around..." I remembered the scene. The horrible, senseless, catastrophic loss of life I'd seen when I emerged from the train car. "I just see bodies. Everywhere. They'd shot them....c-coming out of windows...and..."

Matt stroked my hair and held me until, finally, the tears stopped flowing. The thunder sounded again, but I didn't cringe.

"You are so brave. You're the bravest person I know."

"No. Bravery is acting in the face of fear knowing the situation you're up against. We were nothing more than lucky. That's all. I've wondered every day what would have happened if our car hadn't tipped. We'd have gotten out, and we'd be...we'd be dead. Lying on the ground there with everyone else. Me and Percy, Edgar, Gigi..."

Matt kissed my forehead. "But you're not."

"No," I said. "I'm not."

"That's what you see in the nightmares?" Matt asked.

"I see them. All of them. Those dead bodies. Everywhere around me. Lying there. Usually I'm being chased or...shot, or I can't escape."

"You're safe now. You escaped. You're here with me."

The thunder clapped once more, though not as loud, and my body sagged, as though having been through a war in the twenty minutes since I'd told him about the train. We lay there against each other, his arms around me, and I wondered if I'd relive it again that night, trapped in the same nightmare... forever.

The rain was still coming down when I awoke, although the thunder and lightning had long since passed. Matt was damned near lying on top of me, his body heavy and relaxed in sleep against mine. Our legs were tangled around each other, and his arms were still wrapped around me from last night. I allowed myself to close my eyes for one second more and pretend that no time had passed. That I hadn't left Matt in Los Altos. As if the last few months had been a bad dream—the train crash, the invasion— as if all of the pain was just gone. I sighed. I couldn't do it. Because letting go of the last few months meant letting go of my time with Percy. And I could never do that.

It was late morning, and the fact that Charlie hadn't gotten up yet was a miracle. Matt stirred against me, mumbling in his sleep. He had always been a light sleeper. He was also big on talking in his sleep, but not really anything you can understand. On more than one occasion, I'd listened to him talk about a car he wanted, closing arguments of the last case he'd been working on in college, and finally –my personal favorite – the lyrics to his favorite song. He vehemently denies this habit although I threatened him with a tape recording when we were together. This morning, his face relaxed, he was mumbling incoherently and moved a hand down to my backside. Knowing Charlie or Carrie would be getting up at any minute, I attempted to reach back and move his hand but succeeded only in pressing more tightly against him. At which he groaned. Loudly.

"Shhh!" I said and held my finger against his lips. "Matt, wake up."

"Kate," he whispered, still ninety percent asleep. "Mmm. Horrible dream."

"Yes, I had a horrible dream," I said. "Now you have to get up."

"Okay," he said, eyes still closed. His lower body, unlike the rest of him, was beginning to wake up, and I knew I was going to be in a very big mess if I didn't get the situation under control immediately.

"Matt..." I half pleaded, half hissed, "please."

"Love it when you beg me." He pushed his hands under my shirt.

This was not working out well. All I needed was for either Carrie or Charlie to come in and see this, and I would have a lot of explaining to do.

"Matt!"

"Yes?" he said, becoming more awake. "Oh, Kate, I love it when you call my name."

He pushed his face against my cheek to gain access to my neck. Butterflies fluttered in my stomach. "Say my name again," he urged, and his mouth opened over mine.

My body, was coming to life, in ways it wasn't supposed to be. "Matt," I said, and he groaned, his breath hot against my neck. I moved one of his hands and the other slipped inside the back of my shorts. "Knock it off!" I said and pushed him.

"Oh God, I want you."

"Stop this! We ca—"

His mouth was warm and covering mine before I could finish my sentence. His legs, already entwined around mine, pushed between my knees and he rolled on top of me. Our bodies fit together incredibly well, and he was determined to make me remember exactly how well. His hips held me against the couch and I gasped at the feeling of him. Matt was awake. In every sense of the word. My thin blue pajamas were almost as bad as having no barrier at all and he deepened his kiss. Wearing only his boxers and an undershirt, Matt was determined to make me remember how good it felt to be against each other. Unfortunately, my body was remembering.

"Oh God, Matt..."

He kissed me again. "I know."

My resolve was weakening. "I'm..."

His mouth covered mine and he took my lower lip into his mouth. Unfortunately, the moan that I heard was my own.

"You feel so good." His hands were all over me, his breath hot against my neck, and the length of him was pressing against me. Reaching down between us, he took my hand and placed it underneath his shirt, against the hard line of his chest. This, I remembered.

"Kate, I've wanted you for so long."

It was on the tip of my tongue to respond. To tell him that I'd wanted him as well. That I needed him. That I needed to feel him against me. I pulled my hands away, gripped his shoulders, and pushed him away. Hard.

"Ow!" Finally, he rolled to the side and I moved a few inches from him. "What the...what was that for?"

I looked at his face. Finally, it had dawned on me what was missing. "Because if we have sex right now," I said, "I won't be having it with you."

"You've lost me."

Not looking at him, I said, "It would be your hands and your lips and your..."

He leaned in towards me again, but my hand on his chest stopped him.

"It would be Percy that I was with, in my mind."

And suddenly, everything stopped.

CHAPTER TWENTY-SEVEN

"Wh…what?" Matt pulled away as if I'd burned him. His chest was heaving and his face was flushed. He raised his head and looked at me in the eyes. "Were you thinking about *him*? When we were…?"

I nodded and he swore under his breath. I could tell he was trying to rationalize what had just happened.

"Kate, what's going on with us?" He rolled to the side away from me. "One minute we're kissing like we're seventeen. The next you're sending telegrams to…" He blew out a breath. "I tell you I've got this plan for us, and you haven't said anything! We've cleared the air about what happened in Los Altos. I'm not sure what else I can do to—"

"It isn't about clearing the air between us."

"Then what the hell is it about?"

"You told me about *your* plan," I said. "But I don't think your plan is what I want."

"How can you say that?" He was looking down at me, his face registering pain.

"Because it's not. Because I want more than simply being a wife and mother." Saying it out loud, I knew that I was finally ready to forge ahead in my life, even if it meant I did it alone.

"Would you want it if I was *Percy*?" I knew how much it physically pained him to ask the question and for once, I was ready to answer it.

"No." Staying in Percy's shadow as the perfect *Warner wife* wasn't going to work for me. Not in the long run. And lying there next to Matt, I knew it. "I know that we've kind of danced around this issue for the last two weeks," I said, "but really, it doesn't come down to who I care more for— you or Percy.

I care for both of you. And I hate myself for admitting it out loud, but there it is."

He made a scoffing noise that I ignored.

"What it comes down to is what I choose. And I guess it took these last three weeks out here, close to my, well, my *family,* to figure it out."

"And what do you choose?" he asked gravely.

I sighed. "I love it here, and being with Carrie and Charlie. To me, this will always be home. But it's not where I want to end up. It's not where I want to be. So, I choose *me.* I've never done that before. My college chose me; they offered me a scholarship. Percy chose me to come to Wind Cave with him. I've been a passenger my whole life." I slid an arm around him, wondering if he would recoil. He didn't. "I followed you to Los Altos because I was afraid. Of losing my family, of losing what we all had. Before that month I'd never had friends that felt like a family before."

"Yeah, I know."

"I think I just wanted to hold onto it a little longer. However, I lost a little bit of myself in the process. That's something I can't afford to lose anymore. I have to choose what's right for *me,* even if it means losing the things I've been fighting so hard to keep. Staying with you means I can't do all the things I need to do to be me, which means we won't work out. Not in the long run."

"I could go back to a city. Finish law school?" His eyes raised to me hopefully.

I shook my head and touched his jaw with my index finger. "You wouldn't be happy. Not for long. Seeing you here, I think you're more at home here than anywhere I've seen you before."

He nodded. "Yeah. I am."

"You've found yourself. You're ready to start the home and the kids, and I'm still searching. I'm not sure if med school is it for me. I'm twenty-two, and I have time."

"And Percy?"

"Percy is...changing. I don't know who he is anymore. He's so distant all the time."

"But you love him. Edgar said you're going to marry him."

I laughed softly. "Edgar is fifteen. And he's very protective. I have a new family that accepts me, that wants me as a part of it." He winced and I knew I'd hurt him. "Sorry, Matt."

"S'okay. I know what you meant."

"But I can't stay with Percy just because I care for his family."

"And you've been hopelessly in *love* with him for three years?"

"I wouldn't have put it exactly like that."

"You could use the word *once*, you know. It wouldn't kill you to say it. Just once."

"I get that."

"It's kind of true."

"He's been such a part of me for so long. When I'm without him, I feel…"

"Like you're missing half of your heart," he finished. I looked into his eyes and knew that he was telling me how he felt about us.

"I don't want you to think that I don't care for you, or that I don't want to be with you, Matt."

"Just not as much as Percy."

"When I was with you in Los Altos," I said, "some days all I thought about was him. And that's not right."

"Wow. That's…hard to hear."

"I'm sorry."

"When you're with him do you…did you think of me?"

I smiled and touched his face. "I care for you so much. Of course I thought about you."

A knowing look covered his face and he nodded. "But not in the same way."

I shook my head slowly. "No. Not in the same way."

"I thought he was paying more attention to his work than you lately."

"He is. And when he's working all the time, I feel like I don't even know him anymore." "Have you talked to him about it?"

"Yeah. A little, before we left."

"I can't believe I'm about to say this, but Percy's been through a lot, too. He lost his parents. And his brothers."

I pushed against him and looked into his face, my mouth open. "Are you actually defending Percy?"

"No. I'm saying that hearing you tell me last night about the train crash, I see why he stayed behind."

I drew my brows together. "You do?" He nodded. "Enlighten me."

"He feels responsible. For dragging you there, for the train crash, for everything. And he's trying to make it right. Settling into a career, trying to make, a life."

"How do you know that?"

"Because," he said, closing his eyes and sighing, "that's how I'd feel, if I was a jackass like Percy."

I chuckled and slapped him lightly. "Nice."

"I didn't say I wanted to be lifelong friends with the guy. I said I might understand where he's coming from."

"Well, unfortunately, that life he's building isn't for me. I want *him*, but I don't want that life. Him in a lab twelve hours a day, never talking, never seeing each other. Being the perfect *Warner* wife, the perfect *Warner* mother. That's not for me."

"You gonna tell Percy that?"

"Yeah. When I get back to Virginia."

"Where're you gonna go from there?"

"I don't know. I've got some money left. Not sure if I want to go back to med school, or do medical research. I'm not really sure."

"Well, until you figure it out, would you consider coming back here?"

"I'd be treading water, Matt. And misleading us both."

He sighed, then, "Kate?"

"Yeah?"

"Does this mean we're not gonna have sex?"

I giggled and kissed him, hard. "Yes. That's what it means."

CHAPTER TWENTY-EIGHT

When Carlie awoke the next morning, the familiar sounds of a hospital around her, she pretended it had all been a bad dream. That she would wake up and be back in the trauma center at Bellevue. That everyone she'd worked with for all those months would still be alive. That David would be coming into the on-call any minute to rouse her and complain she was laying down on the job. That she hadn't had gone into battle and taken a life.

Some mornings were easier than others. She could keep her eyes closed and imagine for over an hour; dream about what she would tell David when she saw him, and how he would look. Other mornings were impossible. Since this wasn't a civilian hospital, there was no privacy. A curtain was all that separated her from the sounds coming down the hall or passing by out in the CSH. If a heavy load of traumas came in, the screaming and barking of orders was impossible to concentrate over and she longed for the end of the week so that she could finally leave here and be somewhere to think. To grieve. And then, remembering John's offer on his visit last night, she opened her eyes.

Carlie had considered contacting her uncle. There had been no activity in Denver from what the soldiers around her had said. It was contacting him and getting there that presented the problems. She had no address to send or receive a letter at. She could send a telegram, but he'd still have to mail her money for the ticket. With the mail system the way it was, it could take three weeks or more to get a letter back. She'd sent a letter to Kate. At first Carlie was thinking that Kate would come to her, bring her money, take her to Denver where she'd be safe. Then she heard of the attacks on the East Coast and decided she couldn't ask Kate to endanger her life like that. And again, how would she receive help with no address?

She was stuck in a hopeless situation, and here was this doctor – that she hardly knew – offering her his home, his family, and his protection, asking nothing in return. She could use his address to write a letter to her uncle, get a response, and then travel to Denver; have the baby there. Alone. Tears squeezed out of the corners of her eyes and she wiped them away. She had been crying a lot in the last week and a half and she was sure it was mostly from the stress. The shock. The hormones. Everything.

A doctor came in, dressed in surgical scrubs, a mask on his face. "Jane Doe?"

She sighed. "No, I'm not a Jane Doe."

The doctor pulled her chart from the end of her bed. "Says here Jane Doe."

"I realize that, but it was changed. The Army hasn't changed it over yet from when I was loaded on the MEDEVAC." She wiped the tears away with the back of her hand.

"You were wounded in battle?"

"Yes. If you'd just read the chart, doctor, it—"

"In a firefight?"

She looked up in irritation at the doctor examining the chart. "It says so right there, Doctor."

He gave her a non-committal sound. "Jane, what was a civilian doctor doing in a combat zone under heavy artillery fire?"

"I told you, I'm not—"

"Didn't your attending teach you," he said, setting down her chart, "to duck..." he pulled off his surgical mask and threw it on the bed, "drop..." he came to sit next to her, "and roll?"

For a moment, Carlie couldn't speak.

"Say something," he said, a smile on his face.

"You're not real," Carlie said staring at him. "I'm dreaming. I'm still asleep."

David reached his hand up to touch Carlie's face. "No. You're not."

She backed away, positive she was having a delusional episode.

"Carlie," David said softly, and he leaned forward, his hand outstretched.

The second his hand touched her, she grabbed it, clutching to it as if her life depended on it. She kissed the palm of his hand, tears wetting his fingers as the threaded them through her hair. Careful of her bandaged shoulder, he leaned forward on the sides of her bed to embrace her.

"They told me everyone..."

He nodded solemnly. "Shhhh."

"How...?" She still didn't believe it was him, but her free hand dug into his shoulder blade like a vise. She wasn't going to let him go.

He kissed her on the cheek and neck over and over. She turned her face to his, her lips kissing anything that was within her reach.

"Carlie?"

"What?" She moved her cheek to rest against his, but she didn't release him.

"You actually have to let me go. My shoulder is about to fall off."

"Sorry," she said, and they both laughed. She took him in with her eyes, shaking her head in disbelief. Reluctantly, she released her grip on him, and he sat back on the edge of her bed. "I could look at you forever, David."

"I'm here."

"I'm never letting you out of my sight again."

She reached her hand towards him and touched him, to make sure she wasn't going to wake up and find him gone. He was wearing the same scrubs he'd worn the last time she saw him and he hadn't shaved.

"I'm going to hold you to that." He pulled her chart from where he'd tossed it. "The things a girl will do to impress her attending."

"Where the hell were you!" she said, her voice high.

He took her hand and kissed each knuckle in succession. "Got pulled out of x-ray by a soldier. He said there was one transport left and I was the only one still in the building."

"What the hell were you doing in x-ray?"

"Getting some films for the private that came in with a shattered sternum."

She sniffed. "Oh."

"They pulled me out of x-ray and threw me in the back of the last transport with them."

She listened intently to him, so glad that he wasn't letting go of her hand.

"We didn't make it more than ten miles before we came under enemy fire. They hit the transport and we had to make it out behind the hot zone on foot."

"That's where you've been?"

He nodded, his face tired. "The last three days we spent holed up in a building, trying to get out."

She slid her hand up to his face. "Some attendings will do anything to impress the new residents."

"Speaking of impressing people, I met a friend of yours."

"A friend?"

"That's how I found you. Major Phillips?"

"John?"

"John? Hmm. I don't know him as John, but I met Major Phillips last night as he was coming into the Med Ward on Command 4. I was getting our soldiers that had been wounded getting out of ground zero situated."

"I was with John when...it happened."

He looked again at her chart. "Multiple GSW to the shoulder, thigh, and side. Shattered clavicle, fractured femur..." his face darkened. "I went crazy when he told me. "Why the hell didn't you get out of there? Why didn't you take the transport with Maria and Ynez?"

"David, the transport that took Maria and Ynez, everyone, their command post was attacked that night."

A blank look covered his face for a moment and then he ran a hand over his face. "No. Oh my God."

"They told me," she began to cry again and her hands started to shake, "that my whole unit had been...that there were no survivors. What was I supposed to think!"

"I didn't know," he said, over and over, and leaned in to kiss her again, gently. "I didn't know."

"If I would have been with them..."

He crushed her to him, causing a small yelp to come out of her mouth.

"Oh God! I'm so sorry."

She tucked a strand of hair behind her ear. "It's fine. I'm getting better."

"Major Phillips told me what you did."

"Which part? The part where I got shot or the part where I killed someone with your gun?"

"The part where you saved men's lives."

"I think I missed that part."

"He told me you spun and fired. Emptied the clip."

"I can't stop thinking about it."

He nodded. "I know."

She looked up at him for the answers that only he could give her. "Will I ever forget?"

He knew what she wanted him to say, what she needed him to say. But he couldn't lie. Not to her. "No. You won't. But it will get less and less."

He placed his hand on her abdomen. "And here?" Their eyes met and she smiled. "How are we doing here?"

"He's good."

"He! Oh, you're already convinced it's a boy, huh?"

"Well, he's caused so much trouble, I figure it's gotta be a boy."

He grinned at her. "Sorry it took me so long."

Her eyes welled up with tears again. "Don't ever leave me again."

"Don't worry," he said. "I'm not going anywhere."

True to his word, David stayed with her, sitting on her hospital bed throughout the day, never going further than his arm could reach. A nurse came in to change her dressings around dinner. She looked over at David, who was watching the nurse carefully.

"David, would you..." she closed her eyes, "turn around?"

He walked over to her right side. "Why?"

"Because it's awful." The tears came again, and David knew it was mostly hormones and the emotional roller coaster she'd been on for the last few weeks. "Now I'm going to be scarred and—"

David looked over to the nurse. "I've got this."

"Wha...what are you doing?"

David took the scissors from the nurse's hand. "This," he said, the pain evident in his voice, "is my penance. For being so selfish that I kept you with me." He cut through the top four layers and peeled the tape off the perimeter of the dressing. "I have to see what I've caused." He pulled back the lump of dressing from her shoulder.

Nothing could have prepared him for the sight of her wound. A bright red mark the size of a silver dollar surrounded by purple and blue skin. The bullet entrance was still angry and red, and the back of her shoulder looked like she'd been sawed in half where the bullets had exited. She averted her eyes from his as he eased her forward and cleaned the wound, applied more antibiotic cream, and re-dressed it. He repeated his inspection on her leg and then her side; checking the stitches for discharge, heat, redness and infection. Finding none, he cleaned the wounds and re-dressed them then she leaned back against her pillows.

He didn't look up at her for a long moment. "Carlie, I'm so sorry."

"Me, too," she said.

He choked back a sob. "What do you have to be sorry for?"

She reached for his hand and kissed it, placing it against her cheek before replying. "I lost your gun."

CHAPTER TWENTY-NINE

That afternoon, all sitting on the couch or on the floor, the men surrounded the radio, waiting to hear any new news about the fighting. Ano, Carrie, and I, talking quietly, fell silent when the announcer's voice came on.

"Today, we have received this recorded message from a secure location within the United States. We will play it for you now, in its entirety." A pause filled with dead air and then we listened with baited breath and the recording began to play.

My fellow Americans. I speak to you today from the newly relocated command center here within the United States. My deepest regrets on the losses that many of you have suffered in these last few months. The battle that we have waged has not been without serious consequences...or sacrifices. For the first time in almost three hundred years, a war has been fought on American soil. Unlike the Revolutionary War, where we fought for our right to be heard, to be represented, this war has been about survival. Survival of our way of life, survival of our ideals and dreams. Much as it was with the Revolution, we have learned that these ideals and dreams come only when its people are committed to its ability to endure .

"We, as Americans, banded together across the country to fight back the oppressive force that attacked us with such violence and lack of provocation. We have, even now, reports of civilians who – at great personal risk – joined together with our military to further our cause. In what was certainly the darkest time in U.S. history, our military was aided by the skills of men and women – Americans – who were willing to make the ultimate sacrifice to preserve the sanctity of who we are, and who we will continue to be as a country.

"Two days ago, I issued an executive order that any and all foreign vessels or personnel occupying U.S. air, land, or waterways would be destroyed if not removed within twenty-four hours. Unfortunately, that order was not taken with the gravity with which it was issued. As we speak, three large weapons ships have been fired upon and sunk off the coast of New York. Two more vessels were destroyed off the coast of California by our Navy only hours ago. For the first time in U.S. history, I have authorized the use of nuclear weapons to be used on American soil to drive out the insurgents that still occupy much of our country.

"The message that has been sent out today is clear: the United States will not tolerate these terrorist acts. We will destroy the forces that have invaded our borders. We will drive them from our lands and our waters and, when necessary, eliminate them completely if our warnings go unheeded. For, when you see the shores of America, you will see us as a one and united people. When you see the lands that have been ravaged, you will not see a people defeated. You will see us rise up with our heads held high saying 'We will survive. We will overcome.'

"I speak to you tonight as a neighbor who sits by you, waiting for the war to end. I speak to you as a fellow American who has suffered grievous losses, as you have. I speak to you as one angered by the acts of terror but emboldened by our response. I speak to you no longer hiding from those who threaten to assassinate our members of government. I speak to you as your leader, Commander in Chief. I am the President of the United States. Good night, and God Bless America."

For at least thirty seconds after the end of the transmission, we were all completely quiet. Jazz leaned forward and switched off the radio, and Ano walked over to sit on his lap. Matt, leaning forward with his elbows resting on his knees, looked up to me, and I smiled at him.

"Well," Charlie said finally, getting up from his chair, "sounds like we're at least fighting back now."

"I think we were fighting back before," Jazz said. "We just weren't hearing about it."

"Nuclear weapons," Carrie said quietly, "within U.S. borders. Never thought I'd see the day."

"He wouldn't do it unless he had to, Mother," Charlie said, and walked to her, touching her cheek lightly. I don't think I'd ever seen a tender moment like this between them.

"Do you think we can go home now?" Edgar asked me.

"I don't think it's safe to travel yet, Edgar."

"Well, more fighting or not," Carrie said, "I best get the roast on. Girls?"

Ano kissed Jazz and got up to join me in the kitchen.

"Katie, can you cut us some bread?" Carrie asked. "I think we still have a half loaf."

"Actually," I said, walking toward the bread box, "we'll need a fresh loaf. We only have a few pieces left over from the last one."

"Really?" she asked, peeking over to where I stood from the cutting board.

"I had a snack earlier today."

"Okay, honey. Get a fresh one."

I reached for the bread knife and the new loaf in front of me.

"Ano, do we have any more of those carrot slices?" Carrie asked.

"Oh, sorry Carrie," I said with an embarrassed laugh. "I got hungry last night and ate them. Want me to cut more?"

Edgar's face shot to Carrie's and she turned hers quickly.

Charlie saw the exchange and looked from one to the other. "What's that all..." Carrie shook her head sharply at Charlie. "What?. I can't ask what—"

I turned around and looked at Ano and Carrie. "What's wrong?"

"Nothing, honey," Carrie said. "Eat as much as you want. We'll cut more carrots."

Jazz and Matt, sitting on the couch, leaned in towards Edgar curiously. "What's going on?" Jazz asked.

I looked at Carrie's face, to Edgar's, to Ano's. "What's this about? You guys, is there something I should know about the carrots?"

"No. You seem awfully hungry lately is all."

"Edgar," Carrie warned.

"Holy crap!" Jazz said. "Kate, are you—"

Matt's face blanched. "Kate, no."

"What?" I asked, looking at all of them at once.

As if on cue, a knock sounded at the door and Charlie crossed the room to open the door. "Somebody better tell me what's goin' on."

"Edgar," Carrie warned again, and Edgar stood, followed by Matt, who looked like he was going to faint.

"We're just worried about you." Carrie said gently.

"Because I ate the carrots?"

Jazz laughed and looked to Ano. "Why didn't you tell me!"

Ano's face was pale and her hand was at her throat. "Kate, did you take a test without telling me?"

"Ano!" I said, looking around the room, "Shut up!"

"Oh my God," Matt said. "Oh my God."

Charlie stepped aside, and a very wet Percy entered the room and dropped his duffel down by the door.

"Percy!" Edgar ran to his brother and embraced him.

Having heard half of the conversation coming through the door, Percy kept his eyes on me. His hair was in dark, wet curls all over his head and his clothes were soaking wet.

He looked down at Edgar, who now stood by his side. "Apparently, I've missed something," he said, the meaning not lost on at least three people in the room. He turned to Edgar. "Got your telegram."

Edgar nodded solemnly. "I'm glad you came."

"Edgar," I said, moving a step closer, "what did you say to him?"

"Apparently, not enough," Percy said sternly. He placed a hand on Edgar's shoulder. "Is this what you were talking about?"

"Yes. But I couldn't tell you the rest."

"Edgar," Carrie said, louder this time, "don't!"

His eyes were apologetic. "I'm sorry, Kate."

"Percy," I began.

"Percy, Kate's pregnant," Edgar interrupted.

"What? No!" I screeched. "Edgar—"

"I heard you!" he protested. "Outside the cot—"

"You were listening to that?" Ano yelled at him.

"Carrie sent me out to get you!" he explained. "I didn't mean to hear!"

"Kate," Matt said. "Why didn't you tell me? You said—"

"Is that why you've been acting so weird?" Jazz asked.

Ano squealed. "Kate, girl, why didn't you tell me?"

"Everyone, calm down," Carrie said, her words lost among the other six voices talking in the room.

Percy and I, our eyes locked amidst everyone else talking loudly, were quiet.

Charlie's whistle echoed through the room, deafening everyone and making the room silent within seconds. "Everybody, shut up!"

Matt took a step towards me, and Percy stopped him with a hand to his chest. "You were right. This *is* a man's job." Their eyes locked and Percy stepped in front of him, towards me. "And I'm here to do it."

Percy walked over and stood in front of me. "We need to talk."

He took me by the hand and led me out back, towards the cottage. The rain soaked my hair within seconds and by the time we entered the cottage, I was as drenched as he was.

He closed the door behind us and I reached for the light. "No, leave it off."

I came to him, reaching up to touch his face and hair, which were dripping wet. "How did you get here? Why didn't you tell me? We would have come and picked you up."

"I caught a ride at the station. No time for telegrams by the time I got on the train."

I looked at his face, so perfect. "Percy."

He leaned towards me, his forehead touching mine. Shrugging off his jacket, he let it drop to the floor and I ran my hands over his shoulders.

"I missed you," I said.

His face showed relief at hearing it and he led me over to sit on the edge of the bed. "I missed you, too."

I sighed at the sound of hearing him admit something so tender. After not being with him, *really* with him, for over three weeks and missing him terribly for the two weeks before that, I badly needed to touch him.

I touched his face, his hair, and he turned his face to kiss my hands as I did. His hair fell in loose, wet curls and I ran my hands through it. I wanted to melt into his arms and have him tell me the last month was all a bad dream. I settled for opening my mouth against his and tasting his lips.

"Kate, wait." He slid his hands to my waist and held me gently. "Do you have something you want to tell me?"

"No."

"Kate," he said, "I want you to...please. I just want to know."

"Percy, Edgar's wrong. I'm not pregnant."

"Then why did Ano say something about you taking a test?"

"Because I'm late. But it's stress. From the train ride and everything else." I didn't want to add this, but felt like it was the right time, so I took a chance. "Of feeling so distanced from you."

"That happens when you run thousands of miles away."

"That's not it."

He nodded, a small smile at the corner of his mouth. "I know."

I couldn't help myself. I ran my hands through his wet hair again and down to his shirt. It was unbuttoned at the top and I kissed the base of his neck. "I swear," I reiterated against his skin. "I'm not." I could tell he was weakening against my advances.

"But you *have* taken a test?"

"No, but—"

"Kate," he said, closing his eyes in frustration.

"Percy, I'm fine."

Finally relaxing a bit, he flicked his tongue against my jaw. I gasped and pressed against him. My fingers worked on the next few buttons on his shirt and I tried to kiss him but his mouth was working its way down my neck. He lowered his hungry mouth to my breasts. I wanted to taste him; needed to feel him.

"Tell me again how much you missed me," he said as he lowered me to the bed. I finished the last button on his shirt and stripped it from him, tossing it to the floor.

"I'm not going to *tell* you." Rolling over him, I slipped from the bed, stood, and unbuttoned my jeans, then removed the rest of my clothing. "I'm not going to *tell* you," I repeated, crawling on top of him and kissing my way from his stomach to the base of his throat. "I'm going to *show* you."

Between the two of us, we unfastened his jeans and he kicked them to the floor, his mouth never leaving mine. Gently, Percy touched me, whispering against my neck and mouth, until I begged him to give me what I needed.

Sliding his hand behind my knee he rolled, driving inside me, and I cried out with pleasure. Percy's hands were everywhere, touching me, caressing me. The rain got harder and beat down against the roof and sides of the cottage. I wrapped my calf around the outside of his, pulling him tighter against me.

"You're not playing fair," he gasped and closed his eyes in rapture.

"No," I said, my own breath ragged, "I'm not." Knowing it was the one thing I could do to drive Percy over the edge himself, I moved my hips against his until he called out my name and dug his fingers into my sides. He moved his hands up to my wrists and held them above my head, his thrusts faster until I arched my back, explosions coming from within me so hard I saw stars. Seconds later he came, calling out my name, covering my mouth with his until the beat inside us slowed.

We lay together, listening to the rain, and Percy reached over me to pull a quilt around us. Tucked up against his chest, smelling his skin, I was where I belonged. The rain had increased, and we listened to it, my arm draped over his chest and my head resting against his shoulder. The pulsing beat within me had faded and in its wake was rapture.

"I came here to...I need to tell you something."

"All right."

He exhaled. "I quit the lab."

A relieved sigh erupted from me, and quiet laughter came from my chest. I covered my mouth with one of my hands. "You did?" He nodded. "Why?"

"Because it caused something I love very much to go away."

I blushed, but the sound of him telling me he loved me made me smile. "But you love the lab. It's your dream."

"No," he said. "The lab was my *plan*. The plan my father laid out for me. When I went to Stanford... not *my* dream."

I was quiet for a moment, thinking. "But you said it was—"

"What I really want to do is be a teacher. A college professor."

We were silent for a minute and I smoothed a curl back that had fallen over his forehead. "Why didn't you say that, then?"

"Because," he said, "I was following someone else's idea of what I should be. What I should do to provide for my..." his eyes locked onto mine and he said the word, "family."

I flushed warm and smiled at him, moved closer to him and kissed his mouth.

"I want us to be a family, Kate. I want it so much."

Percy wanted me. All of me. Wanted me to be a part of his family.

"I need you to know, though," he said, holding me tight, "that I might not be able to give you what my father gave my mother. We won't have the Manhattan penthouse, or the—"

"Percy."

"...expensive cars...and perhaps not even—"

"Percy."

"...a house as large as my grandmother's."

"Percy! I never wanted any of that."

"You didn't?"

"No. All I wanted, all I have *ever* wanted...was you."

His arm tightened around me and his voice was low. "You have me. But..." he lowered his eyes for a moment, "do I have *you*?"

I knew what he was asking. The same question Matt had asked of me, and yet, now somehow different. "Percy, I don't know if I want to go back and do medical school or not."

He tucked a loose strand of hair behind my ear. "All right."

"And I don't know if research is what I'm suited for."

His face took on that look of concentration I had loved for over three years. "I see."

"In fact," I said, going a step further, "I'm not sure what I'm doing." I paused. "At all."

Despite my admission, a smile touched his lips. "You don't have to know right now," he said, touching my nose. "We have time."

His kiss was without reservation, without restraint, by far the most passionate I'd ever received.

Pulling slightly away, he held my face in his hands. "You still want me? Without money. Without—"

I pulled his mouth to mine again. "Yes."

"Then I need to give you something," he said against my lips.

I whispered seductively against his cheek, "I think you already did that."

"No," he said gently, and he looked down at me. "This is something else."

I wrapped my arms around his neck and kissed him again, barely able to breathe. He granted my request by opening his mouth, letting me taste him once more. In that fraction of a second, I knew. It was raw emotion, sweeping through me. And finally, like something long missing had snapped into place, I said it.

"Percy," I whispered as he lowered his mouth to my neck. "I...I love you."

He stopped instantly, pulling away from me, his face flushed with our kisses. "Say that again."

"I love you."

So often stoic, his eyes welled up with tears. "Kate, I need to ask you something."

"Yes?"

He shifted nervously. "I need you to sit on the edge of the bed."

"Um, all right." I was flustered, having never uttered those words to anyone, wondering if I'd done it wrong. I sat up, and Percy left me on the edge of the bed to wrap another quilt around himself.

He looked excited, nervous, and terrified all at once, searching the floor for his discarded jeans.

I looked down at him from my perch on the bed. "What are you doing?"

"I'm - oh, God. Normally, I'd have gone through your family, and...and all this would have been arranged." He swallowed nervously. "At least I'd have asked your father's permission, and we'd have had a – oh, this all would have been done before now. But..." his eyes came up to meet mine, and it suddenly dawned on me what he was about to do. And I began to shake my head.

"Kate, I've been thinking of what I'd say to you right now for the last twenty-four hours. Well, really, for the last four months."

My heart was going to explode from my chest.

"I lost three years with you because I was too blind to see you." He smiled and I realized I'd never seen Percy like this, almost giddy. "You know, Matt was right. The first time he told me about you. He said I didn't see your heart. He was right, I think. Because, Kate, I was in love with you for those three years. I was just too blind, or foolish, or scared to do anything about it. I'm not now."

Percy knelt in front of me, and this time he brought up one of his long legs so he was—literally— down on one knee. I smothered a giggle at the quilt wrapped around him and his half undressed state.

"Kate, I could ask Charlie for his permission. Really, though, this is *your* decision to make. I want to build a future with you. Although not me stuck in a lab with you lonely at home. I want to build a future. Together." He moved closer – no small feat considering he was down on one knee. "I've only loved one person in my whole life." He looked up at me in the darkness and for once, the look of intense concentration was gone. In its place was the look I'd only seen on his face a handful of times. The look I'd now come to know as *my* look. The one he only got with me. "I intend on being in love with that person for the rest of my life."

His eyes captured mine, as they always did when I looked right at them. His hands, shaking as he did so, reached into the pocket of his jeans and retrieved an enormous diamond ring mounted on a thin, white gold band. "Kate, will you marry me?"

AFTERWARD

"You look beautiful," Ano said, while Carlie twirled back and forth in front of the mirror. "Really. The most beautiful bride I've ever seen."

"Thank you."

"David's gonna flip when he sees you in that dress!" I added.

"Hope so!" Carlie gushed.

Ano and I stared at Carlie in the full-length mirror. "I can't believe you're getting married," I said.

Carlie turned towards me. "I'll see you in Philly in three weeks doing the same thing, Mrs. Warner!"

"The *future* Mrs. Warner," I corrected her, and Emily fussed from her playpen in the corner.

"I'm surprised you guys didn't fly!" she said to me, examining the back of the gown in the mirror as I crossed to Emily and picked her up.

"Percy still doesn't want to fly." I shrugged. "He's still nervous when I take the car to class every day."

"I know," Ano said. "Grandma got a car and Jazz is still nervous when she drives it after dark. Even around the seminary."

"Um, Carlie, where's Emily's bag?"

Carlie pointed to the large overstuffed chair in the corner of the bride's room. "There, why?"

I stood with Emily on my hip rummaging through the bag. "She's wet."

Carlie came towards me with her arms out.

"Uh uh!" both Ano and I said, stopping her.

"You wanna get baby diaper on that dress?" Ano said, motioning to the pristine white wedding dress she wore.

Carlie kissed Emily's hand as I walked by. "No."

"I've got her," I said.

Ano grimaced and pointed at me holding Emily. "For someone without the baby gene you sure got the touch."

"She's an easy one, isn't that right, Em?" One-year old Emily cooed on my shoulder and sucked on her hand. "Oh, Carlie, it's not in here."

She turned around and looked at everything at our feet. "Um, David has the other bag. Can you..."

"Got it."

"Thank you, Kate."

Ano grabbed at me as I was leaving. "Hang on, girl. You don't wanna go out there without being zipped up all the way."

I stood holding Emily while she pulled the sides of my dress together. "It's not...you gained weight since your last fitting?"

"No."

"Damn, girl! What the hell is wrong with this dress?"

"Just zip it, please."

After a few moments of tugging, inhaling, and cursing, the zipper went all the way up and I turned.

"Wow, Kate!" Carlie admired me in my bridesmaid dress. "That dress makes your, um, you look really great!"

Ano's eyes got wide and she covered a smile. "You're kind of bustin' out of it, though!"

"Yeah. Um, I'm gonna go get another diaper for Emily. I'll be right back."

Walking towards the far end of the church, I waved at Carlie's uncle and his friend Damon. I could hear the laughter and male voices as soon as I walked into the large room at the end of the corridor. Percy's baritone mixed with Jazz's, Matt's, and David's voices and I smiled at the sound.

"Hello?" I called, peeking around the corner.

"There she is!" David said, obviously not talking about me. He swooped down and reached to take Emily from my arms, but I turned the other way.

"Sorry, there. She, uh, needs a diaper. Save your tux."

"Oh." He looked around him. "Does Carlie have the bag?"

"She says you have it."

He held up a finger for me to wait and ran into the changing room for the other bag.

"Hey, Kate," Jazz said, hiding a smile.

"Hey."

"You look...oh, wow, Kate. You look good in that dress."

Matt slapped Jazz upside the back of his head.

"Matt, I saw Sarah inside." I smiled at him.

"Goin' somewhere with that?"

I kissed Emily's cheek. "Nope."

"Here, Kate," David said, handing me the bag. "Take the whole thing."

I slipped the bag over my shoulder and waved to the room with Emily's hand. "Bye, guys!"

Percy followed me out into the corridor. "You, uh, seem to have the touch with her."

My eyes lifted to his. "Well, let's hope that luck holds, right?"

Leaning in closely to me, he whispered in my ear, "You are driving me crazy in that dress." He reached out to caress my abdomen.

"Another week and I won't be able to zip this dress. My chest is about to explode out of it."

His eyes opened a little wider and he grinned wickedly at me. "I know."

I looked around and made sure no one was near us. "You keep looking at me that way, Mr. Warner, and I will have to notify my fiancée."

"Your fiancée is an idiot if he doesn't look at you this way."

I turned on my heel. "I'll let him know you think so."

I set Emily down on the couch to change her.

"Thank you, Kate." Carlie looked down at Emily, who was really fussing with her wet diaper. "Did Auntie Kate get you brand new panties?" She blew kisses to Emily, who, as soon as I took off the offending diaper, was happy as a lark. "Kate, have some champagne."

I finished folding up the old diaper and worked on closing the deal on the new one. "Oh, um, I'm gonna stick to water. I'm kind of parched. Thanks anyway." I looked around. "Where's Ano?"

Carlie stood looking at me for a second, a bottle of water in her hand and didn't answer right away. "She went to go see if Jazz had their camera." She paused. "Kate?"

"Yeah?" Clean diaper finally on, I pulled on the ruffled tights and bloomers of Emily's outfit and placed her back in her playpen then crossed to grab a bottle of water myself.

"Kate?" Carlie said again, and stood behind me, hand on her hip.

I sighed. "Yes?"

"Turn."

I turned to face her. "Yes?"

She tapped her shoe on the ground impatiently. "I've known you too long."

"Possibly why I chose you to be a bridesmaid in my wedding," I said, and smiled.

"Your dress is too tight." I shrugged. "And your boobs are huge!"

I turned and looked out the window.

"And—"

"Carlie, is this going somewhere?"

She smiled at me. "Your wedding is in three weeks."

I nodded. "Yeah."

She leaned in close to me. "And I'm a doctor."

I didn't say a word, but our eyes locked.

"Percy know?"

I nodded.

"He excited?"

I tried unsuccessfully to hide a smile. I couldn't keep this to myself anymore. Not from Carlie. "Jubilantly so."

"I knew it!" She jumped up and down, and Emily made loud gibberish noises from her playpen. "Oh, Mommy's sorry for yelling, baby!" she said. "So? How far along are you?"

"Eight weeks."

"Really? That's it? Cause your boobs are—"

"Yes. I know. Percy's been...admiring that benefit as well."

She lifted the train of her dress and sat on the large arm of one of the chairs in the room. "You feeling okay? Taking your prenatal—"

"I've got it. Trust me, Edgar now monitors everything that goes in and out of my mouth." In fact, Percy had gone so far as to make a chart before we left. Everything from my daily water intake to how much food I should be eating was tracked. I'd commented to Percy that I felt a little like a prize heifer and he and Edgar had both laughed.

"It's good to have someone keeping an eye on you," she reassured me with a pat on my hand.

"Um, let me clarify. I don't have *someone*? I have Edgar. And Percy. Which is worse than having the entire Marine Corps sitting over your shoulder forcing you to eat all the time."

Carlie's laugh was contagious and I joined in.

"I poured a cup of coffee for breakfast and I thought they were both going to come over the table and tear it from my hands."

"Well," she said, her doctor voice on, "one cup once in a while isn't going to hurt you or the baby."

I liked how she thought. And it gave me an idea. "You think you could tell Perce that?" I snapped my fingers. "Better yet! David! He's an OB, and he's a guy. Have David tell Percy that it's okay for me to drink coffee in the morning!"

"Gotcha covered," she said, her face completely aglow.

"Thanks."

She grinned, ear to ear. "It's great, you know. You and him?"

I looked up at her. "Is it still weird?"

"It was a little, in the beginning," she admitted. "Now it's not." A little smile tugged at the corner of her lips and she looked over at me. "Is it weird for you?"

"That one of my bridesmaids slept with my soon-to-be husband?"

Her laughter was loud and echoed through the bride's room. "Yeah."

"As long as ya don't do it again, I think we're good."

"Oh, hey. Does Ano know? About the baby, I mean."

"No. We found out a week ago."

"You haven't been sick?"

"Nope. I feel great, actually. Except for the fact that none of my shirts fit anymore and that I'm really tired all the time."

"That will pass. Another few weeks and you'll stop being so sleepy."

I laughed. "Thank God! I need more time to study."

"Did you tell Gigi?"

"Not yet. The only ones that know are Percy and Edgar."

"I can't believe you told Edgar."

"I had to!"

Edgar, my shadow, rarely allowed me to go anywhere without him. With Percy working on his PhD at Penn, and me finishing my Masters, we'd found time to "raise" Edgar through a private high school in Pennsylvania over the last two years in addition to planning a wedding. Granted, there had been little time for wedding planning over the last twenty months. Somehow, though, between Gigi's constant pushing and our schedules, we'd managed to pull it together.

"He excited? About being an uncle, I mean."

"Oh my God," I snickered. "He almost didn't let us come."

"I'm so happy for you guys."

I looked over to where Emily was now standing in her playpen, holding the side. "You and David gonna have more?"

Carlie dipped her head toward her midsection and I opened my mouth in surprise. "No way! Another one?"

"Well, Emily's a year old, and I found out a few days ago as well."

"Does David know?"

She laughed, the sound of it echoing through the room.

Ano reappeared. "What's so funny?"

My mouth was hanging open. "Carlie's pregnant again!"

Ano smiled widely and hugged her. "Congratulations! That's, wow. Oh wow. Two. So, you're gonna have two!"

Carlie shrugged. "David wants four."

"FOUR?" Ano said and made a face. "Aw, hell no!"

"I heard Jazz say last Christmas that he wanted four," I said, ribbing her.

Ano pursed her lips and inspected her nails. "Mmmhmm. And did you also hear that pimp slap upside his head right after he said it?" Carlie and I both laughed. "No, thank you. He's nearly done with seminary and I'm almost done with my Masters."

"You could finish the PhD and be pregnant," I said. "Happens all the time."

Carlie shot me a knowing look.

"Well," she said firmly, shaking her head, "it's gonna have to happen to someone besides me. I'm gonna have a practice within five years and then we'll talk about a baby!"

"Carlie and David have a practice," I persisted, "and they're gonna have *two*."

Ano put a hand on her hip. "Isn't it hard working with him all day and then going home with him at night?"

"We never see each other unless it's between patients or for a quick consult."

"Yeah, I see you've been *consulting* a lot lately!" I said, laughing.

"Can't help myself," Carlie grinned.

Ano grabbed a glass of champagne for herself and handed one to me. "I'm gonna stick with water for now," I said, shaking the bottle.

"Well, photographer's ready," Ano said, hugging Carlie again. "You are crazy. Four."

Carlie nodded towards me. "Percy came from a big family."

"Yeah," I admitted, "his mom had five boys, and Gigi had five boys."

"My girl here is not gonna have five. She's gonna wait like me," Ano said. "Till her PhD is D-O-N-E done."

Thinking of the baby growing inside me, I said, "All the Warner men have boys. Lots and lots of boys." I wasn't going to add this, but the thought of five little red-haired boys that looked exactly like Percy and Edgar running around didn't scare me as it once had. Remembering Edgar's face when Percy and I had told him, I knew what an amazing uncle he would be. I was going to have a *very* big family.

As if on cue, Emily squealed from her crib. I walked over and to pick her up and Carlie said, "No! Kate! Let Ano get her. She's much too heavy."

Ano looked at me, then Carlie. "She gain weight in the last fifteen minutes? She's not any heavier now than she was when Kate changed her diaper."

"No, it's..." Carlie faltered. "I just want you to hold her."

"Oh. Well, long as you don't expect me to follow suit?, I can do that."

"C'mon, Ano," Carlie said, changing subjects, "you and Jazz have been married two years."

"And her mom and grandma are *buggin'* her!" I said.

Ano took Emily from my arms and kissed her cheek. "Yeah, go on, both of y'all. I'm finishing my PhD before I have a child!"

I laughed and followed them out into the courtyard. If I'd done the math correctly, I would graduate with my Masters six months before I had the baby. And Percy had promised that I could go back and finish my PhD as well. He already had a job offer from Penn as a professor in their science department, but he'd applied to the newly constructed New York University and several colleges in Boston and Connecticut. By the time I had my PhD, he will have been a professor for at least three years. After I finish my PhD I would join him as a professor in our chosen field.

Edgar will graduate in May, and go off to college. He'd promised me last Christmas that he wouldn't go far for his undergraduate degree and I knew, especially with Gigi's age and me being pregnant, he would never go very far from home.

Everyone gathered in the courtyard and Ano handed Emily to Carlie's uncle to hold while the photographer moved family members in and out. Carlie and David looked blissfully happy, kissing each other and Emily, smiling and laughing as if this was truly the greatest day ever. Just before we moved into the church, Carlie turned to everyone around us.

"I wanted to thank everybody for coming, and sharing this day with David and Emily and me."

"You want to save this toast for the reception?" David asked her.

"Nope. This isn't gonna keep till then."

Ano pursed her lips next to me and downed the rest of her champagne. "Girl is crazy."

"There's something David needs to know before he marries me."

An actual look of worry creased his forehead as Carlie stepped towards him and wrapped an arm around his neck, pulling him towards her. She held him, whispering in his ear until he pulled away quickly, his face lit up and he spun her in his arms. "You sure?" She nodded and he leaned down, capturing her mouth in a kiss that caused several catcalls and whistles from onlookers.

"All right, all right," Jazz called out from next to Ano. "Save it for the honeymoon."

"Looks like they already had the honeymoon before the wedding," Ano mumbled back and I laughed.

"My soon to be wife," David said, his smile never fading, "is going to have another baby!"

Congratulatory cheers went and Carlie kissed David again, heartily.

"Kate, can I have some of your water?" Ano asked. I held onto the bottle and looked straight at her.

"I don't think you'll want it."

"Why?"

I tilted my head towards Carlie. "It's catching."

Ano and Jazz both laughed and she took my bottle from my hand. "She drink out of it?"

"Nope. Just me."

Ano's smiled faded and we stared at each other for ten full seconds. "For real?"

Jazz looked at me, then at Ano. "What?"

"FOR REAL?"

"*What?*" Jazz asked again.

"You're pregnant, too?" Ano shrieked.

Grabbing the water bottle from her hand, Jazz threw it over his shoulder.

I nodded with a big grin, and Ano pulled me hard into her arms and squeezed me tightly. She was crying and I held onto her just as hard. "I never thought—"

"I know."

"Everybody's crying over here," Matt said, and we turned, Ano wiping away her tears. His arm was around Sarah and I smiled at them both. They fit.

Ano pulled away to look at me. "Percy know?"

Matt looked at her, then at me. "Does Percy know what?"

Ano hugged me again. "I can't believe it! Oh my gosh! And Percy knows?"

"Percy knows." His deep baritone voice sounded from right behind me, and he kissed the side of my neck gently, his hand drifting down to cover my abdomen. "Percy definitely knows."

Ano shook her head in disbelief and Jazz reached out to shake Percy's hand. "Congratulations, man."

"Thank you."

Even Matt, despite the somber smile he gave me, shook Percy's hand. "Oh, wow. Hey, congrats, Perce."

Percy accepted the handshake and Matt leaned in to kiss me on the cheek and hug me gently. "Be happy," he whispered.

"Hey, you guys!" Carlie called. "I gotta get married! C'mon!"

"Wait!" I turned to the photographer, who had started to pack in his gear to go into the church. "Can you hang on one sec? Don't pack up yet."

"What's wrong?"

"Carlie, can we do one more shot? Humor me?"

"Sure, Katie," she said. "Okay."

I turned to face them. My friends. The five of them. My family. "Percy, Matt, Jazz, Ano, Carlie, come up here. Please?"

They all gathered in a group and Ano nodded at me, knowing exactly where I was going with this. I moved Percy and Carlie to the far right, Matt and Jazz to the far left, and Ano came to stand next to me in the middle of the group. Over three years had passed since the original photo had been taken. So much had changed. Paths not taken, love lost, hearts broken, friendships mended. A country nearly destroyed. Above all, we had remained, the six of us, together in the end. A family.

"Okay," I said to the photographer. "We're ready."

"Kate," Jazz said, "you wanna tell me what we're doing this picture for?"

Ano smiled at me and I began to cry.

"C'mon, Jazz," I said, my voice quavering. "Just one. For posterity."

ABOUT THE AUTHOR

Michela Montgomery graduated with her B.A. in Creative Writing from California State University, Long Beach. She completed the Claims Law Program with AEI and occasionally teaches classes on negotiation, litigation and investigation at her Corporate University. Although born and raised in California, Ms. Montgomery considers Boston her second home. She enjoys singing, dancing, yoga, cooking, the Red Sox, the Patriots and a good cannoli from Mike's Pastries. She lives in Northern California with her two children, a feisty Yorkie and a teacup Chihuahua named Killer. *The Battle* is her third novel.

CPSIA information can be obtained at www.ICGtesting.com
Printed in the USA
BVOW02s1149201115

427402BV00001B/2/P